A Novel

EDISON

NABORS

BRIAN PIETRO

ZUMAWORKS
ET HISTORIA EST RE

I've been walking forty miles of bad road,
If the Bible is right, the world will explode.
I've been trying to get as far away from myself as I can.
Some things are too hot to touch
The human mind can only stand so much.
You can't win with a losing hand.
People are crazy and times are strange
I'm locked in tight, I'm out of range.
I used to care, but things have changed.

"Things Have Changed"
by Bob Dylan,
written for the movie "The Wonder Boys", 2000.

Notes from the Editor

Brian's first novel, the sprawling *Milton Stubbs,* is like a kaleidoscope, in book form. It will be completely overhauled later this year, and re-released. Brian edited it, which is like not having an editor at all, and it is glaringly apparent for those who chose to read the original, ridiculously long book. At over 600 pages, it weighed as much as a good-sized trout, but it was fun.

Brian's true-life scandalous second novel, *Rory Gooze,* also created without the aid of an editor, was substantially shorter, and in fact, too short. Brian could have benefited from filling in the numerous holes and cracks in the story, with the help of an editor. There was so much more he could have told.

His entertaining and quirky third novel, *Stan Hurts,* had Colin Plotnik as the editor, and while he did an exemplary job, he seemed terribly confused, and sought therapy. I'm not sure if it was due to working with Brian, or due to the unusual subject matter.

Quentin Hollis, was Brian's fourth outing. It is a good and solid piece of writing, loaded with surprises, and aided by his editor, Lawrence Pedazz. From what I can discern, he too, did some good editing, but like Colin, Lawrence came away very confused. I'm beginning to think it has something to do with working with Brian.

And now, there's me. I'm known as a stickler for getting facts right, and getting things in chronological order. That's probably why Brian hired me. *Edison Nabors,* proved to be challenging, but I think I was up for it - you be the judge. I think I am being auditioned for the upcoming overhaul of *Milton,* since that will be a much larger task, of a similar manner. I have to admit however, that working with Brian can be quite...what's a good word for it? Labyrinthine. Yes, that's the perfect word.

Zantoon Nickelbob, editor

Excerpt from an interview of Quentin Hollis, filmed at his home in Ventura, California. He and his father were longtime friends of Edison.

The interview was conducted by Paula Zahn, for her Discovery Channel documentary and news show, "On the Case".

It aired in September, 2021:

Quentin: "Edison was a smart guy. Came from big money back East. A Navy Captain. A rocket scientist, for God's sake. Also, a very religious kind of a guy, but you couldn't talk religion to him, no way. Best to steer clear of that subject, if you did not see things just the same way as he did. Nice person though. He was a good friend of my dad's. They loved to go sailing. He was a genius in his own kind of a way. Changed the world, I guess you could say. But it's a funny thing, as strong as his beliefs were, as much as he held tight to his religious convictions, he also talked a lot about the metaphysical, "the boundless universe so full of dreams", as he would always say. He was, well, he was so damn narrow about things. You'd think a person that smart, and so full of knowledge, would be more open-minded. I mean, I've seen things, experienced things, out of this world, you can hardly imagine...and all it did is open me up, not close me down. I've heard what they say about Edison, that he robbed a bank, maybe killed somebody. I doubt that could be true. It must be an exaggeration".

Illustrations drawn by Edison, posted on his
childhood bedroom wall, 1942
(it's interesting that he knew Pluto would be excluded)

"Our Solar System"

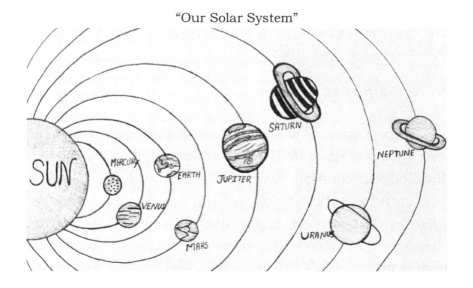

"Jesus playing with kids and a dog"

Posted on the wall of Edison's homeroom class at the Trinity School, 1967

PERIODIC TABLE OF THE CHEMICAL ELEMENTS

MAJOR GROUPS

No.	M 1	M 2	M 2'	M 3	M 4	M 5	M 6	M 7	M 8
1					H 1				He 2
2	Li 3	Be 4		B 5	C 6	N 7	O 8	F 9	Ne 10
3	Na 11	Mg 12		Al 13	Si 14	P 15	S 16	Cl 17	Ar 18
4	K 19	Ca	Zn	Ga 31	Ge 32	As 33	Se 34	Br 35	Kr 36
5	Rb 37	Sr	Cd	In 49	Sn 50	Sb 51	Te 52	I 53	Xe 54
6	Cs 55	Ba	Hg	Tl 81	Pb 82	Bi 83	Po 84	At 85	Rn 86
7	Fr 87	Ra							

TRANSITION

	T 3		T 4	T 5	T 6	T 7	T 8	T 9	T 10	T 11
4	Sc 21		Ti 22	V 23	Cr 24	Mn 25	Fe 26	Co 27	Ni 28	Cu 29
5	Y 39		Zr 40	Nb 41	Mo 42	Tc 43	Ru 44	Rh 45	Pd 46	Ag 47
6	La 57	Lu	Hf 72	Ta 73	W 74	Re 75	Os 76	Ir 77	Pt 78	Au 79
7	Ac 89	Lw	104							

INNER TRANSITION

6	Ce 58	Pr 59	Nd 60	Pm 61	Sm 62	Eu 63	Gd 64	Tb 65	Dy 66	Ho 67	Er 68	Tm 69	Yb 70
7	Th 90	Pa 91	U 92	Np 93	Pu 94	Am 95	Cm 96	Bk 97	Cf 98	Es 99	Fm 100	Md 101	No 102

Posted on the walls of Edison's home offices

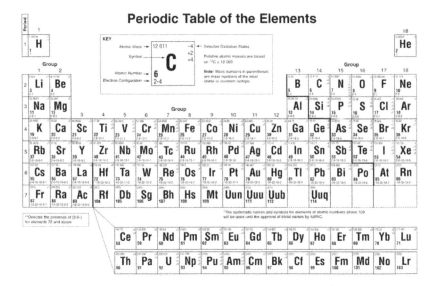

Periodic Table of the Elements

TITAN FAMILY OF MISSILES AND SPACE BOOSTERS

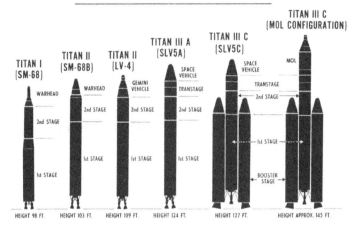

TITAN I (SM-68)
- WARHEAD
- 2nd STAGE
- 1st STAGE

HEIGHT 98 FT.

TITAN II (SM-68B)
- WARHEAD
- 2nd STAGE
- 1st STAGE

HEIGHT 103 FT.

TITAN II (LV-4)
- GEMINI VEHICLE
- 2nd STAGE
- 1st STAGE

HEIGHT 109 FT.

TITAN III A (SLV5A)
- SPACE VEHICLE
- TRANSTAGE
- 2nd STAGE
- 1st STAGE

HEIGHT 124 FT.

TITAN III C (SLV5C)
- SPACE VEHICLE
- TRANSTAGE
- 2nd STAGE
- 1st STAGE
- BOOSTER STAGE

HEIGHT 127 FT.

TITAN III C (MOL CONFIGURATION)
- MOL
- 2nd STAGE
- 1st STAGE

HEIGHT APPROX. 145 FT.

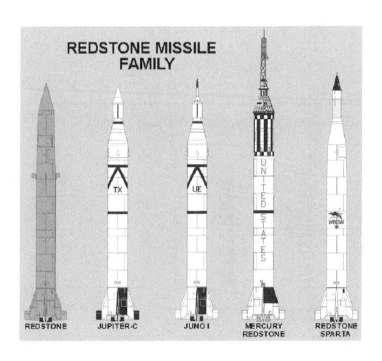

REDSTONE MISSILE FAMILY

REDSTONE | JUPITER-C | JUNO I | MERCURY REDSTONE | REDSTONE SPARTA

CONVAIR - GENERAL DYNAMICS ATLAS FAMILY

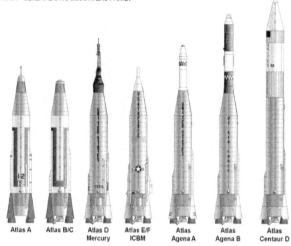

| Atlas A | Atlas B/C | Atlas D Mercury | Atlas E/F ICBM | Atlas Agena A | Atlas Agena B | Atlas Centaur D |

G. DE CHIARA (C) 2012

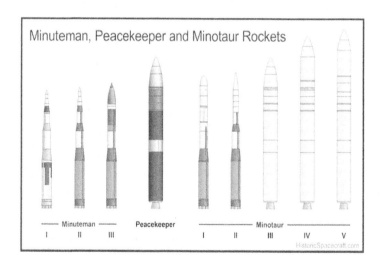

Minuteman, Peacekeeper and Minotaur Rockets

— Minuteman —   Peacekeeper   — Minotaur —

I   II   III   I   II   III   IV   V

MINUTEMAN MISSILE COMPARISON

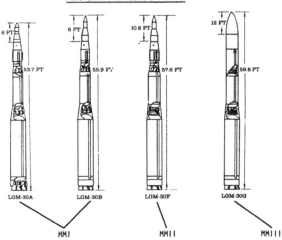

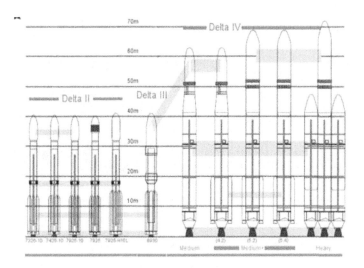

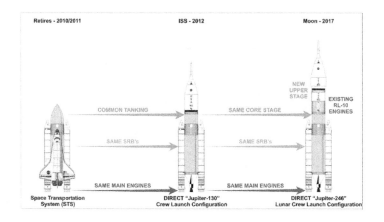

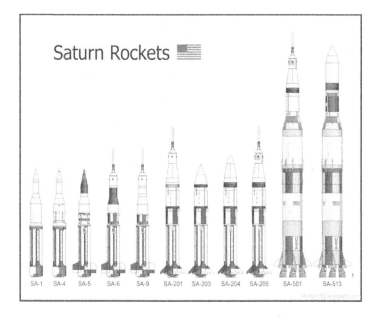

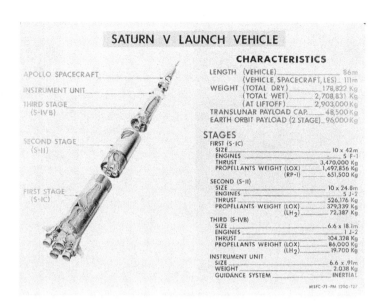

SATURN V LAUNCH VEHICLE

APOLLO SPACECRAFT

INSTRUMENT UNIT

THIRD STAGE
(S-IVB)

SECOND STAGE
(S-II)

FIRST STAGE
(S-IC)

CHARACTERISTICS

LENGTH (VEHICLE) _____ 86m
(VEHICLE, SPACECRAFT, LES) _ 111m
WEIGHT (TOTAL DRY) _____ 178,822 Kg
(TOTAL WET) _____ 2,708,831 Kg
(AT LIFTOFF) _____ 2,903,000 Kg
TRANSLUNAR PAYLOAD CAP. _____ 48,500 Kg
EARTH ORBIT PAYLOAD (2 STAGE) _ 96,000 Kg

STAGES

FIRST (S-IC)
SIZE _____ 10 x 42m
ENGINES _____ 5 F-1
THRUST _____ 3,470,000 Kg
PROPELLANTS WEIGHT (LOX) _____ 1,497,856 Kg
(RP-1) _____ 651,500 Kg

SECOND (S-II)
SIZE _____ 10 x 24.8m
ENGINES _____ 5 J-2
THRUST _____ 526,176 Kg
PROPELLANTS WEIGHT (LOX) _____ 379,339 Kg
(LH_2) _____ 72,387 Kg

THIRD (S-IVB)
SIZE _____ 6.6 x 18.1m
ENGINES _____ 1 J-2
THRUST _____ 104,328 Kg
PROPELLANTS WEIGHT (LOX) _____ 86,000 Kg
(LH_2) _____ 19,700 Kg

INSTRUMENT UNIT
SIZE _____ 6.6 x .91m
WEIGHT _____ 2,038 Kg
GUIDANCE SYSTEM _____ INERTIAL

MSFC-71-PM 1200-127

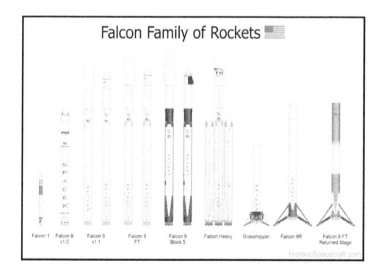

Falcon Family of Rockets

Falcon 1   Falcon 9   Falcon 9   Falcon 9   Falcon 9   Falcon Heavy   Grasshopper   Falcon 9R   Falcon 9 FT
            v1.0   v1.1   FT   Block 5   Returned Stage

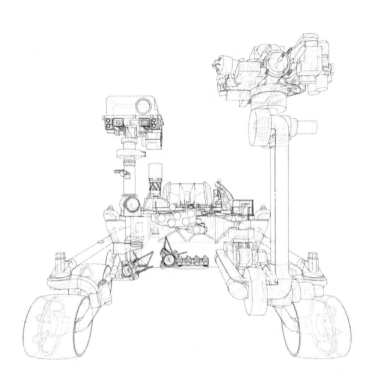

SPACE SHUTTLE

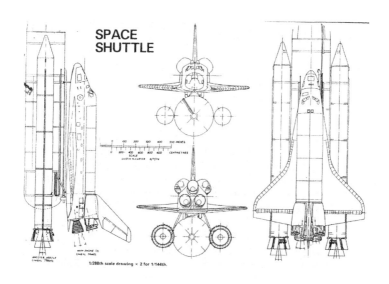

1/288th scale drawing × 2 for 1/144th.

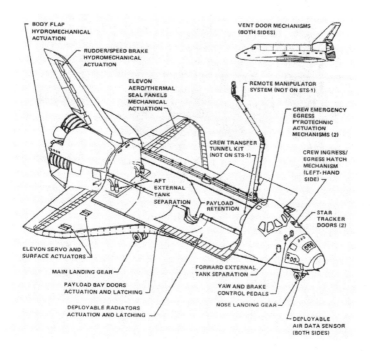

BODY FLAP
HYDROMECHANICAL
ACTUATION

RUDDER/SPEED BRAKE
HYDROMECHANICAL
ACTUATION

ELEVON
AERO/THERMAL
SEAL PANELS
MECHANICAL
ACTUATION

VENT DOOR MECHANISMS
(BOTH SIDES)

REMOTE MANIPULATOR
SYSTEM (NOT ON STS-1)

CREW EMERGENCY
EGRESS
PYROTECHNIC
ACTUATION
MECHANISMS (2)

CREW TRANSFER
TUNNEL KIT
(NOT ON STS-1)

CREW INGRESS/
EGRESS HATCH
MECHANISM
(LEFT-HAND
SIDE)

AFT
EXTERNAL
TANK
SEPARATION

PAYLOAD
RETENTION

STAR
TRACKER
DOORS (2)

ELEVON SERVO AND
SURFACE ACTUATORS

MAIN LANDING GEAR

PAYLOAD BAY DOORS
ACTUATION AND LATCHING

DEPLOYABLE RADIATORS
ACTUATION AND LATCHING

FORWARD EXTERNAL
TANK SEPARATION

YAW AND BRAKE
CONTROL PEDALS

NOSE LANDING GEAR

DEPLOYABLE
AIR DATA SENSOR
(BOTH SIDES)

Aztec style shirt

Aloha style shirt

CHAPTER 1

He had been looking down at his Levi jeans, realizing he had outgrown this pair as well, as the bottom hem sat a good four inches above the top of his Keds. He had rummaged through his dresser drawer at home, and this seemed the longest pair of the three that had been in there, folded neatly by his mom. Maybe she would be able to get him a new pair this weekend, so he wouldn't be teased at school come Monday?

It was a hot sunny afternoon, and he squinted as he looked out, leaning on the wood railing of the viewing platform. He could see across an expanse of flat empty dirt, to a spot about two-hundred yards away. There was a rocket engine, a large one, perched upside down in a huge metal platform, with a hole cut out in the middle to cradle the engine. *It looks like a giant metal pear,* he thought to himself. The outer shell of the engine was indeed pear-shaped, the narrower end placed in the platform's hole, and the "business end" pointing to the sky. That's what his uncle Edison had said to him just moments before, about the "business end". He thought it was a pretty nifty expression, having not heard it before. Maybe that's how all these rocket scientist and engineer types talked. It was pretty cool. The headphones that his uncle had placed on his head were beginning to itch, and small beads of sweat were trickling down his neck, and into his ears.

People were talking to one another, and there was an excitement in the air. And then, the steady murmur of the invited guests came to a halt, and the last-second, short staccato comments between all the "rocket guys", ceased. A silence fell over the entire platform. Without anyone having to say so, with no announcement over the outdoor speakers, everyone seemed to know that then was the time to stop talking, and pay attention to the large metal pear. Anticipation and adrenalin climbed, as the ignition sequence began.

A detonator was used, the primitive forerunner of NASA's Standard Detonator (NSD), which they began using with the advent of the Gemini program. For a rocket scientist, the design is alarmingly simple. For the layman, it's odd and complex.

The NSD is about the size of a turkey roasting pan. Inside, it bursts a thin seal, with an electrically charged wire, which then ignites a pyrotechnic charge, known as the "booster charge". The booster charge then ignites a small portion of the solid propellant, which is housed in an igniter initiator, which is inside the NSD, and attached to the booster igniter. This charge fires down the entire length of the solid rocket motor, lighting the entire surface of the core of the booster, simultaneously. In this test, there was no actual large ninety-foot-high cylindrical booster rocket, but there was a 200-gallon cylindrical container serving that purpose, filled with the propellant. The beauty of the solid fuel that was being tested, is that it is much simpler and more reliable to ignite, than liquid propellant. The one enormous downside is that once solid fuel has been ignited, you cannot down throttle it down, or turn it off. What is not wanted is for any one of the dozens of things that could go wrong, to go wrong. If it does, it's called a RUD (Rapid Unscheduled Disassembly) which is another term for, an explosion.

Everything that happened next could be counted in small fragments of seconds. Tony saw a small flash of a squib, and then another, which instantly ignited a miniature explosion, like a firecracker. It was hard to see that far without binoculars, but Tony had great vision. The family doctor had told him he had 30/20 vision, which was way above average, and he could make out details of something at a twenty-foot distance as if he were standing only ten feet away. It made Tony feel special. He needed that ability now, squinting into the bright sunlight, looking at the odd-looking structure across the open field of the sun-bleached dirt, which was reflecting the sunlight, making it even more difficult to see. Tony looked down at the dirt down below, in front of him, and noticed small pieces of gravel beginning to vibrate, and then bounce.

It reminded him of popcorn kernels in a sauce pan. His mom always made it that way, with a little oil, moving the Revere Ware back and forth over the flame of the stove top, as the kernels exploded into life. She'd hold the pan lid over the action to prevent the kernels from flying out onto the floor. Sometimes, it was a funny thing to watch, in case she was caught off-guard, and one or more of the popped kernels had launched itself out of the pan and across the kitchen. Their French Bulldog was sure to scoop it up in an instant. The melted butter would come next, and a dash of salt. It was 1958 and electric air pop machines hadn't been invented yet. Jiffy Pop, with the disposable foil-covered aluminum pan, wouldn't come along for another year.

His mom was standing next to him on the platform, and she also began to notice the gravel bouncing on the ground. Her name was Rachel. And then, ever so slightly, he could feel the wooden viewing platform they were standing on, begin to tremble, at a high rate of speed. And then there was a jolt, as if a truck had slammed into their platform. Some of the visitors were a little scared, with a couple of men exchanging nervous smiles, and one woman letting out a short small yelp.

The rocket engine, powered by the experimental solid fuel propellant, had come to life, and blew its top, blasting a stream of fire straight into the sky. Tony was astonished. He had expected a much smaller flame, maybe as tall as a person, he wasn't sure, not being experienced at this kind of a thing, but this was enormous. Also, it was loud. Very loud. Tony hadn't expected that either. But he had been supplied a pair of headphones, so maybe he should have expected it? Tony thought the flame must've been fifty feet high. Much taller than their house. But Tony was a kid, only eight years old, what did he know about distance and measurements? Not much. The flame shot straight up in a column, almost three-hundred feet. Bright yellow against the blue afternoon sky in Chatsworth. Tony reached for his mom's hand and clenched it tight. The ground shook as if from an earthquake, the smoke belched from the bottom of the rocket's platform in huge dark plumes, the roar of the engine was deafening, growing louder, and the platform shook hard. Tony clasped the headphones tight on his ears. Was it going to get even louder? Would it explode? Would the flames engulf them? For those answers and more, Tony looked up at his uncle, who stood next to him, looking straight ahead at the rocket. He was Rachel's kid brother. He was dressed in the rocket scientist attire of the day: tan dress pants with a sharp crease, black dress shoes, and white socks, white short-sleeve shirt, with an undershirt, pocket protector, black tie, tie clip, horn rim glasses, regulation military haircut neatly combed and slicked back with hair cream, and a lanyard with his I.D. around his neck. Tony and his mom had lanyards too, but theirs only said "Visitor". Uncle

Edison's said "Solid Rocket Team CHIEF". Tony felt his uncle's, was much cooler.

Perhaps more noticeable than how his uncle was attired, or his very cool lanyard, was his size. He was a tall guy, standing at six foot five, and large-framed. He wasn't ripped, but had only a suggestion of flab at his belly, and his upper body was fit. He had dark hair, receding somewhat, cut short as mentioned, was clean-shaven (of course) and had a very distinctive cleft in his chin, as pronounced as Cary Grant's. Also, he had an easy and winning smile. This did not indicate he was an extrovert, far from it, but when he felt like it, he could melt ice with that smile.

Edison had a big sloppy grin on his face. He eased his binoculars down and let out a loud hoot like at a ball game, and began to clap. All the others around him, mostly other youngish white men, similarly dressed, also gave out hoots, and were clapping. Tony gasped in surprise when he noticed that some of the men were crying while laughing.

This moment lasted half a minute, and just as abruptly as it had begun, the rocket engine shut off, the flames retreated in a blink, the huge clouds of smoke dissipated, drifting over the sandstone rocks and scrub brush surrounding them. Their ears were buzzing, and the adrenalin was pumping. And then all fell silent, with Edison and the others standing, gazing at the upside-down rocket in awe, soaking in the spectacle that they had just created and witnessed.

It was history. What the rocket scientists had done that day mattered. It would allow mankind to venture into the vast unknown. "Deep Lift" would become a well-known phrase, and synonymous with what they had accomplished that afternoon. This was just the first test of many, but it proved to Edison that he and his team had developed a formula that would work, something that had eluded other teams in the past. It was a significant step, and the weight of their accomplishment was just beginning to sink in.

Later, his uncle Edison would explain to him that the fuel wasn't really "solid", but more like the consistency of the Minute Maid frozen orange juice that his mom bought at Ralphs. A gooey sludge. Tony, for his part, was glad he hadn't been burned to a crisp, or blown to smithereens.

The fact that invited citizens were allowed to witness the test, that they were allowed to stand on a wooden platform, sturdily built yes, but nevertheless, made of wood, with no protective sheet of glass or acrylic, entirely exposed to the outdoor environment, not housed in a shelter, and only a few hundred feet from the rocket, and all that fuel, was at once very dangerous, and quaint.

Currently, there are official labels, expressing warnings from the Federal Government, that are affixed to transport trucks, storage containers, cylinders containing various gases and liquids, warehouses, and so forth. You get the idea. They come in three levels. The first and least concerning is "Caution", followed by "Warning", and then lastly, "Danger". Had a label been required to be posted on the viewing platform that day, where this rocket test would fall might not be found on this list. It would be on an expanded list, if there were one, terming the test either "Treacherous" or "Potentially Lethal". But this was 1958, and so many things of this nature, had that quality about them. Warnings were not in vogue then, on rocket tests, or with much of anything else. Even barricade tape (aka caution, or construction, or barrier, or police, or hazard, or danger tape, did not come into wide use until well into the 1960's, for example). The dichotomy between that more innocent decade and our current one, heavily draped with every imaginable warning, is stark:

Back then, automakers had begun to voluntarily put padding on car dashboards in the late 50's, about the time of the rocket test, advertising that the dash pads offered a touch of elegance, that they were a luxury, and the vinyl-covered foam, a mark of sophistication, veering away from the minimalism of earlier car designs. There was no mention of safety in the sales pitch. It wasn't until the early 1960's, that legislation began requiring them to offer the padded dashboards, at which point, the car companies began extolling the virtue of safety. A little later, in 1966, vague cautionary health warnings appeared on cigarette packages, after decades of people smoking them with abandon. Seat belts in cars became a "Motor Safety Standard" in 1968. Warnings of lead poisoning arrived, but not before kids poured molten lead into molds to make toy soldiers in the 1950's. It wasn't until 1993 that the Consumer Product Safety Commission provided a recall of Slip 'N Slide, requiring warning labels, after numerous injuries and cases of paralysis (but they were terribly fun). The Commission wasn't even created until late 1972.

Nowadays, we are perhaps over-burdened with countless warnings and recalls of various foods, drugs, equipment, and toys, making many numb, or angry, but back then, life was simpler, and most dangers were neatly tucked away and kept out of sight. Out of sight, out of mind.

Another example would be live A-bomb tests in the Nevada desert, with soldiers and guests hiding in dirt trenches or cement bunkers, unprotected except for tinted goggles. But not to worry.

Cancer-causing additives were common in food to enhance taste, texture, shelf life, and color. Jonas Salk had, after much testing, introduced his polio vaccine to the general public by 1955, however. But, with few restrictions or penalties, oil refineries belched poison into the air, and famous name-brand American factories, such as General Electric, dumped highly toxic chemicals into rivers, such as the Hudson. It was different back then.

So, it was in this context, that eight-year-old Tony was standing on an unprotected platform, only a few hundred feet away from a rocket connected to enough solid fuel propellant to blow up the entire mountain, or if not the mountain, then most certainly Tony, his mom, and his Keds, plus a couple of dozen other witnesses. It was a very real potential reality.

But this story is not meant to throw water on what was the single most exhilarating experience in the young boy's life, or on the significance of this successful test.

Tony looked up at his mom, and she seemed ready to faint. Edison, also noticing that, asked one of his cohorts to grab a glass of water for her, as he helped her sit down in the folding chair behind her, spotting her against a fall. Tony didn't get it. How could something this completely amazing cause his mom to get light-headed? She didn't like it? She didn't find it to be the most exciting and stupendous event she ever witnessed? It made no sense. But the kid was only eight, what did he know? And from there on, he was hooked on anything to do with rockets, jets, launches, satellites, you name it, and looked up to his uncle with unharnessed admiration, hanging on his every word about rockets that would take them to the moon, and beyond.

At times, his uncle would get dreamy-eyed, and talk to Tony about deep space, about voyages to other solar systems, and to other galaxies one day, and about worm holes, time travel, string theory, portals that could take you to other places in time or space, other dimensions, traveling a hundred times, or a thousand times, faster than light, about parallel universes, and how all of it was God's creation, God's plan.

Tony was mesmerized one afternoon, shortly after the rocket test, when Edison took Tony out to their big front lawn with a small bowl of apples. Edison loved to explain "scale" to Tony. He would've made a terrific grade school teacher.

He told Tony to stand still while he walked around, pacing in large steps, and placing an apple, here and there. He then came back to the boy, who was amused at the silly display. Edison explained to him how there were billions upon billions of stars, like the Sun, in our galaxy. He told him it would be like filling a Sparkletts water jug full of marbles, with each marble representing a star, and then lining up tens of thousands of those jugs, and that would only represent just a fraction of how many stars there were. "You'd need a lot more than that", he would say. And then came the grand finale. Edison would point out to the lawn, where he had placed the apples sixty feet apart, and tell him that was, to scale, the average distance between all those hundreds and hundreds of billions of stars, if a star was the size of an apple. Edison would then crouch down to Tony, at eye level, and say, "All God's work, all time, all space".

Tony didn't entirely understand how God fit into all of this, and hadn't spotted him on the platform the other day, but knew that his uncle felt this God stuff very strongly, adamantly some would say. Tony would ask his dad about it when he got home from work, but he knew his dad wasn't much on religious talk, and was a casual Catholic, attached to the Church, more by culture and family, than any deep thinking about God or any of his plans, but he'd ask anyway.

Tony and his mom had joined a small group of other friends and family on the platform that day, all of them there to cheer on their family members. All of the scientists and engineers assembled, had comprised the small army of Edison's work mates from Jet Propulsion Laboratory in Pasadena (JPL). They were at a high security testing facility tucked away in the picturesque rocky hills of Chatsworth, overlooking the western San Fernando Valley, known as the Santa Susana Mountains.

The area was famous for movies from the silent era, and later, for the talkies and TV shows, that needed a rugged and interesting outdoor location.

It was a fairly short drive from the Warner Brothers, Universal, Republic, or Disney studios, and just over the hill from all the others. There had been Tom Mix, Gene Autry, Leo Carrillo, Clayton Moore, Guy Madison, John Wayne, Roy Rogers, and Dale Evans with Nellie Belle the disobedient Jeep. They were but some of the many, who rode their horses in front of the cameras, among the craggy and beautiful eroded rock formations, that were once a slurry of sand and molten rock from long ago. Tony's science teacher would tell him later, that they were a combination of igneous and sedimentary rock.

On those rocks, the actors and stunt people got ambushed, got into fist fights, and gun fights, got their stagecoaches robbed, fell off rocks onto thick pads, and vanquished the bad guys. Not far from there, were old western town movie sets, with main streets, and churches, saloons, barber shops, hotels, livery stables, wood sidewalks, water troughs, and the Sheriff or Marshal's office, and jail. The credible authenticity of these fake old towns, were recorded by the camera, and allowed the suspension of disbelief to live. There was Corriganville, Bell Ranch, Iverson Ranch, and lastly, Spahn Ranch, made infamous by Charlie Manson about ten years later.

But in time, after many decades of filming up there, the rocks and dusty trails had served their purpose. They were being slowly replaced by distant locations made possible by smaller and more efficient cameras, better truck and airplane transport, and hiring local talent. Western town sets were being built all across the west, placed in authentic settings.

It might require the Teamsters to pick up the cast and crew an hour or two earlier in the morning, than they would have needed to in the L.A. area, as those more authentic locations were more remote than traversing Pacific Coast Highway from Malibu, Beverly Hills, or Burbank, or Culver City. John Ford was most probably the first director to significantly break the "location barrier" with his famous "Stagecoach" in 1939, partially filmed in Monument Valley. But most directors and studios lagged far behind his vision, and continued with the rocks of Chatsworth, or the Alabama Hills outside of Lone Pine, below Mount Whitney.

Audiences wanted locations that looked real, partly because they wanted to see different settings and landscapes, wanted to see the real thing, out in the expanses of Arizona, New Mexico, Colorado and Montana. Having the Lone Ranger, Zorro, and the Cisco Kid, ride along the same dirt road, under the same rock formation, had gotten old, and the Dream Factory needed some auxiliary support.

During the transition from old TV and movie westerns, was also the transition from prop-driven planes to space-age rockets. The remoteness and security of those same rocky hills had helped to forward Rocketdyne's purpose and usefulness, and it emerged in the mid 1950's as a key component with the testing of critical rocket engines and their specialized fuels.

The general location had some residential sections, but were not directly next to the facility, usually tucked up into one of the many small canyons nearby.

The facility was reached by way of Woolsey Canyon Road, a windy two-lane asphalt road built for the test site, and at 2,700 hundred acres, was one of the largest sites in the country. Larger ones would follow, for testing even mightier engines, but for its day, it was the crown jewel. What happened there the following year, would make even bigger history. Eventually it would be called the Santa Susana Field Laboratory (SSFL) and later, all but abandoned.

The space program was just then coming into its own, and the excitement in the air was palpable on that hot afternoon. It wouldn't be long until the prototypes of lunar rovers, "robots on wheels" as Edison called them, would be getting their workout trials in the Mojave Desert. The little vehicles looked like dune buggies, and were powered by cables attached on the other end to remote control boxes, some with joy sticks. The grown men operating them were like kids with a radio-controlled toy car. Back hoes created a test course for them, featuring craters dug in the sand and boulders placed here and there. The first LRV (Lunar Roving Vehicle) was created for NASA in 1969 by Boeing, in its test labs in Kent, Washington. It was first used in July of 1971, as part of the Apollo 15 mission to the Moon. Since the gravity on the moon was only a sixth of the gravity on Earth, much invention went into building an extremely light weight vehicle. It was so light, it could not be tested on Earth, for the weight of an astronaut passenger would have crushed it. But the U.S. was not living in a bubble when it came to such enterprises, and a constant undercurrent with all of these projects, whether it be rocket and fuel testing, or rovers, was about competition, about the "space race".

The Soviet Union had successfully landed their Lunokhod on the Moon in 1970, a year before the first U.S. LRV arrived. They were the only two competitors for decades, until finally, China successfully landed their Yutu rover in 2018, followed by India in 2023. There were many failures along the way as well, including attempts by India, Japan and Dubai, and one American venture called Peregrine, launched recently in January of 2024. As of the writing of this book, China is about to land an un-manned "lunar probe" to the far side of the Moon, called the Chang'e-6 probe.

The "space race" was really more of a "Moon race". It called for the scientists and engineers to focus their considerable knowledge and skills, and create components of almost unimaginable complexity, while under the enormous pressure put upon them by JPL, NASA and the military.

As for Edison, this day in Chatsworth had been the culmination of countless hours of work and invention, and a about a life that had seemed to be on an unchangeable trajectory, until it changed on him later. But for the present, he didn't see that change coming. On the walls of his primary ab at JPL, there were two signs posted, for everyone to see. Edison would take a quick lunch outside, weather permitting, and would always sit on a particular bench, under a Japanese Maple, and look across the expanse of the concrete that made up the main courtyard of the campus, lined with small bronze plaques, and miniature models of past rockets and satellites.

There was a break between two buildings, where Edison could see between them to the large grassy area behind them. This is where the deer would collect, and munch on the grass, steering clear of the Humans. There was a large herd on the campus, perhaps a hundred or more of them. They would have their fill and then retreat up the hill and settle in for the night in the woods. Sometimes, during these lunch breaks, he would think about the signs posted on the walls back at the lab. One of them was the JPL motto, "Do Mighty Things." The other was the mantra, "Follow the Water". Edison knew that ultimately, all of this gigantic level of industry, all of this invention and exploration, was to seek out life beyond our own planet. And where there is water, it is very likely that life exists in some form, or it used to. It wouldn't be until fifty years later that JPL would confirm that water was on Mars, below the surface of large ice-covered lakes. Clean, clear and drinkable. In fact, there was so much there, that the first human explorers wouldn't have the need to bring any with them, it was in such abundance.

Edison would look up through the branches of the Maple, and get dreamy. His mind would wander and begin to conflate his science with his beliefs. He knew that in order to believe in his god, he first had to not believe, that's the way it worked. But that was a long time ago, his non-belief. He knew that for him, it was all part of a spiritual journey, with the ebb and flow of life allowing him to experience and understand. He further knew that it was not necessary for him to understand how it all worked, how God and the Universe, and his rocket scientist life were woven together, all seemingly pointed in one direction, sharing the same outcome. He knew that science and his spiritual knowledge were now seemingly on parallel tracks, but it was an illusion, he felt. Each track was slanted toward the other, ever so slightly, so slightly that it could hardly be detected, but he knew that one day, and perhaps it would take a thousand more years, but that one day, those two parallel lines would converge, and become one. All he had to do is believe, and all would be revealed to him. It was not a scientific approach, nor entirely spiritual. It was a blend. The stark contrast between the work he did inside the building across from him three-hundred feet away, in some way, was directly related to his belief in a god, the God, that was as large as the entirety of the Universe, yet lived inside of him.

He thought about what it would be like to become miniature, microscopic, so small that molecules appeared floating in the air, the size of planets, and that perhaps all of creation was designed this way, galaxies containing solar systems, containing planets, containing atoms, containing electrons, containing protons, containing quarks, and ever smaller living round structures? His ability, his willingness, to see it this way, he knew, was the right path, the only path, as Jesus had once said.

"Is my heart restless?" He would ask himself this, almost daily. And he wanted his answer to be 'no', but it was always 'yes'. He was restless to know more, and often wondered if he had discernment, in the Christian context. He didn't consider himself "gifted", or especially "special". He cringed when someone would call him a scientist, for he was modest, he always strove to be accurate, and knew inside he was simply an engineer, perhaps a clever, inventive, and intuitive engineer, and that any special talent he might have, was God given, simple as that.

He would sometimes admonish himself for being so very curious about the all of it, the entirety of life, and its inner workings. He would counsel himself. If he was ignorant of something, whether it be something that was of minor importance, or something to do with the immensity of space and time, then it was meant for him to be ignorant. There was a constant inner battle, with the Christian Edison compelled to accept things as they are, and the scientific Edison, compelled to know more, to explore. What he did know, or perhaps more accurately, what he sensed, was that he was here for a special purpose, not yet revealed to him, and he knew he was somehow in touch with the Source, he could hear it, not literally, but could feel it, and it would give him direction and purpose. For there was a purpose to all of this, that much he did know. For the time being, he felt as if he were in a bubble, protected, but that there would be a time when he would be called to stand apart from all the others. He knew that at some point, he would need to be tested, or rather, that the strength of his belief would be tested, and he relished it, knowing it would be the only way to test the true depth of his sincerity.

His backstory and his inner thoughts matter, because they inform us of his desire to break away, make his own mark, to stand alone and be counted. Those are all traits that usually create the accomplished, the famous trailblazers, the ones that make a difference.

On the flip side, those same traits can also serve as indicators about some people that aren't able to carry that weight. Often times it's young people just coming into their own, that are socially awkward or inept, who retreat into books with their over-average intellect, and their ability to absorb information. Perhaps they have been hampered by indifferent, or overly attentive, parents, or a broken family, and the accompanying trauma? Sometimes it can be a physical thing. Or if the young person is not in the normal range of appearance, whether it be height, weight, or facial characteristics. Or perhaps it's something missing inside? If they don't have the ability to laugh at themselves, they have no perspective, and drill down on an idea or belief with intensity, lacking a balanced viewpoint. Edison would score high points in that test, if there were such a thing. But in a way, there is such a test, which is called school, and the kids were not kind. Edison was tall and gangly when he was a kid, a teenager, and his face was slowly developing into something some might call handsome, but then, that was still years away. Inside, things were churning, for Edison, even back then, knew that he was destined for something great, undefined as of then, but most definitely great.

Innumerable books have been written on the daily pressures and stings on intellectually exceptional young people coursing through these first years in school, in terms of their social skills and dealing with people, both in terms of friendship and trust, and with adversarial situations. Edison could be included in that broad brush stroke, concerning kids of higher-than-average intellect, with lower-than-average social skills. Young Edison in school, fielded the incoming barbs as best he could. He was a bright kid, and nimble on his feet, when dealing with insults or put-downs. He knew he was meant for bigger things and could look beyond the petty little jabs, but they still hurt.

Edison's early life was spent in the Bronx, the densely populated borough of New York City, about forty-two miles square. If it were ranked as a city, it would be the ninth most populous city in the entire country. It had as its inhabitants, a broad range of nationalities and cultures, not as true in Edison's young days, in the 1930's, as in present day certainly, but the roots were there. Edison was spared most of the barbs or pleasures of being raised in a city such as this, for he lived a comfortable sheltered life with his parents, and older sister Rachel, in the Hudson Hill section of Riverdale, one of the more swank, neighborhoods in all of New York. This is before his dad's business success propelled the family to an even more swank neighborhood, the up and coming, Upper West Side of Manhattan.

This needs to be put in perspective. Edison was born in May of 1930, and while much of the country was in the throes of the Great Depression, Edison's dad, Nelson, was a very successful businessman, busy tucking away an ever-growing nest egg, having managed to zero in on his main client base, the affluent. His type of potential customer lived in the upper reaches of the economy, nearly impervious to the chaos and grief around them. They carried on as if the economic free fall were an inconvenience.

Nelson owned a small chain of car dealerships, across various nameplates, primarily within the borders of the city and its boroughs, with three more up-state. When the economic collapse occurred, it only put a dent in Nelson's business, resulting in two of his dealerships closing down. It also birthed other consequences, including one of his sales managers committing suicide one night, after the dealership had closed for the day.

Nelson, upon hearing of the tragedy the following morning, sped up the road to his Cadillac dealership, in White Plains. Upon arrival, he was shocked to see that a large crowd of onlookers had gathered, and made his way through the crowd, to the inside. The police sergeant in charge of the scene spoke to Nelson in hushed tones about how they had found the man, slumped over in the front seat of one of the cars in the showroom. Nelson listened to the sergeant as attentively as he was able to, but was highly distracted, and kept peering over the sergeant's shoulder to get a glimpse of the scene. It was grisly. The manager had apparently decided to launch himself into the next life by blowing his brains out while seated in a brand new, bottle green, with rich tan upholstery, Cadillac V-

16 Convertible Coupe. If there was a better representation of the pinnacle of high-class American motoring, Nelson hadn't heard of it. After the sergeant was done filling him in on some of the basics, he walked away, allowing Nelson to approach the scene. The body had already been removed and was on a gurney in the corner, draped by a sheet. The sergeant had said he'd need a positive I.D. before Nelson left.

Nelson, being the devout religious man he was, prayed silently for the sales manager, and his family, while walking slowly toward the elegant automobile. It was the best car on the lot, by far. Only about fifty had been produced that year, with production being crippled by the depression, but there were still some citizens out there who lusted for the 6,600 pound, 18-foot long, two-door "Cadillac Sixteen", with a sticker of about twelve grand (that's about $230,000 today). It was the longest mass production car ever made, but now, with the leather upholstery soaking in the aftermath of his manager's decision, with nauseating small chunks of evidence splattered about the dash and windshield, Nelson rushed to the men's room to heave out his hurried breakfast of toast and coffee, from two hours before. When he returned, there was a police photographer taking photos, using the recently invented flash bulb to illuminate the aftermath, with his large format Graflex Speed Graphics camera. Nelson knew the camera well, having purchased one himself, for family events and outings.

Nelson felt it was necessary for him to be dragged through this experience to reach a higher level, for it was only due to the shock and raw vulgarity of the scene, that Nelson realized that his sales manager, a devout Catholic, might not make it to the pearly gates, as his was a religion of ritual and dictation, while Nelson's was about grace and acceptance, so he thought. But looking down at the gruesome results of this event, he began to rethink his position.

Was this man, as imperfect as he obviously had been, not worthy of God's grace and forgiveness? How horribly distraught and lost he must have felt, to be drawn to this act? And, why did he choose to do it in *this* car? There were so many others to choose from. Was it a message to Nelson? Was it some kind of a "fuck you", being sent to the Quaker? He had been with Nelson for years, having worked his way up the ladder. He had always gotten along well with the manager, never once having an argument, or even so much as a mild disagreement. The sales staff at the dealership had always been top shelf, as they needed to be, and Nelson never had any complaints. The Nelson Nabors, mild-mannered dealership chain owner, was a much different person than Nelson, the hypercritical and hypocritical Quaker.

Nelson, always sure in his beliefs, was now, quite unsure. He prayed again for the man, knowing he was with God now, whatever that meant, exactly, for he wasn't altogether sure, but when he walked away from the dealership, he had been changed. He realized that his beliefs had been too judgmental, too severe, and it was no wonder why his son felt unconnected to him. On the drive home, he resolved to make an adjustment, to be more open, less critical of others. For Nelson, it was a huge turning point, and done silently.

He hadn't a clue that Edison was going through a change of his own.

As for his mini empire of a car business, Nelson did quite well, spurred by his cloyingly memorable magazine and billboard advertising. As an example, he would have a photo of a young boy or girl, usually at the beach with a toy metal pail and shovel set, looking impishly at the camera. Next to them would stand a parent, looking at them admiringly, while leaning on the hood of a new car. For the day, it was an amusing and darling eye-catcher. He used his last name, Nabors, with bold-lettered zingers like, "Be a Good Neighbor, buy Your Next at Nabors", or "Nabors is your Neighbor", or "You Can Trust Your Neighbors at Nabors" and other equally corny slogans, but they worked. Word of mouth was strong, and the word was that his prices were fair, and his sales people not overly solicitous, or pushy. His dealerships sold Cadillacs, plus Buicks, Plymouths, Chryslers and in an expensive and large street level showroom on Fifth Avenue, took orders for the Rolls Royce Phantom II, using his one and only floor model, for display. The salesmen at this location, wore fine suits, tailored in England, and if they weren't actually British, they were required to put on a faint British accent. Usually, the prices were set well above sticker.

His family had made the move from Hudson Hill to the Upper West Side when Edison was in the transition from grade school to junior high, so most of his social interactions and confrontations happened in his new home in the city, where most of the kids looked upon him with suspicion, being the son of a "blue collar millionaire".

As Edison grew older, he gained an inner strength, a determined sense of self, but had never managed to harness many friendships, or be invited to parties, or to join clubs or sports teams, because he was never taught how to be, and never thought of friendships as being reciprocal. Out of self-defense, and by observing his dad, he figured people would, or should, come to him.

Worst of all, he failed to win the affections of Gail Nussbaum, a freckle-faced blonde heartbreaker he had always longed for. He had hit puberty three years back, and his physical reaction to seeing her at lunch or recess, or having her as a classmate, would often result in an embarrassing reaction, forcing him to sit still for five minutes and concentrate on multiplication tables, or the periodic table, going through the elements in their exact order from Hydrogen to Plutonium. There was a rumor that a 95th element was about to be named, "Americium", but it hadn't been made official yet. If those techniques failed, he'd take an exit with his books strategically placed in front of him. After much effort and heartache, the highest form of communication he ever accomplished with her, is when he passed her in the crowded busy hallway in ninth grade, as he was making his way to Intermediate Algebra, and her, to Advanced English.

It was September of 1943, and the first day of school. He had waited impatiently all summer break, not having a clue as to where she lived or knowing her phone number, and had decided to turn a new page, to forge a relationship with the pretty young girl. As they passed one another in the crowd, his heart pounding, his throat dry, feeling dizzy, he said to her, "Hi Gail", and she replied "Hi" without even looking up. She didn't even seem to know his name. He stood motionless, looking at her walk away, her pony tail bobbing up and down and finally getting lost in the crush of fellow students, and vanishing. He was destroyed. He was too shy and inept to make another attempt, and instead, wallowed in pain.

His entire plan, what there had been of it, had crumbled.

She was supposed to have said, "Oh, Hi Edison. How was your summer?" Or something along that line.

He would then stop and answer, "It was great. We went camping, and to the beach, and visited my uncle. We went to the Paramount to see "Bambi", they brought it back, did you get to see it again? Aren't you glad we're pushing back the Japs? They aren't going to beat us." He wanted to convey that he was a busy guy, doing this, doing that, aware of what was going on in the world, had an opinion, and was not just hanging around, leaning on trees, waiting for summer break to end, so he could bump into her in the hallway. He desperately did not want to come across as desperate.

The notion of going to his parents, or older sister, for advice on how to win the affections, or even merely the attention, of little Miss Nussbaum was dead on arrival, for he knew he would only get admonished or made fun of. He had nowhere to turn, no mentors, no older brother. He knew he had to white knuckle the pain. After school, instead of going directly home, he took a detour to the F.W. Woolworth store, sat on a counter stool, and drowned his sorrows in two chocolate fudge sundaes.

No doubt, the enormity of his rejection by his first love, propelled his adolescent self to be dedicated to achieving greatness. He became attached to the un-breathing, to the inanimate, for those things could not hurt him back. His desire to achieve something great was fueled by the enormity of the rejection. The familiar refrain of "who needs love when I can make lots of money?" tumbled around in his head for quite a while. He looked up to his dad for many reasons, not the least of which was his dad's command of business, and his ability to make a handsome income. Certainly, one definition of "greatness" could be attaining lots of money, the young man reasoned.

But, as a breathing contradiction to that, his parents were not as inclined to go along with their son's concept of greatness, as they were strict Quakers, or doing their best to impersonate them, and found his ambitious dreams to run counter to their professed beliefs of humility and serving God. They wanted to instill these values in their son, even while his dad accumulated ever more wealth, even during the Great Depression, and then followed by the war, with much of the country in dismal condition, and many making daily sacrifices.

Through this lens, Edison may have developed a different take on religion, one that centered around giving, rather than taking and keeping. Ironically, his parents had given him an unintended life lesson about humility in the face of God, all the time worrying that they may have raised someone arrogant and Godless. It was the one big elephant in the Nabors' home, for on the one hand, the parents believed in modesty and humility, while simultaneously working like beavers to support and accumulate ever more wealth.

As he became older and more independent, he would make his way on foot or by trolley, to one of a few picture show houses. Sometimes he would see a movie multiple times if the plot or leading actors were especially interesting. 1943 offered up *Casablanca, Heaven Can Wait* and *For Whom the Bell Tolls*. The following years did not disappoint either. *Arsenic and Old Lace, To Have and Have Not, Gaslight, The Lost Weekend, The Big Sleep* and *It's a Wonderful Life*. He would get lost for hours in the theater, devouring Junior Mints and Almond Joys. His escape into these movies became a necessary antidote to his real life, as an awkward and friendless teenager.

His home life was not only sheltered to the degree possible by his parents, but heavily attended. Not a day would go by, not even a Sunday, when there was not someone in the house, or in the yard, doing some kind of work. They had a specialized gardener for the lush flowering garden (performing careful pruning, planting, and fertilizing), a separate gardener for maintenance (for weed pulling, grass mowing, and tree trimming), a pool man, for maintaining the three-thousand gallon Koi pond, and the Koi themselves, another who maintained the three-tiered Romanesque fountain in the center of the circular driveway, stocked with goldfish, another who cleaned all the glass on the outside of the house, a live-in maid who worked tirelessly to keep the entire two-story Victorian ship-shape, which included being sure to clean, dry, and fold the bath towels properly. There were towels, embroidered with a fancy "N", that were an ivory color, that had to be stored in the ivory-colored bathroom's cabinet. There were also white towels of a similar description, that had to go in the white bathroom. And then there was the light blue, cobalt blue, and tan towels that had to be placed in their respective homes. There was another worker who came in once a week to do a deep cleaning of the interior, another who placed fresh cut flowers in the many vases throughout the home, a fix-it person who came weekly to repair and maintain the various mechanical nuisances, from loose door handles to a leaking under-sink pipe. They had two dogs, Harlequin Great Danes, who were brothers. They weighed in at about 170 pounds and stood at nearly 3 feet at their backs. They were affectionate, playful and could be ferocious. His dad had named them "King" and "Champ". Although Edison attempted to teach them the joys of fetching, they weren't all that inclined, and preferred an energetic game of keep-away between the two of them, with Edison looking on. They had a dog groomer visit them once a week, for a bath and brush.

This ever-constant parade of people nearly gave Edison a nervous condition, never knowing when someone would, by accident, see him through a window while dressing, or walk into the bathroom while he was doing his business (if he had forgotten to lock the door), or if he was downstairs, trying to have some peace and quiet during breakfast, and enjoying a bit of buttered toast, or a bowl of the 1941 sensation, Cheerioats cereal (changed to "Cheerios" in 1945).

He felt that there were always eyes on him, and that he was living in what seemed a public hotel. In spite of the fish-bowl lifestyle, he was out-going, and was sociable, getting along quite well with all the workers. Cristobal, an older man from Argentina, and the koi pond specialist, was his favorite. Friends his own age, were non-existent.

Cristobal would point out the many varieties of the koi, some of them having grown to be quite large, and tell Edison all about them. There were about a dozen, and some stood out. They had two, of a variety developed in the 1890's, (and nowadays the most well-known) that was the brightly colored, orange and white, Kohaku. There was the Showa variety, developed in 1927, with dazzling black, white, and orange patches. There were three of them. There were other varieties swimming about as well, but Edison's top pick was the Hikari Muji ("metallic, single color") variety, specifically the Kin Matsuba (yellow/gold). It was the only one in the pond of that type, was very large, and swam gracefully around and among the others. It never seemed to be a bully, and would calmly go for its food, allowing others ahead of him. Cristobal taught Edison how to feed the fish during the week, while he was not there, and when he did arrive, usually every Thursday afternoon, Cristobal would toss out a head of iceberg lettuce, and it would float like a ball, as the Koi would surround it, eating it bit by bit until entirely gone. It was perhaps the high point of Edison's entire week.

Cristobal would repeat the same comment to him nearly every time: "Most of these fish, will out-live you". Cristobal explained to him that unlike the goldfish out front in the fountain, the koi could withstand the winters, and when the top of the pond water would freeze over, the koi's metabolism would slow to a hibernation level, and they would nestle together, side by side, and wait out the cold freezing water until it warmed again, in the Spring. Edison could not help but think about all his dad's commentary, concerning the "natural order of things" and how God had designed and mapped out every little detail. As for the goldfish, if Cristobal didn't net them, and put them safely inside in time, they'd freeze to death.

Staring down into the deep pond, and watching the fish glide elegantly under the water lilies, it crossed Edison's mind that the fish came from the same country that they were at war with. Edison's young mind was made curious by the lack of pure "evil" on the other side of the ocean, and dove into books that detailed Japan's natural beauty, its ancient culture, religion, and ceremonies. These books were all at the public library, certainly not on the shelves of the study at home. He would spend hours soaking in all that he could about the country that had named itself Nippon (for "origin of the sun") and later, "land of the rising sun". Their culture, beliefs, and myths were at least as involved and tangled as anything that the West held onto, far as Edison could tell.

This is where things became murky for the maturing boy, the young man, trying to make sense of the difference of what he was constantly preached, and what he constantly observed or read. He had opened a window to the East, about a culture older than his, and a people steeped in spiritual beliefs.

What made so much of this difficult for Edison was that he was, to be kind about it, a humorless person. He rarely found the light side of any issue, rarely thought or expressed any humor, taking in most everything, with a sober interpretation. But, to be fair, he was still developing as a person, was self-absorbed, partly as a defense, and once older, he would loosen up somewhat. But it would take time.

Not that there was anything to joke about when it came to the war. But he had been surrounded by only the one perspective. Most adults he encountered, parroted the blood thirst for a Japanese and German defeat, while Edison truly detested the idea of war. He knew that the "idea" of no war, of the complete and total refusal to participate, or in any way support it, could be a hard thing to accomplish. It seemed to him, that there had been examples in history of the apparent tragic necessity for it. When he thought about the attacks on Dansk in 1939, or Pearl Harbor in 1941. He knew that in this case, war seemed the only recourse for those attacks. Or were they? Could they have been prevented, could the seeds of those attacks have been removed years ago? He knew it was unrealistic to think so, but sometimes it seemed that the adults thirsted for war, as if they had wanted the attacks to come, as an excuse to counter attack. He knew to keep these thoughts under wraps, not wanting to be seen in school as an enemy sympathizer, or worse yet, a pacifist. He had made that mistake once. The Quaker credo, "people can only hurt themselves" kept revolving around in his head, but it had not attached itself to anything real, and remained an aspiration, not a blueprint for him to live by.

His dad and mom fell into a the more conventional middle group, that found it necessary to grasp tight their Quaker Bible while silently demonizing all people of those countries we were warring with, not making a distinction between their government's will, and the citizens actual desires. People who they would see in the city, who had been born here, but were of Japanese or German or Italian descent, were to be avoided and ostracized. It seemed, every time he turned around, Edison could identify another hypocrisy.

Non-slanted or complete news of the day was virtually non-existent, but over time, Edison came to be sickened by whatever news he could read about the Japanese internment camps, primarily located in the western half of the country.

The government had organized them into three categories. There were "Civilian Assembly Centers" which were temporary camps, often located within cities, at race tracks or fairgrounds. The people they had just rounded up, that had been yanked from their homes, businesses or jobs, would be placed there. They were located in Arcadia, Fresno, Pomona, Portland, Sacramento, Salinas, Stockton among others. From there, the Japanese were transported to "Relocation Centers" also known as internment camps. There were ten of them, the most famous being Manzanar, at the foot of the Eastern Sierras, in California. There was one other in California, in Tule Lake, and then others in Arizona, Colorado, Wyoming, Arkansas, Idaho and Utah. If someone was considered dangerous, disruptive, or of "special interest" to the government, they would be sent to a "Detention Camp". These facilities often housed German-American and Italian-American detainees as well. There were nine of those, from Montana to Georgia.

A strong reaction by our country and military from being attacked was to be expected, but the overt and irrational racism it helped to create, or unveil, was to Edison, repulsive. Even the President had deeply held racist views about the Japanese, long before the attack. Most of the country was in favor of the prison camps, but one of the lone exceptions were some Christian groups and churches, and among them, the Quakers. There were individuals, not necessarily associated with a church, who would drive to the camps to lend aid, bring food treats, and magazines, but they were watched by government agents, and considered potential adversaries, working for the enemy. Edison would mention some of these details to his parents over dinner, but he was always rebuked, for Nelson and Nadine didn't see things the same way.

His parents had found a niche that allowed them to conduct their lives under the umbrella of their declared religion. By necessity, it was a customized niche. Beyond any other principle of the Quakers, the absolute nonacceptance of war, regardless of who the perpetrator or more righteous appeared to be, or indeed was, was rule number one. His parents would always declare that they were in line with the Society of Friends. In general, Quakers were also opposed to the internment camps.

Edison, learned about all of this from his visits to the library, not at dinnertime. Also, he learned a hard lesson about how to lay low, after having said he was a Quaker in English class, and being teased, and deposited into a trash can after class, by some Cro-Magnon types.

Edison knew that the war had been made necessary by the aggression, warmongering and invasion by the other countries, but had always wondered, that if it had been put up for a vote in those invading countries, before years of propaganda had influenced their opinions, before failed economies, before demagogues, and xenophobia had all done their work, would they have voted for war? They had lived for years, steeped in hatred, fear and self-loathing. Following that would be small-minded bigotry, greed, and nationalism. And what had his country done to perhaps provoke them, to poke the bear with a sharp stick? Perhaps nothing, or perhaps something?

Edison was developing a point of view, or if not that, at least the ability to question, and develop his own opinions. The governments of those countries, he felt, dove head first into war as a solution to their problems, little caring about any opposing public opinion. But they had conditioned their citizens first. Sometimes war serves as a way to mobilize the citizens, improve the economy, and direct their anger and fear away from their leaders and onto a common enemy. Sometimes it was a manifest on the part of the leaders, as if they had had a vision, a message from God. Certainly, he thought, this was a good overarching view of Japan and Germany, but how much of that could be applied to his country, he wondered? These were the kind of thoughts that rolled around in the young boy's mind.

At home, he was given the boilerplate sermon of the day, delivered by way of the dinnertime grace, usually spoken by his mom, but for Edison, growing evermore sour, it was the classic "do as I say, not as I do" moment.

Why would his parents lay claim to a religion that they did not live by? Why did they talk about Krauts and Japs when dinner guests were over? On one occasion, Edison could remember his dad saying to a prospective customer, "I wouldn't lie to you, I'm a Quaker". Was the whole thing just as act? Was it to boost sales? Were his parents knowingly imposters? Did this mean there was no God? Were other people, who held different beliefs, more truthful in their belief? If so, was there a belief, a religion, that was in fact, more truthful, closer to the universal truth? Did the Japanese have a more truthful and pure religion?

Most boys of his age were spellbound by Baseball cards, or fixed on trying to get a peek up some girl's skirt, but not Edison. Since he had been born into a home of sanctimony, did it mean there was no truth about a god, or could it mean, there was no truth about his parent's belief? He instinctively knew that his parents, as much as they adored him, were not living truthful lives. Edison was starving for some truth. He knew he wasn't old enough to venture out into the world to find it, but determined that one day, in the not-too-distant future, he would be.

His parents, with their beehive lifestyle, the many dealerships, and the spic and span efficiency at home, wanted to give the appearance of being moral, hard-working people, who were fortunate, and not people working to simply acquire more and more wealth. For Edison, the possession of the wealth wasn't the issue, but the ardent desire to acquire it above all else, was. Edison straddled the line that divided a truthful and righteous life, from a life made of shadows and lies. On a daily basis. His parent's mythical life was not something Edison wanted to help carry, or make apologies for. He appreciated all the material benefits, from the nice house, the good food, being safe and warm, the nice clothing and toys, but as he grew to understand the reality of the situation, he realized, with increased clarity, how he was an accomplice to the deceit.

Of course, when a person is young, they often think they have all the answers, and most certainly, better answers than their parents. They grow uncomfortable, and itch for change, for their own identity, that is not tethered to the parents. They rebel. They act out. But Edison, was a different kind of a guy, and seemed to have the perspective of someone who knows his limitations, due to age and immaturity, due to a lack of experience out in the world at large, and a profound ignorance of what it was like out there for others. He had been incapsulated for so long on the West Side, he didn't have a sense of self.

As for the deceit? He was constantly reminded of this, because it was the war era. There were magazine ads and posters, proclaiming sacrifice to be a virtue, a duty, all with the aim to help the country at large, to support it, through self-sacrifice and hard work. And all of it by way of honor and honesty. This was the "Yes We Can", and "Buy War Bonds" generation.

Not that Nelson Nabors did not work hard, for he most certainly did, but his posturing as being an everyday normal citizen was a preposterous and futile attempt. Everybody but everybody was onto him in the neighborhood, but it didn't seem to impact the success of his dealerships, not even a little. The Nabors wanted to acquire it, but not show it, for that would be brazen. That plan would have worked had it not been for the conspicuous presence of their immaculate and huge brownstone home, and always-new vehicles parked in the drive or on the street, not to mention the army of hired help. Edison never could square the huge paradox that was his parents, and didn't wish to call it hypocrisy, and instead, aspired to counter it, to do something "great" and selfless, that was not defined by money, he finally concluded. It was more of an emotion, than a defined plan, but it resonated with him, making him feel in touch with himself.

Before Edison was "Edison", the newborn child, his dad had named him in advance, not knowing if their new baby would be a girl or a boy. The name had been chosen, with the eighty-three-year-old and 1,093 patent-holding inventor, firmly in mind.

His dad had nothing but unbounded praise for the famous inventor, and no doubt hoped that by choosing that name, some of that genius would magically rub off onto his son, like pollen. His dad did not hold the inventor's best friend, Henry Ford, in nearly as much esteem. Ford's overt antisemitism was too much for Nelson, in spite of his own feelings about "certain people from those other countries". His dad embraced racism when it came to the Japanese, but hated bigotry when it came to the Jews. Edison's cynical belief was that since a sizeable chunk of his dad's customer base was Jewish, supporting those with anti-Semitic beliefs might hurt the bottom line.

Edison's mom had campaigned for a family name for the boy, such as James or Kenneth, both ancestors on her side, and nearly wept blood when her husband had flatly refused to consider Scott, which was her father's name. All of this was based on the inexact assumption that the child would be a boy. The girl's name was not an issue, as they both loved the name Doris.

His father had wanted his boy to grow up and become someone who would create something wonderful, or be a king of industry, in this blooming industrial age, and become someone who would make headlines, and acquire great wealth. Of course, he could never share that information with anyone outside the walls of their home, especially to fellow-

Quakers, to avoid being labeled an immodest hypocrite, and a rich one at that.

The comedy of the entire act, was that for a certain stretch of time, Edison shared his father's dreams for himself. Edison too wanted to achieve something important, and meaningful. You'd think, they would have had a meeting of the minds, but they kept it a secret from one another. More likely than not, it was because both sensed that the other's dreams were not a match. Nelson wanted his son to achieve greatness, within the confines of what was considered normal and acceptable business practices. He expected Edison to follow a traditional path, blazed by others before him. Edison wanted to also achieve something great, but even as a young boy, knew that in order to achieve it, he'd have to smash conventional patterns, and write new rules, and take his own path.

By the time Edison was about ten, it became apparent to Nelson, that his son's behavior and interests did not seem to be conforming, or fitting into his idea of "normal and acceptable". Edison, in his view, did not fit into the proper way to go forward in life, in terms of his interests, his tastes, and educational abilities. His son spent far too much time staring into the koi pond, playing with a scale model of the solar system he had fashioned using balls of dried clay, which he had painted, and sitting at the public library reading God knows what? Also, just the week before, Nadine had called Nelson to come up to look in Edison's room. When Nelson came up the stairs and went inside, he was aghast at what he saw. On the wall, was an art print of a wave, but not just any wave. It was a reproduction of the famous "Great Wave off Kanagawa" by Hokusai. The fact it was done by an artist over one-hundred years ago, or that it was beautifully rendered, or that it had revolutionized Japanese art with its use of Prussian blue, was of no importance. The only thing that was important was that it had been painted by a Jap.

Edison was quite bright, but didn't make a show of it. Worse yet, Edison knew that to his dad, he was someone operating outside of the conventional norms. He wanted so much, to be accepted and admired by his dad, but it wasn't to be. Being a nonconformist in this household was not considered a good trait. And what Edison had begun expressing at the dinner table about Eastern culture, the Japanese in particular, and about a path for nations to follow, that did not lead to war, had made Nelson quite uneasy, almost suspicious, of his young son. Who had he been talking to? What was he turning into? Perhaps he needed to march down to the school and check up on his teacher, and her political views? There were German sympathizers everywhere.

He knew that Edison did have an aptitude for math, and was equally adept at chemistry, but from what he could detect, did not possess that certain flare, that kind of fire in the belly that was required for greatness. Being smart was important, but knowing how to maneuver, to move sideways, when necessary, to be diplomatic without being dishonest, was an acquired skill, not one that his son seemed interested in learning anything about. In spite of this, Nelson thought he might be able to groom Edison toward business, and perhaps take over the family concern, all the dealerships, one day. That is most any father's dream in that position. While this kind of private thinking was going on, Edison's attitude about his future was steadily shifting away from any plans his dad may have had in mind.

Much stayed the same for Edison as he traversed Junior High, and High School. The adjustment from a semi-rural affluent environment, to an affluent urban one, had some challenges, mostly having to do with the hustle and bustle of a city expanding.

In more modern times, the Upper West Side of Manhattan has become one of the most expensive and desirable places to live in all of New York, but in the 30's and into the 40's, it was a checkerboard, with some streets being quite upscale, such as where the Nabors lived, while other streets were dangerous to walk down, even in broad daylight. The police were not in abundance, and half seemed on the take. Not all the streets were paved, and the concept of water flow design and control was not part of the building codes, creating deep puddles of water during a storm, or deep drifts of snow, making walking or driving, an issue.

The surge of immigrants, one culture clashing with another, showed on the streets and alleyways. Each group was feared and despised by the other, whether they be Irish or Italian or God forbid, from an African or Caribbean country, and dark-skinned. Burglary, purse snatching, muggings, and the occasional murder were not uncommon. Edison was very cautious by nature, and had inner radar that steered him, and helped him to avoid being a victim. His social life remained essentially the same, near flatline. His body had filled out somewhat, making his above-average height seem less awkward in appearance. And his ambitions of doing something great, had gradually downsized into the simple ambition of getting away from his claustrophobic parents and riches, and entering the "real world", as he put it.

The war years had interrupted many lives, and ended quite a few as well. As for the Nabors' family, the war dramatically impacted their business life. By early 1941, Nelson had acquired two more dealerships, featuring the new Chrysler Town and Country station wagon, which was an instant hit, with people signing up and willing to wait for months for their new car. He was also a silent partner with other dealerships selling the new 1941 Packard. Nabors Family Enterprises, Inc. had never been so profitable.

December of that year had brought war with the Japanese, and four days later, war with Germany. A month later, in January of 1942, by Presidential order, all production of consumer vehicles was frozen. The manufacturing plants that made all of the nameplates, had to do what they could to immediately start producing tanks, large troop-carrying trucks, bombs, guns, cannons, ambulances, torpedoes, and even helmets. All car parts, and sheet metal, either raw or already stamped into the form of a car hood or fender, was melted down to be re-purposed into anything needed for the war effort.

His dad was quite well known in the auto industry, being one of the top selling dealership chains on the east coast, so he was in the loop. A friend clued him in on the production of a new type of rugged military vehicle being developed in Ohio, and his dad threw an enormous amount of money into the start-up Ford Willys Quad prototype, later known as Ford GP, and then simply GP, and finally, Jeep. His having been at the right time and place, allowed him to reap huge profits, keep his family light years away from the nearest bread lines, and except for a few inconveniences, such as shortages of fresh eggs, new shoes, and anything made of rubber, the Nabors' household continued on with very few sacrifices.

As Edison continued to make his way to graduating from high school, he excelled in some subjects, while scraping by with a C- in others. He felt the weight of guilt resting upon him, more and more. But it was guilt by association. He knew that his parents were essentially good people, but that they were religiously corrupt in many ways. And sadly, racists. His parents had created a pathway for him to follow, but he had no interest in it.

No one could fault his dad for not being a good provider. He had worked tirelessly for a long time to achieve the success they all enjoyed. Furthermore, Edison knew that everyone was imperfect, for his exposure to religion had taught him at least that much. He had grown up observing that his parents were devout in outward appearance, preaching humility before God, and exhibited this belief only when it could be seen, while denouncing selected nationalities, and their religions, under their breath, or out loud to a select few others who felt likewise. It all made Edison feel dirty and complicit, and scared. Perhaps, underneath all of his revulsion, he was somehow the same, would turn out the same? He would attend their Quaker Church every Sunday, and listen to the sermon, but with each successive year, he would find ways to not always attend, and when he did go, he only half-listened.

Edison would revisit the topic of his parent's professed beliefs from time to time, looking for a different and kinder interpretation of them, but came away disappointed. Did he want to denounce this false life, this enormous pretense? Did he want to be "down there" with the majority of the people in the country? Struggling to make ends meet, sacrificing personal comfort and convenience, having just enough to get by? No, not especially, but he felt a responsibility toward all of those people. He owed them something, maybe a form of penance? Again, he couldn't share his feelings with his parents, for he knew all that would come of it, is another lecture, another acidic comment about him "sounding a lot like a Catholic", and other similar accusations about his feelings, his worth, and his character.

And finally, it happened. Taking up the entire front page of the *New York Times*, was a photo taken on the deck of the USS Bennington, a large, and late model aircraft carrier. In the photo, were a group of sailors holding a newspaper up to the camera, and beaming. The headline on the paper, in large bold print, read simply, 'PEACE". The war was over.

Edison had been attending the highly regarded Trinity High School, established in 1709. When he graduated, he was in the upper 90% percentile group, hammering out most of his classes. He excelled in Chemistry, Math (Algebra, Geometry, Trigonometry) and Astronomy. He did fairly well with History, but anything better than a "C-" in Biology, would have to wait for another lifetime.

American society was still in great turmoil and economic chaos, recovering from the long hard years of the war, but things almost immediately began to settle down, and people were eager to put the war behind them, and to find the new normal. The president from an elite background, who had bravely led them through the war years, almost up to the very end, had died, and had been replaced by a tough and pragmatic Midwesterner. Citizens were buying the small six-hundred square foot "cracker box" houses, which were prefabs created by Sears and Roebuck. People were buying vacuum cleaners, clothes washers, garden hoses, fresh fruit and bread, and new cars from his is dad's dealerships. The imprisoned Japanese were being released, and returned to their home towns but stripped of their former homes and businesses in most cases, and had to start over.

Edison, still in school, but out of a sense of obligation, spent a few afternoons a week at his dad's Chrysler dealership. He'd help to file papers, run errands, answer the phone, and sweep the showroom. Saturday mornings were for washing off and drying the cars.

There was another son, belonging to the sales manager at the lot. His name was Tad, and Edison had taken an instant dislike to the kid. He thought of him as a "kid" because he behaved like one. He was in fact, two months older than Edison, but seemed years younger. Even though Edison had been raised in comparative opulence, surrounded by service people, he had fended for himself, to the most part. This was one aspect of his upbringing he appreciated, and it all stemmed from his parent's strict "Quaker rules". He often made his own breakfast, packed his own lunch, carried his dirty laundry to the wash room, and always hauled the trash cans to the street every Tuesday. Tad, on the other hand, seemed to be someone who had grown quite accustomed to being served and pampered. He would be driven to the dealership every morning by his mom, whereas Edison took his bike, and he lived further away. The dealership was on Eighth Avenue and West 53rd Street, pretty much a straight shot down the west side of Central Park for about ten blocks and then, six blocks down Seventh, to the corner showroom. Tad lived three blocks away on Seventh and 55th Street.

Edison's dislike of Tad was how willingly Tad took to being pampered, even at age 15, and it bothered Edison, to see one of his own, behave as if he was still a little child. His mom would pack him a lunch, always the same lunch, which was a peanut butter and grape jelly sandwich, on white bread, with the crust cut off. Included would be an apple, with the skin peeled off, and wrapped in some aluminum foil. For dessert, there would be some Jell-O gelatin, usually cherry flavored, secured in a Ball Mason glass jar. Edison, ever the junior chemist, wondered if little Tad would be so eager to eat the confection if he knew what it was made of? (Gelatin, produced from collagen that had been extracted from boiled bones and connective muscle and ligament tissues, and other animal products).

That Tad's presence could annoy Edison to such a degree, was simply an indication at how small Edison's world had become. Sometimes, after work, or on a day off, Edison would pedal over to Central Park and find himself sitting atop his favorite large rock, with a view of the ball fields and the skyscrapers, one going up every week it seemed. The days with white puffy clouds, or thunderheads approaching, were his favorite. He would lay on the rock and gaze at the clouds, the day's light fading, and get lost in thoughts and daydreams. He could, for those moments, escape the dull routine that had become his life.

It wasn't entirely his parent's fault, and in fact, it was mostly his, and he knew it. The expectation from his parent's, now that they had abandoned dreams of his being a business titan, was that he would, upon graduating Trinity, go to a university somewhere in the east, and after graduating with a Masters or PhD, become a renowned mathematician, perhaps earning tenure at an ivy league university. They knew that their son would need to be in the protective shell of a well-established institution, such as Princeton or Harvard. They knew he did not have what it took to forge a new path, or a leader. They had resigned themselves to this.

Edison did not see things that way. The ever-present shadow of his parent's, that cast itself over Edison every waking moment, haunted him. He knew of an alternative viewpoint, that told him that no matter how great and accomplished he might become, in whatever field that might be, it would all be due to God's hand. Edison was merely the instrument. To their credit, his parent's had instilled this in him from the moment he could walk. But to achieve a firm foot hold as a professor in a highly traditional and wealthy university, was not Edison's ambition, but his parent's. Yes, he wanted to achieve something remarkable, but if it happened while he was living with sherpas in Tibet, and living in a tent, and hardly had two nickels, that would be fine with him, and in fact, it would be preferable.

Regardless of his high aptitude for science and mathematics in general, he knew he would have to start at the bottom, somewhere, somehow, but he did not want to join the ranks working at a large corporation. It was the "ranks" part he recoiled from. He liked being alone, liked doing things on his own, and wanted to create something he could call his own.

At last, It was 1948, and Edison was now 18, having had his birthday a month before his graduation ceremony. Even though he knew that the birthday was a significant one, or said to be, serving as the line that separated boyhood from adulthood, he also knew it was an artificial line, one that some had crossed when 16, and others not until they were in their twenties. Regardless, it felt good to Edison, and he could sense being lighter, not as burdened with his parent's foibles and follies, and now entering the phase of his life where he could begin to make his own decisions, chart his own course.

But he languished. Week after week went by, and then the months, with Edison working at his dad's dealership, having to tolerate Tad, who incidentally, had moved from "lot boy" to sales, and even had his own desk with a nameplate, "Thaddeus Monkley". By the time Tad had secured his foot hold, he had just turned the ripe old age of 18, with Edison close behind. His sales numbers were somewhat anemic, with most first-time visitors to the showroom, veering away from the over-eager, and quite obviously young, salesman. His appearance and manner did not evoke confidence in the shoppers, it was fair to say. Edison would observe this from across the showroom, and learn from it. Learn what not to do, learn how not to be.

Those three years after the end of war had sped by, and Edison watched the world of Manhattan become more confident. The war was now receding in the collective memory of the people who busily walked by the showroom windows, focused on their lives, unburdened by the material sacrifices they had suffered, but some, were burdened by the pain of having lost a son, a brother, or a husband to the war, but those people had been swept up in the general pool, absorbed, and the creature that was the swarming crowd, moved on, looked ahead, did not forget the nightmare, but did not linger, for they were going to survive and succeed. There was an energy to this, that Edison could feel, almost see. That is what he had wanted to be part of. But how could he grab it, become part of that thing, whatever it was?

Two months later, in the Fall of 1948, he felt a strong desire to serve. And impulsively, enlisted in the Navy, being led to believe by the enlister, that his strong math and chemistry knowledge would be put to good use. The promise of being able to utilize his G.I. Bill once out, supplied him with the confidence that he could make it on his own, if need be, without being supported by his parents. His parents, upon hearing the news at the dinner table that night, were astonished and crestfallen.

His dad had already secretly set him up as the assistant sales manager at his Buick dealership in Midtown, having abandoned visions of even a professorship for his son. Once Edison had graduated Trinity, Nelson had nagged his son almost daily, about applying to a top shelf university, and then to a second-tier one, and finally, to a local state college. Edison, wanting to avoid confrontation, would promise to look into it "tomorrow", but that day never came. Upon hearing that Edison, without any hint of advanced warning, would be joining the Navy, as a mere Seaman Recruit, sent Nelson to his doctor with heart palpitations.

His mother took the news with resignation, having long realized that her son had no ambitions of fortune in the retail car business, or had a desire to be a professor. She knew that her son would lead an unconventional life, and would need to carve his own way with a career of his own choosing. As for his religious inclinations, she had lost all hope, and prayed for his soul nightly. Internally, she had said goodbye to him years ago.

By the time Edison had finished his basic training outside of San Francisco, it was the end of the year, and the young sailor turned heads almost immediately, impressing his superior officers with his mature manner and obvious level of education. Their appreciation of his knowledge would come later.

He was first assigned to a naval supply ship, carrying food, linens, equipment, and mail from war ship, to war ship, up and down the California coast. Edison, ever the introvert, did not partake in the wild weekend leaves while in port, and chose instead to stay aboard ship for some peace and quiet, or walk the streets of San Francisco, Seattle, or San Diego, in his whites. The war was not that far in the distant past, and people everywhere, enjoyed speaking to him, thanking him, as if he had been on Iwo Jima, and always offering him free lunches or Coca Colas. He would get his share of teasing by his fellow crewmen, but there was something about Edison, that caused them to take it easy on him, to give him some room. At six foot five, and now entirely filled out with some muscle, they referred to him as the "gentle giant".

1949 was well under way, and with tensions rapidly coming to a boil in the Korean Peninsula, President Truman had ordered there be a readiness with the Navy, and subsequently, war ships were busy cruising the coast, doing drills, getting ready for what might follow.

There was mass denial among most American citizens, and most Navy recruits, that another war might be in the making so soon after the close of the last one. Some people felt it wasn't a new war, but an extension of the last one.

Regardless, it seemed like science fiction to Edison. Especially so, since in those few short years, the entire landscape of war, of "theaters", had changed. Now, there was the atomic bomb, developed by the Soviet Union, in addition to the U.S., with other countries surely coming on line soon. These bombs could of course, wipe out entire populations, and be transported not just by plane, but by missiles. Much of this was high tech, and most of the bombs being tested, and the missiles to go with, failed at launch or ignition, but many didn't, and the race was on.

Japan and Germany had both mistakenly seen a weakness in American resolve and fortitude, and now it seemed that Russia, the new gorilla in the room, looked upon America that way as well. They wanted to seize the upper hand, if possible, while America was distracted with yet another war on the tail of the last horrific one. World War Two involved seventy countries in armed conflict, but this new one on the horizon would be much more confined, restricted to one geographical area, involving four countries. It might be highly distracting for a U.S. government, its military, and citizenry, with post-war trauma still spinning in its collective head. That was the Soviet thinking.

The environment Edison found himself in was surprising. The last thing he had imagined was the likelihood he'd be caught up in an active shooting war. The idea of more atomic bombs being used loomed over everyone's head. But as of yet, war had not been declared. Edison's sharp mind and ability to improvise allowed him to pass by most of his fellow recruits, and virtually skip the title "Apprentice" and in short order he was an official Seaman. The Navy was in a hurry to pluck the most capable from the ranks, and push them into areas of responsibility.

Within months of duty, he was promoted to Petty Officer Third Class. His home base was shifted to Long Beach, and his tour continued, with more promotions, landing him up the ladder to Ensign aboard the USS Sturgeon, a large auxiliary storage ship, modified and upgraded from the former war.

His ghosts went with him everywhere, however. He would recognize them, and do an inventory. He called it his "fear inventory", and equated it to the devil's work. It would whisper to him that he was inadequate, that he should always strive to please people, to make them like him. Edison would resist these messages, knowing that with the strength of God, whatever that meant, he would not let others define him, to determine his destiny. He would not let the opinion of others become his higher power. He knew he was different, and would undoubtedly always be alone.

The war in Korea commenced in 1950, and the notion of a casual Navy life for a young man, a life with military structure, but allowing for some travel, and interesting experiences, quickly evaporated. Korea, formerly a Japanese colony for thirty-five years, had been divided along the 38th parallel by the U.S. and the Soviet Union, creating a north and south, after the end of the Second World War. It was a ticking bomb. The northern half was communist, and its citizens were forced to conform and obey, but there was unity. The southern portion, was a democracy, and had a long-tortured history of factions within the former colony in opposition to one another, on both political and cultural grounds, resulting in very little unity. What greatly complicated matters, was that both of the newly formed countries had their big brothers to lean on.

Americans were being informed on the front pages of every newspaper that the North Koreans, aided by Russia, were pouring over the border into South Korea, and before long, they would occupy that country, with an eye for more conquests. It was the beginning of a whole new struggle, but unlike the world war, it was shadowed by the prospect of it growing into mass annihilation. It wasn't long before China got involved, helping North Korea with troops and weaponry.

Edison had two more years to go in his four-year hitch, and he was promoted yet again to Lieutenant, given a course in sonar operation, and sent back to San Francisco, so he could eventually step aboard the USS Iowa battleship when it was ready for re-commission from the former war. His preparation and training took much longer than anticipated, with many idle days, what with the retrofit of the battleship taking much longer to finish, than originally planned.

During this extended time, Edison was given some leave, and flew back east on an Army transport plane to see his parents. They were like so many parents, proud of their son but terribly nervous, one could say terrified, at the prospect of their son being killed or maimed. Edison had been given a two-week leave, and he spent most of it revisiting his former younger life. He dropped in to one of his local movie houses and caught *The Day the Earth Stood Still* and at another, *The Lavender Hill Mob.* He still loved the movies, but the prospect of being in a shooting war had taken a lot of the fun out of it. He visited his dad's showroom to see the latest styles and do a little reminiscing, and couldn't avoid bumping into Tad, who was now the sales manager. The draft had been reinstated, but Tad had been given a 4-F deferment for low vision, and being hard of hearing. These were both conditions Edison had never noticed when working next to him, but perhaps, they had both developed while he was away in the Navy? As for Edison, more than one fellow Seaman had asked him why he hadn't deferred, as a conscientious objector (a "conchie") since he was legitimately a Quaker? Edison's motive for joining the Navy was to escape his former life, that had felt like a prison. Had he known he was going to walk head first into another war, he might've considered using his religion as a reason for deferment, but Edison didn't, in his heart, see himself as a

Quaker, but as some kind of an unformed Christian. The reality of the war, he viewed in the abstract.

He spent most of his time at home, visiting with Cristobal and the koi, catching up with the small army of hired hands as they came and went, all very glad to see him. King and Champ had passed, and been replaced by Thor and Hercules. Unlike the former two, Edison managed to teach them to fetch. He had shown up in uniform, but had quickly shed the clothing for his own, once home. He was required to wear the uniform only if he went out in public, and had grown weary of being constantly stopped by people on the street and elsewhere, wanting to hear the latest news about the war, and if he had seen "any action yet?" It did come with benefits however, and he couldn't help but enjoy being handed free popcorn at the movie house, or a free sandwich at the diner, or having a door held for him. The rush of warm feelings this delivered to him melted away rather quickly, as he was just then beginning to fully absorb the fact he was in the military, bound for war. This point came home for him, literally, when seated at the dinner table with his parents, who were doing their level best to put on a happy face, and be supportive. He knew that his dad severely disapproved of his decision to join up, having a dual feeling of rejection. He felt that his son had betrayed his Quaker roots, and that he had thrown away an opportunity to step into the family business. His mom remained mute.

On their last dinner together before he had to return to base, his dad had said to him, "You know, once you get out of the Navy, there'll be a job waiting for you right here".

Edison had stopped chewing his pork chop, looked up and said, simply, "No thanks dad, I'm thinking about rockets".

"Rockets?" And looking at his wife, asked rhetorically, "Did he say 'rockets'"?

"Yes dad, rockets".

"What does that even mean?"

"I'm not really sure".

Nine years prior, there had been considerable pushback from a vocal minority about the country entering World War Two, especially in the beginning. Many prominent citizens wanted to be isolated from the European war, and in some cases, almost seemed sympathetic to the Nazi ambitions. Some of that feeling emanated from overt anti-Semitism, while others were of the more pragmatic mind, wanting our money and efforts to be turned inward, and not spent on another country's problems. The larger world view had won the argument, reasoning that if we didn't help end the war over there, war would come here eventually.

The Korean War, was not even classified as a "war" but as a "police action", and it involved more than just American troops and weapons, but also the United Nations, with many allied countries joining in. This war, arguably an extension of the last one, had also received much pushback, but after two months of war, with the South Koreans nearly defeated, the United Nations stepped in, pushed the North Koreans back, and drove over the border into their country. Ultimately, the U.S. supplied about 90% of the troops. Later, the success of the counter-offensive was so dramatic that General MacArthur was urging Truman to allow him to push deeper into the North Korean real estate, and take the whole country back. Truman was not nearly as convinced as MacArthur, as to the wisdom of that a strategy, and insisted on re-establishing the 38th parallel, but not before a considerable amount of bloodshed had been created.

Before any of that, Edison realized that the ship he was about to be on, was a super star, the twin of the famous USS Missouri, the "Big Mo", that hosted the surrender ceremony of Japan in Tokyo Bay, only a few years earlier. The ship was constructed in the New York Naval Yard, and as it was being built, it attracted all the workers from the entire yard, who gazed up at the behemoth, almost in disbelief, and finally, it launched in 1942. It was nicknamed the "Big Stick", and had been in attendance with 250 other allied ships, at the surrender ceremony, in Tokyo Harbor. It had participated in many Pacific battles, being the decisive weapon in the Marshalls Campaign, the capture of the Marianas, the Palaus, and sea battles in the Philippines Sea and Leyte Gulf. It was responsible for decimating what was left of the Japanese carrier-based war planes. It was a beast, at nearly 900-feet in length, with nearly 3,000 crew members, powered by four, steam-driven sets of turbine engines, and carrying 2.5 million gallons of fuel oil. Officially, it did 33 knots. It sailed out of San Francisco Bay with Edison, toward Korea in April of 1952, about five months before Edison's discharge was up. He was put in charge of the sonar room, with few chances to see the open sky or daylight.

The first stop, was on the east side of North Korea, just off of the port city of Wonsonjin, destroying supply warehouses and roads. It was Edison's first experience with weaponry, let alone with nine, enormous 16-inch guns, and his first time at war. It scared the daylights out of him, but he kept a cool demeanor, so he thought. The force of the enormous gun batteries shook his internal organs, and he found it difficult to get any sleep.

Immediately following this, the ship steamed to Suwon Dan and Kojo, destroying gun emplacements and a division headquarters, and the very next day she sailed into Wonsan Harbor and destroyed more warehouses, railroad yards and depots. After this, she moved northward and shelled railroad lines at Tanchon, destroying four tunnels. Then onto Chindong and Kosong for two days of non-stop bombardment of various North Korean positions. She then went into the waters off of Chongjin, an industrial center, only forty-eight miles from the Russian border. She seemed indestructible, but in actuality, was protected by a flotilla of other war ships, and air support from carrier-based Grumman Hell Cats.

The battleship struck fear into any enemy personnel on land, who first spotted it through their binoculars. This type of movement, bombardment, and movement again behavior, continued without pause, and all of the Iowa's crew members had to get along with minimal sleep, and basic food. Edison subsisted mostly on hot dogs, mac and cheese, and vanilla ice cream, while it lasted. Edison's tour of duty was extended into late October, by decree, whereby he participated and witnessed numerous other bombardments, up and down the coast of North Korea. Twenty-seven operations in all. 16,689 rounds were fired. Each round weighed as much as 2,700 hundred pounds, or put another way, each one as heavy as a VW Beetle or a Honda Civic.

Surprisingly, the death toll exacted on the enemy was low, for two main reasons: 1) The Iowa could move in reality, at about thirty-five to thirty-seven knots, depending on conditions at sea, which is quite fast for such an enormous war ship, but slow enough to allow the terrified enemy personnel to evacuate, 2) which made for mostly empty buildings, warehouses, depots, factories, harbors and roads. The ship had earned a reputation, and with nearly fifty anti-aircraft guns ringing it, it was a suicide mission for a war plane to get near it.

In spite of the relatively low body count that Edison participated in, it made him feel very strange. At first, there was the fear and exhilaration of being part of such an extensive wave of attacks on a despised invading enemy, and being a crew member on such an illustrious ship, but "war" was not something Edison had ever factored into his consciousness. Before this, it was an abstract thought, but after his bones and guts were rattled almost without pause, and his ears rang from the thunderous roar of the mighty guns for days on end, he took on another perspective. It might have been the Quaker hiding inside of him, it might have been some inner spark of ambition inside of him, wanting him to do something that mattered, that did good. Whatever the cause, Edison's purpose in life had surfaced, by way of the deafening roar of the guns, hurtling shells over twenty-five miles, onto enemy positions.

For Edison, whether this war was justified or not, was not the issue. For him, the future had to present something better for his life, and for the world. What war would come next? What justifications would be created, or recognized, on the way to killing millions more? He became caught up in a mission to do something significant, something that mattered. Mixed in with this, was his increased ardent Christian faith, that in his mind, was undeniably linked to his sense of destiny. He would rob naps when he could, drifting off, ear plugs firmly in, his bunk shaking from the guns, thinking of the Prince of Peace. Nearly as a chant to himself, he would say over and over, his various memorized quotes from the Bible. His favorite was from Matthew 5:0. "Blessed are the peacemakers, for they shall be called the sons of God". Was he a peacemaker? Was he a Quaker at heart? Was he making peace now, detecting enemy ships nearby? Maybe it wasn't the sounds of the roaring guns that had kept him awake.

Upon his discharge from the Navy, he enrolled at Caltech in Pasadena (California Institute of Technology) on a G.I. Bill, with some additional financial backing for housing, from his supportive but puzzled parents. He was still on the hook for two more years in the reserves, and he hoped the Korean "conflict" would not spread across other borders, and become larger, which would pull him back onto a war ship, no doubt. When he arrived back in San Francisco, he planned on giving himself a little vacation before commencing his studies.

His parents flew out from New York on Pan American Airways, aboard a four-prop Super Constellation, newly improved by Lockheed. It was the state of the art in those days. Turbo props were being experimented with, and increasingly in use, and the notion of jet engines was just coming on. He realized that with his strong aptitudes in math and chemistry, the obvious choice would be to focus on those disciplines once his general courses were out of the way. He still hadn't stumbled upon, or teased out, his "mission", his purpose, but something was pulling on him, motioning for him to follow this particular pathway, for it would lead to something of consequence. "Rockets" were still on his mind.

He had heard a pastor in church once, at the Navy base in Oakland, speak about pathways. He held that when Jesus said to people, "This is the way, I am the way" it was in context to what was happening at that moment. The streets of ancient Galilee were clogged with poor people, desperate for clean water and food, and there were other people, sinister people everywhere, taking advantage of the poor, claiming to be messengers from God, that they had the true answers, and they were seeking followers. According to the Navy pastor, who spoke in plain non-lofty phrases, that when Jesus showed up, and took all of this in, is when he stated, in essence, that "No, these others are imposters. They will lead you astray. Come with me, for I know the way, I am the way". Edison hadn't finished connecting the dots, but he knew that his faith and his destiny were going to meet, to cross paths one day, and that day could be soon.

His parents could only assemble a small number of sentences when talking to him. It was as if he had been somehow transformed, not just because of his appearance, in his crisp white dress uniform when they would go out to dine, or his notably more trim and muscular body, but it had to do with something inside of him which they hadn't a clue about. They were happy for their son, and glad he had not been hurt in the war, but remained puzzled as to what he had in mind. They were happy he had chosen a good school, but not entirely happy. They reminded him that there were many good schools back east, and that maybe he should consider one of them?

C altech introduced him to yet another new world. As with most things in Edison's young life, things then don't compare terribly well with things now, such as the scope and appearance of the school currently. For example, it wasn't until the 1980's, long after Edison departed the campus, that the Beckman Institute was established, housed in a beautiful Spanish style building with arches and breezeways, and a beautiful reflection pool. It is dedicated to the study of biology and chemistry. When Edison went there, there was no Beckman building, but there were certainly serious courses of study in those two areas. Caltech was aligned with the Army and then later with the Air Force, as it came into being. It had been recommended to Edison, as he was exiting active duty, that he enroll in that school, for he would be given preferential treatment, and have access to proprietary information and discoveries, linked to various military research projects, in particular, projects involving rockets. He had told his rank superiors in the Navy, many more times than once, of his avid interest in rockets. It was so often that it had become a running joke aboard the ship. Even though the war for him had been detached, never once seeing an injured or dead soldier, never seeing blood, or the results of their bombardments, the notion of war, and peace, was still conceptual. He knew that the military was on the cutting edge of discovery when it came to anything involving technological advancements, so he wanted to use that access as a stepping stone, to where, he wasn't sure, but to him, it had to involve rockets.

Edison had studied with fascination the lore of this new world he was entering. Much history had already occurred in the world of rocket science, and the people at JPL had been given the nickname, "Pasadena Rocketeers".

Starting in the 1940's, and flowing into the 50's, Martin Summerfield and Frank Malina, two scientists who had pioneered liquid rocket propellant during World War Two, had done much experimentation with jet propulsion. They had been joined in their quest by other scientists, Jack Parsons and Theodore von Karman, being the two most prominent. They established Aerojet, that had ties to Caltech and by extension, JPL. They became known as the "suicide squad" for their risky tests. But then came a wrinkle. Malina had expressed misgivings about the use of their fuels and rockets for military use, and was immediately branded a Communist sympathizer by some, and sidelined, but not before being the first director of JPL. It had been his partner, von Karman, who had gone to post-war Germany, and brought Werner von Braun back to the States for his work as a "space architect". By the late-40's, Malina knew that future liquid-fueled rockets, made possible by him, would carry the newly developed atomic bombs, and was further convinced that the U.S. was gearing up for a first strike world war. Due to the pressures of his circumstances, his wife left him, and shortly thereafter, he quit the rocket program and joined the newly established UNESCO, but his past always haunted him. His life hadn't turned out quite the way he had imagined or hoped.

In this same chaotic and politically-charged atmosphere, Oppenheimer was being openly criticized for his negative comments about nuclear bomb development, and Oppenheimer's brother openly admitted he was a Communist, while also implicating Malina. Finally, Malina in desperation, fled to France, where he was sought by U.S. authorities for espionage. He remained in France, and became a kinetic artist, having become quite rich from his Aerojet stock.

As Edison walked the hallways of Caltech, and across the expanses of lawn, lost in thought, he contemplated the unseemly mix of science and politics, and as he considered those two worlds, at odds with one another, it served as a sieve, allowing him to separate the two, and focus on what was important to him. He was developing, not so much as a person against war, a "peacenik", which in those days was often conflated with being a pinko or commie sympathizer, but instead, being a pragmatic someone, who had no time or inclination for war, or its mechanics. His mind was riding higher than that, his eyes cast on faraway ideas and theories. He wanted to help propel mankind into deep space, blaze new frontiers, and not be involved in the constant push and pull of geopolitical maneuverings and strategies. He couldn't prevent the gamesmanship, but he could at least shut it out of his world, and not knowingly participate. He thought it would be simply wonderful if he could be left alone to help develop a way to reach deep space, leaving the political jousting behind, and out of mind.

However, there is one person who distracted his gaze into the future. Her name was Marcy Ann, a tall and slender young woman, of approximately his age he reckoned, with dark blonde hair, brushed back and then to the sides. He was certain it was a movie star style, with a name, but he didn't have a clue as to what it might be, he just knew it seemed to fit her very well. Marcy was a part-time student, living at home with her church-going and bible-touting parents, in town, and studying of all things, nuclear fusion. Her demeanor was Southern proper and sweet, even though she had been born and raised in Pasadena. They immediately hit it off, sitting together at lunch under the Japanese Maple every Tuesday and Thursday. It took Edison what felt like two centuries, to build up the courage to ask her on a date, and when he did ask, she cheerfully responded to the affirmative, glad that the suspense was at last over.

Edison was developing into his own living-breathing paradox, being full of wild imaginings inside of his head, but in his personal manner, was very quiet and non-assertive. Upon meeting Marcy, this personality trait soon melted away, and he became much more buoyant, outwardly happy, and even made the occasional joke, which in some cases, was funny. Marcy by contrast, receded more into the background, allowing Edison to talk and expound on any number of scientific topics. She had a firm grasp of her religious beliefs. Perhaps "un-bending" would be a better term? Her steely-eyed belief didn't always mesh well with Edison's devout but unformed beliefs, but they recognized that they were both in the same room, so to speak, so there was rarely any conflict. As time went on, they ventured into movie houses, into church (her family's Lutheran church), took small hikes in the adjoining hills, tried their hand at bird watching, and after an arduous process of false starts and missed signals, had "intimate contact" about six months into their relationship.

The author is conflicted as to how much to divulge, as to how completely their first night of lovemaking should be described in these pages. This conflict arises not out of prudery, but out of modesty. The entire story is about modesty, about a modest man, in an immodest time, so it might not be in keeping with the tone of the overall book to become too graphic. But this important moment in their lives does deserve some description, on the other hand. Actually, nothing remarkable happened, given that this was a romantic and lustful encounter between two amateurs, and all of the usual mishaps occurred, from zippers that wouldn't unzip, buttons that were snapped off of clothing, non-sequential undressing resulting in, for example, pants trying to be being pulled off prior to shoes coming off, that kind of thing. As for "performance", Edison was a stud and Marcy was his immodest equal.

Once that happened, the wheels fell off, and they were both convinced they were meant for one another, and whatever future lay in store for Edison, would carry them to great spiritual, and economically acceptable, heights.

It was the 50's, and it was assumed the woman would take the rear seat to the man's ambitions. This was certainly the case with these two love birds. Marcy was very bright, but her heart wasn't into nuclear fusion, and all she had really wanted when enrolling there, was to be exposed to some higher education, and be around people who wanted it also. The proximity of the school to her home was a big influence on her choosing Caltech due to her parent's neighbor, who was the Assistant to the Dean of the school, and got her to the head of the line.

Edison diligently plowed through his general course requirements, anxious to get on with some hardcore math and especially, chemistry. Perhaps it was the influence of Marcy and her studies, or the notion that was widely believed in 50's America, that grasped the imagination of many people: that DuPont's "better living through chemistry" slogan was the new mantra, and much more than a catchy slogan to push the latest cold remedy, or clothes detergent.

The more he attended Marcy's church, the more he realized that while it may have said "Lutheran" on the sign outside, it seemed very Pentecostal on the inside. He went along because he wanted to get along, but quietly resolved that ardent organized religious belief was not the path for him. He held onto his quieter and more modest Quaker self, as much a believer as ever, but quietly, without the thunder and lightning. This required a certain level of deception and evasion, when visiting her parents for Sunday supper once in a while, but watching evasive maneuvers inside the sonar room had taught him a few tricks, when it came to maneuvering, redirection, and anticipation.

He had been attending Caltech for a full three years, and was just beginning his fourth and last year. It was early 1956. By now, he had figured he would have developed a game plan, his path forward to destiny, but had nothing to show for it. Certainly, a solid education in the application of known chemistry, and much study on theory was his, but in terms of making his mark, on doing that one important thing, he was at a loss. He would look out into the night skies, at the stars, and wanted to be a part of that, but didn't know how to achieve the dream.

Various manufacturers had already been in touch with him about employment. On his list of choices were good offers from Clorox Chemical Company Detergent Division, Proctor and Gamble Detergent and Toiletries Division, Johnson and

Johnson Lotion Division, Natone (later Neutrogena) Soap Division, Colgate-Palmolive Company Personal Hygiene Division, and lastly, offers from the dueling Mobil Oil Corporation and Chevron Corporation, both of them step children of Standard Oil.

There's a funny thing about chemistry in the modern age. Usually, a lone chemist develops a new formulation, perhaps in an effort to apply it to a specific need or use. Often, it is discovered that the chemical has other uses, perhaps "better" uses. Also often, at some point, a major chemical company will hire that chemist, buy the formula from him, or simply adopt it (steal it). In many instances, the development of the chemical into various applications for industrial, military or consumer use, will have a history of many companies or people having played a role. Of note, the DuPont company was especially keen on netting Edison to help them with one of these types of chemicals. In the late 60's, they had further developed a liquid chemical, originally invented in the late 1930's, to spray onto army tanks and other military vehicles, to waterproof them. (It was later, primarily manufactured by the 3-M company). Their chemical formulation, first known as PFOA (perfluorooctanoate), later changed to C-8 (8 carbon chain structure) and known to the consumer as Teflon, had endless possibilities, and they needed bright young chemists to help them develop variations (synthetic compounds). It ended up famously as a cookware coating, but was also used in clothing, carpeting, upholstery, floor wax, and in various toiletries. Regrettably, the chemical also found its way into the water table near one of the manufacturing plants, the Washington Works plant, in West Virginia. It also was in the air, spewed out by their multiple smoke stacks. Livestock, fish, birds, various other types of wildlife, and people inadvertently consumed it, causing numerous cases of cancer and birth defects. Like so many of these accounts, the company fought the accusations ferociously for years, until finally, years later, the EPA fined them an enormous amount of money and had the product(s) pulled off the market. But the damage had been done. It is estimated, that every species of animal on Earth has the chemical in their bloodstream, including 99% of the Human population. It is a "forever chemical" (persistent organic pollutant). Of course, Edison couldn't have known about any of this in advance, but his "true north" senses had told him to avoid helping large corporations develop chemicals. That was not his purpose.

While Edison's self-esteem was given a cautionary lift with all of the offers, his dreams of achieving something great, something that mattered, were slowly disappearing. He knew that he could, blindfolded, throw a dart at a paper listing the offers, and take the one found by the dart, for they seemed all the same, and it killed him inside. Although a skilled student, he went to class heavily distracted by his powerful but vague ambitions to achieve something great, but all he could see was the end of the road, not an endless one. He agonized over the prospect of a career making a better bar of soap or a better food preservative. Marcy was an expert at consoling, but her best work fell far short.

In long distance calls, his dad could detect his disillusionment, and remind him that he could come home and start to take over the business, starting with running a Buick dealership on Long Island. No matter how Edison couched his feelings, no matter the topic, his dad would find a way to bring the conversation around to the latest model of car on one of his showroom floors, as an enticement. The car could be his, and a down payment on a nice little house as well, if he were to come back home. A typical segue from Edison describing his feelings about deep space, would be to hear of the features of the newly improved Buick Roadmaster, with a larger 236 horsepower engine, equipped with "Dynaflow" for "quicker and smoother acceleration", air conditioning by Frigidaire, rear seats with armrests, a padded dashboard, and "the convertible base model could be had for only $3,521" (close to $40,000 in 2024 dollars). His dad had been selling cars for so long, it was in his DNA, and would slip in and out of a sales pitch seamlessly. His dad was trying the best he could, and the offer from his dad was heartfelt, and meaningful, and no doubt promised a much higher income than working anonymously for some large chemical company on a new type of toothpaste, but in all the offers, there was a vital ingredient missing: Magic. Edison had to feel the magic, had to feel he was in new territory, and doing it with an aim to make things better, somehow. New car smell, or a cute bungalow as a starter home, were no match to exploring the outer fringes of the solar system.

The first big fight he had with Marcy was about the Buick dealership offer. "The package", as his dad had called it. She was flabbergasted that he didn't want to continue the family business, a very lucrative one at that, and that he instead, had some nebulous idea about achieving something "great" but had no idea what that meant. She was getting pressured behind the scenes by her parents, both of whom felt that Edison was one of those unfocused, over-educated, and noncommittal types, and she should get on with her life, find someone with defined goals, someone whose head wasn't in the clouds, and whose nose was in the Bible.

They weren't the only ones beating Edison up. He was doing a good job on himself as well. He would torture himself as to his actual, down deep, motives. Was it that his ego couldn't allow him to be an anonymous worker ant, that he had to be in a spotlight, getting attention, getting noticed? Was his ambition really about fame, and not doing something for the greater good? Was it all about him, and not something aspirational? And where was his Christianity hiding all of this time? Where was his humility, his quiet reverence for Jesus? He prosecuted himself on a daily basis, nearly talking himself into moving back east and selling Buicks, and making a ton of money running the entire operation when his dad finally retired. It pulled on him. He took the long way back to his place on foot that day, with dusk coming on, and a beautiful scarlet colored sunset. He had resolved to pick up the phone, and work out the details with his dad. He'd do it first thing after school tomorrow. But, of course, life loves to dish out curve balls.

It was raining that next day, and a cold nasty wind swept through the campus and found windows cracked open, doors not secured, and blew papers up into the air, and if caught outside, the men's pompadours blew over their foreheads, and ladies skirts traveled up over their thighs.

The two men that walked across the common lawn toward Edison's class during second period, seemed completely un-phased by the cold wind, and battering rain drops. They walked side by side, holding their briefcases in one hand, and clasping their Fedoras on their heads with the other. They entered the classroom, spoke in confidential tones to the professor, and the professor motioned for Edison to come forward, to the front of the room. Once there, Edison was introduced to Mr. Black and Mr. Red (that's really the names they used) and was asked by them to step out into the hallway for a moment. Edison did so, and once out, they both gave him a thorough up and down look, as if he were a product, a slab of meat, they had just purchased sight unseen, and wanted to be sure they were getting the goods they paid for.

Mr. Black and Mr. Red were in the employment of the nearby Jet Propulsion Laboratory. It was known to some, but not many, that Caltech was essentially overseen by the U.S. military, and that Caltech oversaw much of what JPL was imagining and developing. These two had come to see Edison with a job offer. Edison's heart nearly stopped. He had of course heard about JPL, knew some details about the facility, knew of its secrecy and ties to the government, knew it was heavily involved in missile development for both exploration and military use, but never in his wildest imaginings, had he thought he would be approached. He had many times thought of inquiring with them, and had gone so far as to drive to the facility, and fill out a generic employment application, but he had never heard a thing back in response. He did this three times. He knew that this place was for the elite and already accomplished, not a freshman like him. Apparently, he was mistaken.

The two men, dressed in bland no-press dual-fabric grey suits, with standard accessories from head to toe, had bland personalities to match. They laid out a brief outline to Edison, as to why they had come there. Everything they said came out as a brief stilted outline, and Edison soon realized that if he wanted more details, he'd have to ask someone else. The core idea was that they had been directed to find some young and very capable talent in the field of chemistry, for developing a new and top-secret project. The idea was that JPL wanted fresh eyes, fresh ideas, and not the same old tired ideas. They said "out of the box" more than once. They needed youth and smarts. They were intending to approach a few others on the campus as well, but Edison was their first stop. They said that the pay, once employment probation was complete, would be "quite generous".

At nearly the last moment, just hours before Edison was going to pick up the phone and make that fateful call to home, here were these two guys offering him to come over and be part of a place he barely had the courage to dream about. The project they alluded to, whatever it was, just had to be interesting, cutting edge, he figured. And it must have something to do with math or chemistry, and rockets, or else why would they be pulling him aside? It was one of the more stupid thoughts he had had with himself, of which there had been many. Of course, it had to do with math and chemistry, and most probably, rockets. It was JPL.

As he was standing there in front of them, the only adverse thought he had, that crossed his mind in a flash, was whether he'd have to end up looking like them, dressed like them? Edison preferred Keds and cardigans. He liked his quiet and modest individuality. He smiled faintly, but not faint enough. Mr. Black wanted to know what was so funny? Mr. Red seemed mildly irritated. Edison assured them the smile was from being happy they were there, and he thanked them more than twice, for having bothered to come over to his class in such nasty cold weather. The two JPL men slipped Edison their business cards and left. Edison's head felt light, hardly believing his good fortune. He had to stay in the empty hallway, pacing back and forth, for about ten minutes, to compose himself. He laughed out loud. He hadn't laughed a real laugh for months. He felt like he could float. Once he had calmed himself, he realized the reason he was so giddy was because he was on his truthful path, at last, and he looked up at the ceiling as if he could see through it to the heavens, giving God a personal thanks.

He marched himself back into class, with all eyes on him, and sat quietly, looking straight ahead, doing his level best to appear nonchalant, as if he had just been asked something completely inconsequential out in the hallway, such as what was his favorite flavor of ice cream?

It should be noted that his favorite was Pralines and Cream, which he treated himself and Marcy to, every Saturday afternoon at the Pasadena Thrifty Drugs. They'd always glance at the large black and white framed photo on the wall, showing Errol Flynn cutting the grand opening ribbon to that store in 1941. Even someone as great and famous as Flynn, had to suit up and keep himself in the public eye, to keep himself relevant. Edison would wonder if that was a necessary ingredient to keeping your career alive? Many of the rocket scientists of the day and in the past, were not afraid of the camera, or flattering publicity. *What if that is something I have to deal with, one day? I don't want to. I want to stay hidden, in the shadows.*

After his hallway meeting, he felt much lighter, with a great sense of relief washing over him, and the dreadful weight of a future filled with managing car dealerships, lifted from him. But that lasted about one day. His lightness was tamped down by the reality that he wasn't in JPL yet, and he had to prove himself worthy. He was facing a series of sit-down interviews at the lab, with exams, aptitude tests, a physical, a psychological exam, and interviews conducted with Marcy, and finally with his parents and sister Rachel, by phone. Much of the thoroughness made sense, since he might be dealing with highly sensitive government secrets, and he needed security clearance. If even one friend or relative was considered sympathetic to Communism, or was associated with someone with those beliefs, it could sink his chances.

Before he fully realized it, the school year was nearly over, all of the JPL interviews and exams had been conducted, and all that was left were the remaining two weeks of wrapping up school by taking final exams. Some were surprisingly difficult. Others were almost laughable, as he flew through the answers without even double-checking himself. For the tough ones, he had studied with intensity, barely sleeping, rarely eating. Edison knew that at the very last moment, it was possible to stumble, to somehow go blank on questions he knew the answers to, and the intense pressure he felt could screw it all up. He prayed frequently, but found it hard to concentrate on talking to God, or anyone else, for more than a minute, his mind skipping and hopping from thought to thought, and menaced by his racing emotions.

In the end, he aced all but one of his tests, with scores in the 90's, and the lone exception, an 88. The offers from Clorox and the others kept flowing in, the starting salary figures kept going up, with some offering to pay for moving expenses, or to help with a down payment on a sweet little house in a new tract, near their headquarters in the Midwest or back east. Most anyone would have been seduced, but Edison had always had his eye on much bigger things, and he had a look of fierce determination on his face when at last, he exited JPL's main office, having been officially hired, on a three-month probationary basis.

His new employer wasn't going to take any chances, and would be looking at his performance through a microscope, but Edison didn't care one bit. He knew he had come face to face with his destiny, the place and time where he was supposed to be. He knew in his heart that God had sent him to this place and would guide him through every day, every decision. It only took about two weeks for him to adopt the same no-press suits, available at the nearby Sears and Roebuck. His probationary salary only allowed him to buy the one suit, so he chose the darkest grey he could find, right off the rack.

CHAPTER 2

This is a story about a modest man, a man of God, a scientist of sorts, and a dreamer as well, a man driven by a sense of destiny, who knows quite a bit about chemistry. This is not however, a history book. He experienced a lot of history, first-hand, so to that extent, by necessity, history will be told, some of it, common knowledge to many, and more obscure to others. Had he been born in another age, a different place, then he would have found his niche in some other way, but it seemed to him, that it was all about providence, and God's will, not luck or serendipity.

After his tour of duty on the Iowa, and after his education at Caltech, this was most certainly, a whole new chapter in his life, requiring a good deal of chemical knowledge, but as importantly, it necessitated a creative mind, a mind unbound by convention, or old tired rules. Of course, he was bound to the realities of chemicals and the compounds of them, but was not bound by lack of imagination. It was during this era, that the term Mr. Black and Mr. Red had said, "thinking outside of the box", came into being.

This is important because we want to follow Edison the man, his emotions, his thoughts, his dreams, and not Edison, the chemist. This story tells of his personal journey, his emotional relationship with God, and is not intended to be a tedious accounting of his outer world, made up of chemical formulations, and absolutes. What drove Edison the most, were those things he could not see, could not formulate. For something much more technical and in-depth, we suggest you refer to Linus Pauling's "General Chemistry" available in hardback for $24.00 as of this writing.

The late 50's, were a time of great turmoil all around the world, and America was no exception.

Tensions were high, the threat of nuclear holocaust was growing, social upheaval was exploding, class wars were pitting citizens against one another, racial tensions were exploding, extreme nationalistic views were on the rise, "right-wing Christians" were forming an army to oppose "socialists and commie sympathizers". Politicians, some of them demagogues, always glad to seize upon these differences and to exploit them to their advantage, were honing their skills. Some people wanted to expand America's reach and influence, while others wanted America to concentrate on only matters here at home. Technologically, America was in a race for its survival. The first fallout shelters were being constructed underneath people's homes or in back yards, air raid drills at schools were beginning to occur, with kids being taught how to dive under their wooden desks to protect themselves against flying shattered glass, or the instant scorching heat of an atomic blast. People were scared.

If you were a young American, a teenager or younger, there was lots to attract and distract you: Bobby Soxers, drive-ins with milk shakes and cheeseburgers, served by short-skirted girls on roller skates, rock 'n roll, Buddy Holly, Elvis and his gyrations, James Dean, flying saucers, *Leave it to Beaver, Father Knows Best, Lassie, Sea Hunt, and The Lone*

Ranger beaming into people's living rooms on their new televisions. There were hot rods, Brylcreem and Butch Wax, Bill Haley and the Comets singing "Rock Around the Clock" on the 45's, Chevy Bel Airs, Hula-Hoops, Frisbees, Mickey Mantle, and small transistor radios.

A former general and war hero, was now elected President, who looked and behaved like their grandfather, and the threat of the "red menace", seemed faraway and other-worldly to these young people.

If you were in a lower income class or not white, there were lots of distractions of a different type, and not pleasant ones. Rosa Parks had lit a fuse for rebellion, along with sit-ins at diner counters meant for "whites only", and marchers being blasted by high pressure fire hoses.

Many were attracted by the thought of space aliens and rockets to the moon. Extremes of every sort were coming on strong, from the clash of generations, defining what it meant to have allegiance to the flag, looking skyward to invading space aliens, or to who was allowed to move into a particular neighborhood. These elements flying around in society were all the more reason the young generation was preoccupied with their own needs, and their own dreams.

If someone was slightly older, the fear began to sink in, and concerns of a good future for themselves and their children, seemed threatened by the ominous threat of nuclear war and annihilation. Or the insidious invasion, like a virus, of the Communist threat. But they continued to mow their lawns and wax their sedans, prune the roses and go to the Saturday matinee at the nearby picture show house. These two parallel conditions, between the younger and the somewhat older, began to blend together, so when news of bomb drills at school came home, when salesmen pitching the latest and greatest fallout shelter knocked on the door, even the most inattentive school kid, or parent in denial, knew that a wooden desk was probably not a good deterrent for a hydrogen bomb blast, and that a metal box buried in the ground was not going to save them. The fact that the Soviets had as their premier, just a few short years later, a person willing to pull off his shoe and thump it repeatedly on his desk, at a meeting of the United Nations, spoke volumes as to his willingness to smash norms, conventions, and quite possibly, "the rules of war".

This bizarre and macabre post-war scene, served as a backdrop to much of the lab's purpose of being. They were deeply involved in developing missiles that could carry warheads to enemies, working tirelessly to develop even bigger and faster rockets. It was during this time that they attempted, unsuccessfully, to re-brand themselves, and no longer stated they were developing "rockets". They felt that the word "rocket" held visions of Buck Rogers, to the public, that it suggested they were in the realm of science fiction, instead of actual science, and they wanted to be taken very seriously. So, developing "jets" and "launch vehicles" were better terms going forward. But the term, "rocket scientist" stuck, nevertheless.

That's what Edison had become, in essence. A rocket scientist. He certainly now looked the part, having blown past his probationary period with flying colors, having adopted his new conforming wardrobe, and being observed working very long hours into the night, far past the requirements for his salary.

He was given only small pieces of information at a time, being strictly inched out on a need-to-know basis. He was immersed in studying the chemical properties of propellant, in terms of their capacity, their mass, volume, viscosity, and their propensity to explode at the proper moment, or their likelihood of exploding at the wrong time, or not at all. The process of safely igniting the propellants was a discipline all unto itself. It wasn't like lighting a match to a gas stove jet, but more like having to light a series of matches in just the right sequential order, to a series of gas jets, that were very sensitive, and sometimes unpredictable, that were all connected to a time-delayed five-hundred-pound bomb, while you stood next to it.

As his tests and experiments grew in size and difficulty, he would need to add an assistant, and then another, and another. At a certain point along the way, one or more of the assistants couldn't take the tedium, or the long hours, or the possibility of being blown into a thousand pieces, and would ask to be removed. Others would join on, take to the work, and contribute above and beyond. Word around the campus was getting out, and the word was that a certain newcomer by the name of Edison, was doing some "sensitive" work in Lab #3. Everyone was curious, and some pleaded with their supervisors to be allowed to join Edison's experiments.

Edison had joined JPL a year prior, and now he was half way into 1957, and had been led down the path to his real purpose: JPL wanted him to stop experimenting with conventional liquid or gas propellants, and instead, create a reliable solid fuel propellant for use in heavy launch vehicles headed for the moon, and planets, and the stars beyond. They wanted Edison to choose his best assistants, and create a team, a crew, that would work with him to develop the right mix, the correct recipe. Solid fuel was not a new thing. Many had tried to develop a trustworthy formula before, and had ultimately failed. It was a highly explosive cocktail, that could succeed wildly or fail with catastrophic results. Edison was no longer in school, he was now deeply immersed in the real thing, for keeps.

One of the reasons Edison had been attractive to JPL from the very beginning, as with the Navy, was his calm and reserve. Lots of people have deep knowledge, are book smart, but their attitude, their temperament weighs in as being just as important. He took the scientific approach seriously, never skipping a step, never taking unnecessary risks. Measure twice, cut once, his dad would always tell him. He had remembered that mantra because it made sense and also, because he had never in memory, seen his father anywhere near a saw or measuring tape, so it was comical.

The Soviets had been very industrious with their own experiments, including those with solid fuel. Many of theirs resulted in explosions and deaths. They made up for their lack of technical knowledge with boldness. They were willing to lose people in order to achieve a goal. JPL, and the American government at large, was not willing. It was a philosophical difference, but also a military strategic one, as well.

Edison had zeroed in on a formula using most of the conventional ingredients already developed, but he had the "genius" to add into the recipe, aluminum. No one had thought of that before, and it created a propellant that was highly explosive, stable, durable, transportable, and had a very long service life, and most importantly, it was reliable.

Miniature tests were conducted, both inside their lab building, now labeled as "Top Secret" on the door, and outside in the fresh air behind the building, in the small outdoor lunch area, under the eucalyptus trees. They had cleared a space, removing some of the tables, and had an open area about twenty-by-twenty feet in which to work. The tests used various formulations all based on Edison's new recipe, and done in miniature, so that if there were a mishap, it would only cause minor damage, such as a scorch mark on the patio, or making a loud noise, heard all across the campus. They had to the most part, gone quite well, and the team was exhilarated. There had been no significant explosive mishaps, only the occasional disappointment of a test not fulfilling the desired results. Management was pleased.

Edison was not only pleased, but elated, because he knew that if his development of an effective and reliable fuel was successful, it would lead to the potential for serious space exploration shortly thereafter. People on the campus, people on TV, people writing in magazines, politicians, social activists, moralists and scientists, all had an opinion to offer, as to the possibility and value of such exploration, but Edison knew that without the nuts and bolts to achieve it, it was just a bunch of talk. He was determined to be the one who broke it all open. The cost would ultimately be, enormous. It would over-shadow many other actual or proposed government programs. Was it possible that his invention would allow some the unfortunate to go un-fed or un-clothed? Or for a bridge to go unbuilt, a railroad line to not be improved, a federal program to improve health care to not be funded as well? Yes, no doubt about it. But Edison's head was in the clouds, concerned with all of mankind, not individuals. This was about exploring the great unknown. About mankind lurching forward into infinite space. And possibly, about discovering life on another planet. He saw all of this as a directive from God.

The Air Force had already developed large rockets, but they wouldn't do for near-space exploration. What was needed, was the lift of a fuel that could carry them into the outer reaches of the Earth's atmosphere and beyond. The liquid propellant currently in wide use by the Air Force was adequate for a five-thousand-mile, one-way trip to Moscow, but JPL needed something much more powerful, something that had much more propulsion by the pound than liquid, and that would last longer while in storage. The Atlas rocket would be the vehicle to use for near and deep space. It had been tested extensively, and was already in use, on a standby basis, as an Intercontinental Ballistic Missile weapon, capable of reigning hell down on any chosen target on the globe. There were officially hundreds, but more likely thousands, already in position, ready for launch, at various Air Force bases in the country, as well as various discreet locations in corn fields, and next to empty farm houses, throughout the Midwest.

Edison's new formulation would propel satellites, space probes, and ultimately, astronauts, into the heavens. He knew this to be so, because this is what he had been told by his superiors, repeatedly.

Edison handled the bureaucracy of decision making well, only expressing his frustrations privately to Marcy, and on occasion to his sister, Rachel. By then, Rachel, and her husband Pete, with their son Tony, had moved out west, and lived in a nice bungalow-style place in the San Fernando Valley. The place was next to a huge orchard bulging with navel oranges. The owners didn't seem to mind Tony hopping the fence to pick a few. Simpler times.

On the rare occasion that Edison had time to make the drive and visit, usually on a Sunday afternoon, he would sit around the back porch with Marcy and Rachel, talk about old times and new, watch Pete handle the BBQ, and play catch with Tony. Edison would always bring Tony a present of some kind, whether it be a toy model of a rocket, a mobile of the planets to suspend from his ceiling, or a jersey from the newly transplanted Dodgers.

It took lots of time, and endurance, but at long last, JPL had arranged an actual field test at the Rocketdyne facility, that was, as you know, tucked away in the rocks above Chatsworth. Everyone was confident that the test would go off well, but then, the reason it was called a "test" is because there was always a chance it would fail.

This site happened to be virtually next door to the Nike Hercules launch facility (1958-1974) hidden a few miles away, near Oat Mountain, in the no-man's-land region between Chatsworth and Simi Valley. The designated name was LA88, and it was there that twelve of the missiles lived, in three separate silos. This was one of hundreds of such sites all over the country, but the first to be armed with nuclear war heads. The radar control station, positioned on the ridge of the mountain, could scan 150 miles in all directions, and with an assist from the Laguna Point facility, and one near the quaint town of Julian, plus others in the San Fernando Valley, they had a full scan of the area, should any unfriendly missiles be headed their way. The Nike's could either be sent to a faraway target, or more likely, be used to intercept incoming ICBM's. Los Angeles, in particular, was ringed with these bases due to the large number of aerospace and military sites in the general area, needing protection and a deterrent.

The irony of the location for Edison, was that when he had first started going to Caltech, and had garnered a small circle of friends, every one of them a movie buff, they'd take an afternoon and venture out to these very hills, and drop in on old western movie sets. Their favorite had been the Bell Ranch, not more than a mile from Rocketdyne, at the time, unknown to Edison. He and his friends would visit the old couple that served as the guardians of the western street, bringing them cold sodas and snacks. The couple, Hal and Dorothy, had a huge dog, a wolf-shepherd mix, that took an instant liking to Edison. They'd walk the wooden walkways that tied together the saloon, barber shop, undertaker and livery stable. Hal and Dorothy lived in the Sheriff's office, which was, upon entering, a sweet little one-bedroom house. This entry into a world of fantasy, made of hollowed out buildings, false fronts and a fake church at the end of the street, served as a wonderful escape for Edison, not imagining he'd find his future working virtually next door.

Back then, as mentioned, there was a seeming naiveté to tests such as these, where it appeared that the unspoken rule, was not to appear overly cautious about a possible mishap, for it would telegraph the wrong message to any onlookers. So, it wasn't naïveté after all, but boldness in the face of questionable odds. Some of the onlookers would be from the government at the behest of the President, or a politician, or from the military, and in a position of power or influence, to slow down the pace, or put the kibosh on future studies and experiments. Nobody at JPL wanted that. Any trepidation, or outward signs of anything short of total confidence, could be a tell. Even if the test was a total success, any sign of relief by the scientists and engineers, could invite Congressional inquiry and years of bureaucratic meddling. It was fine to give out hoots and cat calls at the finish of a successful test, but never the look of surprise.

The test, as you know, went off without a hitch, and Edison had earned the status of demigod in the eyes of his nephew, Tony.

With the success of the propellant, Edison and his team were given full unfettered access to the entire lab facility, should they need a particular piece of equipment, a certain laboratory formerly off limits to them, and wonderfully, very large increases to their weekly salaries. Word got out on the JPL campus that this five-man team were super stars, and most everyone not in the know, attempted to casually pull information from them. Sometimes it would take the form of Sunday backyard BBQ parties, a night of bowling, or an invite to the local watering hole near the facility after clocking out. Not once, did Edison or his crew reveal anything of any import, but they did enjoy the BBQ's.

The team's sense of loyalty and steadfastness, was underscored by alerts, that had been sent out, to hundreds of government, and quasi-government, facilities throughout the country, to be on the lookout for Soviet spies. This hyper-vigilance was not without cause. There had been some foreign agents caught in a handful of places, and the thinking was, it could be the tip of an iceberg.

These spies would work hard to infiltrate a company or military installation, would be your neighbor or close friend, would be a bowling partner or give you advice on how to fertilize your lawn, or what kind of oil to put in your Ford sedan. They could be drinking buddies, or your kid's piano instructor. They would look American, act American, and speak American. This was because in most cases, they were American. Rarely, if ever, would a Russian spy attempt to impersonate an American, for there would always be a giveaway to their impersonation, if not a dozen of them.

Many Americans were terrified by, or opposed to, the huge build-up of the American nuclear arsenal, and equally alarmed by the Soviet's. To some, we had started the weapons race with the invention, and use, of the first two atomic bombs, and we were not the good guys. And to many, their use had been a necessary evil to stop an enemy, who refused to surrender even in the face of insurmountable odds, or with the deaths of many of its citizens.   Some of the contrarians, who were otherwise law-abiding citizens, felt it their duty to do what they could to thwart the aggressive American war machine and help to prevent the world's destruction. Others felt that the country had to do anything and everything it could to thwart the threat of attack, by being too strong to attack, with a mighty and dangerous ability to counter-attack. This had become an ongoing and heated argument between these two factions within the government and Congress, with John and Jane Doe citizen, being on the outside, looking in.

Adversaries, and outright enemies of the country, were determined to gather as much information on the military, and on the new fuel, as they could. This was all the more reason to keep their lips sealed about what Edison termed, the "secret sauce".

There was a time, many years prior, that the military had begun using remote locations to test their new devices, such as Truk Lagoon, situated northwest of Papua New Guinea, and southwest of Guam, essentially in the middle of nowhere, in the North Pacific. What Edison was involved in required lots of infrastructure, access to various sophisticated pieces of equipment and personnel. Certainly, the military continued to maintain various remote locations for testing, but someplace like Truk, could not support the kind of work Edison was involved in.

Additionally, there was a level of deceit that had to be maintained on the team by management. Edison was not alone in his passion for helping to make space exploration possible, and if he and some of his crew knew of how deeply the military was involved in their work, they might have rebelled.

Edison conducted two more tests at Rocketdyne, using even larger rocket engines with more fuel, and again, the tests went off without a hitch. Because every agency involved in this new fuel was getting nervous about secrecy, guests were no longer allowed.

Although the field tests had been successful, there was much more work to be done. Larger amounts of the "sauce" had to be developed and experimented with, most carefully. Additionally, solid propellant rocket boosters, which were simply called, solid rockets, had to be designed, and fitted to the Atlas launch vehicles, and to the upcoming larger Delta family of rockets. The notion of re-branding these objects as "jets" fell to the wayside, as the general public had gotten used to the idea of real-life space exploration, knowing it was a real thing, and not something from comic books or Saturday matinee serials at the local movie house. An Air Force aviator, being groomed as an astronaut, was referred to as a "rocket man".

The calendar turned to 1959, and Edison and Marcy got married in the early spring. It was a small ceremony held in the gardens of the Huntington Hotel, Pasadena. Both sets of parents attended, and all the siblings, nephews and nieces, and a few assorted good friends. Their honeymoon was fun, but brief and local, with a duration of four days at the historic Ahwahnee Hotel in Yosemite. Their time away from their hotel suite was spent wandering the many trails that lazily crisscrossed the valley floor, some leading to wildflower meadows, and others to stupendous waterfalls, spraying mist on them until they were soaked.

From the moment Edison returned to work, he was beginning to get restless in the small cramped rental house that he and Marcy were now crammed into. When he was single, it worked just fine, as he had command of the whole 700 square foot unit, but now, it was ridiculous. The backs of kitchen chairs served as clothes hangers for the over-crowded closet, and if dishes, pots and pans were not cleaned immediately and put away, there was no room for anything else on the small kitchen countertop. Ambient traffic noise, people walking on the nearby sidewalk, and a general sense of having little privacy, came into sharp focus, whereas when Edison was alone, he put those things out of his mind. It was most definitely time to move.

Edison's salary had now reached a fairly high and comfortable plateau, with a promise of endless employment. Buoyed by the promise of a bright future, they began looking around for a place of their own.

First, it was a local hunt, involving various neighborhoods in the Pasadena neighborhoods, but even then, in early 1959, the prices were fairly steep, and as much as they liked the idea of living in a Green and Green, on an old and shady, street in Pasadena, it wasn't in the budget. They would need to aim lower.

They had realized, they both wanted the same thing - a larger place, big enough for a family, with a large yard, and for that, they'd have to venture further out. Altadena, La Canada, and Flintridge were examined, followed by Sierra Madre and Arcadia, and further east. Nothing they found checked all the boxes. They'd get input from friends, from real estate agents, from storekeepers, and work mates. Marcy had taken up substitute teaching, but they both resolved that once they found a place, wherever that might be, she could quit that work and focus on being at home, doing some writing, which had always been her dream, and tending to the future kids. They wanted three.

During all of this, they attended a local church, not her parent's Lutheran, but another, that seemed less judgmental to Edison, and acceptable to Marcy. The truth was, she was never entirely comfortable with the fire and brimstone slant of her parent's church, and was glad for the excuse to go elsewhere.

And then, as if from Divine Providence (Marcy would say later) a friend of theirs at church informed them over cookies and coffee after a service, of a small mountain community tucked away in the San Bernardino mountains. It was a fairly long drive, about an hour from JPL, but it was a beautiful community, she said, and at about six-thousand feet, with lovely homes, that had four seasons. And perhaps most importantly, the location of Forest Roots. That was the name given, many decades earlier, to a Christian camp, complete with a beautiful A-frame church, rental cabins, camping sites, a "kid's camp", and a large community hall. The facility had grown exponentially over the years, mostly due to the largess of some key donors. Many of the people who lived in the community of Forest Falls, either attended that church, or were of a like mind. Their friend said, "if you're an atheist, you won't feel too comfortable up there".

Edison and Marcy had looked most everywhere, at least it felt that way, so they decided to take a drive to Forest Falls the next weekend. Their friend was correct, it was not a short drive.

Near the mountain community, down in the flatlands, was Redlands, and they stopped at a real estate office, took some hand-outs on places for sale up there, some of which had price tags they might be able to reach. The last few miles of their drive took them up a winding mountain road with a large boulder-filled wash next to it, and as they climbed higher, there were patches of snow, and before long, dense stands of pine trees. Once they got into the area, there were some narrow streets leading this way and that, all anchored by a small general store and cafe. Just from its outward appearance, tucked away as it was, it was obviously a very laid-back kind of a place. They couldn't help but notice Forest Roots, with the impressive looking church, and the various out buildings. There were two other churches in the community as well. It appeared that the population couldn't have been more than a few hundred (but in fact, was hovering just under one-thousand, which included full-timers and weekenders).

They drove up and down the many little streets, some of them dead-ends, taking notes when they saw the occasional "For Sale" sign, matching it to the hand-outs. There weren't a lot of places for sale, only about six. Most people had a 4x4 truck or Jeep of some sort, parked in their driveway, which Edison took note of as he piloted his two-wheel rear drive sedan, occasionally slipping and looking for traction on the icy roads.

They liked the neighborhood, and the overall feel of the place. Edison was able to rationalize the long drive from there to work, if their dollars would take them this much further. The notion of a Christian-based community appealed to them greatly, so all they needed now, was to find a candidate. None of the homes they had seen, did much for them. They tried to force their thinking toward one or the other, but they were in their Goldilocks moment and found them to be either too small or too large, too isolated, or crammed too close to another house. Most had yards, some fenced, some not. Mostly not. Some were nicely designed, and looked like a mountain home, and some were very ordinary in appearance, and belonged in a tract development down below. They decided to go to the cafe and grab some lunch, and make a call or two to agents, from the pay phone outside. There was one house that they somewhat liked, and was probably within their budget. Marcy did the talking when she got the agent on the line. Edison went inside to claim a table, and the realtor was able to give Marcy all the basic information on the house.

Marcy sat down with Edison at a table, and they ordered some sandwiches and coffee. The place was almost full, obviously a popular stop for locals. The price on the house they had spotted, was within their budget, but it didn't do much for them. It seemed plain, and too ordinary. They wanted to talk themselves into it. They weren't the types who needed an architectural statement of a home, but they wouldn't mind something with a little character, a place that looked like it belonged up in the mountains. Some of the places, this one especially, looked like it had been transplanted from a very conventional neighborhood and plopped down on the lot. And, after all, this was to be their first, and perhaps, permanent home, and they wanted to get it as right as they could, given their limited budget.

Their sandwiches arrived with a smile, and as Edison looked out at the view through the window, he spotted a "For Sale" sign. It was across the street, and up from the cafe a few hundred feet, planted at the head of a long driveway, that led gently uphill to a tan, two-story house. How could they have missed that? He nudged Marcy so she could turn and see the place too. They were hundreds of feet away from the place, and had only a partial view, but from what they could determine, it might be the place for them. They wasted no time with lunch and made their way across the street to the head of the driveway, looking at the sign. They double-checked their hand-outs, and it was not listed. Then they noticed in small print, "by Owner" at the bottom. It was a two-story, but not a box, as some of it was only one-story, what's called a "split-level ranch". It had two chimneys, a large deck out front, an attached garage and a fairly large lot, about a quarter acre or more. It looked to be in good shape, but not great shape. The paint was beginning to peel in places and the fiberglass shingle roof looked a little worn. But it had strong potential.

About three months later, in May of '59, they moved in. There was work to be done, much more than they had noted standing outside that day when they first saw it. When they had done the walk through, it was as if wearing blinders, looking past all the things that would need attention. The price pushed their budget some, but if they conserved, they could swing the payment. Macy could volunteer at a church, maybe work her way into a paying job, and Edison could make the drive five days a week. Weekends could be spent fixing and replacing, working his way down the list. Edison determined that he'd have to invest in a used Jeep of some kind, just to get around town, during the winter months, and had to also think of a car he could commute in. Included in the gymnastics they employed to talk themselves into Forest Falls, was the fact that the drive to JPL was much more than an hour. His Ford Fairlane sedan was in okay shape, but the eighty-five-mile trip would age the sedan quickly. But those were all details, to be taken care of, one by one. The important thing is that they had found a wonderful four-bedroom house, plenty big enough for their intended brood, and someplace they could stay for years to come, maybe permanently. It wouldn't be all work on the weekends, for they intended to take advantage of the numerous hiking trails nearby. All in all, it was pretty idyllic.

Then came the phone call. It was a Saturday in August, and Marcy picked up the receiver, and was greeted by a serious voice. She handed the phone over to Edison, who had just come in from chopping some firewood. He held the receiver to his ear, barely saying a word, and hung it up, staring ahead, processing what he had just been told. He looked at the expectant Marcy, and said, "There's been an accident, I have to go". With that, he went into the bedroom, changed clothes, hopped in the Ford, leaving behind an anxious Marcy, and made his way to the field lab in Chatsworth.

Being a large test facility meant that on occasion, there would be an accident of some sort or other. There had been a few of them, involving their sodium burn pits, their plutonium fuel facility, another building with uranium carbide fuel, and some relatively minor mishaps at the "hot lab", which was where they handled radioactive materials sent to them from the Atomic Energy Commission or the Department of Energy, to be broken down and safely housed. There had been a fire in this facility, just two years prior, which resulted in a significant escape of radioactive particles into the air. The entire facility was a busy place, and they had conducted hundreds of engine and fuel tests over the years. Everyone was aware of the risks involved, but all involved had their eye on the prize.

On this particular Saturday morning, they were conducting a sodium nuclear reactor experiment, and one of the chemicals clogged one of the lines, resulting in some of the core shutting down, and then melting down, releasing a large amount of radioactive iodine into the air. And it wasn't just a "large amount", but stands today as the largest release of radioactive iodine in American history, one-hundred times the amount released at Three Mile Island. The good news was that this substance, only had an eight-day half-life (that is to say, in eight days it would be only half as potent, half as dangerous, which for a toxic or dangerous chemical, is quite fast) but eight days is plenty of time to find its way into nearby dairy cows in neighboring regions, and their milk, or into water storage facilities, or into people's lungs. It all depended on the direction of the wind.

It would be hard to imagine a more serious accident at the facility, short of an atomic bomb explosion, which was impossible since they did not have actual bombs there. A nuclear bomb explosion, even from a so-called "low yield" bomb, would have been worse, in theory, but this type of mishap was high on the horrible list.

Edison was privy to the information surrounding the accident, but only to a degree. The government blacked out all news and restricted access to the facility, and to any information related to the accident. It wasn't until many years later, that they became transparent about it, partly due to numerous law suits claiming that the explosion had led to a dramatic spike in cancer cases in the rocky hillside communites surrounding it. The combined harmful effects of the other radioactive materials, and toxic materials, released by the facility over the years, paled in comparison to this terrible single event.

Fortunately for the infant space program, and for Edison's role in it, the accident had no adverse mechanical effect. Of course, a mandatory safety review was ordered of all operations on the JPL campus, and the Rocketdyne facility was closed for a few months, before gradually coming back to use.

This incident did have an adverse effect on Edison's morale, however. It began his slow downward spiral, in terms of his belief in the program at JPL. He realized that the people he ultimately worked for, were willing to block information to the public about how incredibly dangerous this accident had been. The iodine-131 that was released into the air, is a radioactive form of iodine, and is extremely radioactive. It's produced in nuclear reactors when uranium is split, and from that, energy is generated. Bodies, both human and other, initially treat the iodine as if it were safe, and it goes to the thyroid. The radiation, of course, damages the thyroid, greatly increasing the chance of cancer, and in children, it can destroy some or all of the thyroid. It is quite lethal. To be clear, the thyroid is a gland that controls many bodily functions, from metabolism, to heart rate, to breathing, to cholesterol levels, and women's menstrual cycles. It eats its way into people's bones, slowly disintegrating them. It can take a person a year to die from it. At best, when a child is exposed, and made sick from it, it can have serious developmental effects. Radiation poisoning in general is horrible, with sometimes horrific results, affecting various organs. Sometimes death comes quick, but sometimes slowly, as with this particular type.

Edison already knew of all the potential hazards long before the accident, as did Marcy, what with her studies at Caltech. For Edison, it was a micro-version of what would happen if a nuclear device had been set off. He knew his history, and knew that the Word War Two bombings of Tokyo and other Japanese cities by the allies, caused vastly more deaths and destruction than either the Hiroshima or Nagasaki bombs combined, but this fact was sometimes used by apologists for the bomb, wanting to mitigate history, as if to say, things could have been worse. In the end, dead means dead. Either way a person wanted to view it, this accident in the hills just above a large population center, was incredibly serious, and jolted Edison into doubting the people and organization he worked for.

Edison wasn't entirely naive, and knew that the juxtaposition of his faith, and the hard realities of life, were sometimes quite difficult to square, but only a very small percentage of people on the planet had Edison's particular vantage point, coupled with a deep religious belief in doing good, in bettering mankind, in living by the code of love and kindness. He sensed that his faith was going to lead him somewhere important, and that his particular type of faith, yet to be clearly defined, had primacy.

There was still much research to be done on the fuel, and a considerable amount of time had to be devoted to making the equipment harmonious with that fuel. By now, Edison was recognized as a senior team member of the campus, not simply the "Chief" of the solid rocket team. His rise to such a place of respect had come to him quickly, and at an early age. He was only twenty-nine, going on thirty.

It was then that he began to take the long drive to Lompoc, where the Vandenberg Air Force Base was located. It was there that the military developed and tested many of its larger rockets, including the Redstone, Atlas, Delta, and Titan families. Edison's mission was to interface with the scientists there, in an effort to create a launch vehicle using solid propellant that would allow an astronaut to be launched into space just above the Earth, and orbit it. Project Mercury, as it was so named, was the beginning of what evolved into the Gemini program, and Edison wanted in on it, for he knew this would be the beginning phase of what it was all about.

Just as with Rocketdyne, the history of rocket development was sprinkled with many accidents, some of them deadly. The fuels that the Air Force had developed to propel the enormous rockets skyward, were exotic liquid concoctions, some of them unstable, and most, highly toxic, flammable, and explosive. There had been various flash fires in silos from Arizona to Kansas to Arkansas, due to simple mistakes with welding torches or accidental small leaks of fuel. By the time the latest rocket had come online, the Titan II, the rockets themselves were much improved, but the fuels, one after the other, remained highly dangerous.

As the Air Force was struggling to develop safer fuels, the guidance systems had also been greatly improved, developed by the AC Spark Plug company, and then improved upon by Delco Electronics. The ever-present fear of a "nuclear exchange" haunted everyone, and the deterrent of MAD (Mutually Assured Destruction) did little to quell people's fears.

It was also to the advantage of the government, and the industry that supported it, to stoke those fears, by reminding the general public in various ways, of the need to keep the military strong and ready. While there was some considerable truth to that, the one detail that the government neglected to communicate, was that our primary enemy, the Soviet Union, had guidance systems that were highly unreliable, and would likely fail, should the time of war ever arrive. Their guidance systems relied on air pressure and altitude sensors, to guide their horrible rockets to the target. America's equally horrible rockets used much more complex GPS-like systems, to assure accuracy. In the event of such an "exchange", thermonuclear blasts disrupt the sensors on an altitude-based guidance system, rendering them virtually rudderless. It was theorized, that most American rockets would find their targets, while most Soviet rockets would ditch in the ocean. It was the most grim and ghoulish of conversation topics, and no one at JPL cared to discuss it, for it was so abhorrent and contrary to their mission, but there it was.

In a way, connected to that odd and morbid fact, would be another revelation, years later, in the 70's.

At that time, the Kennedy Space Center opened its doors to the Soviets, as part of the joint venture to create the International Space Station (ISS). The Center felt the need to share technological information, to assure a successful mission. There was much controversy surrounding the decision to "open our secrets to the Soviets", as it was said. Nevertheless, the doors were opened, and we shared, and the mission was a success. It wasn't until later, that John Glenn, by that time a Senator from Ohio, revealed the necessity for the sharing. Apparently, up until then, many of the Soviet rocket technology depended not on miniature circuitry, transistors, or semiconductors, but on vacuum tubes, similar to the ones found in American televisions in the 50's. In order to assure a safe mission, the U.S. had no choice but to help the Soviets abandon their old technology.

Edison was only vaguely aware of the "tech wars" between an ever-growing list of countries, for he was laser focused on his assignment, which transcended mere technology, as it was inexorably linked to God's mission for him.

Most of Edison's time at Vandenberg was all business, and rarely were friendships forged. The lone exception was Edison meeting Ned Clausen, an engineer-designer. Ned lived with his wife Betty in Lompoc, in a very nice two-story country home, where they were raising their two kids. Ned and Edison hit it off immediately, in part because Ned did not come across as an MIT or Ivy League-educated jerk, but a nice down to earth guy. Years before, his parents had underwritten his schooling at the University College in London, so he came away without the supplemental trappings of a privileged or entitled American "rich kid brat". He was as relaxed, casual, and witty as one could be. This type of personality sat in stark contrast to the button-down seriousness of the overall mission at hand, and the people who were part of it. Edison found Ned to be refreshing, and began spending a lot of time with him. Sometimes, Ned and Betty would insist he spend the night, instead of allowing him to bunk at the base in an antiseptic room. They had a lot of shared interests, and Betty made a mean lemonade.

Only once could Edison persuade them to make the drive to Forest Falls for a weekend. They had a good time, but Ned preferred staying close to home, tending the garden, reading a book, and clearing his mind of the dense tangle of thought he had to live with, five days a week at the base.

Sometimes, Edison and Ned would discuss their shared discontentment with their mission, in the face of so much pressure and bureaucracy. It clouded their shared vision of exploring space, and distracted them from remembering why they were there in the first place. Ned would say "I can't remember what I'm forgetting". This was far more than simply a job for the two men, it was the extension of a dream, to go to space, to explore the unknown, and perhaps discover life forms.

It had been just months before, in late 1959, that the Air Force officially broke away from JPL, but had done so behind closed doors, so they could focus on its own needs concerning rockets, and fuel, and armaments. Perhaps the terrible accident at Rocketdyne had something to do with their decision, no one knew for sure. Just months before, the National Aeronautical and Space Agency (NASA) had been created out of various other agencies, as the urgency of developing space and military missile capability was growing. Obviously, the creation of NASA at the same time the Air Force exited JPL, was a coordinated effort.

The space race, and the arms race, seemed on parallel tracks, both headed straight ahead without hesitation. The Russian Sputnik 1 satellite had gone up successfully, and was quickly followed by the American Explorer 1 satellite. NASA became the lead in civil space exploration, taking over the management of JPL, among other facilities and programs, and also became the military space lead.

As terrifying as the arms race was, it did nothing to dampen the excitement in Edison's head about unexplored frontiers. Concentrating on the good he was achieving helped him to mollify the potential bad, and it had come as a relief to him that the Air Force had split away from his home base. He figured, there wasn't a whole lot he could do as an individual chemical engineer to stop the potential for war, but now, he and his efforts would be divorced from military application, and instead, pointed to the stars.

The arms race, and space race, proceeded, and they had carved out two distinct lanes in the road, and Edison didn't want any part of the former. President Kennedy declared that the country would put a man on the Moon by the end of the decade, or more precisely, eight years and seven months from then. And ironically, that same President came incredibly close to End Times with the most dramatic nuclear confrontation in history. Edison mused that it seemed the President was balancing two balls in the air, promoting the use of the enormous rockets for near and deep space, while combating their possible use in mass destruction and death.

The declaration by Kennedy in May of 1961, had caught everyone at NASA and JPL by surprise. It was both exhilarating to know that the full force of the President was behind their mission, but also frightening, for they were caught flat-footed, and from what they knew, at least two decades away from the ability to successfully launch a rocket to the Moon, not to mention, a rocket carrying astronauts, not to mention, landing them safely on the surface of the Moon, not to mention, bringing them back to Earth safely. It was an assignment with such enormity, of such gigantic scale and complexity, that the entire campus was in a near state of shock.

Then, with events following one another in rapid succession, the Russians put a man in orbit, and quickly thereafter, Alan Shepard became the first American to enter space. That was in late 1961. The following year, John Glenn became NASA's first astronaut to fully circle the Earth, three times, before returning safely to a "splash down". Space age terminology was now showing up in normal conversation, on TV news and talk shows, and in movies: "Big Bang", "binary star", "black hole", "cosmic ray", "dwarf star", "event horizon", "gamma ray", "intergalactic", "light year", "pulsar", "red dwarf", "red giant", "supernova", among others.

Along with this, the 50's and 60's, ushered in a spate of sci-fi movies, having to do with flying saucers, alien encounters, radiated monsters including giant ants, vegetable alien humanoids, pilots turned into radioactive monsters, and of course, Godzilla. It was a new genre of entertainment, but it was also seeping into the hearts and minds of the general public. Things were changing.

In the scientific world, it was an amazingly busy and inventive time, and it seemed the moment a record achievement was made, it was replaced by another one, that was higher, faster or larger. Edison was embroiled in much of that. He was still the chief chemical engineer, developing not only the solid propellant, but helping with all the mechanical components that would use the propellant. He was surrounded by a large circle of people who were hardcore scientists, not a hint of humor among them. Rumors and wild theories swirled around them, but they were oblivious. It is no wonder that

Edison missed noticing something important. Horribly important.

A dizzying pace had been set for detonating above-ground atom and hydrogen bombs. The Nevada desert had hosted many of the first explosions, and then a location in the North Atlantic, the Bikini Atoll, was the recipient of many that followed, including setting off a thermonuclear bomb in 1954, called Castle Bravo, which was 1,000 times more powerful than the Hiroshima or Nagasaki bombs. Its name was "Shrimp". The funny thing, the odd thing, about H-bombs, as opposed to A-bombs that split atoms, is they are all about fusing atoms together, making a fusion bomb. It simulates the Sun. There's no limit to the size of one. When they had detonated Castle Bravo, and the smoke had cleared, three small islands were gone, and an enormous harbor had been created on the Atoll, in the round shape of the bomb's blast. As a homage of sorts, or as a sardonic joke, at the Los Alamos Lab in New Mexico, where the A-bomb was first developed, their main street, is Bikini Atoll Road.

Some people say it was intentional, others say it was due to ignorance and carelessness, but either way, the radioactive contamination from this blast spread to Australia, India, Japan, and even to the United States and parts of Europe. What was supposed to have been a secret test, quickly became an international incident, with many calling for a ban on above-ground tests. Buried in the commotion and controversy, were the native inhabitants on the neighboring small islands, all of whom were infected with the radioactive fallout. The Navy sent out doctors and their aides to conduct medical tests on many of them, to treat their open sores, draw blood, and perform complete exams. The idea that the military would have intentionally exposed these people to radiation for the purpose of study, was a despicable thought. *What if it were true,* Edison thought to himself?

The treatment of the natives prior to these blasts could be an indicator. As an example, years before, just at the close of World War Two, natives had been relocated from Bikini Atoll, to the smaller and much less hospitable, Rongerik Atoll, allowing the military to conduct their bomb tests. The natives initially objected for a number of reasons, one of which is that they believed that Rongerik was haunted by demon girls. They were moved anyway.

When the Castle Bravo hydrogen fusion bomb was set off, it was the first and largest of its kind, and the radiation spread over Rongerik, and the Rongelap Atoll. The natives were evacuated from those two locations, two days after the detonation, and tested. A third and more distant strand of atolls, the Utrik Atolls, were not evacuated, and many of those natives there were tested as well. The natives from all three strands of atolls showed signs of "active radiation syndrome". Those signs included a severe drop in both white and red blood cells, nausea, vomiting, abdominal pain, dizziness, fatigue, fever, redness of the skin, blistering and ulceration, leading to death. Not a pleasant way to go.

Edison knew all about this kind of thing, as a requirement of his studies and research, but also because he wanted to know his enemy, to know what his enemy was capable of. It made Edison sick to his stomach to contemplate the horror suffered by these natives, at the hands of a giant country, his country, a super power, that professed equality and freedom for all. But always, it was done in the name of self-defense. Edison answered to a higher power, and his patriotism waned, not in favor of the Soviets or other players, but in favor of God.

The early sixties had arrived with the thunderous roar of rockets, but back home, the Nabors' were expecting their first child.

They tried to block it out, but could not help but know that sabers were rattling around the world, that there was mighty unrest in the country with civil rights, and the rocketeers were busy launching missile after missile, as they edged closer to a Moon landing. Up on the mountain, they lived in a bubble, but Edison continued his trek down the mountain to JPL, still harboring deep emotional turmoil inside of himself, about what he had apparently done to aid the creation and potential use of these horrible weapons. He was making good money, was respected around the campus, was now in his early thirties, and before he and Marcy knew it, a second baby was on the way. He and Marcy would attend church, listen to the pastor, read the passages recommended once home, attend Wednesday night Bible study if he got home from work in time, continue to fix up the house, but all the while, Edison was becoming radicalized.

When the Air Force had exited JPL in 1959, declaring their interest was in military application only, and that they were no longer going to be involved, or participating with JPL in its goals and experiments, it wasn't entirely the truth. In fact, it wasn't even close to the truth.

It was in Building G, where Edison was conducting a series of experiments, involving different recipes of plastisol, which is a member of a family of high-performance propellants, known as electric solid propellants (ESPs). He was working alongside two of his regular team members, and some other chemists, he did not know as well.

There are many components to an ignition system and firing system, and if one small characteristic of the propellant were off, by even the smallest of fractions, it could cause a catastrophic chain reaction, involving the cones that the ignitors were in, or the discharge flow, or the seals, or the burn rate, or temperature. So many variables, so many potential failures. One of the chemists came over to look at what Edison was doing, how he was coming along, and made what was supposed to be a quip. "I wonder if the Birds are gonna want this formula too?"

Edison looked up at the chemist, startled, feeling instantly sick, because his curtain had been ripped open. Edison had successfully hidden from himself his concerns, his internal war of conscience about his work, about the applications of his work, and believed, or very much wanted to believe, that he was toiling away for God, and for mankind.

He had from time to time, allowed himself to speculate about his formulations being used for warfare, or for the intention of possible warfare, but as quickly, dashed those thoughts from his mind. This single small wisecrack about the "Birds" caused a rupture in his entire belief system, his firewall so to speak. It didn't take much, just an unanticipated comment that caught him off guard, for it was a very fragile belief system, made of his own custom formulation, using denial and delusion as the key ingredients.

He had known all along that the Air Force was an extremely determined creature, and that they were going to do anything and everything to see to it that the country had the best, fastest and biggest. Rules and assurances didn't matter. He knew that the comments he received from his superiors on the campus, pertaining to the clean split between them and the Air Force, were probably not entirely true. He knew intellectually, that in the real world, this "clean split" could certainly be a lie, but he had held onto the assurances, held onto his own private fantasy, that his work would be only toward the good, the future of space travel, and exploration.

But for someone in his field, someone in the same lab working by his side, perhaps closely tied to various secrets, perhaps more closely than he was, to make such an off-hand snide remark, spoke volumes. If this fellow chemist was relaxed enough to make a joke like that, then it followed that this was common knowledge, knowledge that Edison had filtered away. If he accepted the idea that the Air Force had been using solid propellant in their own tests, using formulas that he and his team had developed, and that these propellants would be used to bomb the living hell out of some country, someday, killing millions, Edison's lofty Christian principles would not tolerate it, could not.

All the rest of that day, he couldn't concentrate, couldn't get his mind to focus on anything other than this deep sense of betrayal. In a way, he was a clown, and he knew it. Who was he trying to kid, anyway?

It never crossed his mind in any real way, that the Air Force had taken his formulas with them? Of course, it had. And realistically, why wouldn't they? They had in essence, owned him, and he thought to himself, *I'm their court jester, their trained monkey, their property.* On the way home he had to pull over so he could dry heave on the shoulder of the road.

His dream ended that day. He knew that he was a purist, because that was the only way to be, and that his intense beliefs about space exploration, were shared by practically everyone on the campus. But for Edison, he had a higher power to answer to, to serve. He wasn't the only person of religion there on campus. Most of the people held to one kind of belief or another. But Edison was apparently different, or thought he was. He took his Jesus quite seriously, not to mention narrowly, and couldn't see or tolerate exceptions, or compromises. In an odd and unexpected way, his belief in

Jesus had become radical, unwavering, due to his intense feelings of both betrayal, and destiny.

This awful twist, inside of ten seconds that afternoon, plummeted him into a dark and brooding mental state. By the time he got home, and walked in the front door, Marcy saw the distorted look on his face, and his eyes that looked past everything.

At first, Marcy thought he was experiencing a delayed reaction to the shooting of the President, the week prior. They had both loved him, and felt a surge of youthful excitement having this handsome, intelligent, tough and witty person as their country's leader. They especially liked him because he was a huge proponent of space exploration. His untimely and gruesome death, had stunned the nation, and the world in many ways, and the Nabors' were no exception. Many tears had flowed that week in their home, and there was a pall over the campus. It went beyond mere politics, as most people were deeply saddened, and frightened, by this most horrible of events. Nobody wanted to doubt the developing official version of his death, but most on campus harbored serious doubts as to its credibility. All of the facts given seemed to be false, to have been canned. A deep skepticism began to develop seemingly everywhere, with few immediately realizing that this single event would mark the beginning of a permanent deep-set suspicion of the government, from both sides of the political spectrum. For Edison, it had been a time to embrace God even closer.

But John Kennedy was not what was on Edison's mind that day. It had been a Friday, so he could decompress and give some long thought to his situation, take in the whole picture. Marcy knew that something deep down was troubling him, as he was far from his usual even tempered and quiet self. He seemed angry, confused, stomping around the house, going from room to room, robotically, half the time not even seeming to know she was in the room. She knew to stay clear of him, so he could sort it out, whatever it was. They both had an unyielding faith, so they both knew that whatever the problem, and however troubling it was, that they had the world's best safety net in Jesus.

Later, once Edison had calmed down, Marcy would bring him tea as he sat at the fireplace, staring into the flames, as a way to inform him she was there, in the background, and available. His anger and confusion had morphed into a deep depression, and he barely spoke five words all of Saturday. When she got up at two in the morning on Sunday, to investigate why the bed was half empty, he was still seated in the chair, looking at embers.

"I can't physically leave now" is what he said to her over coffee later that morning.

Edison had reviewed every morsel of information he could, examined his own heart and conscience, slapping them up against Jesus, since Friday night. His conclusion was that he would have to leave JPL immediately, in spirit, but stay on in body for another few years. They were making good money, money they needed for a growing family, money for the church, to which they had contributed generously, and then they could leave, get away to some other place. He would go into work, perform his duties as required, work on formulations that he would be sure to have quirks, requiring more research, more experiments. He would never release or approve a formulation for use that might later endanger lives, either in real use, or at the field lab, but we would be sure to come upon failure after failure with his tests and research. It would prove elusive for him to improve on his original formulations. He didn't see it as sabotage because he had permission from God to protect mankind, and his family. If he was older, if they had a much larger nest egg, then things would be different. He couldn't, wouldn't, in good conscience approach his dad for any financial help. His dad had semi-retired a few years earlier, but was still involved, over-seeing the operation, occasionally dropping in on a dealership for a surprise visit, and while his dad and mom were proud of him, and what he had so far accomplished, they saw him in the abstract. They couldn't relate to anything in his life. His extreme and intolerant religious views had alienated many from his life, including many family members. His refusal to be "patriotic" and support the military irked his dad, and was the spark of many arguments over the phone. Edison did not want to go to his dad for help, for he knew it would lead to recriminations and disapproval. Edison figured his charade would last about three years, before he could escape. It turned out to be many more than that.

Part of the long delay was that he was emotionally tied to the space program, say what you will about the military applications of the formulations. There were times he would sit in the viewing section above the mission control room, watching the various people at their stations, monitoring a spacecraft shooting out into deep space, and communicating back information. Back then in the 60's, it was a somewhat active place, and in more recent years, has become a bee hive, having evolved into the nation's primary control center for orbital and deep space satellites, and robots, such as the Mar's Rovers.

Once a mission had been a success, from launch to successful orbit, sometimes a satellite doing a sling shot around a planet to gain momentum, to go even further, the exhilaration of the moment in the control room was overwhelming. People wept, cheered, laughed, hugged, and were at once, intensely happy, and crushed. Many had to seek therapy with the psychologists brought in for grief counseling, as the separation, and ending of a mission, could be so deeply traumatic.

By outward appearance, the strait-laced members of a mission, seemed impervious to emotion. But that was far from the truth. It would have been a project worked on with intensity, perhaps for many years, culminating in the launch and monitoring of their craft, as it traveled from Earth to its intended destination. It was the majesty of the launch and mission, the knowledge that mankind was on the leading edge of probing deeper into our solar system, to the furthest reaches, and beyond. It was also a love affair. These men and women were dedicated believers in what Edison also felt, and in that, there was a strong kinship. He would wonder to himself, why it was he couldn't be much more like them? He wanted to be. But for him, above the intensity of that emotional attachment to a mission, and the extreme separation anxiety that followed, was his God, that he knew well, and had a relationship with. Could he not be like the others because they were all Godless, and he, the lone believer? He recognized that many had spiritual beliefs, but for Edison, that was far from adequate. For him, your belief had to be specific and intense. No grey areas, no wishy-washy beliefs, no Christian Smorgasbord would do. It had to be the absolute pure real thing, or nothing at all. There was no middle ground. As his disenchantment with JPL and its collusion with the military grew, so did his religious intensity.

He knew that he hadn't always felt that way. He knew that his beliefs had become much more extreme. But he defended his extremism, for it was the only legitimate and pure belief to hold. All the others were imposters. Yes, God was love, he would think to himself, *but it was conditional. God was conditional.* You had to seek him out, go to him, ask for his forgiveness, take him into your life and heart as the only true God. He wasn't going to seek you out, and come to you. With three-billion souls, on the planet and counting, who has time for that? Did Edison think of himself as being too severe, too judgmental? Certainly not. He didn't think that God was talking directly to him, but he did feel that he could hear his voice, as he spoke to others as well, and that he, Edison, was one of the chosen few. He felt that he understood the true meaning of Christianity, and that the world was infested with the devil's sympathizers, and at the least, were enablers of evil. By not believing purely and completely, meant you were cast out to the wind, worthless, unimportant in the grand scheme of things. He knew that his true mission in life would not be rockets, but about sharing his knowledge about God, and offering people an opportunity to join God properly, that is to say, in the one true way. Seeking to learn about the unknown, and to venture out into limitless space was a tool, a device by which, he and millions, perhaps billions, would come to know God. He didn't see himself as an apostle, for that would be quite a prideful thing to think, it would require an enormous amount of un-Godly hubris, he would tell himself, but he also knew he had a special place, but needed to guard this special knowledge closely.

He knew himself, and knew when it came to this, this most vital and important of things, he was not a patient man, nor should he be, and *I won't offer anyone the opportunity for surrender, for salvation, more than once. You'd have your chance, and if you didn't take it, it was on you. You would be the one going to hell, not me.* If he knew you well, if you were a loved one, he might approach you more than once, but never more than three times. He knew, perhaps from his special communication with God, that *everything was a creation of God, whether in form or thought, whether expressed as love or hate, as acceptance or rejection. Every emotion, every thought, was a creation of God. In essence, God owned you because he created you. Yes, you were a separate entity, and yes, you could "become one" with God, but in the end, as in the beginning, you were a part of him. Your parents were merely organic vehicles that you were housed in as an embryo, when you received the spark of life, and then you grew, and at last, emerged into the air and sunlight, but the whole time, you were God's child, his actual creation, as were your parents, and their parents.*

Edison knew that His majesty spread to every far corner of the Earth, and all of the vast limitless Universe. He transcended other religions, cultures, languages, all of history, all thought and invention, all creation. If you had a thought, it was his thought. If you dreamt of something, of some achievement or goal you sought, it was his dream, his goal. If you did not achieve it, it meant he did not want you to, or did not need you to. All of life, all dreams and thoughts and actions and all objects and physical reality, and all of the great unknown was created and owned by God, and stored in his own enormous mystical warehouse. All of everything imaginable, and everything not yet imagined, was in his purview. You could claim to be a Muslim or a Hindu, but in the end, you would either claim the true God into you, or perish, perhaps for all eternity.

Edison didn't pretend to know all the particulars. For example, the actual definition of "eternity"? Maybe eternity, to God, meant actually that, as in "forever", or maybe it meant "a long, long time"? That was God's business to know, and Edison's business to serve, and be the best he could be. He wasn't so deranged that he claimed to know every detail about Heaven and hell. About all the machinations of God, as that would be quite presumptuous to think that way. Edison knew he had to find a niche by which he could do his best work in service. And then, he would have done his part. "Do my best" he would say to himself out loud. "Do my best. Do my best".

This became Edison's mantra as he made the drive to JPL to put in one more day, week after week. It was a very aggressive form of rationalizing, but it was the only way he could justify continuing to aid and abet the devil's work. He would trick the devil, outsmart him, lead him to believe that he felt the work he was doing at the lab was justified, honorable, and that he, the hard-working chemical engineer and scientist, was oblivious to the destruction and cruelty his work was capable of unleashing. Edison knew that the devil liked the unwitting. Liked the person who thought they were doing good while actually creating more harm than imaginable. Edison knew that the devil was cunning, relentless, but not all that smart. He could outwit him at every turn.

E dison became comfortable in his disguise, toiling away in the lab, or scribbling notes and formulas on the newly invented whiteboards, which Edison felt were far superior to chalk boards. To disguise his contempt for everything and everyone around him, he would talk about such things, about the advantages of the wipe away boards and their special markers, over the much more primitive chalkboards and their sticks of chalk. How much neater the new boards were, and how dusty and messy the old ones were. Some people would stare in confusion or embarrassment, as Edison would talk for minutes about such things, talk like a man obsessed. Edison thought he was pulling off a clever distraction, covering his true feelings, but it only helped to fuel the rumors around the campus, of how Edison was "going nuts" or "coming unglued".

His inner adjustment came willingly. He now had a clear vision of what he was meant to do, and what sacrifices he would need to make. It actually wasn't all that bad. Yes, he had to hide his real self, his real mission, from all of his workmates, but that wasn't all that difficult to do when your environment is a serious research facility occupied by self-absorbed, and to the most part, droll studious introverts. He didn't realize how odd his behavior was, and to what degree his subterfuge was failing. Everyone on campus gave him wide berth, and Edison interpreted that as his disguise working, and that he had everyone duped, including the devil.

He thought it rather easy to step back and disappear into the crowd. The buzz that had been created on campus with his newly developed rocket propellant had calmed down, and now he was upstaged by any number of amazing feats, with the development of ever more sophisticated satellites, rocket, and the approaching Gemini program. About a year after Kennedy was gone, Gemini 1 went up, and from there, another, and the third, carrying for the first time, astronauts in 1965. Then came Project Apollo, designed for human spaceflight. Up to that point, a tragic exception to the success of the program was when the very first Apollo command module craft, Apollo 1, suffered a malfunction, and internally exploded in flames while conducting pre-flight tests with three astronauts inside. That same year, the Soviet Soyuz 1 crashed after malfunctioning, killing the Soviet astronaut.

Later, after many successful flights and improvements to the modules, Neil Armstrong was chosen as the lead astronaut of Apollo 11, slated to land on the Moon within Kennedy's aspirational deadline, with only six months to spare. The self-described "Ohio farm boy", was deemed the most steady and reliable of the top candidates, and had presented himself well in terms of public relations, interviews and his square-jawed American appearance. His name didn't hurt matters either.

Fortunately, in addition to those public relation attributes, they had picked a very capable pilot, with a strong background flying combat jet fighters, and assault helicopters. This came in handy when they were about to set down on the Moon in July of 1969. The computer models that had been created, had them unintentionally landing the lunar module in a crater, with boulders the size of cars. The "unflappable" Armstrong took the module off auto-pilot, and in a heart-stopping few seconds, hand-flew it past the crater, and onto a field of soft Moon sand, in the Sea of Tranquility, for a successful touch-down, with very little fuel to spare. Had it been anyone else piloting the craft, the chances were high they would have crash landed on the Moon, killing everyone aboard. One of the more remarkable takeaways for Edison, was the rumor that the entire thing had been fake, had been staged in a large converted warehouse in Palmdale, and broadcast to the world as being real. *Humans,* he thought to himself, *will bring onto themselves, their own destruction.*

All of the Apollo missions were powered by the enormous Saturn V rockets designed by Werner von Braun's Marshall Space Flight Center, for NASA. They replaced the former Jupiter family of rockets. The Saturn's were manufactured by a combined effort from Boeing, North American Aviation, Douglas Aircraft and IBM. They were "super heavy-lift launch vehicles", and burnt liquid hydrogen fuel. As rocket technology developed, the Air Force had pulled the Titan II rockets out of their silos in exchange for the much more reliable "Peacekeeper" solid fuel rockets, introduced in the mid 80's. By May of 1987, all of the Titan's had been replaced. Prior to the Saturn family of rockets, the Titan's had many successful versions, and were used extensively in the Gemini program, using solid fuel boosters. Other "families" of rockets were developed, many new versions overlapping the exiting older versions.

There were, in sometimes overlapping chronological order, the Redstone, Jupiter, Thor, Atlas, Juno, Titan, Saturn, Delta, and presently, the Pegasus, Taurus, Athena, Minotaur, Falcon, and Antares families. The Neutron and Terran families are in the development stage.

What it all amounted to, was that both the space program and the military, bounced back and forth, using various launch vehicles, using solid and liquid propellants, as they continued their learning curves. It was a constant state of cross pollination. There was no clear-cut line dividing the applications of the fuels, or which rockets were employed, or for what purpose. It was a vast, complex, and ever-changing world of rocketry, with the exploration, communication and observation sectors, co-mingling with the military sector. Edison had entered this world of rocketry with the belief that there was a hard line of separation, but as he discovered, there never was such a thing.

The Apollo 11 had used a Saturn V launch vehicle, propelled by enormous amounts of liquid hydrogen and liquid oxygen. These propellants were found to be lighter in weight, for long hauls, and were more controllable, could be throttled up or down, as the situation demanded. Gruesomely ironical for Edison, solid fuel propellant was better for the military, because the whole idea behind an ICBM for defense and as a deterrent, was that the Peacekeeper and later, the current Minuteman III missiles, could be launched within a very short time frame, in less than a minute, and the solid fuel keeps well, and is stable. Liquid propellants don't store well, which means the missile needs to be "gassed up" shortly before launch. That takes precious time. Also, the liquid propellant needs to be treated with great care, and is volatile. In a war situation, that kind of delay and extra-gentle handling would prove quite unworkable. All of the country's silos are presently armed with Minuteman III missiles, and all nuclear submarines are armed with Trident missiles, both propelled by solid fuel. Edison's work made it all possible, for the whole point of it was to have the missiles launch reliably and quickly, and get to their targets rapidly, evaporating their targets in a flash.

CHAPTER 3

Believing wasn't enough. Subterfuge wasn't enough. Edison was sinking into a depression. Had he seen fit to seek therapy, he would have been diagnosed as having PDD (persistent depressive disorder). His creative and optimistic side was increasingly less able to combat it, and slowly, he was losing that war. He began to think of himself as a mad scientist, an out-of-control inventor. He likened himself to Victor Frankenstein, and although the character and story was all fiction, he could see distinct parallels. "The best fiction is based on the truth" he would tell himself. At other times, he saw himself as Matthew in the Bible; financially stable, a nice home, wonderful children, a good life by all appearances, but that he was losing his way, and was becoming one of the "lost sheep" (Matthew 18:12).

His mind wandered to the musings of the early Christians as they spoke of the "plurality of worlds", that is to say, life on other distant planets, all part of God's Universe. He thought of the "Jesus pin", a slang term from his Iowa days in the Navy. The chopper pilots came up with the sardonic name. It meant that if a bullet shot at their chopper, in a one in a million chance, hit the pin that connected all the blades, and shattered it, it would make the blades fly off in all directions, and the chopper would drop like a rock, and the occupants would be "seeing Jesus, real soon". He then thought about panspermia, and how entirely likely it was that life, as mankind knew it, originated elsewhere and began when microorganisms landed here, like pollen from the Cottonwood tree outside his office window, all sent by God.

He thought about his belief being the other side of having no belief, or of having lost belief, and what that must be like? They were opposites, but must coexist so the other can exist. Was that true of him? He could not exist were it not for non-believers? Did it apply to accepting or denying other religions or beliefs? Did God create those as well? Would they exist even if he did not believe in them? He knew that Matthew was correct, and those who come late to knowing the true God are as equal as those who came early. Did he arrive late? Was he as worthy? What could he do to demonstrate his worth?

He and Marcy had traveled far together in life, making their charming mountain house a true home, now populated by three children. Ed Junior, Ellen, and Billy. Edison's commute was now habit, and his demeanor at the campus was that of a low-profile secret combatant, not unlike a member of the French or Italian underground resistance. That's how he looked at it. He would be social at lunch, when called for, and give back a cheery "Hi" or "Good morning" when cued. He was careful to always look the part, never let his ever-deepening disillusionment affect his attire or grooming. To the outside world, he appeared to be the very same Edison that everyone had known for years at the lab. He now seemed more stable, not as "unglued" as before. He no longer went into long commentaries pointing out the pros and cons of wipe-away boards, or other equally pointless subjects. Perhaps he was depressed, some speculated, but others felt that maybe he was a quiet and reserved person, and that was all there was to it?

The enormous success of the Apollo 11 mission, having achieved putting a man on the Moon, began to effect the overall program. The gigantic Saturn V rockets, using liquid fuel, continued to be the launch vehicles for the program, and by the time NASA and JPL came to Apollo 15, in 1971, the focus had changed from being a space race/Moon race (for the U.S. had finally won a decisive victory) and into an earnest attempt to discover the origin of the solar system. This was what Edison had been waiting for, and the reason he had joined up with JPL all those many years ago.

One of the quests of JPL was to find anorthosite rock on the Moon. This igneous rock, found on Earth, but from down very deep, far below the Earth's crust, has great geological implications if found on the Moon, and would help NASA and others to define the origin of the solar system. It is a by-product of magma, and usually found in tectonic zones. It has two basic forms, one of which is sodium-rich, and the other and more common form, calcium-rich. The latter of the two typically contains a variety of feldspar, called labradorite, which some people have invested with spiritual qualities. The whole point of it was to see if the Moon was made of the same basic materials, which would go a long way in confirming the theory that the original molten Earth was hit by a large meteor, causing a large chunk of it to fly off into space. If this rock is present on the Moon, it might define the other rock planets, and possibly, all rock planets everywhere in the entire solar system. (It was found by the astronauts of Apollo 16 and 17, both in 1972).

These Apollo missions had brought back hundreds of pounds of Moon rock, which was examined every way imaginable, and they had some significant help, a lunar rover, which allowed the astronauts to venture further than a few hundred feet from the landing craft by foot, and venture into craters, inspect rock formations, and take soil and rock samples, perhaps miles from the craft. Various types of vehicles had been developed and tested, but the one that won out was a co-creation of General Motors and Boeing, and looks very much like the rovers in use today on Mars, but a much simpler, and more primitive version.

All of this slowed Edison's downward emotional spiral, for now at last, the company he worked for, was fully committed to space exploration and discovery, the Moon being the first stepping stone, and with Mars in their sites. Space probe budgets had already been created and some approved. Jupiter had been orbited with the arrival of Pioneer 10 in 1973, and later, another would be deployed to Saturn (Voyager 1 in 1980), both sent to inspect the atmospheres of the far-distant gas giants. But physically landing on a moon or a planet, with an exploratory robot on wheels, was as compelling a thing as there could be. It didn't change any of the facts regarding the military's Minuteman program, but it helped to assuage Edison's tortured conscience, allowing him to stay at the campus longer. In the background, his inner turmoil, his "storm clouds" as he called them, would persist, and grow.

Increasingly, Edison felt that by being passive, by allowing the betrayal from his rank superiors, to go unanswered, to allow it to go by like a parade, and to do nothing reactive, was not acceptable. He knew he was just one man, and for now that man had to lay low, keep building up his nest egg, so he could go to some other type of life and do something, as yet undetermined, to serve God more properly, and importantly. He knew, that for now, he should be committed to doing something affirmative. And then, it came to him. The idea was so simple, so obvious, he laughed at himself as to why he hadn't dreamt it up long before. But then, as quickly, realized that once again, the idea was not really his, and the timing of it was not his. He was simply the tool.

Marcy, with reservations, helped him create some basic and plain pamphlets. They consisted of four, letter-sized sheets of paper, folded in half, and stapled together, to form an unpretentious newsletter about God, that he would laboriously type up and have copied down at the newly opened Kinkos in Redlands. It was the mid-seventies, and by today's standards, the appearance was primitive, and amateurish. Edison was aware of that, and had no illusions about the "look" of his pamphlet, and was unconcerned. He felt that the message was the important thing, and not the "medium", as professed by his antithesis, Marshall McLuhan. But on the other hand, he felt that the crude unpolished look of his pamphlets could lend a sense of sincerity to the effort, and therefore more effectively communicate his messages about God, than something that appeared more professional or "slick". So maybe McLuhan was correct?

Regardless of who was correct in that argument, the pamphlets were made, and on the weekends, Edison would walk around the community, from door to door, and to the cafe, the fire station, the general store, and hand out his latest edition of *The Palm*. Most days, he was all too glad to get out for a long walk, with the opportunity to share his knowledge with his neighbors, person to person.

The upswell of smooth TV preachers was still in the future by about two years, and it would be heralded in by the ardent televangelist, Pat Robertson, on his Christian Broadcast Network on cable TV. Many would follow him, some of them brash, and with the glitz and showmanship of Las Vegas, and others oozing with emotion, and predicting the impending apocalypse, bellowing into their microphones. Some would weave into their sermons, various political proclamations, and candidate endorsements, most always of a conservative bent, helping to give rise to the "religious right". Others would snag some inexpensive late night air time to advertise various books and potions, including "miracle spring water". Much of this approach began in the post war years, but with the advent of cable TV, it blossomed rapidly. But it didn't spring from nothing, it had its roots in revivalist meetings, tent preachers, and tub-thumpers, with proclamations of doom, spoken from pulpits and wooden orange crates since the turn of the century.

The early signs of this change in society were already appearing, and Edison had to push back against all of it, by showing people he was a down to earth and sincere fellow. In order to not be considered a "mealy-mouthed white-shirted Mormon", as one community person had stated, or a "pushy" Jehovah's Witness, as another had said. He wore his weekend attire, calibrated to the weather. It could be a polo shirt with cargo shorts or a winter jacket and jeans. The point was, he wanted to let his neighbors know about Jesus, in a friendly and non-aggressive, neighborly manner. Edison had a warm smile and he put it to good use. He knew that he came across as a sincere person, and tried to present himself as such.

Of course, one could argue that McLuhan had gotten to him, since he was very self-aware of his attire making the strategic non-intrusive impression. To a large degree, he was literally preaching to the choir, as many of his neighbors were members of the Forest Roots Church, or went to the other churches nearby, and attended services regularly. But for Edison, Forest Roots was missing the mark. Sure, they were a Christian organization, a very well-endowed one at that, and so were many others like them throughout SoCal and beyond. But they seemed more consumed by their size and influence in the greater religious community, than on delivering the goods. Edison knew he had the goods because he could hear God. The message being conveyed by Forest Roots each Sunday was boilerplate to Edison, and he had a higher calling.

Just because Forest Falls was inhabited mostly by Christians, didn't mean it was entirely inhabited by them. There had been some challenges that he was eager to accept in that regard with a small assortment of agnostics, atheists, and the lone Muslim that lived at the end of May Road. In other cases, some neighbors were ready to ambush him and whip out their Bible, and quote verses to him, and in some cases, questioning his sincerity or knowledge. Other people were less dramatic, and listened to him patiently up to a point, before cutting him off, or listened to him, in agreement. He tried to be strategic, visiting different streets on different weeks, and trying to not repeat a street more often than once a month. It was not a large community, but when walked on foot, half the time up hill, it seemed much bigger.

As to how many souls Edison had managed to wrangle into his exacting Jesus Corral, is hard to know, and maybe he did gather a few, but he knew that achieving a goal number was not the point. It was about serving God, and if he had managed to turn one head, or a hundred, it didn't matter, for God was in charge, and whatever number of people he did bring over, was the number he was supposed to have brought over. It was not like working for a company that dished out end-of-month sales "goals" that were actually requirements for continued employment, such as with his dad's car dealerships.

If his knock on the door turned into an amicable visit to a neighbor, and the conversation wandered outside of his intended topic, that was okay with Edison, for he knew this venture was about developing relationships, and trust, and from there, a sense of kinship and shared values, which would lead to shared belief, or as Edison put it, shared "knowledge". The only time he got his hackles up is when somebody challenged his sincerity, or his truthfulness. It was okay if someone didn't believe, but to challenge Edison's character, was entirely a different matter. This usually earned the homeowner a grim or fiery speech about hell and salvation. Also, his message was not to be confused with a sales pitch, as if offering a customer, a better choice in a new vacuum cleaner. This was about imparting the ultimate truth, and nothing could dissuade Edison from his mission.

He disliked being referred to as an evangelist, by some of those he visited. That was a term being tossed around extensively in the 70's, and seemed to Edison, to be a craze. For Edison, it was superficial, with people showing off, brandishing their beliefs like billboards, and was an impersonation of true belief and commitment. It was probably the humble Quaker inside of him, waging war with his louder and more adamant self, and one would think that the evangelistic style would appeal to him, but it didn't. To him, it was extravagant and ungracious, and when he would encounter someone like that, it was all he could do to not denounce them. He would rather come upon a self-identified non-believer, than deal with someone he considered an imposter.

Of course, those that were evangelists, felt equally strong in their convictions, and would have been deeply offended by Edison's dismissal of them. If he had sat down with them, and put down on paper his beliefs and theirs, it's likely they would have matched almost perfectly. But Edison's tunnel vision did not let him enjoy that kind of perspective, and he did not consider them as being on the "same team", as some would say to him. For Edison, it wasn't about teams, or who could talk faster, or quote the Bible more, or sacrifice their time and money the most, but simply and only, about the one true path. If you weren't on it with him, walking in lock-step, you were likely going to hell.

Edison's beliefs were being honed and intensified by these door-to-door's, which for Marcy, was not an entirely good thing. His walks went from about one hour on a Saturday morning, to three hours or more. He then spent time at the breakfast table, typing out the next pamphlet, often times snapping at the kids who were making too much noise. The time slot, that had at one time belonged to him and Marcy, had been consumed by his pamphlet, and Marcy was not overly pleased about it. His list of fix-it jobs had been shoved to the side as well. Also, he had adopted the idea that their sex life, was something only for the expressed purpose of procreation (of more Christians) and not for pleasure. For a man in his forties, that was an unusual position to take. God had made it pleasurable in order to get the job done, but now that they had a house full, that job had come to an end. Whatever private time, Edison and Marcy had enjoyed, even something as simple as a short hike or talking about a book or movie, was on the fade. He had no time for movies, most being packed with insidious anti-Christian messages, and books were considered clever distractions, often feeding the unsuspecting reader more of the devil's propaganda. Edison's world was slowly being carved into two distinct sections: The Good and The Evil.

Marcy was not without her own skills, and after failing to get Edison to come back around, to return to his old normal self, she decided that if he could put his passion into something more productive, with measurable results, that maybe it would help him, and improve their relationship.

She approached the Superintendent of Church Activities at Forest Roots, to see if there might be some room for him within the organization? Not a paying job necessarily, for he already had one that was quite demanding, but something he could do for one day a week, on Saturdays, to help the church in some way? This church, like most any, welcomes help. And from their point of view, Edison was a valued member of the congregation, had volunteered to help them in the past with the Fourth of July, Christmas, and Easter festivals, their Community Yard Sale, as well as other events, so he was well known and well liked.

Marcy's intent was to have Edison agree to volunteer on a regular basis, and her hope was that it would slowly replace his frenetic pamphlet writing, and would redirect his energies, putting the proselytizing behind him. This was a sharp point, for too often, in the general store and elsewhere, Marcy would be met by a glare from a fellow community member, having just experienced one of Edison's less than open-minded visits.

The redirect seemed to work. Before long, Edison was happy helping out the church with various projects, and within a couple of months, he was helping to put out their quarterly newspaper, that had a "Message for the Community" section. Edison would write up a one-page article, expressing views, which were often pretty blunt. He would turn the work in, at which point, a couple of members of the Governing Board would soften his language into something much more digestible and welcoming, before going to print. Edison's adamant style of writing, in their view, was off-putting, and they were in the business of attracting members and dollars, not scaring them away with forecasts of doom and hell. They had a complex to protect, and had over the years, built small homes for the elderly, a barn and stable for member's horses, a basketball court, completely remodeled the church building itself, and built other structures for meetings and community use. There were over two dozen bungalows for people visiting from far away, who wanted to take in the week-long summertime seminars, and retreats. There was a lot going on, and the organization had grown in size impressively. They valued Edison and his enthusiasm, but had to regulate it. He behaved like a "born-again", but they detected something else in his eyes as well; a faraway brooding look.

It's called an atmospheric river. It's a strong weather system that hits the Washington, Oregon, and California coasts, either from the north or the south, and dumps unusually large amounts of rain within a few short hours, or for a few days. Sometimes it hovers over those regions or moves on eastward, bombarding other states. On or near the coast, it causes widespread destruction in the form of mudslides, or cars and front porches being swept away in torrents of water, with trees and boulders, swept down a street or gully. It's especially bad near the mouth of the storm driven river, if it is being channeled between two hills or high spots. It can become ferocious. Houses can be destroyed, pulled off their foundations and turned into kindling, and people, pets, and livestock are killed. The road that Edison drives, connecting Forest Falls to the freeway down in the flat lands, is a serpentine mountain road, the only way in or out, climbing over four-thousand feet in elevation after leaving Redlands. For much of the drive, a large wash can be seen, usually dry, and laden with small and large boulders, and the occasional sapling trying to make a stand. In the winter months, it has a small stream coursing down the middle of it, and is frequented by the animals in the area, from deer to bear to raccoon, and the occasional mountain lion. But when a large wet weather system rolls into the mountains, it turns into something very dangerous.

It was a Tuesday in February of 1976. The rain was coming down in Pasadena in sheets, and the prediction was for even stronger rainfall that night. Rainfall records were being broken all across the L.A. region. It was just before lunchtime. Edison got paged to a phone call. It was Marcy, and she was frantic.

The torrential rain had created a fast-flowing river only two-hundred feet from their house. It was growing larger and more ominous by the minute. It had already ripped apart two homes further up the street, and carried away one Volkswagen Van and two pickup trucks. Boulders the size of a cow were being pushed by the current, tumbling uncontrollably, with some rolling or bouncing out of the flow into people's front yards, or on top of their porches. It carried with it much dirt, that had turned into a slurry of mud, rocks, vegetation, fencing, gravel, tool sheds, and potted plants. She was terrified that it might edge closer to the house. She had the children with her, and was huddled in the living room near the fireplace. Edison at one time had told her that one of the safest places, structurally, in the house was next to it.

Edison dropped the receiver and shot out the door like Superman. He was on the freeway, going as fast as the steady rain and traffic would allow, weaving and bobbing from lane to lane. He arrived at the turn off, drove about a mile, and could see trouble ahead. He kept going, but the higher he climbed, the harder the rain pelted the windshield. The wipers couldn't keep up. Around a bend, about three-quarters of the way to home, the road had been entirely eroded and washed out. The entire mountainside had slid down and eliminated a five-hundred-foot span of road. There was no way to drive further, even if he had some kind of a tough 4x4.

The wash to his right was full of muddy water, about fifty feet wide, and appeared to be at least six feet deep. Pieces of houses, trees, huge boulders, car doors and bumpers, pieces of wooden stairways, what was left of a piano, and the occasional whole car tumbled down the fast current. He was soaked to the skin in an instant as he exited the car, and scrambled over the rocks, finally getting past the wash-out.

He continued up the road, always wary of tumbling rocks from the hillside on his left, or more erosion on his right. Near the beginning of town, about an hour later, he came upon a pile of boulders and other objects, that had been pushed up against the hill, and created a damn. Water flowed over it, and Edison had to climb it, in order to continue, pushing against the current. He fell twice, banging his head and his knee. Bleeding, and limping, he made it up the street, seeing the cafe and general store flooded out, but still standing. He made it to his house on the other side of the road, and it was still intact.

Marcy had been correct to worry, for the gushing water had shifted to within about a hundred feet of their home. The tall sycamore in their front yard was listing far over, the roots having been exposed by the current. It probably wouldn't make it. He came in through the kitchen door, at the rear, as the whole front yard had turned to deep mud. He rushed to Marcy and the kids, hugged them all, blood streaming down his face, and went to the garage to dig up some candles and flashlights.

Something deep in the often soft-spoken, and gently-mannered Edison, had turned him into a hero. He could have easily been killed attempting his drive, and the risky walk up the mountain road. All it would have taken is one small sized boulder, or tree limb, to whack him from behind. By luck or

Intervention, he made it. His wounds looked worse than they were.

Maybe it was his time on the Iowa that had prepared him for this? Just as a simple matter of survival, of keeping his wits, it had been necessary for him to adjust to the fear, and deafening sounds, of war aboard the ship. The fight or flight instinct had to be clamped down and replaced with rational thinking, in the face of potential death, or dismemberment. There had been some swarms of the fearsome Russian MIG 15's attempting to do damage upon the Iowa, but the heavy defensive guns aboard the ship, coupled with counter-attacks by the superior F-86 Sabre's, pushed them back. It wasn't just the jets, but the pilots. They had been trained quite well, and began to earn their reputation as the best. It might sound like patriotic zeal, but even the enemy knew that was the case. Other than a few rounds from the MIG's formidable guns making their way to the ship, punching holes in the wooden deck sections, or part of the structure, no major damage was exacted. Two crew members got hit by shrapnel produced by the impacts, but the injuries were fairly minor, not life or limb threatening.

But all of this is in the comfort and safety of retrospect. Back then, in real time, as it was happening, the constant fear was that one of those times, when the MIG's were swarming, they would break through, and the Sabre's wouldn't be able to stop them, and they'd do some very serious damage, kill some sailors. Who could not have been afraid of that, gone to their canvas and pole bunks to get some sleep, and not think about that? So maybe, Edison was more or less conditioned to handle fear and panic? He gave that some thought, as he fetched some firewood stacked up in the garage, and got it going in the fireplace.

Once it was putting out some real heat, he ventured out into the yard, still being pounded with rain, and the street next to them now totally transformed into a roaring stream. The flow had moved closer, to within about fifty feet from their foundation. Any closer, and they'd probably have to evacuate to higher ground, somewhere. He scanned the hill that was adjacent to their yard, looking for an exit they could take on foot. He determined that an outcropping of rocks above them, and about a block away, might do as a safe perch if need be. He went back inside, checking out the front window every five minutes to gauge if the stream had moved closer to them. A few times, he went outside to get a closer look, and to see what erosion it had created, possibly threatening their house. After about an hour, the rain began to let up, and the stream became less fearsome, and had slowed just a little. Each time he checked on it, the stream had become a little slower, a little smaller in volume, and the rocks and debris it was pushing, became smaller in scale. The worst was over.

The family huddled under blankets all that night, and sometime in the early morning, the rain had backed off to a small misting. The power was off and would probably remain off for days. Power poles and trees were toppled everywhere, and cars had been pushed down the roads, slamming into other cars or people's homes. Edison hauled out his portable generator from the garage, gassed it up and got it going. It wasn't all that powerful, but was enough to keep the fridge going, and fire up the electric stove.

The Forest Roots complex was largely undamaged, just due to a chance of the terrain, and the way the water was being directed downhill. There had been some damage to the main stained glass above the doors to the church entrance. It had been smashed by a flying limb, and some subsequent water damage inside, but beyond that, they escaped unscathed. Edison was concerned there might have been lives lost, considering the ferocity of the flooding.

It was too soon for the grapevine to be working, but there were many rumors to be had at the cafe. There was a community spirt that the flooding disaster had brought out. People had gathered there at dawn to shovel out mud, clean up the debris, and by noon, the place was giving out free lunches to one and all.

One bit of very bad news was confirmed, however, by a reluctant young firefighter who had walked down the road from the county station. He stood, awkwardly, in the doorway, clearing his throat, and announced some terrible news. Apparently, the elderly woman who lived up the road from the Nabor's place, a one Mrs. Shirley Glade, born in Gary, Indiana, transplanted in 1956 to Forest Falls by her husband, but then widowed, with no children, had been swept away in the torrent. She must have been attempting to flee her small home as it was being deluged with mud and debris. It was so horribly tragic. She had been discovered wedged under a fallen tree, and her death, judging by the injuries, had come fast. People stood in the cafe, thawing out, holding their plates of enchiladas and burritos, and were stunned into silence. People began to cry, people hugged one another. The one bit of good news was that her wonderful mixed breed dog, Rusty, had survived without injury. The firefighter had Rusty on a leash.

"This is horrible, we're so sorry" said Marcy, to the people in the room. Others uttered similar comments, but the whole room was stunned. Edison nodded in sorrow, saying a prayer to himself for the old woman. He didn't know her very well, and had paid her a visit a couple of times during his pamphlet days, and she had always been polite, but not terribly interested in his message. He had met Rusty as well, petting the affectionate young dog on the head while delivering his message. Rusty, as you might guess, was a dark reddish-brown color, and looked to be a mix of Irish Setter and possibly Black Lab.

Edison looked up, gave a glance to Marcy and the kids, all huddled around her, and impulsively said, "Can we have Rusty? We'll give him a good home".

The firefighter, just a young guy doing his first year up on the mountain, looked around the room, not wanting to be put in that position, and everyone gave back a nod of approval.

He said, "Sure Ed, sure. He's all yours", and handed over the leash.

Edison took the leash, and the kids were instantly in love. Marcy gave Edison a long hug, and thanked him. Maybe her husband had come back to her, had become Human again?

Hours later, in the living room, the fireplace was going strong, blankets and pillows were strewn over the floor, and the kids huddled around Rusty, giving him pets and pieces of bread. Once the roads were cleared up and they could make it down to the flats to the grocery, they'd get him some proper dog food, biscuits, and other goodies, but for now, he'd have to subsist on people food. He seemed to be quite fond of canned vegetable soup, served cold. The kids hauled out their crayons and markers, creating dramatic images of the flood, while Edison and Marcy sat in chairs pointed toward the fire. The last of the day's sunlight was coming through the window, and Marcy looked at Edison and said, "Ed, huh?"

With a small grin he said, "Yeah, Ed".

"You don't let anyone call you that."

"Yeah, I know. But what was I supposed to do, correct him, right there on the spot?"

She just smiled. "You know, it's going to get out, your new nickname. Everybody is going to call you that".

A worried expression crossed his face. He gave Rusty a good rubbing behind his ear, and the newest member of the family sat down near the fire, contentedly.

Edison examined the scabs, on his right-hand knuckles, flexed his stiff knee a little, ran his fingers over the cut on his forehead, feeling the bandage Marcy had put on so carefully. He stared out the window, thinking of the last twenty-four hours as if it had been a dream. He damn near had lost his life, going over the rocks like that, and if things had gone really bad, his wife and kids could have been taken. He went over the logistics. It would be a week or two to get some electricity and phone service back, and the yard will take months to repair. He had turned off the valve for the propane tank out back, assuming the line must've gotten ruptured someplace. As far as they knew, there was only the one fatality, and he and Marcy quietly prayed for her. After this, he got up, put on his coat, and headed out the door to pick up some dinner from the cafe. The stove worked, and he could've thrown something into a pan but he figured everyone needed something more special than scrambled eggs or canned soup, and the cafe needed all the help they could get. The owners had tried to insist that meals would be at no charge, but after the first giveaway, no one permitted that, forcing cash, or IOU's on them.

He walked down the road a few hundred feet, and walked across toward the cafe. This would be repeated for another few nights. Emergency crews started showing up the next day, cleared debris, and opened up one lane at the wash-out two days later, so people could go to and from.

He made it to JPL a few days later, and as most everyone lived much closer to the campus, most of them in conventional neighborhoods with street gutters and engineered run off, they were fascinated by Edison's story. He downplayed it to the max, but people pressed him for the details. For a few days, the campus was buzzing once again about Edison the hero, Edison the brave, and although he professed to hate the attention, deep down, he enjoyed it. He had missed the sense of belonging to the group, the warm feelings of being part of a team. It made him almost forget how much he detested the arms race, the equipment of mass annihilation, and how his work had directly contributed to it.

On his way home that day, as he turned off the freeway and headed up the mountain, he noticed a car that was stranded in some thick mud, by the side of the road. The owner, an older man, was standing next to it, looking forlorn. Edison pulled over and ended up pulling the guy out of the mud using his never-used trailer hitch, and a rope tied to the guy's bumper. Not more than two months earlier, Edison had seen an ad in the "Redlands Daily Facts" paper and gone down to check out a gently used Chevy Impala being sold by a retiring school teacher. It was clean, with low miles, and priced right. Luckily, the guy in the mud had a smaller compact. and the Impala could pull it out with ease. The man, Frank Hollis, would become a good friend of Edison's, in part because Frank owned a very nice vintage sailboat. It was harbored in Ventura, which Edison developed into a fun detour, as he made his way to Vandenberg every once in a while. Sometimes, Frank and Edison would take a sail, usually just for the day, but once, made it out to Santa Cruz Island on a hot summer weekend and camped out on the deck.

This change in routine gave Edison some off-time to reflect on his life, and on the path, he was on. He sensed that Frank wanted no part of his viewpoints on God and Heaven, or salvation, so he stayed away from the topic entirely. Edison, as with all things in his life, interpreted this need to silence the topic around Frank, as a directive from God, and was satisfied that there must be a reason he had been introduced to Frank, and that he, and no one else, had been chosen to pull Frank out of the mud that day.

Edison knew, that by the strict standards of his faith, as he understood it to be, it was commanded of him to believe without question, to be absolute and stark, in the belief of Jesus being the only one true God, and the only portal by which one could reach Heaven. But something was beginning to nag at Edison. It wasn't so much a thought, but a feeling, as if there was an empty spot in his belief, a tiny black hole. As devout as Edison considered himself to be, as dedicated to serving God as he was, there was something inside of him that was instructing him to go down a different path. Not so different that it would defy his beliefs, but it would require him to look at things differently, in order to reach the people, he was being directed to reach.

Edison did not reveal to his new friend his internal thoughts. Frank was not nearly as spiritual, with his thoughts usually reserved for his metal fabrication business, and women, which was a far cry from rocket launches into space, so Frank was always fascinated by anything Edison could tell him. Edison, having little in common with him, at last came upon the reason he liked him so much. Frank knew how to have fun, and Frank knew how to enjoy life.

Frank had a son, Quentin, who was just a young kid, but liked being on the boat, and sometimes they'd sail around inside the breakwater, or take short trips outside, if the wind wasn't too much. It made for a fun day. As a rule, Quentin didn't join them, but when he did, he too was riveted by anything Edison could tell him about satellites, missile launches, and lunar vehicles. If the conversation ever strayed into the subject of strategic missiles or bombs, Edison would deflect, and become suddenly unfamiliar with those topics.

By the next year's end, Edison's time with JPL had come to an end, in his mind. JPL would have more than likely kept him around until a forced retirement. They had had him on so many different projects that he hadn't needed to do much of his intentional incompetence, which had allowed him to stay on for all those extra years, beyond his original projection. They had developed him into their tunnel rat, exploring the soundness of a new idea, whether it had to do with a chemical formulation, but often, about a mechanism on a lunar rover prototype or a rocket engine valve. Edison hadn't been brought aboard years ago for engineering work, but he had demonstrated such a strong ability in that area, that he was often brought in as the "fresh thinker" on a problem that had others stumped.

But, as much as he knew how appreciated he was around there, he also knew that he had run the clock out, and it was time for a big change. He had stored away a good amount of money, and he and the family could make things work for a while, he reasoned. He had become so adept at living a double life there on the campus, he hardly gave it any thought. The spiritual Edison was kept under wraps at all times, and no one there suspected him of harboring extreme views on anything, let alone Jesus, God, Christianity, Eternal Damnation, Salvation, Repentance, the devil or hell, and the impending End Times. Anyone who could have somehow tapped into his burgeoning inner thoughts, would have been scared witless.

Edison was not deranged, and probably not potentially violent, but he was very motivated. Extremely so. His level of devotion had come full circle, and had been redefined. This is why he had seemed calmer, and less severe. Before this latest version of himself, he had always been "calm" and "soft spoken" but just underneath that veneer, he had seemed a man about to explode with anger and frustration. It was noticeable. It tended to keep people away from him. But now, perhaps because he had shifted into a new viewpoint about the whole "God Thing", he seemed more at peace. Quite resolute, but at peace, determined, and self-assured.

He had worked at Forest Roots during this transition, had enjoyed his field trips to Vandenberg, and enjoyed the sailboat and friendship with Frank, and Ned, and all of this, encouraged by Marcy. But what had been dormant and vague inside of him, was now rising to the top, and he was now reignited by his fanatical and increasingly defined views, stimulated by them, and had a focal point. But he needed a sense of purpose, an outlet.

On a blustery day in November of 1977, Edison went to his supervisor in the main JPL administration building, and turned in his letter of resignation. He had written, and rewritten it, several times, hammering it out on his typewriter at home. Marcy had insisted on proofing it for typos, and for editing out any mention of God, destiny, or the mention of "a pathway".

Once finished, he folded it up neatly, placing it in the only envelope he could find at home. It was in their "everything drawer" in the kitchen, with yellow and light blue daisies printed all over it, and he tucked it away in his suit jacket. When he handed his supervisor the envelope, with extreme solemnity, his boss couldn't help but smile at the stark contrast between the daisies, and the stern expression on Edison's face. He read it, and seemed genuinely surprised, and even sad, upon reading that "JPL did not fulfill his life's dreams" or that "the age of rocketeers has ended".

The usual conversation ensued, with pleas for him to reconsider, to accept a different assignment of some type, something that better suited his desires, something that might reinvigorate him, and with each suggestion, Edison found it increasingly more difficult to restrain himself, to avoid mentioning God or his life's mission here on Earth. It wasn't that Edison was ashamed of his feelings or knowledge, and he didn't especially care what people like his supervisor thought of him, for his life was now about to dramatically change, under the watchful eye of God, creator and master of the Universe. What his boss, or any other person thought about him or his knowledge, was no longer an issue. Edison had reached a point where he knew that his knowledge was special, and was reserved for the select few, so he understood their bewilderment about his chosen path. Due to his modesty, he didn't care to think of himself, or his calling, to be better than someone else's, or that his particular belief was his because he was among the "chosen" few, but he knew that was exactly the reason he was on the path he was on. They simply weren't dialed in like he was. It wasn't their fault. God hadn't spoken to them. Edison had promised Marcy to not make any mention, to say "not one word about God" to the boss. She felt it would harm him should he later decide to get work there again. He agreed with her, not for that reason, but because he had come to realize, that people who did not understand him were not simply non-believers, people not dialed in, but were possibly agents of the devil, and it was important for him to conceal his true feelings, as if also a secret agent. He worked for God now.

At first, the transition from badge-carrying chemical engineer at JPL, to private citizen working for God, went smoothly. The first Monday of his new life seemed a little weird. He got up at the usual time, but dressed in his "mountain clothes", drank coffee more leisurely, enjoyed a second piece of toast with marmalade, and to relieve Marcy, volunteered to drive the kids to school, who were glad to have their dad around for a change. Everything continued on in this new normal, with Edison finding a variety of long delayed chores to do around the house, and finding himself becoming a little less severe, less judgmental, about how Marcy washed the dishes or did the laundry. In fact, he started doing both himself, insisting that Marcy take a walk outside, study birds, do some sketches.

It's possible that his overall demeanor was directly tied not to God, but to the balance in the savings account. They had begun this new life with a substantial amount tucked away, but each month took a bite out of that sum, as most of the expenses continued on. About the only thing that went down was how much he spent on gas for the Impala. He continued to work for the church complex, even volunteering for more assignments, which kept him hopping two and three days a week. Marcy kept an eye on the ball as well, and would check in with the bank every so often, to see where their balance was. She created a house budget, which they stuck to, but economize as they may, the balance kept slowly creeping down. Marcy calculated, that at this rate, they had enough cash on hand to see them through the next four years if they tightened their spending just a bit more. But that was it. There was no indication that Edison, now forty-nine years old, was going to invent another career, or do anything that paid any significant money.

Marcy was a more traditional type of Christian, and dutifully went to church, and Bible study, but had never felt about matters as intensely as her husband did. He was obviously driven, felt compelled, to pursue his "path", and it worried her. She kept this to herself, and the kids kept getting taken to school, the laundry and dishes continued to get cleaned, and Edison kept getting up early in the morning. But something underneath all of that was shifting, changing.

Marcy had a part time job at the church complex, and one day, suggested to the administrator, that they could or should, consider Edison for something there, that paid. She sold it well, and got them to thinking. About two weeks later, she was approached by the administrator and told that they needed some organizational help, some bookkeeping, some paperwork management, someone who could oversee the annoying details in the office. This seemed like a good fit for Edison, and Marcy mentioned it to him that very afternoon when she returned home.

The less severe version of Edison instantly vanished upon hearing this idea, and he flew into a rage. He accused her of scheming behind his back, of not believing in him, and of betrayal. Betrayal seemed to be a central theme in his rage. In the most condescending way he could manage, he explained to her that his life was not his, never had been, and that his main purpose, his only purpose, was to be on the path he was on. When she inquired as to what path that was, he started screaming at her, and pounded out the door and down the road. This was the first time that she began to think that her husband was mentally ill, or if not that exactly, then deeply disturbed, as if he had PTSD after learning about the actual use of his formula. She sat down on the front steps, away from earshot of the kids, and cried. But that didn't last too long, because she was fed up with all his God nonsense, as if he thought himself the second coming. She wasn't going to take it anymore.

For lack of a bar in town, he had no choice but to go to the cafe and drown his sorrows in bottles of Modelo. This being a very tight knit community, virtually everyone who came through the front door knew him, and would give him a nice "hello", or at the least, a nod. Seeing the conservative and often modest Edison, sitting alone at a table drinking beer, many of them, was definitely something new for them to see, and naturally, before sundown the next day, word was out that Edison was a drunk. Not everyone was that unkind, but it only takes a few to start something like that.

After a few bottles, he made his way home, barely affected by the beers, and quietly entered the house. Marcy was in the kitchen, sitting at the counter, thumbing through the latest copy of "Better Housekeeping". Edison approached her meekly, and gave her a heartfelt apology for not only his behavior, and his horrible words of earlier, but for his overall behavior of the last number of months. Marcy's anger subsided, and they hugged for the first time in weeks, but her hurt lingered for more than a couple of days.

He had been outside, the following day, doing some repair on their cute decorative picket fence out front, when she approached him with a cup of tea, and said, "Hey, Edison, maybe we need to think about selling, moving on from here, find a place more practical...".

He looked up at her, surprised at how simply and directly she had couched this revolutionary idea, and he nodded.

She continued, "Not anytime real soon, it's not an emergency, but I mean, in time, give it a year or two maybe, then we can start looking around, you know?"

He stood and gave her a big hug and a kiss. The enormous weight had been lifted from them with this simple plan, and things became easier and kinder around the household. Edison said he'd go in and see the administrator about the job.

The same qualities that had turned heads for him in the Navy, and impressed colleagues at the campus, were still with him, and everyone at the complex was glad he had joined them. He created, step by step, an organizational template that they could all follow with their paperwork. He created sections and sub-sections, cross referenced people and subjects chronologically, alphabetically, and numerically. There was no way someone searching for information could not find it easily.

CHAPTER 4

Some folks are of the belief that God puts certain people and situations in front of them, on purpose, for the person to deal with, for a reason. If someone was weak in the empathy department, for example, a person or situation would be put in front of them that demanded empathy. Same went for kindness, generosity, forgiveness, understanding, and any other type of need that another might be hungry for, that the giver could supply. Sometimes it could be a pleasant encounter, and at other times, it would be uncomfortable.

This category of belief, is what some would refer to as an example of God as Manager, that he was a Managerial God. God created the chessboard, so to speak, created the pieces, created the rules, but that people had a choice to move the pieces, or not, and that was up to them. It was up to the person to figure out why the other person or situation had been put at their feet, or perhaps, it wasn't meant to be figured out, but simply experienced, with the reason to be revealed later.

Edison had come to believe that this perspective was hogwash. He felt that God was involved intimately in every decision, every event, and that nothing was left to chance. God did not look upon the Human experience from a distance, but was intimately involved. It was not for Edison to know the inner workings and intentions of the Supreme Being, and he did not seek answers to the multitude of Earthly problems and challenges, just directions as to what he should do next.

He would immediately interpret every chance meeting or occurrence, however minor, as a message from high above, sometimes veiled, sometimes transparent, sometimes obscure and confusing, sometimes quite obvious, but always with specific intent. He felt this way about how he came to know Frank, and little Quentin, and Ned. It was no mistake. It was as if he had received an encrypted message from the One and Only, to be put into their lives, and theirs into his. He felt this way about everything, about his wartime experience on the Iowa, about the years at JPL, his quest to help reach deep space, his disillusionment with his work, the flood, even his having met Marcy. Everything had an origin, a purpose, an intended reason, and an intended conclusion. Every moment, every conversation, every chance meeting, were like links in a chain, and it was not for Edison to question them, or allow his ego to alter what direction he was being purposefully sent in. It was important for him to keep his head clear, so he could "receive" the messages, receive the voice of God, clearly.

The notion that God had set up the Earth, and its inhabitants, in what amounted to a pin ball arcade game, a game of some skill, but mostly chance, that people had complete free will, and were but loose leaves gliding on the wind, was absurd to Edison. It was obvious to him, simply by looking around, that the Earth and everything on it, was not simply an accident of nature, or a random happenstance in the vast Universe. There had been an intentional plan.

This thinking had made things tidy for Edison. He could take his hands off the wheel, as he knew that the Almighty was driving, making all the decisions. This gave Edison comfort, and a release from many of his daily concerns. It also had a way to infiltrate his personal ambitions, for there was no longer a "personal", no longer an entity called "Edison", in the true sense, for he had never been a separate entity, something apart or detached from the greater Universe.

None of this thinking did he dare divulge to anyone, not even to Marcy. As he always had, he knew that these thoughts were not actually his, but being supplied to him by Divine communication. He knew that his special knowledge had to be protected, and that his weak Human traits could not be trusted.

He forgave Marcy her naivete, she thinking that her traditional form of worship, her standard arsenal of belief tools, were adequate. It wasn't her fault. Her heart was in the right place, but she had much to learn, much to realize. But that was okay, for like everything else, they were together for a reason, and his ability to see beyond the ordinary, was going to save her. The same applied to the kids.

There had been a lapse in his pamphlet-making, and it was now time to start it up again. His months of writing the Community Message for the church had grown stale, and he did not want to waste any more time on resenting their severe edits. But to get his pamphlet going again, he had to up the game, and make the pamphlet more appealing. He drafted his kids in a contest, the winner's prize would be a Hershey bar. Only the youngest had a strong desire to win the chocolate bar, and the older two were doing it because it was all about pleasing dad. The goal was to come up with a crayon-rendered front cover. It had to feature a depiction of Jesus, or their idea of what God looked like, and anything else they could think of that was appropriate. They went to work, knocking out over two dozen pieces. Most of the creations were below par for Edison's needs, but once in a while, one of the kids would come up with something charming and effective. Edison was attempting to be clever, by showing something cute and approachable, to put some sugar on the medicine he was delivering. He chose a well-drawn rendering of Jesus washing the feet of poor people. What could have been better?

Edison, armed with his revamped pamphlet and a color crayon rendering, went door to door. People would stand in their doorways, and smile or give a little pleasant laugh at how adorable the crayon rendering of Jesus was, and how well his kid had illustrated farm animals, or trees, in the art work. The pamphlet had grown thicker by a few pages, and included other illustrations that Edison had found in books or magazines, to help illustrate faith, love, devotion or conversely, craven devilish acts leading to hell. It was quite the assortment. Before and after these appropriated images, would be Edison's words of both the love, and the severity of God. He would cherry pick Bible passages to make his points, attempting to supply the reader with hope and inspiration. But his alarming and dire undertone always had a way of seeping through, so in the end, the pamphlet, for all its child-art covers and additional purloined materials, fell flat. Only those who already agreed with him seemed to welcome another issue.

The color covers had cost him significant extra dollars down at Kinkos, using their new Xerox 6500, and even he had to admit that his "articles" were becoming repetitive and tedious to read. He felt that God had given him the opportunity, the inspiration, to create *The Palm,* and was now retracting that same inspiration, so he could travel onto a different branch of his pathway. After one especially exhausting afternoon trudging up and down streets in the heat, he knew he was again, being sent a signal. It was time to put aside his pamphlet.

It hadn't helped matters that the last pamphlet had a cover rendered in only black crayon, done by his oldest child, depicting a very disgruntled God, perched inside of dark stormy clouds. He had delivered this over the course of two hot afternoons. Inside the pamphlet, people could read three articles, all having to do with the various reasons for the imminent end of the Earth.

Edison, if he was feeling especially charged up, would include the warning signs, and the evidence pointing to the catastrophic end, coming soon, which included a seething description of the apocalypse itself. Edison would point to the increase in hurricanes, volcanic eruptions, earthquakes, wildfires, never linking it to climate change, for God had created climate change, had created the invention of toxic chemicals that were destroying the atmosphere. The same could be said for war and the threat of mass annihilation, for disease and pandemics, for moral decay, false prophets everywhere who were promoting false gods and beliefs, people embracing deities, or symbols of the devil, the oppression and persecution of true Christians around the world, and lastly, people who claimed to be Jesus, or the Second Coming. Edison had developed an Elmer Gantry intensity (but without the drinking and serial womanizing). The list, and the way in which it was delivered, was exhausting to the average Forest Falls neighbor. It was hard to turn away from him, or shut the front door on him, but shut the door they did. Even to Edison's most supportive fans, (and there were some scattered about) it was over the top. Edison, who was blinded by his zealotry, could at last see, that having doors slammed in his face was taking the Word of God, in the wrong direction.

To make matters worse, Marcy was receiving much more than glares when she would go out to the general store or market. The people who encountered her, and some of them were close friends at the church, were outspoken, as to their disapproval of Edison's cynical, and stark predictions. Their words were harsh, and sent her home in tears, and shaking, one afternoon. What she didn't know that day, is that Edison had come to realize he had to stop, and go in another direction. He had delivered his last hair-raising doorway sermon, that same day, and his decision, or as he put it later, his "revelation", was that he had been given a new directive.

But she didn't know this at the time. She had gotten home, washed her face with cold water, and paced in the kitchen, waiting for him to return home with the kids after school, summoning her courage. She would have to be quite blunt, to penetrate his thick shield of belief and counter-measures. She would have to convince him, somehow, to stop his pamphlet campaign, or else. She saw the Impala turn into the driveway, headed for the back parking area in front of the garage. She watched as her three kids poured out of the car, greeting Rusty, and dropping their school backpacks so they could run and play.

She saw Edison get out of the car, and he seemed strangely different. His usual body language of late was that of a person carrying a heavy weight, but now, he walked lighter. Sensing he was being observed, he looked up at the window, and spotted Marcy. He waved a friendly wave, and started for the stairs to the house. Marcy was pushed off balance a little, by the seeming difference in his demeanor, but she had a job to do, for the sake of the whole family, and for the community as well, if they were to remain living there any longer at all.

Edison walked into the kitchen from the rear stairs, and immediately walked over to Marcy, delivering a kiss and a big hug. She was disarmed. He hadn't greeted her like this in, how long had it been? Maybe a year, or two?

Before she could begin her prepared speech, centering on his off-putting, radical and militant views, he had surprised her.

Edison planted his feet and spoke directly to her. "Sorry I took so long, but I went over to the church, and asked them for more responsibility, for them to give me something I could do over there, to help out more. I'm done with that pamphlet".

Marcy couldn't have designed the conversation better, and discarded her ultimatum. In the following minutes, Edison detailed his conversation with two Board members who had happened to be there, going over the details of a new expansion, involving a seasonal community garden with dozens of raised outdoor beds and multiple greenhouses. His timing couldn't have been better, for they were discussing which funds should be allocated, and more importantly, how much the project would realistically cost? Edison, always the planner, and extremely good with numbers, chimed in, and after a few minutes, had made some common-sense suggestions, not seen by them, for they had gotten too buried in secondary details, having to do with aesthetics. Within five minutes, he had seen through the fog to make some simple observations, without judgement, and he convinced them of altering the design. They had been consumed thinking only of how the garden area would look, while Edison was primarily concerned with the angle of the mid-day sun in Spring and Summer. At one point, he excused himself and asked the kids to go out to the playground for a few minutes while he finished up inside.

They were so impressed by his comments, that they had ushered others into the impromptu meeting, and before long, it was suggested that they bring Edison aboard the planning of the project, as a paid consultant. Part of his job would be to organize the budget, allocating funds to be released for the various stages of development and construction of the garden center. Additionally, so that one set of hands would be on the controls, he would transport their collected funds, from church services and contributions, all in the form of cash and checks, to the Bank of America in Redlands, where the church's accounts were.

Edison's job would be to count the money received, on a weekly basis, have it double-checked for accuracy by another staffer, and drive the money to the bank, as a virtuous bagman for the church. This would at times involve relatively large sums of money, and they wanted someone highly trustworthy to perform this job, and Edison seemed the obvious choice, for he would also need to consult with the bank officers from time to time regarding the allocation of funds for the project. As a function of operating as a non-profit, with the IRS having full access to their activities, they would be depositing money into a special account set up for the project, with withdrawals happening periodically. A contractor would need to be hired, and materials purchased. They would have to interact with Building and Safety, consult with various entities, from the county fire department to the water department. They'd need insurance, architectural renderings, surveys, and many donations. Some of the work could be performed by handy volunteers, but most of the work would have to be hired out. There would be a check and balance to the entire operation, with Edison being monitored by someone designated on the Board, but oversight, would no doubt be light.

Edison was jubilant at this new direction he had been given. He was still of the belief that this new turn, this new direction, was not something he had created internally, but had been given to him, that this opportunity had been laid before him intentionally, by God himself. He knew that the front door rejections he had experienced were not due to his excesses, but due to God recognizing the dark forces around him, and needing him elsewhere. He was relieved that he was free from the shackles of his pamphlet. He had produced it to spread good news, but it had turned on him, or rather, he had allowed it to turn it into something dark. He was convinced that the devil had led him into a trap, and had been using him to cast away believers, to alienate people from God. And now, Edison was onto him, had been given a window to look out, and was going on a new path. He was convinced that this new attitude would be full of wonderful and uplifting events and opportunities. They would lead Edison out of the dark forest, for in there, it was laced with poison and deception.

Consistent with Edison's beliefs about God's intentional presentation of people and situations, something occurred to him, as he was driving down the mountain, and headed toward the bank with another fat deposit. It had been the third such trip, usually taken at different times, and on different days of the week, which was Edison's idea of being stealth.

He knew how the world could be, and how someone could be unscrupulous enough to lie in wait for him, to steal God's money, to find a ruse to have him pull his Impala over to the side of the road. Maybe it would be a staged flat tire, maybe somebody out of gas, or with the hood up in the universal sign of car trouble. Edison had done it with Frank, pulled over to help a brother in distress, for he was that kind of a guy. It could be found out that he was that kind of a guy. But not everybody was like him, as he so very well knew.

Sometimes, he thought, people would step out of their minds, go haywire, at the thought of becoming suddenly rich, and all they had to do was trick somebody, maybe lure them in, punch them, knock them out, or worse, and they'd have a bundle of cash. Edison gave this a lot of thought, with beads of sweat forming on his forehead, knowing that on any given errand to the bank, *there wasn't a huge amount of money with me, a few thousand bucks, sure, but not a fortune, not something somebody would risk prison for, or would they? Maybe they think I'm carrying much more, and all they have to do is surprise me, knock me unconscious, maybe shoot me, throw my body down the embankment into the wash, steal the car, and maybe never get caught. And only then, they'll discover that it had been for only a few thousand bucks. Stupid thing to do, right?* he thought. *But it could happen, happens every day.*

It was only then that he realized that this kind of thinking was sucking him down into a dark place, and he pulled the car over, got out, paced around the car, the engine still on, idling, and he realized that once again, the devil had been playing with him, making him nervous, paranoid, making him hateful. He was not a hateful person, but full of love and kindness, and carried a message. That's why he was *such a threat to some repulsive low-life belly-crawling creature like the devil,* he thought to himself. He laughed out loud, realizing that once again, he had outsmarted the son of a bitch, and hopped back into the car and took off.

As he continued down the canyon road, he felt lighter and safe. He had expunged the rotten and insidious devil thoughts from his mind, and knew he had reached a new higher level of consciousness. He laughed out loud, at how inventive God was, offering him this opportunity, not in some tree shaded alcove at a retreat, not in a church, but while driving down the road in broad daylight. His God was smart and inventive.

His mind wandered, and now he knew, more than ever, that he was continuing on a pathway supplied to him, ostensibly to help the church to construct its next project, helping them to facilitate all the moving parts. But now he knew it wasn't about that, not at all about that. He was beginning to open up, and think differently about all the aspects of his life, and what he had experienced and accomplished thus far. It was 1982, and he was in his early fifties, and wanted to have something to show for it, but hadn't gotten there. He felt that God was loosening his leash a little bit, and that now, he could begin to make decisions for himself, as if he had been promoted, and been given some independence, some free will. His experience with *The Palm* had honed his thinking and beliefs, but it also taught him about communication. About not just the information he had, that he needed to share, but how it was to be shared, in what kind of a "package". He began to think that McLuhan had been correct all along.

He had lots of time to think these kinds of things through, as he travelled the thirty minutes each way, to and from the bank each week, and it helped to air out his head, to get him to think more clearly about matters. He thought about his wonderful and understanding wife, his wonderful kids, all following the course he had set out for them, in God's path. He was grateful for everything. He still harbored deep regret for his participation with his chemical engineering work, and would pray on a daily basis, that it would not lead to mass destruction and death. But now, he was content in knowing that the pathway ahead for him, was going in a new, positive, and enlightened direction.

This new slant on life continued for quite a long time, for quite a few months, actually. During this, Edison always had a button-down attitude, was usually thoughtful and serious, rarely making remarks to staffers at the church complex, witty or otherwise, and keeping to himself, as if he imagined himself a double-agent for God. There was one exception to this. He took a shine to Michael Florentine, the lead groundskeeper, and quite perhaps, the only Black person anywhere on the mountain. Maybe God wanted him to meet Michael? It had been quite some time since he had been given a directive, and maybe this was it?

Edison enjoyed talking to him. Michael had a small staff of two part-timers, local guys in their twenties, to help him out, but he was there, rain or shine, six days a week. He lived down in Yucaipa, which was an older but growing community a couple of freeway exits southeast of Redlands. He had two teenage sons, both of whom went to the local high school, one entering, and one about to graduate. His wife, Louella, was a bookkeeper at the University of Redlands. Michael had worked at Forest Roots for many years, "near twenty", he told Edison.

From the very first time Edison saw Michael, as he was walking to his Impala parked in front of the church office, he liked him. Edison hadn't invested much time or energy trying to figure out why he liked Michael so much, but had he, he would have concluded it was about how casual and friendly he was. Michael reminded him of Frank somewhat. In a way, he envied them both. Edison liked being around people who felt comfortable with themselves, something that Edison had never achieved.

Edison's years at the JPL campus had conditioned him to modest ways, to low volume "inside voices", even when outside, and emotions kept in check. People had been friendly enough, it wasn't as if people weren't nice to one another, but the general feel was that of a strictly run library.

The first time Edison met Michael, informed him of everything he needed to know. Michael had simply given him a casual "Hi there Mr. Nabors, how's it goin'?" Edison didn't mind the familiarity of the person saying hello to him, didn't question as to why he knew his name, and walked over to Michael, with a smile. There was something warm and inviting about the man, obviously an employee, what with his khaki work clothes, and a sewn-on patch of the church's logo on his left upper arm. At JPL, Edison was the same way, often engaging in long conversations with the groundskeepers, secretaries, the security people, all the support people, the underlings. He had always been that way, even as a kid.

As for Michael, they ended up talking for well over an hour that day, and on many subsequent days, Edison would seek him out, and find him in various places in the complex, doing electrical work, plumbing repair, fixing a door knob, doing a paint job on a front door, and more often than Michael liked, picking trash up after some "naughty bears" had raided a dumpster. His young assistants had not yet mastered the art of locking the lids of the dumpsters after throwing some trash in. His two assistants were both the sons of Board members, so the traditional routine of warnings, and threats of consequences, were not in use. Michael just had to live with it, and get along.

Without question, Michael was the singular person on the grounds that Edison truly liked, confided in, shared feelings with, and simply enjoyed being around. Initially, he wondered if he was doing this out of some type of "white guilt", but quickly threw that idea out, knowing that yet again, God had pulled him by the collar and made him meet Michael, and that anything between them, anything discussed or confided, was all part of the plan. Their backgrounds, cultures, ancestors, their skin colors, disparities of incomes, or differences in education didn't matter, and in fact, might have been the mutual attractant. Also, it wasn't lost on Edison that of all the names this man could carry, it had been "Michael": The lone archangel, the staunch opposer of the devil, with sword in hand, the commander and chief of all angels. It was obvious to Edison, that God had much loftier plans in mind for him.

Much of their talk, initially, was reviewing their lives, where they had been, what they had done, and of course,

Edison had a rather colorful background, what with having been on the Iowa in wartime, and then his years at JPL.

Edison danced over most of the details of his time on the Iowa, not being one to tell war stories, and besides which, the Iowa was not as colorful and "romantic" a subject as it had once been, considering the tragedy of just a year ago.

Edison knew many of the details of the horrible incident, which he shared. Why did he share it? It wasn't as if he had been aboard the ship then, or he had known any of the crew. Perhaps it was his sense of belonging to her, as if a member of an elite club. For Edison, and many of her former crew members, the Iowa was like a living thing, an immense steel creature, that ached and moaned in heavy seas, that cut through swells like a knife, and seemed to be conscious, a sentient being. When he had heard the news, it had hit him, personally, as if hearing about a friend who had been in a bad car accident. Michael listened in rapt attention. The story went like this:

In 1989, while on fleet exercises near Puerto Rico, one of the Iowa's guns misfired, and killed forty-seven crewmen, that had been in or near the gun room (inside the turret).

The Navy's initial investigation as to the cause of the explosion, was something straight out of the Maury (Povich) Show. The Navy released a report, detailing how a rejected, and love-lost seaman, had intentionally detonated a bomb inside of the turret due to his heartbreak over another seaman on board the ship. A romantic relationship gone tragically bad. He had triggered the explosion electronically, in order to kill himself due to extreme depression, was their somber conclusion.

People inside and out of the Navy, having serious doubts as to its validity, were outraged by this finding. The evidence given was scant and mostly hearsay. Both the Senate and House were highly critical, and the House conducted their own investigations, releasing reports disputing the Navy's findings.

What they had discovered, is that accidentally, the large bags of highly explosive powder used to propel the huge projectiles out of the cannons, had been improperly loaded. Although the guns were huge and fearsome, in a way, they functioned like old time-muskets, that used a gun powder charge to propel a bullet or load of pellets.

With the Iowa, depending on the range needed, there could be multiple bags used, all weighing hundreds of pounds each. If the bags, had gotten rammed up into the gun breech too far, or too quickly, it could have triggered an explosion.

The House Committee's conclusion was that this was in fact the cause of the explosion, not a romantic entanglement. The Navy disagreed with these findings, but admitted that such an accident was possible. Added to this were the findings of additional investigations, which told of a refurbishment and modernization of the huge warship in the mid-80's, that had been rushed, with much attention given to the condition of the guns, but not nearly enough attention given to training the seaman, manning them.

Later, the Navy Chief of Operations would apologize to the accused seaman's family, for there had never been any real evidence to support the claim that he had been depressed, or heartbroken over lost love, and certainly nothing to indicate that he had planted a detonator. What they did discover is that he was not especially liked on the ship.

Edison said to Michael, "How can you ever really take back something like that? The harm was done. How do you erase that? With an apology?"

Michael was also intrigued by Edison's days on the campus, helping to develop the space program. Edison carefully skirted around the solid fuel propellant part of the story, and instead, wowed him with stories of launches, rovers, and mission control. He spoke with excitement of the Voyager 1, launched in 1977, and still headed deeper into space. It was the one that famously had a message aboard, from Carl Sagan, and a gold record with a stylus, speaking of the Earth and some of its features and facts. The Voyager days had had three or four satellites aloft, and currently, it was closer to three dozen. He spoke, of how everything is designed to travel in a curve, to coordinate with the constant motion of the solar system and galaxy at large. There was so much to tell of, and it gave Edison an audience, someone he could dazzle with the immensity of space and the challenges of venturing into it. He discussed the sixty moons of Jupiter, four of them being the most intriguing, with Europa the most likely to have life in its ocean. He spoke, of the gas giants, Jupiter and Saturn, and the ice giants, Uranus and Neptune, that take 164 years to orbit the Sun, and the likelihood that there are a trillion planets in our galaxy alone. There was always the risk of traveling thru the asteroid belt, just beyond Mars, that was simply rubble left from the formation of our solar system.

Edison was not accustomed to having an audience for his life story, and all the mystifying facts about space, and was careful to not mention how he could hear God speak. This affable, honest, hard-working man might be his only real friend on the mountain. He intentionally avoided discussing his childhood years, which was no doubt opulent compared to what Michael's had been. Edison had been tempted to segue into a discussion of Michael's religious beliefs, as if the Iowa story, and space exploration, were both parables, but Edison had the good sense to protect this friendship, and not introduce the topic.

Michael's stories were not nearly as dramatic in nature, most centering around his kids in school, with Baseball and other sports, how he met his wife, about his family's roots in New Orleans, and his last name. Michael was Edison's junior, by around twenty-some years, and had done some time in the Army, but nothing nearly as gripping. He had been swept up in the Vietnam era draft, but had spent the entire four years at the massive Fort Benning, in Georgia, named for the Confederate General who vigorously defended slavery and was a leader in the secession. This last fact earned some conversation as well. What neither man knew was that many years later, the name would be changed to Fort Moore, in honor of an esteemed U.S. Army commander.

Edison's routine in Redlands would be to walk into the bank, trying to not park in the same spot each time, and would carry the cash and checks in a small manilla envelope. Sometimes he'd have the envelope in his briefcase, sometimes not. There could be a combined total, upwards of $12,000, on some days, and only $4,000 on others. He became familiar and friendly with many of the bank tellers and officers, usually dropping by the assistant manager's desk to check in, to make sure everything was going smoothly with the inflow and outflow of money. Some of the money was to be pulled aside and put into the special project fund, the "Garden Center Fund", but that was usually performed by the chief teller and an assistant, with Edison looking on. Edison would have already counted the money back at Forest Roots before packing it into the envelope up at the church office, and after it being verified by another, usually the girl-Friday secretary in the other room, Marjorie.

A minimum of ten percent would be pulled at the bank and deposited into the special "Garden Account", up to $1000. Anything over that would be kept in the main account, and not diverted. It was a good and reliable system. If the project needed a little cash infusion, it was easy enough to instruct Edison to take care of that upon his next visit. One of the matters Edison was able to think about during his drives, was the wellness of his own bank account. He had been away from JPL for quite some time now, and they had been living carefully off of the nest egg. But that egg had been consistently shrinking, even with the help of Marcy's small church income, and even now, with Edison's consulting income. It had been a situation of one dollar in, three dollars out, for a long while, and with both of the new incomes it had turned into two dollars in, three dollars out, and it was beginning to nag at Edison.

He had established a fund of $50,000 in 1977 when he left JPL, which is today the equivalent of about $257,000, for perspective. It was a substantial amount, but it wasn't a million, it wasn't going to get them into their senior years. But it had been a few years since then, and now the fund was down to around $38,000 (about $130,000 in today's world). Not only were the actual dollars evaporating from his fund, but it was not bearing much interest, and inflation had caught up and passed it. The value of the dollars was shrinking, even without spending any of it. He was good with numbers, with figuring things out, good at abstract mathematical problems and solutions, but bookkeeping was not in that field. He had thought of sitting down with one of the bankers to look into higher yield accounts, but Edison was very meek about such things, and considered these options as too risky, so he never pursued it. Again, he knew that any meekness on his part, any need to change their financial situation, would be taken care of, for he was being guided.

But, in spite of that special knowledge, the more he thought about it, the more he pondered his diminishing fund, contemplating selling their house, and the more he thought about it, the more he began to worry. Perhaps worrying was part of God's plan, he couldn't be sure, but he knew that he had to take some kind of action, before it became critical.

They had a small mortgage payment, and if they sold their house today, paid off the mortgage, they'd have about $150,000 toward a new place, in some other town. They could combine that with the remaining nest egg of $38,000 but even with that, it would be not nearly enough for a house or neighborhood nearly as nice as what they had now. Forest Falls was a great place, but in terms of resale value, the homes were not strong. Most desirable towns and neighborhoods had values much higher. Put simply, the money they could generate now wouldn't be nearly enough. Evidently, God had put this problem in front of Edison, and he had to be given a solution, or rather, his solution would be God's solution.

Edison, almost at the bottom of the mountain road, on the usual Mill Creek Road route, driving toward the bank, got a sickly feeling. He knew that he was intercepting a message, like so many before, directly from God. It had been a long time since he had received one. But he knew what it felt like, it was unmistakable. He nearly had to pull over so he could dry heave on the shoulder, but got a hold of himself, steadied his breathing, wiped the sweat from his forehead, gripped the wheel, and kept driving. It was then he looked down at the passenger seat and saw the manilla envelope. It had $6,885 in checks, written to the church all during last week. Some had been in-person donations during a service, some had been mailed in. There was also $4,632 in cash. Large bills, small bills. He didn't care about the checks, but the cash was something else.

It wouldn't be until 1995, five years from then, that Wells Fargo Bank would be the first domestic bank to add "account services" to its website, that is to say, electronic banking, with deposits and withdrawals. All the other major banks would quickly follow. The people at Forest Roots were traditional and slow to change, to the extreme, and whatever bookkeeping practices they had established in the 60's, were plenty good enough for them in the 90's. Even when electronic banking had become the norm, Forest Roots stuck to their old ways. Pastor Ragnoli, the senior and lead pastor of the congregation, with a chuckle, always used to say to those palming some twenties into his hand after a service, "cash is king" and then glancing upward, "but he's the real king". Folksy as all hell, but he got his point across.

Edison calculated, hypothetically, that if about ten percent of the cash were pulled, in this case, about $460, each and every week, after a year, it would amount to about $24,000 (about $62,000 today). He could pull up in the bank's parking lot, and after pulling his share from the envelope, could present the deposit, and it could be distributed in the usual way. Not every week would be this bountiful, but some would be more. It was a good average number, he felt. *Yes, that's it,* he thought to himself. All he'd have to do is pull into the bank's parking lot, find a remote parking space, and pull God's money out of the envelope, and stick it in the glove box. It wouldn't have to be an exact number, not exactly ten percent, but close to that. He would then make the deposit, and then drive across town, to a different bank, and make a deposit into a secret savings account that he would open, making weekly deposits. As for taxes and the IRS, he would deal with that later, and find a way to hide the money. He was more fearful of his wife than the government, so it would need to be a clever but simple plan.

He knew for a fact that no one at the church office ever examined the account statements to see if the amount of cash counted and put into the envelope up on the mountain, was the same as the amount deposited in Redlands. Nobody had the time or inclination to figure that out, to comb through the records and justify the deposits, one made to the general account, and one to the Garden Project, and to cull out the cash totals from the check totals. It was far too confusing to track, what with money being constantly pulled out of the project account by check for construction needs, or money being transferred from the main account to the garden project account. That's why they hired him, to keep track of all that, should it be necessary.

This was not simple-minded and lowly thievery. This was a Divine Intervention, Divine Creativity, Divine Necessity, that would allow him to go forward with God's word, perhaps in a new location at some point in the future, after gathering enough money. As he drove the final miles to the bank, he began to giggle, and then laugh, uncontrollably. He couldn't stop himself, and finally, stopped trying. It had felt good to let it out, to let himself relax and express happiness. It had been a long time.

He figured he would begin by resurrecting his *Palm* newsletter. This new directive allowed him to think bigger. His original pamphlet had been fine for its use, limited to homes up on the mountain, distributed in person, but now, he realized that was only a jumping off point. He could make it bigger, allow it to be seen not by hundreds, but by thousands. He was just one person, but knew that even one person can make a huge difference. It was the reason he was here on Earth. He knew it. The notion of "right" or "wrong" was irrelevant, for he had a directive that transcended such Earthly concerns and man-made rules.

It was on this very day, a sunny and moderate sixty-four degrees, with a slight breeze coming from the west, that Edison conducted his first "impound", as he liked to call it. He arrived at the bank's parking lot, pulled in under the shade of a tree, pulled out the cash and stuck it in the glove box, smoothly. He walked into the bank and it all went just as he had imagined, without a single hitch. No one suspected anything, and why should they? Everything seemed exactly the same as always. Here was the moderate mild-mannered Edison, dressed in his usual moderate way (tan slacks, brown leather shoes, casual plaid shirt in pastels, blue windbreaker jacket) walking into the bank with his briefcase and envelope, and being his normal self.

The beauty of this newly created plan was that there was no guilt involved. He did not feel badly about skimming the money, he didn't feel defensive about it either. All of it was completely justified, depersonalized, and virtually victimless. Sure, the church might have to wait a little longer in order to afford a new golf cart, or for replacing office chairs, or getting a new printer, but that would be the height of their suffering. It was so negligible that it wouldn't be felt. But that same negligible amount would perform wonders used elsewhere. It would allow Edison to reach out and touch people, to reach into their hearts and minds, and discover for them, their oneness with the true and proper God. It was such a beautiful plan, he wondered why he hadn't thought of it sooner. But then, he already knew the answer to that. It wasn't his idea. It had come from the One and Only.

After opening up a savings account down the street, being careful to park a block away, he drove up Mill Creek Road, headed home, giddy with his new accomplishment, full of purpose. He had found the pathway again.

Upon arriving home, he was handed a note from Marcy to call Frank Hollis's son, Quentin. Edison stood at the kitchen wall phone, dialed the number, and Quentin picked up. Edison stood, motionless, listening intently for over a minute. He spoke quietly into the phone, and hung up. Edison looked down at his feet, lost in thought, and then at Marcy. He informed her that Quentin's dad Frank, had died yesterday.

Quentin had told him, choking back tears, that Frank had been keeping his terminal cancer a secret from everyone, even from Quentin, until about two weeks ago. Frank had broken up with his latest wife, but had not gotten a divorce. He had sold off a few personal items, had stashed some special small items for Quentin in a shoebox. He knew he was checking out, and didn't believe in prolonged medical treatment that would slowly drain him, sap whatever strength and spirit he had left, and keep him from his boat and the water.

Frank and his *Lulu*, a beautiful vintage sailboat, was his main love, quite perhaps even over his own son, some detractors would say. Quentin was no longer a child and was old enough at eighteen, to have been around to notice things over the years. He had known his father to be a drunk at times, horribly irresponsible at other times, and had the worst taste in women. Quentin had never forgiven him for breaking up with his mom, but he understood how his dad could be, and had to accept it. Frank in truth, had treasured his boat and had in fact loved Quentin deeply. He had brought Quentin aboard the *Lulu* at a young age, and by twelve, the young boy knew his way around the boat quite well, and could damn near sail her himself.

Quentin had invited Edison to the service, which was to be held at the marina, on the boat.

Edison's first thought after hanging up the phone, was whether he should volunteer a parting statement for his friend. He had never spoken in public about the recently departed, or ventured publicly into words that would undoubtedly reveal his fervent beliefs. He chose to not think too long on the subject of his friend's departure, or more correctly, his arrival gate. Edison knew, felt he knew, that not everyone was going to enjoy the top Empyrean tier of Heaven upon arrival. He felt there were many tiers, all designed to educate or advance the soul to a higher plane. Some would arrive, and be deposited into the basement, but that had another name. He was worried for his friend's eternal soul. This was the first instance of someone close to him dying since he had fully given himself to his pathway, to his destiny. But then, inexorably, he thought of his parents.

He said to Marcy, "I need a minute", and walked down the hallway to the smallest bedroom, which he used as his office. In there, he'd read the paper, or hammer out another edition of *The Palm*, or simply sit and think, staring out the window at the trees. He scanned the walls, looked at his posters of rocket families, and then in the corner, on a small table, he looked at what he had created, that was in effect, an alter for his parents. He had set it up five years ago, and every once in a while, added something to it.

His parents, getting up there in years, had decided to take a cruise along the eastern side of the States, dipping into the Caribbean for two nights, and then for a week's stay, visiting Bogota, Columbia. His dad had always been interested in South American antiquities, and its rich exotic history. About eighty miles away from Bogota, nestled in the Andes Mountain Range, sat the dormant volcano, Nevada del Ruiz (aka La Mesa de Herveo), at a majestic 17,713 feet. About two million years ago, the volcano began its activity, and had waited until November 13, 1985, to have a seemingly small eruption.

His parents had been visiting a town adjacent, Armero, in the Tolima Department (District). It had a rich history dating back thousands of years with the natives, and then with the Spanish. His parents went there to take in the sights of this town, situated close to the equator, with majestic views of snow-capped mountains, and known for wonderful cuisine and music. His parents wanted so very much to be with and among the native people, and had studied Spanish for months prior.

When the eruption occurred, little attention was paid to it, for it shook the ground only mildly, blew off some smoke, but not much. His parents had been enjoying a late lunch at a cafe, and were worried about the political unrest that had begun in Bogota. Like the Marxist insurgents who had stormed the Palace of Justice, the volcano too had a history, and had given warnings.

High levels of sulfur and carbon dioxide gasses were an indication to volcanologists, that the volcano was ready to erupt again. It was not the first time in recorded history. It had done so at least a dozen other times in the last 10,000 years. The local government had gone as far as distributing leaflets to the inhabitants of nearby towns, suggesting they evacuate, or at the least, take precautionary measures. What was not known is that the volcano had unleashed an underground pyroclastic flow, which in turn, at about three o'clock on that afternoon, turned the surface dirt and snow into a "lahar", which is an intensely hot mud and debris flow. These flows can roar down a mountainside at incredible speeds, and be quite deadly. This one was, to the extreme. 26,000 souls perished that day, two of them, his parents. It is to this day, the deadliest lahar in history. For comparison, the Mount St. Helens eruption was vastly larger, combining many lahar flows, with pyroclastic flows, and 57 people killed.

Sometimes, when sitting in his desk chair, he'd swivel it over and look at his improvised alter. It had photos of his parents, snapshots of him and Rachel, on vacations or at home. There were objects placed there by Edison, from candles, to a rock his mom had found on a hike once, with beautiful striations of dark blue and burnt yellow. There was his dad's Fedora, and his favorite tie (yellow and brown alternating diagonal stripes, by Brooks Brothers), some dried flowers, and other items in the same vein. In the center was a Celtic cross made of brass, and a handmade woven small tapestry, about eighteen-inches square, of the Quaker symbol. It was an eight-pointed star, or more correctly, a four-pointed red star overlaid by another four-pointed star, but black, and in the middle, a silhouette of a dove holding a sprig in its mouth.

He imagined that his parents had perhaps seen some smoke or ash coming from the volcano, and had been of course, alarmed. But no one near them at the cafe had seemed especially concerned, so they continued their meal. Then would have come, a rumbling sound, and a vibration, the kind that heavy earth-moving equipment creates. And then, with only a few seconds of warning, they would have seen the smoke and debris flying in the air, over the roof tops, or what had been roof tops, only a few blocks away, with homes being consumed by the unseen flow, perhaps they would have heard screams? They would have probably stood up, with his dad grabbing his mom's arm, and taking a step or two in the direction of the street, so they could flee. And then, it would have been on them, in an instant, before they had a chance to think about it. The immense wall of undulating hot mud carrying the debris of blocks of houses, would have probably enveloped them and killed them instantly, and if not, would have knocked them unconscious instantly. In other words, except for the seconds of concern, followed by a sudden jolt of fear, their end would have come quite suddenly, with no time for thought or terror. This gave Edison some comfort.

He walked over to his alter, picked up a framed photo of them, and stared, blankly. He hadn't gone to their memorial, convinced they were going to hell. Rachel had attended. *I can be such an asshole*, he thought to himself.

He then thought about the dockside ceremony he was going to attend. Edison saw it as a test. And a chance for penance. Could he, would he, go to the dockside ceremony and impart what he knew about his friend's journey into the afterlife? Or would he step back, blend in, and be there to silently participate with the others? He decided that it wasn't his decision. It would be left up to the guidance he received at the time, through his unique spiritual antennae.

He couldn't help but think of his own mortality. Here he was, at age sixty, a man with a plan, and if he lived long enough, Frank would be the first of many other friends and acquaintances that would pass, his parents having been the first. Edison had so successfully shut people out of his life, that he would be saved the inconvenience, and the wrenching pain of loss, he realized. *Hopefully, I'll go before Marcy. I hope so.* But that thought did not bring him comfort.

He knew from observation, and stories he heard from Frank, that his friends were not as a group, church-goers. Often times when he would visit Frank at the marina, there would be one of Frank's pals there, someone who lived a few slips over. They were, to the most part, good people, Edison felt, but certainly not touched by any sort of Divine inspiration or guidance.

There had been one fellow in particular, whose name was Alphonso, who favored loud Aloha shirts, a size too small to cover his ample beer belly, complimented by a large gawdy gold necklace, as worn by millionaire Baseball players. Alphonso looked and sounded Hispanic, perhaps Mexican, perhaps from some Central American country, but more importantly, he identified himself as being Jewish, which ran against his entire outward persona. It was nearly comical. He sported a long billy-goat goatee, entirely white, and his short-cropped hair was salt and pepper, and sweaty. Alphonso, would speak in rhapsodic terms about the Almighty, life after death, and angels, not knowing that he was speaking to one of God's very own emissaries. This brief relationship, which spanned only two encounters, entirely by chance, Edison interpreted as yet another person that God had placed before him, as if a stunt man suspended on cables, being lowered down to him. Edison never did reveal to Alphonso his inner life or belief system, and let Alphonso hold forth to his heart's content. At one point, Alphonso spoke of his time in a hospital after a bad accident on his boat, which for a time was considered "touch and go". During his four-night stay, he claimed to have seen an angel, in the bed next to him. The angel appeared to be Human, dressed entirely in black, and spoke to Alphonso about his past life, what he had accomplished, and comparing those accomplishments to his dreams and ambitions. Apparently, the angel was satisfied with the inventory, and blessed him.

Edison was reasonably sure he would be among a group of nonbelievers, skeptics and atheists, Alphonso perhaps being the lone exception. He could handle that. Every day, he was exposed to people like that, whether at the general store or the cafe on the mountain, of which there were not too many non-believers, or his days at JPL, and in the Navy, where there was an abundance. The mountain had offered the densest number of the faithful, per capita, but there were still plenty of doubters.

During the fiercest bombardments of the Korean coast, there had been some believers created, however temporarily, but to the most part, the guys were the average American, from the Midwest, or on occasion from an inner city someplace. Most were not the most educated, or from families with money, but he had enjoyed that, being among "real people". But back then, Edison also had his blinders on, his spiritual blinders, and had not reached the point in his life where he could see clearly, as now. The whole point of being "saved", was that there were people who *needed* to be saved. Many of them. He could have done a tremendous amount of good on that ship had he known then, what he knew now.

Edison fired up his aging Impala and headed for the Channel Islands Marina, that the *Lulu* called home. He decided to dress in a dark suit and tie, knowing he'd probably be the only one attired that way, but that was okay. He would be the lone wolf in a number of respects. And not just with his spiritual knowledge. He thought, *how many of them, standing next to the Lulu, a medium-sized, thirty-foot-long schooner, with a full displacement of about five tons, had ever stepped foot on a Naval vessel? Not to mention the likes of the Iowa, at 887 feet long, thirty times larger than the Lulu, and a full displacement of over 55,000 tons? How many had served in the military? How many had been officers? How many had seen action?* Edison's guess was that some would have checked one, maybe two of those boxes, at best. How many, had been rocket engineers, had helped the advancement of heavy launch vehicles to the stars? And what of the one glaring difference between him and all those others? Edison knew he was walking into a spiritual black hole by attending, but his greater obligation was to honor his good friend, and to show respect for his son. Edison would be protected. He was being dispatched there as an agent of God.

Edison made pretty good time, catching sluggish traffic only twice, and arrived at the marina just before the one o'clock scheduled start of the service. Quentin saw Edison walking down the dock ramp, and hurried over to him, giving him a spontaneous hug. They spoke a few words, but it was obvious Quentin was highly distracted, trying to organize his father's ragtag group of friends, and keep them away from the kegs until after words were spoken. Edison earned a few looks, dressed out as he was, and not being recognized by a single one, other than Alphonso, who rushed up to him and hugged him, as if he were a long-lost friend. On this day, Alphonso had dressed in a formal fashion, with a black and white Aloha shirt, featuring plumeria blossoms, and clean khaki board shorts.

Edison knew all along that his friendship with Frank had not been the usual kind of friendship, for either man, and that Frank's usual set of friends and acquaintances were quite different than he was. But now, at this moment, this difference was apparent on a grand scale. There were the various "dock rats", the single men, who lived out their scant lives on their boats, and then an outer ring of friends that were fishing boat captains, first mates, barkeeps, strip club managers, bouncers, and a professional astrologist named Lucille, with miles of beads complimenting her dark blue dress. There were others as well, including some nattily dressed people who owned some of the larger boats, a few docks down, where the big motorboats were moored. The harbor manager was there as well, along with Paul, the generously proportioned security guard. There was Sam and Ricky, who operated the marina's all-in-one bait and tackle shop, general store, and fuel station. Mixed into this group of about sixty people were some women, who Edison guessed, must've been former girlfriends of Frank's. They held back and did not speak to many, and made a point of not speaking to one another. Some of the men appeared to have rolled out of their bunks five minutes ago, while others had bothered to comb their hair. Loud Aloha shirts were the typical choice for the men, and short dresses for the women, of all ages.

Would Edison want to speak to this group? Had he been placed here to save anyone? Was he to keep silent and pay respects to Frank and Quentin, and leave? How informed was Quentin of Edison's spiritual inner life? Was Quentin at all spiritual, or just a product of Frank? He had been around Frank enough to know that there was little if any, spiritual content to the man.

He hadn't received a signal from high above of any kind, no kind of an incoming message, not yet. But he would keep his antennae on, let in any messages that might be transmitted, for he was not going to assert himself, or presume anything.

Quentin stood on the bow of the *Lulu*, and clanged together a couple of pans from the galley, to get everyone's attention. The group drew in tighter, and Quentin cleared his throat, and started to speak:

"Thanks everyone for showing up". He choked back tears, the reality of the situation suddenly slamming home. "My dad was a special kind of a guy. He didn't always make the right decisions, and he took some chances, but I gotta say, he was the best dad I could have ever hoped for. He taught me so much, partly by teaching me what *not* to do". This was greeted by general laughter. Then he paused, having been surprised by another sudden upswell of emotion, and fighting tears, continued:

"He was a good man. He taught me so much about how to sail this beautiful boat, and how a lot of that teaches you how to sail around life, you know?" With that, there were many people yelling out in agreement, saying "Amen". It was beginning to remind Edison of a revival meeting. But that idea was quickly dashed.

"I'd like to step away now, I'm no public speaker, and allow my dad's good friend, who came all the way down here from the mountains, to step up and say a few words. Everybody, Edison Nabors!" Quentin did a sweep with his arm, pointing grandly to Edison. Everyone followed Quentin's motion, and settled their eyes on the stranger in the dark suit. Stone silence, excepting a couple of seagulls.

Edison had positioned himself at the rear of the group, not wanting to be pinned in, shoulder to shoulder, with this odd bunch, and upon hearing Quentin's intro, wanted to run up the ramp and escape. But in the next instant, he knew that he had been called to do this, and that's why he was there. He pulled on his suit jacket, buttoned it, and snaked his way to the front, and with a hand-up from Quentin, hopped on the boat. He stood at the bow with Quentin, straightened his jacket self-consciously, with all eyes on him. Quentin stepped away, and hopped off the boat.

He of course, hadn't prepared a word, and not even prepared himself emotionally, for this moment. He looked out at the expectant crowd, some already armed with full Dixie cups from the kegs, most with quizzical expressions, having only seen Edison for the first time.

Edison knew to breathe in deep, to focus, for he had to be clear, so he could channel whatever message he was receiving, so he could broadcast it to the group. He thought about his Quaker parents, both still living in one form or another, on one plane of existence or another, perhaps the Atmic Plane, of pure spiritual consciousness, or the seventh and highest, the Adi Plane, the very zenith of spiritual development, all created and overseen by Jesus God.

He thought of Frank, and how he must now be doing, about what kind of a Heaven he had dreamt up for himself, and if he was in the arms of the Savior? And terribly worried he was not there, but in some horrible dark burning place.

Maybe he couldn't save Frank, but the assembled crowd might have some candidates? He looked out at them, settling his eyes for a quick moment on some, not meaning to stare. There was Alphonso, full of expectation, broadly smiling, which seemed oddly inappropriate, and there was the marina manager in his bright red and yellow Aloha shirt, teary-eyed, and Lucille, the astrologist, grasping her Mardi-Gras style beads. He looked down to his right and caught Quentin looking up at him, with hope. Quentin had handed him the baton, quite unexpectedly, perhaps assuming he would have something meaningful and appropriate to say. Did he know about his particular religious knowledge? Was this all on purpose, all staged by the Knower? It was time for Edison to jump off the cliff. In the Navy, they had called this "situational awareness".

Edison cleared his throat, unbuttoned his suit jacket, and looked out to the flock.

In a clear strong voice, one that surprised him, he said, "Hello everyone. My name is Edison. I knew Frank for a few years. We came from much different worlds, different backgrounds. I met him when his car was stranded by the side of the road, caught in some mud, and I pulled him out. And maybe now, this is what it's all about? Frank was stranded, I was stranded, maybe we all are? I have fought evil, and I have helped us reach for the stars. There is a vast universe out there, containing things we can barely imagine, dimensions of life all around us, occupying this very space, where time, as we think of it, doesn't exist, and now, Frank is part of that. He went on a long trip, and he will be meeting his maker, the maker of all of us".

A long pause followed this, and folks were held silent by his earnest and unusual statements, but others looked at one another in complete puzzlement, wondering what in the hell the guy in the suit was talking about. Edison, looked up at the clouds floating above, and then leveled a serious look unto the gathered, and continued.

"If we think of ourselves as lost, we become lost. If we think of ourselves as connected to a higher meaning, to a higher purpose, the highest purpose, we become connected. It is the simple matter of putting belief and faith, before knowledge. And then we have to ask, is it a purpose, or simply an understanding? I think it is a purpose. Is there a final destination? Yes, I have no doubt of that. But is the next destination the actual final one, or just another stop along an eternal route, as if we're all on a train, going from one stop to another? You don't know me. It's not important. But today you will become connected to your highest purpose, through Frank. He will show you. That's why I am here".

With that, Edison put his head down and said a small silent prayer for his friend, looked up to the puzzled crowd, now beginning to mutter to themselves, and hopped off the boat to the dock. He squeezed Quentin on the shoulder, and walked into the crowd. People parted a way for him, as if he were now suddenly very special, or perhaps, dangerous and unpredictable. There was some more muttering, and then one person, followed by another, clapped. And then everyone did, with big broad smiles. Edison was a hit.

They hadn't entirely understood what Edison had talked about. Most of them hadn't invested much time, if any, thinking about the grand scheme of things, but it sounded good, sounded hopeful, and they liked it. The words about space and time, and reaching for the stars, confused most, but it had all sounded so hopeful, so affirmative. It was doubtful that a single person there, would have a moments introspection about it once the beer started flowing and Jimmy Buffett was blasting, but Edison had been called there to deliver a message, and he did. It was not up to him to spoon-feed everyone, to explain it, to spell it out. If they were open to receive the message, they would. If not, then not. Edison had done his part. This had been only one step in his journey.

It was apparent, as he walked up the ramp, to exit the scene, he didn't want to fraternize, didn't want to be involved in a beer bash, and be exposed to whatever base impulses these people might be having. It was time for Edison to depart, and as he walked up the ramp, he had an odd feeling sweep through him. It wasn't nausea, wasn't a sudden headache or a feeling of numbness in his legs, he wasn't dizzy. But he was thunderstruck by an idea. Would it be too much to call it a vision? He didn't know the answer to that, but knew he had to make a sudden turn in his life, had to change, and change now. It was as if everything he had done had led to this sermon on the dock, and now he had to listen to his messages, and react, not doubt a thing. He was directed to follow his next impulse, however grand, however small.

The drive home pulled him off the freeway two exits early and past a line of car dealerships, and forlorn car salesmen waiting for the next consumer to walk onto the lot. Car sales were in Edison's DNA it seemed, and he could virtually see a good deal, as if with X-Ray vision, without having to give a second's thought. He slowed, and pulled over to the curb upon seeing what he had obviously been drawn to: a brand-new Chevy Caprice wagon with a pale-yellow paint job, a medium brown band of faux wood side paneling, wire wheels, and discounted for that weekend only (stated the bright orange sign, but Edison knew better). He climbed out of his Impala, not wanting to park on the lot (a rookie mistake) and walked over to the long enormous car. It would be perfect for their escape from the mountain. Yes, an escape. It would have to be carefully planned out. He had more impounding of funds to do. But at some logical point, in the not too far distant future, they would need to leave the mountain and go elsewhere, to pursue his purpose, his pathway. This he knew.

Edison walked slowly but directly to the Caprice, looked at the "special" price of $19,999, and was intercepted by an older car salesman who seemed to have come out of nowhere, and had outgrown his suit jacket years ago. After the usual cordialities and bullshit, Edison said simply, "I'll give you eighteen-thousand cash, all-in, right now". There was resistance at first, but the salesman had the stench of desperation all about him, Edison could smell it, saw the look in his eyes betraying him, and he invited Edison to sit down inside, go over things. After five minutes of nonsense, Edison stood up and walked out of the place, pursued by the salesman who said, "Okay, you've got a deal. Eighteen-five".

Edison turned with a smile and said, "Good. Now let's talk about how much you'll give me for her", pointing at the Impala on the street. The salesman's face blanched, and he became irritated, not having realized who he had been dealing with. The salesman squinted his eyes and said, "She don't look like much".

"Aw, you can do better than that", said Edison.

After he pulled the Impala onto the lot, and the head mechanic from service checked her out, they agreed on a value of $4,000.

Edison reached under the passenger seat and pulled out a small concealed box, once used to house thin cigars, and counted out the money: $14,500. He had kept a certain amount stashed there, in case of urgent need. About thirty minutes later, he had himself a new car, and had to admit, there was a sense of loss for the loyal Impala, that had carried him back and forth to JPL for years. But it also served as a metaphor. In Edison's life, everything was.

The drive home was spent talking to himself about his next move. He had impounded about $50,000 and figured if he could double that, it would make for the perfect round figure he needed to enter his next phase. Over dinner that night at home, he quietly informed Marcy that the old Impala had seen much better days, that it would cost too much to start keeping it up, and that she ought to go have a peek in the garage. She was ecstatic. She at first wasn't too wild about the fake wood siding, but loved the interior tufted vinyl seats, the padded dashboard, the automatic transmission, the power seats, but once done pouring over it, turned to Edison and said, "But why?"

"I think it might be time to think about doing some traveling".

"Traveling? What kind of traveling are you talking about Edison? Are we going somewhere?"

Later, upstairs, at the dining table, between mouthfuls of pork chops, mashed potatoes, and iceberg lettuce salad with tomatoes, he laid out his plan: They would leave their home on the mountain, and Forest Home, in about a year, maybe eighteen months, just as Marcy had suggested a long time ago. He hadn't thought of a place to move to yet, and he was open to suggestion, wanted to hear from her, but he had made up his mind, it was time to leave. He assured her the money would be okay, that they had plenty, and with the net from the sale of their house, they could find something "real nice".

Their oldest kid, Ed Jr., had already moved out and was working as an intern for a law firm in San Diego. The middle kid, Ellen, was going to Redlands University, wanting to major in computer graphic design. The youngest, Billy, was just about to graduate high school, so they wanted to wait for that big event before pulling him to a new town.

Weeks, and then months followed, uneventfully. Billy graduated, Edison kept making his weekly runs to the bank, and continued his impounding. Marcy kept up the home, continued to work for the church, and spent spare time combing through ads in brochures for housing in other towns. Edison did his yard work, the dishes, and had his nose buried reading the Bible in his office.

It wasn't just any Bible. It was the first complete Bible that had been printed in English. Miles Coverdale had done the translation, finishing in 1535, and Edison had acquired a copy, printed in 1968, from a used bookseller in Pasadena.

When Coverdale did the translation, King Henry the VIII was the King of England, and he was not known for having an easy-going temperament, or having his authority challenged.

Coverdale's predecessor, William Tyndale, an English scholar, had taken it upon himself to translate the entire Bible to English, in such a way that would be understandable, and in the (English) believer's own native tongue. He had begun with the New Testament, which he finished in 1525, and then began work on the Old Testament. When the King read sections of it, referring to God as being more powerful, and of higher rank, than the King, he became extremely displeased, and put Tyndale in shackles, and imprisoned him. The King was in a great turmoil and conflict with the Church of England already, and decided he needed to control the situation. He commissioned Coverdale to do the job.

This was during the famous time of conflict between the King and Sir Thomas More, the famous theologian, philosopher, lawyer, judge, and Lord High Chancellor of England. This conflict became a monumental one (as dramatized in the film, *Becket*), ending with More's execution at Tower Hill in 1535. Tyndale was executed a year later.

Coverdale, all too aware of the lethal danger that came with defying the King, worked tirelessly to do the translation of both testaments. Coverdale was also a philosopher, and a poet. He used his talents to alter certain passages, to "soften" them, allowing them to be less threatening to the King's rank.

He also added passages to accomplish the same thing. It is known only to God what passages he added, deleted or changed. It is believed, that whatever those changes were, were driven by Divine Guidance. He was not executed.

Marcy's search for a new home started close-in, but soon expanded in all directions, from Flagstaff, to Paso Robles, to El Cajon. Each time she presented Edison with an idea or two, he dismissed it, saying it was too densely populated, or not dense enough, too expensive for the square footage, or in a run-down neighborhood. What she didn't know is that Edison was looking for a good town to disappear in, and considerations such as climate, scenic beauty, ease of living, were not high on his list.

Although the world of personal computers was hatching, and their neighbor had just purchased the new Macintosh SE with "super drive", the notion of internet searches was years away. Therefore, Marcy's searches were limited to newspaper classified ads in the "Homes for Sale" section, or fliers put out by various real estate offices. Sometimes, she'd have to go down the mountain to a newsstand to collect the weekly publications. It was a good system, as she had to do the shopping down in Redlands anyway, and do other errands. Now that Edison was no longer anchored to Pasadena, he had the ability to do some of the errands as well, since he was going down into town weekly with the deposits.

Time flew by most weeks, but now it had been all of eighteen months, and there they still were, with Marcy and Edison at the church, her doing a wide variety of jobs, with a small stipend, and Edison making the weekly trek to Redlands for the deposits and impounds. It had all become routine. Edison knew that their self-imposed deadline had come and gone, but the allure of stashing thousands of dollars a month into his secret account, was quite intoxicating.

As he would drive up and down the mountain, he would mutter to himself, "Okay, this spring, we go…" and then later, "Okay this fall, we go…" and so on.

Occasionally, Edison would break the routine and venture down to the Channel Islands Marina with Marcy, and spend time on Quentin's sailboat. On one occasion, they went all around Santa Cruz Island, and then anchored in Twin Harbors at Catalina. It had been a three-day excursion, which they realized, they badly needed. Edison was now firmly into his sixties, and Quentin talked excitedly about his new girlfriend. Edison gave Marcy a glance, sensing that their sailing days would soon go away, in favor of the new girl.

From time to time, Edison would find himself in his office at the typewriter, and type up a few pages, drawn from inspirations he had received from sailing, his hikes in the woods with Rusty, and the Coverdale Bible. He wouldn't have them made into another edition of *The Palm*, but paper clip them together, and stick them in a drawer.

He wasn't sure if his fierce and adamant feelings about God had softened, or if he was simply incubating his messages, waiting for his next opportunity. He hadn't received any Divine messages for quite a few months, the longest dry spell he had experienced in many years. He fretted that he had strayed, had lost the ability to receive those messages due to his own lazy neglect, and lack of fortitude. He would beat himself up on his walks, admonishing himself for his slovenly approach to duty and belief. Just as quickly, he would counsel himself, saying out loud, "It'll be fine, everything is all right - everything that is supposed to happen, is happening".

But even Edison knew that the clock had stopped, that he was becoming entrenched in this new lifestyle, and that his constant rejections of Marcy's ideas for a new town, were a delaying tactic. Had he become too fond of his impounding? He had already blasted past his goal of $100,000, due to the expansion of his time limit, but also because his dipping had become more aggressive, often pulling 15% out of the cash. It appeared he would break the $150,000 ceiling within the next week or two, and he could hear himself thinking of $200,000 (that's about $420,000 in 2024). He wanted to reach that goal, and combined with the sale of the home, they could walk away with a clear $350,000 or more (approaching $800,000 in 2024 dollars). That amount could get them a sweet place in a nice town, in a nice neighborhood. Nothing overly fancy, but plenty good enough for them to retire in.

His next visit to the Redlands Bank of America stuck to the same routine, often stopping and talking briefly to the assistant manager about the Forest Roots account. The Garden Project had been completed, but the church had kept the account open, continuing to divert funds to that account, thinking there would undoubtedly be another project before too long, and this would give them a head start.

The assistant quipped with Edison, saying "I hope you folks have a good accountant, to untangle all these deposits and withdrawals, I hear the IRS is getting pretty nosy with churches".

Edison manufactured an assured chuckle, and walked away, his blood having turned cold. How stupid was he? How could he have not considered, all this time, the implications if the IRS were to discover his "secret" account. He had blithely stolen this money, for years, never imagining that anyone, let alone the IRS, would have the time or inclination to look at the account, or even know of its existence. And if this manager was correct, and the IRS was dialing up its attention to churches, to non-profits, they could easily do an audit, in which case, he would be found out. A chill ran up his spine.

All the way up the mountain, he talked out loud, counseling himself to stay calm, to figure out a plan. By the time he pulled into the driveway at home, he knew what he had to do. He had to hide the money. He resolved that the very first thing the next day, he would go down to his bank, and drain the account completely, and close it. It wouldn't make the history of the account magically disappear, he knew that much, but if it were no longer an active interest-bearing account, it might not be nearly as noticeable, should the IRS want to audit the church, or him, for that matter. Audits were usually delayed responses to tax filings, often coming three or more years after the tax year in question. It was possible, an audit was already in the works, or just as possible, they hadn't begun one. But the sooner he could stick his money in a coffee can or a bed mattress, so to speak, the better.

CHAPTER 5

The next day, it was time for another deposit and impound errand, and, as had become the routine, Edison got himself attired in his usual casual-dress style, which included suit pants, dress shirt, no tie, suit jacket, black shoes. He had always wanted to present himself at both banks, and the church, as someone who looked professional. It wasn't a guise, for he did this from the beginning, long before his acquisition of spare funds began. When he was a kid, his parents made him wear a suit whenever they'd go out to visit a relative, go to dinner, go the church, or worst yet, force him to sit through a presentation by the Brooklyn Philharmonic. Although it must be said, the one concert he did enjoy, was a tribute to Jan Zelenka (1679 – 1745) showcasing his unusual and progressive harmonies. His parents weren't nearly as taken.

He drove the Caprice into the church parking lot, and parked in his usual spot in front of the building that housed the office, next to the church itself. The air was crisp, with a scent of a coming rain in the air, and he walked up the cement stairs to the door, entered, and was aghast at what he saw.

There was a group of people huddled around Louella Florentine, Michael's wife. She was seated at Marjories's desk, pouring over ledger books. The group included Pastor Ragnoli, Marjorie, and a couple of other people he didn't immediately recognize, but they were probably church members. They were intently silent, and Edison, upon seeing this vignette, had a very unpleasant visceral reaction, and slowed his pace, to take the whole picture in.

Marjorie glanced up, having heard the door swing open, and said, "Hey Edison, come on in, we got ourselves a jigsaw puzzle".

Edison didn't care for the situation, for something was telling him this might not turn out so well, as indicated by the hairs on the back of his neck standing up. He thought of the quotation as uttered by Lieutenant Forbes, the Navy Chaplain on the Iowa, during Sunday morning service, long ago: *"Is there an eternal joy and peace for the inevitable losses in our lives?"*

Edison inched closer to the desk, indicating innocent curiosity, but not too much curiosity. He had to concentrate on keeping his hands from trembling. Once he had edged up next to the desk, he peered over the shoulder of one of the people he didn't know, pretending to look at the ledgers, but it was really to more closely examine the two strangers. He was now fairly certain they were church members, probably board members, but then, in a sickening instant, it occurred to him they might be cops of some kind, or bank inspectors. They could be, judging by the drab dark suits they were wearing. One was a middle-aged man, the other a younger but equally serious woman. Everyone was focused on the ledgers, two of them, opened wide.

The books covered 1990 to 1992, and 1993 to 1995. *That was years ago. When did I start impounding? 1990? No, it was before that, right? Or was it? Shit! Shit oh shit oh shit! That was years ago. Oh hell, I'm so screwed.* There were amounts in each column, with dates, and the initials, his initials in his hand, on the far-right column that read "EN" indicating who had made the deposit. There were multiple pages with "EN" in the far-right column. Page after page.

Edison stood silently, trying his best to not break out in flop sweat, and clasped his hands behind him, squeezing the life out of his fingers, to repress his desire to scream. The two strangers were holding what appeared to be printed out bank statements, indicating deposits and their dates, corresponding to the ledgers. It would have taken a third-grader about five minutes to notice the repeated discrepancies.

"You go on ahead Edison, we don't want to hold you up", said the Pastor.

"What's that?"

"Don't want to hold you up, you know, delay you, you might have other things to do".

"What?"

"Edison, the deposit, we already prepared it for you, it's in the back room, you can just go ahead and drive it down".

"Yeah. Right. So, what are you guys up to?"

Marjorie piped in. "We're going over the books, looks like somebody, or a bunch of somebody's, messed up the deposit amounts, or the ledger, or whatever, not sure"

"Oh, I see".

"Yeah, that's why we asked Michael to ask Louella to come up here, and give us a hand, you know, she's a pro, we're just amateurs, you know?" followed by a weak laugh.

Everyone had gathered around, with serious furrowed looks on their faces, in particular the Pastor, who knew that the buck, literally, stopped with him. If the Board were to find out that some kind of horrible bookkeeping had injured their balance, or worse, that someone was skimming, there would be a likely chance the Pastor would be looking for a new podium.

Edison couldn't resist. He had to know. He turned to the two strangers and said, "So, I don't think we've been introduced. I'm Edison, Edison Nabors".

The man looked up, and then the woman. The man said, "We're the Donaldson's, Jim and Jill Donaldson, good to meet you Edison", as he thrust his hand out for a shake.

Edison did likewise, with a big smile, thinking, *Donaldson...Donaldson, yes, I know that name. They write big ass checks.* "Oh well, great to meet you both".

By now, Edison's blood had turned into ice crystals, and the very best he could do was utter canned words. His throat was dry as sand. He turned to the Pastor, cleared his throat and said, "Oh, I'm sure, it's just a mistake, probably something the tellers have been doing down at B of A. It's just messed up paperwork, I'm sure".

"Well, don't you tip them off", said the Pastor. "We need to comb through these records first, don't want to be pointing the Holy Spear at the wrong people", followed this time by a forced laugh.

Edison backed away from the group, and walked to the back room, whereupon he picked up the usual large manilla envelope, stuck it in his briefcase, and turned, walking through the open door, past the assembled group, and outside to his car. The number of calories and amount of psychic energy that took from him, was almost immeasurable. *The energy of the mind is the essence of life* (Aristotle) repeated in his head, over and over. Once in the Caprice, he thought to himself, *I might be a fraction of an inch from jail, once these bobbleheads figure out what is missing, why it is missing, and who, most likely, made it go missing.* He turned over the engine and backed out carefully, glancing repeatedly in the rear-view mirror to see if a small army of people were leaping down the stairs, yelling at him to stop, calling him a thief. But there was no one.

The drive down the mountain was nerve-wracking. He didn't know whether to do his usual impounding, or this time, let it go. But what did it matter? He had been doing this for years, so if they were to discover his treachery, another impound wouldn't make a bit of difference. Or, if he were in a court room, and his defense lawyer pleaded "remorse", it could help him get less time in jail?

He could imagine his attorney saying to the jury, "The moment Mr. Edison found out that there was an investigation begun, regarding the bank deposits, he immediately ceased his behavior, having realized, it was immoral, unethical, and against God's wishes, even though at the time, he believed it was God's wish". Edison figured if the jury or judge bought that, it could trim time off his sentence. But why was he thinking about a sentence at all? Why was he automatically going so dark, assuming he was going to be detected, and thrown in jail?

This was the kind of thinking he employed all the way down the mountain, until he parked in front of the bank. He did his best to act normal, as if this was just another deposit, like hundreds of others. He decided to pull the impound from the envelope, for he felt that it was God who had shown him this pathway, and he was safe in the knowledge that he was being protected, guided, and that God was in charge, not himself.

He walked up to the usual window. "Hi Chrissy. How's it going today?"

"Oh, just fine Edison, things are just fine". *She seems distracted, or is she just tired? Does she know something?*

He slid the envelope to her, and she opened it, sorting out the checks from the cash, and calling over another teller to cull out some money for the Garden Account. He stood and observed all of this, as was protocol, and once they were done, they deposited the money, and gave him a receipt.

During this established routine, which usually took between five minutes and eight, depending on how long Chrissy had to wait for a helper, Edison noticed out of the side of his eye, the manager talking on the phone. He seemed agitated. He put the receiver down, and looked about, with a pale and worried expression. Edison thought, *this could be bad. Very bad. Did the manager just receive a phone call from the Pastor?*

As Chrissy and her helper were wrapping up, the manager came over to them, and motioned for Chrissy to move over, away from the teller window, out of earshot. He said something to her.

Chrissy jolted away and said to him, "What? You've got to be kidding?"

The manager "shushed" her and said something else. Not once did the manager look at Edison or in any way acknowledge that he was standing there.

This is looking bad, very bad, thought Edison.

Chrissy came back to the window, with a stiff smile on her face, and without making eye contact, said, "Well, there you go Mr. Nabors, we're all set." She then motioned at the customer in line behind Edison to move forward.

Mr. Nabors? She has called me Edison for years. Now it's Mr. Nabors?

Edison slid away with a nod to Chrissy, and glanced at the manager, who was now retreating back to his desk. It didn't take a psychic for Edison to figure out that the ground under him had been suddenly jolted loose.

As he walked outdoors to his car, he knew that all of this was a directive, just as everything before had been. He knew he had to stay the course, and improvise, perhaps doing something radical. He got in his car, calmly. Adjusted the rear-view mirror so he could see the front door. *Nothing going on. That's good.* He drove the few blocks to his secret bank, well under the speed limit, made his deposit, and then, just as the teller was making out a receipt, he realized what his next course of action had to be. The thought arrived to his head like an electric shock.

He arrived home, concealing even a hint of anxiety. He shed his business attire, boiled up some pasta, heated up a jar of red sauce, for him and Marcy and Billy, started a fire, turned on the stereo, and chose some generic "light classical" to accompany his unimaginative cooking. Marcy came in from a shower, and Billy wandered in, curious as to when dinner would be. The night progressed, the heaviness in his heart felt like a large rock. He was good at masking, and continued to behave as if everything in the whole wide world was peachy. He turned in early, saying he was "beat", but could not, literally, sleep a wink that night. Once Marcy came to bed and drifted off, he stared up at the ceiling, not thinking or planning, or channeling another message from the Great One, but just laid on his back, staring up, as if suspended in shock. He felt as if his entire life, the weight and purpose of his being, was dangling from a thin weak string. He clenched his fists, and grimaced, trying to detect even the faintest signal coming from God's voice. He could hear nothing, but then realized, and almost laughed out loud, when it dawned on him that he wasn't defeated, but had been intentionally presented with a deep and troubling obstacle to his success. He had to detect the inspiration to solve, not to find a way to accept defeat. The deeper into the night it became, the stronger was his resolve. He was not going to be beaten.

T hat next day, he drove down the mountain to his secret bank, and arrived about five minutes after it had opened. He informed the teller that he wished to withdraw the total amount in the account, in cash, and close it. The young teller, Travis, a thin and nervous young man, went to his supervisor who in turn went to the assistant, who in turn went to the manager, and the manager approached Edison, not wanting to hand over such a large amount of cash, if not necessary.

The manager, Kamal Chatterjee, a man of East Indian descent, almost as tall as Edison, wished to know if he wanted to diversify into other accounts, perhaps accounts that could earn much higher returns, or perhaps an IRA account? Kamal was determined to persuade Edison, which made Edison increasingly nervous with every passing second. It occurred to him that possibly, the church was on to him, and that they had somehow detected his secret account, and the overly polite Chatterjee was simply stalling him, waiting for the police to show up, and at gun point, corner the loathsome despicable rat that was once Edison? He abruptly but politely declined all the suggestions, and tapped his leather briefcase, indicating it was time to fill it up.

This procedure took quite a few minutes, with Helmand Laggard, the sixty-something security guard, standing watch, as the cash, bundled in paper security straps of 100's, was counted out. Each bundle was worth $10,000 (100 hundred's) and there were eleven of them, plus one more, smaller bundle, for a total of $110,560. Chatterjee apologized to Edison, for they only had a limited amount of cash on hand, and had to issue him a cashier's check for the balance of $126,000. It came to $236,560 in total. Edison realized he must have lost track of how much he had stashed in the account, for it was a number much larger than he had expected. Edison played it cool, and placed the bundles and the check, in his briefcase, with the dismayed bank manager looking on, and quietly left the building.

Edison was escorted to his car by Helmand, an ex-Marine on a pension, working part time at the bank for some walking around money, and as a way to steer clear of his wife, Linda Sue. Once Helmand had left his thirty-seven-year career as the chief warehouse supervisor for an enormous clothing company, he had started to get the wandering eye. Once Linda Sue had discovered that Helmand was a major league philanderer, she refused to divorce him, but instead, complained and nagged at him virtually non-stop, and spent every spare nickel of his pension after the bills had been paid. His life was a self-made hell of sorts, and evidently, he deserved it. These were but some of the personal details Edison had learned from Helmand over the years. It had always seemed to Edison, that Helmand was a decent sort, and a gentle soul, the womanizing aside.

Edison thanked him, shook his hand, and wished him well. Helmand, with a touch of sadness, looked at the Caprice as it rolled out of the parking lot, quite likely for the last time. He would miss his rocket scientist friend.

Edison felt as if he had just robbed the bank, but he soothed his jangled nerves, assuring himself that this money, procured over a long period of time, was not for personal use, but to enable him to spread his knowledge. And so much more of it than he had thought! He could begin to feel his blood flow as he headed home.

With this simple dramatic act, he had reconnected to his determination. He had regained his sense of purpose. He felt whole, and knew that the very next place Marcy suggested, would be the place they should go, for he was plugged back in, and whatever place it might be, it was ordained.

He pulled into their driveway, and into the garage, stashed his briefcase behind some old cardboard boxes on the shelf in the garage. He'd have to find a better hiding place for the cash soon, but for now, that would do. As he had shoved the cardboard box back into position, with the briefcase hidden behind it, a smaller box, made of wood, became dislodged and fell to the cement garage floor. The lid had popped open, and inside, was a gun. "What the hell?" uttered Edison, who immediately looked Heavenward and apologized. He stared at the gun, still partly wrapped in a blue work rag. His mind raced, trying to figure out why there was a gun there, and then it snapped back to him.

This was a keepsake from Marcy's dad, who had owned the gun, and had bequeathed it to her, years ago. He had looked at it once, many years ago, in this box, wrapped up in this rag, and had forgotten all about it. But now, here it was. Had this been shown to him deliberately? Was he to take this gun for some purpose? The thought of using it on someone, let alone even touching it, was abhorrent to him. Here was a man, frozen in shock, in thought, about this gun, not wanting to even touch it, a man who had enabled the possible evaporation of millions. The irony was lost on Edison at the moment.

He slowly reached down to the box, lifted it up gingerly, and placed it on the hood of the Caprice. He stared at it as if an ancient treasure unearthed, and found himself confused and worried, that his immediate reaction had not been to snap the lid closed and shove it back on the shelf. It was a revolver of some type, with a dull steel finish, maybe stainless steel he thought? It wasn't a more modern gun, one of those black squarish ones the police have, or all the heroes and villains carry on TV shows, and in the movies. Not one of those. It had a short barrel, but it wasn't a small gun. Maybe it was a "38 Special?" He seemed to remember that. It was the kind of gun cops used to carry, and private eyes. He thought, *yeah, that's right, Peter Gunn carried one of these.* That made sense, since her dad used to be a cop with the Fresno Police Department. He stared at it, wondering if this was a directive of some type?

He didn't know what to do with this discovery, but had learned long ago there was no such thing as an accident or a coincidence. He closed the lid quietly, and went to the rear of the station wagon, opened the big swing door, opened up the hatch holding the spare tire, and placed the box inside. Nobody but him would know where it was. And maybe, for some reason, as dreadful as it sounded, he was going to need it? It was disturbing.

But he wasn't at all confused as to what action to take next, as to the money, and about moving off the mountain, in a hurry. He wasn't all too sure how to put it into motion, however. He knew that Marcy might have a plan for that, and he had to be careful, for he had his lovely wife to consider, and needed to gain her support and participation, on the quick.

Marcy had done her homework. She had assembled numerous clippings and real estate magazines from over a dozen towns, that she thought to be likely candidates, fitting their needs and financial ability. About a week prior, she had mentioned the benefits of Tucson to Edison, outlining the advantages and opportunities there. It was a mid-sized city, with all the modern conveniences, and there would be opportunity for employment most probably, for one or two older people, such as they. It would be a far cry from the mountains and snow of Forest Falls, but it had clean air, low crime, lots of infrastructure, and no doubt, friendly people they could count on as friends. It also had an inordinate number of churches. Per capita, it was one of the densest towns in America, church-wise. Housing did not cost a fortune, but seemed reasonable for a nice standard home on a large lot.

Neither she or Edison had made any plans to actually go there and look for a home, but knew that at some point, they might get serious about it, and maybe take the drive there, to check things out. Marcy of course, did not know, could not have fathomed, that today, this day, would be when they would be driving there, quite possibly never coming back to their home in the forest.

Marcy came to know this as a reality within five minutes of Edison pulling up in the driveway, and tucking the long wagon into the garage, which he rarely did. He darted up the stairs and explained to her that he had just heard of a the opportunity waiting for them in Tucson, of the sudden rush of people wanting to move there, that the bank manager had told him about it not two hours ago, but that they had to hurry, that there were others also wanting to take advantage, and the prices on homes were sure to skyrocket, so they had to leave that very day, get a jump on the competition, and at the latest, depart the next morning, early.

Marcy was baffled at this sudden decision, and protested over the impracticality of it.

"It takes weeks Edison, to pack up stuff, get it in a truck, or hire a moving company, let alone find a house in a new city".

Variations of that complaint continued deep into the night, but Edison waved her off, saying that they would "send for everything" once they got established in Tucson. He did this while furtively glancing out the front living room window to the street, looking for signs of police, the Pastor, or maybe a SWAT team.

Marcy, observing this obvious nervous behavior, challenged him, sensing that something else was bothering him, motivating him, but he successfully deflected, saying he had been called by the Lord to make this radical and sudden decision, and he had to do this, for it was ordained. Marcy knew that Edison could be rather extreme in his beliefs, and in many ways, admired his bravery and conviction, but something was telling her, that he was not being entirely transparent, and that his rush to leave was being caused by more than he was saying.

She had always dutifully listened to him and gone along with him with many prior decisions regarding most everything imaginable. She was not, by current standards, a liberated wife or woman, but subjugated by a very traditional husband, who behaved as if they were living in the 1950's most of the time. She knew that Edison was having a crisis moment, and even though she did not know all the facts about it, she was not about to suddenly stop her established behavior at this critical time. She had to trust him, and have confidence that he knew what he was doing, that he was in fact, being directed by Divine Guidance.

The last time she could remember Edison being this impulsive was when they had first gotten married and he pulled her aside during a beach walk, led her into a small canyon, pulled her clothes off, the pieces that mattered, leaned her up against a rock wall and went at her. She was stunned and fearful of people coming around the bend in the canyon wall, in pursuit of wildflowers, fossil specimens, or similar carnal desires. But she loved it, and had never imagined that her Edison was capable of being so lustful and spontaneous. But that had been years ago, and nothing similar had happened since. Maybe for him it had been a rite of passage?

A statement of sexual possession or dominance? She never knew, but he got his point across in the most passionate way possible. Some of the things he did to her that afternoon she had been raised to think immoral or un-Godly, but she didn't resist.

But now, this impulsive side of Edison was resurfacing after years of dormancy, not sexually, but in another way. He had awakened early the next morning, before dawn, and he woke her up, woke up Billy, but this is where the wheels fell off Edison's plan.

Billy had heard his parents going round and round all the night before, and wanted nothing to do with moving to Tucson. He was now a young man who had just turned twenty, and he figured it was high time, past time, to be on his own, or if not on his own, away from his parents. He had been harboring this feeling for quite some time, but this sudden lurch toward Tucson made him realize that now was the time for him to revolt, and part ways. Since high school, he had held down a steady part-time job at the general store, which was good for some walking around money, and for slowly saving up to buy a used car. His dad had been very strict with money, insisting that he save up for the car, without help from his parents. Billy always resented that, especially since his dad had come from a background of selling and buying cars, but he didn't have a lot of choice, and had felt somewhat imprisoned up there in this community, away from the action, and being dependent on his friends to drive him around, in cars their parents had gotten for them.

He informed Edison that next morning, with a long rambling preface, having found his dad down in the kitchen, rumbling around, quickly gathering food items from the cabinets. Edison at first seemed preoccupied, barely hearing what Billy had to say, but then, mid-way thru throwing some crackers and cheese into a bag, he stopped, and looked at his son. Billy stood in the middle of the room and stared at his dad, imploringly.

"Dad, I'm not trying to hurt you, I just need to be on my own".

"Sure, sure, I know the feeling", said Edison. This was said absent-mindedly, as he was far too preoccupied filling up the bag with food items, trying to remember where he had left his favorite jacket, if the shoes he had on were the right ones, or if he should change them? And now this, with his son signaling his split away.

"So, you get it, right?"

"Yeah, yeah, I get it". Edison did get it. Far more than Billy could imagine. He understood, and more than that, was in a way, glad for the timing of it, since having Billy along would increase the chances of being detected, and might put his son in harm's way.

"So, you're okay with it, right?"

"Yeah...I'm sorry for the big rush, we just have to get over there while the deals are still good, you know? Where are you going to go?"

Not sure he wanted to reveal his premeditated plan, Billy forged ahead anyway, "I talked to Ed earlier, about maybe staying with him for a while, until I get things figured out".

"Oh? You did? Okay, that's good, that's good..." Edison was disarmed knowing his son had already plotted an exit, and felt at once hurt by it, but proud of him. His son was going to be okay.

"You've got to do it Billy, you have to, for yourself".

Spontaneously, Billy walked to Edison, and gave him a big hug. This caught Edison totally off guard, as he was not at all used to outbursts of emotion from people, and certainly not accustomed to being hugged, especially by his kids. He had always thought his kids didn't like him. He hugged him back. The last time this had happened was after an especially good outing at one of Billy's ball games, many years ago, when he had pitched a no-hitter.

"Thanks dad". He stood back from Edison and looked him square in the eye. "So, I have to be out of here now too, right?"

"Uh, hey, listen Billy, yeah you do, and I'm sorry for the rush, but yeah, you do..."

"Are you ever going to tell me what's really going on?"

Edison caught himself smiling at this comment. "Hard to say Billy, hard to say".

And with that, they had reached an accord.

Billy went to his room to throw a few clothes in a suitcase, and Edison resumed throwing some food in the bag. A few moments later, Edison would pull Marcy aside and let her know that Billy was going to stay with Ed Junior for a while, and then join them in Tucson. Edison felt bad about the lie, but didn't have a minute to waste on the drama that would ensue if he had told her the truth.

Edison told them they could leave the doors and windows unlocked, and to simply grab a few clothes, a toothbrush, that sort of thing, and stick them in the nearest duffle bag or small suitcase, throw a jacket on, and they would go. Edison would have to part company with some of his cash once in Tucson, to resupply them in clothes, but the important thing was getting out of there, fast as possible. He wanted to be gone in five minutes. Every time Marcy questioned him, or tried to, he put up his hand, and said "Later, I will explain later". He wasn't nasty about it, or rude, but he was quite insistent.

Seven minutes later they were sitting in the Caprice with Rusty, and backing out of the garage. Edison looked around sideways, checking the surroundings without appearing to be checking. Marcy noticed this immediately. As they pulled out onto the street, and headed away from home, Edison was visibly less tense. Not to be confused with not tense at all. He was still registering an "8" on a "10" scale, but he was becoming less anxious with every passing block.

Marcy had wanted to check in with the church before they left, to let them know she wouldn't be coming around later that day, as usual. But the church was in the opposite direction, about half a mile further up the road, deeper into the neighborhood, and it was glaringly apparent Edison had no intention of doing anything other than leaving. A couple had just walked out of the cafe, and noticed their car gliding down the road, past them. They waved, but Edison just kept looking straight ahead through his Ray-Ban aviators, as if he hadn't noticed them.

"Those were the Peterson's, Edison".

"Yeah, I know".

"They waved".

"Yeah, I know".

"You didn't wave back".

"I know that too".

That was the high point of communication between them for the next few minutes. Marcy looked out her window, saw the community passing by, until they were out in the open, in the canyon, descending away on the winding road.

When they got to the bottom of the mountain, Edison kept straight toward the freeway, and just before the on-ramp, turned into the 7-Eleven to gas up, and to let Billy out. This is where Billy had arranged to meet Ed Junior, who would be coming along shortly. Billy got out of the car, gave Rusty a pet, and stared at his dad, who was busy filling up the tank. No words were spoken. Marcy remained in her seat, overcome with sadness, at the thought of not being with her son for a few days, or perhaps weeks. Once the tank was full, Edison walked over to Billy and discreetly handed him a wad of hundreds. Whatever doubts Billy had been harboring about his dad, had now been underscored by a thousand dollars. Edison climbed back behind the wheel, but Marcy got out of the car, and gave her son a big hug, and said, "I'll see you in a few days, love you Billy".

Billy wondered what she had meant by that, but knew it was all part of a fiction his dad had made up, and didn't want to make waves, or have a scene. "Okay mom, see you soon". He walked across the asphalt to the corner. Edison waved at Billy through his window, play acting as if he would be seeing him soon.

Billy stood, not knowing how to react, and looked at Edison, who returned a nod, giving his son a conspiratorial wink. Billy gave a last wave to his parents, with a sickly feeling coming over him, as if he'd never see them again. The Caprice pulled out of the lot and onto the freeway, out of sight.

Edison's mind was racing. He felt like a criminal. Actually, he was a criminal. The last time he could recall doing anything involving thievery was when he was a young boy, and had shoplifted a Snickers bar. He had walked outside the small grocery store, stood on the sidewalk, unwrapped it, took a bite, but it didn't taste very good. Maybe it was stale? Or maybe, his young mind thought, "He" had made it taste stale? Even at that young age, he had been pumped full of the consequences of leading something other than a sanctified life. Did he return to the store to confess, or hand back what remained of the bar? No. He ate it and threw the wrapper in a trash can. The sugar rush helped to assuage his guilt.

His guilt had been overwhelming that day long ago, and he never again stole. Up until lately, that is. What bothered him more than stealing, was that he was pretty good at it. He hadn't known he possessed this skill set, but he knew that he had already been washed of sin for the stealing, for it had been a directive.

And he knew, that as a mere Human, there could be an unpleasant ending to all this. That was okay, for that may be part of the plan. But in spite of that knowledge, he worried about the ending. Would it involve his wife, his family? *The ending to a loathsome act always gets you, always finds you, makes you pay a horrible price,* he thought. It's those little details that snag you, like barbed wire. You think you've figured it all out, have all the bases covered, but then, after it's too late, you realize there had been a gaping hole left behind for people to discover. He knew he was an amateur at this, and that his plan was risky, and that it was dependent on the sloppy bookkeeping by the church, to succeed. But were his actions wrong? That was the real question. He knew that he had been only the mechanism that had brought life to these actions. The mastermind had been the Creator. It wasn't actually his plan at all, but had been supplied to him. *And you will know the truth, and the truth will set you free* (John 8:32) he repeated to himself silently, over and over, as the miles clicked by on the odometer.

When he had first started his impounding, he had waited for a full week after the first time, to see if anyone had caught the shortage? If anyone back at the church office had bothered to double check? If they had noticed the shortage, he could plausibly say that he had miscounted the money in the office, or maybe the bank teller had? A one-time occurrence would not look suspicious, would not appear criminal. It would appear to be sloppy, careless, but not intentional. That would work for one deposit. But since there had been no reaction, he figured that God had cleared a path for him. He hadn't experienced any of his Snickers bar guilt either. He knew that he was doing this for a higher purpose, with instructions coming directly from the highest possible source. He was clean.

By the time he had roamed through all these thoughts, he looked at Marcy, who continued to stare out her window. He put his hand on hers, and she turned. She had been crying.

"Oh, Marce, don't be sad. We're going to have an adventure, you and me, and Rusty".

"Okay Edison, okay. I'm not used to doing things so suddenly, but I know you have a good reason".

"Would you pull the map out of the glove box? Is there one there for Arizona?"

"Sure, I think so". She pulled out a AAA map of the Southwest. "That's where we're going, you're sure?", said Marcy.

"You did all that work, all that research, and came up with that town as the best choice, right?"

"Yes, but I didn't mean right now, maybe in a year or two..."

"Don't you think we're getting a little stale?"

"What do you mean, stale?"

"Well, you know, always the same ol' same ol', all the time".

"I thought you liked routine. Liked it up on the mountain. Liked the church and your job...?"

"Well, sure, but we're starting to get up there in age, and I figured, why not, what the hell, what the God damn hell?"

"Edison! You can't talk like that".

"Oh yeah, it's okay, I have permission".

"Permission? From who?"

"From God, it's okay".

If you had to pin point an exact moment when something shifted in Marcy's mind about her husband, about his mental stability, about his character, about his judgment, it was at this precise moment. She sensed that she should not challenge his last statement. He had the look of someone who was not all there. He had a faraway look in his eyes. He was her husband, and she loved him dearly, but this was becoming a new version of the man she had been with for many years.

He had for years nearly gone into a rage whenever one of the kids used foul language, especially anything that took the name of God or Jesus lightly or despairingly, he had zero tolerance for it. And now, he has yanked her out of their lovely home, decided to drive all the way to Tucson without a word of warning, and is saying "hell", and worse yet, "God damn hell", as if it was simply a colorful phrase. She decided that there wasn't a thing she could do about it now, stuck in their car traveling down the road, so best to keep her head down, and try to notice anything she could about this strange new man driving Edison's wagon.

"Here, let me find something that'll tell us how to get there...". She looked at the map, folding it so that their route could be seen. She was surprised at how close it was. She had figured it would be a much longer drive, but it was only about four-hundred miles, all of it going east on the #10. Simple. It would take them through lots of desert country, from Palm Springs, to Blythe, to the outskirts of Phoenix, and then have them go southward, directly into Tucson. She figured it would be around seven in the evening when they pulled in, figuring on one rest stop. Marcy had a basket full of small talk she could deploy, to keep things light, and not accidentally challenge him, or his judgment. It was obvious that he had given this some thought, some planning, and she figured, even though he might be behaving in an unstable manner, he would never put her in harm's way or do something completely foolish.

He already knew what address they were headed to, once in town. They would spend the night at a Holiday Inn, and in the morning, go to the house, priced to sell, near the corner of South Fifth Avenue and East 33rd Street. It featured all-electric appliances, new linoleum flooring, a fireplace, decorative rock landscaping with succulents and cactus in the front, and a back yard with lots of potential. All this was information based on the photos, and the always-upbeat description in the ad.

Edison had thumbed through Marcy's papers a week before, and had come upon this one as ideal. The price was low, since it was in not the best of neighborhoods, but one that was checkerboard, some homes being nicely kept and others worn down and depressed. There was a fish and chips place not far, and other small businesses within a mile. No bars on windows, or cars parked on lawns, which were good signs. Edison figured a nice cash down payment is all they would need. The home was vacant, so they could have a fast escrow, and then he could put their Forest Falls home up for sale, and pay off the new Tucson place in full, with lots of cash to spare.

None of this, had he revealed to Marcy. He didn't see it as being secretive or devious, but as part of the fabric, part of the overall plan, that was being written and directed by the Almighty. It didn't matter that Marcy didn't know everything in advance. Half the time, Edison didn't know what was coming next either.

They pulled into Tucson around eight that night. Checked into the Holiday Inn, and had dinner across the street at a Denny's. They bought Rusty a hamburger which he happily devoured in the back seat of the wagon, when they came back out.

As they grabbed their bags from the wagon, and let Rusty run around for a while and sniff some bushes, Edison knew that in order to go forward, he would have to become much more accessible to Marcy, allow himself to be vulnerable, open up and share his confidences, which might open himself up to some deep feelings, which could upset the master plan, *whatever in the hell that is,* but it had to be. He gave Marcy a long hard hug, and whispered into her ear, "I'm sorry Marce, I know all this seems crazy, but I promise you, it isn't".

She took a good long look into his eyes and gently nodded, with a small delicate smile on her face. "Yes, I know, but you worry me sometimes, but I trust you, I know you have a special calling".

With that, they kissed and kissed again, and only stopped because he had left Rusty off leash, and he was trying to chase down an alley cat. The interruption was not welcome, but it made them both feel much better. Turns out, Marcy was much more concerned about their marriage and closeness, than any plan Edison had in mind. She'd do most anything with him, and for him, always had. But she had to know he was truly with her, and not drifting off.

They apprehended Rusty by the swimming pool gate, went in their room, settled in, turned on an old rerun of "Gunsmoke", and drifted off to sleep. Edison woke up quite early in the morning, in the middle of the night, awakened by the thought that someone might break into their car, and steal his duffle bag with the money and checks. It wasn't likely that would happen of course, but it wasn't impossible either. He slipped out of bed, carefully opened the door, snuck down the carpeted hall to the exit, went to his car and unlocked it. He unlocked the back door, swinging it open, and under a blanket, checked for the bag. It was there, just as he had placed it the day before. He lifted up the spare tire hatch and took a look at the gun box. He thought that if he stared at it long enough, a message would come through. No such luck. He looked around to see if he was being observed, but the entire parking lot was quiet and deserted, lit only by one yellowish sodium light on the opposite side. He carefully closed up the car, snuck back to the room, crawled into bed, without Marcy knowing a thing.

So far, all had gone smoothly. Edison had felt the vibrating protective force-field all around him, giving him a sense of balance, of well-being.

At some point in the very near future, Pastor Ragnoli and the bank manager would be having a one-to-one talk, over at the bank, and compare notes and ledgers, which would lead them to the only possible answer to the puzzle, after all others had been dismissed.

It was not going to be pleasant for the Pastor, for he had put complete faith and trust into Edison, and this would erupt into a scandal like no other in the Forest Roots' history, no doubt resulting in his expulsion, not to mention it being a scandal for the entire community, involving not only the church, the anchor of the entire town, but implicating one of the town's most trusted families. There was no way this could turn out to be anything but horrible for many people.

Edison not only was anointed with God's protective bubble, but was able to take advantage of the limited police technology of the day. The FBI had established a nationwide network many years ago, in 1967, that allowed regional offices to communicate by way of enormous and clunky computer systems, but it was still primitive in many ways, the format of the technology having been grandfathered in, version after version. Additionally, large police departments had begun using smaller and more efficient computers, in the early nineties, but that tech had its limitations as well. And now, it was 2000, and some towns, Tucson among them, still hadn't stepped into the latest technology, and relied on the tried and true of past decades. Edison had made a broad assumption about the readiness of police tech in Tucson after reading various articles about the antiquated computer systems that many police departments still used. Some of it had to do with lack of funds in their budgets, while others were stuck in their ways, due to the culture of their departments and city governments. Redlands, for example, didn't have up to date computers or software at their police headquarters, and nor did Tucson. Had Edison fled to New York or Chicago, or any major city, it would have been another matter. The Achilles heel of many smaller departments, was their inability to communicate with one another.

Eventually, Edison knew that this "safe" landing spot would wear thin, and they'd have to leave, but for the time being, and for probably quite a few years, if he kept a low profile, they would be safe, and undetected. He wouldn't need to go so far as changing his name, or creating false identifications, but he'd simply need to employ some common sense "must-dos", such as only banking at a local and insulated institution, not a name brand national one, such as Bank of America or Wells Fargo, or linked to larger banks in other cities. Also, to be careful to pay in cash whenever possible, and have personal checks that do not have his address or phone number printed on them. He would not take out any credit cards, whose information could be shared or tapped. He would sell the Caprice immediately, and get something very generic looking, and used. He wanted to blend in. He would grow a beard, which he had already begun by having not shaved the last four days. He would have to come up with a clever ruse as to why Marcy ought to dye her hair. He would have to be careful to not get too familiar with anyone, and start talking about his rocketeer days, or Navy days. It would be better to make up a past. He'd go get himself some eyeglasses that he'd wear full time to help with his new appearance, and get in the habit of always wearing a ball cap. He heard that a new ball team was going to be established in Arizona, and he could wear one of those, blend in.

But all of this subterfuge was not so they could live the life of Bonnie and Clyde, but so that he could do the Lord's work, as directed by the One and Only. The hiding in plain sight plan was to enable his real purpose. Once they moved in, took care of the long list of "must do's", he would rent a small office somewhere and start up his *Palm* pamphlet. This is where it would begin, and from there, he would see how he would be further directed. He might choose to hand deliver, or perhaps putting them in, or next to a mailbox, would be better? But this would only be lighting the fuse for something much bigger. Tucson was enormous compared to Forest Falls, so the idea of hand-delivery was not a realistic plan. But, like many things past and to come, he would be given instructions on a need-to-know basis. All he had to do was trust, get the ball rolling, and the impossible would become possible.

There was an enormous missing element to all of this, something that had been left unattended, ignored, and now it had developed into an issue. As a chemical engineer, he could appreciate the importance of having all the ingredients to a compound involved, in precise measurements, if a desired result was expected. The question he had for himself was a simple one: *Am I going crazy?*

All of this time, he had been dialing into the directions given by God, had used his internal antennae to get instructions, perhaps not given in the form of a voice that he could hear (for that would qualify him for some serious psychiatric evaluation) but something he strongly sensed, as if being told. And now, he had performed a string of actions, some might say radical actions, and was still fully committed to his path. But what was missing, is that all of these actions were cerebral, and he was doing all he could to keep a lid on himself, so he wouldn't fly off the tracks. Edison had always been very "together", and was able to mask his emotions, but that didn't mean he didn't have emotions. At this critical stage, he could feel himself becoming unhinged, and it scared him.

The next morning, they were greeted by a monsoonal rainstorm, which lasted until mid-morning. It was like a warm continuous cloudburst. It wasn't until then, as he and Marcy were looking out the motel window at the downpour, that he informed her that he had a specific place in mind, and they ought to go there first. Marcy had become almost immune to surprises at this point, and nodded to him, knowing that he obviously had a master plan that he was only going to dole out to her in pieces, as need be. The rain stopped as quickly as it had begun, creating a beautiful full rainbow, arching over the desert. Edison took this as a sign.

They drove to the prospective house and met the realtor, who had gotten there just minutes before, opened it up, and let it air out. The rain had a few more showers to deliver, but was gone to the most part, and moving toward New Mexico.

It was a nondescript and drab little place, with no surprises. The dirt backyard was smaller than in the photos, thanks to wide angle, but big enough. There was a slab of concrete large enough for a BBQ and a table set. A wood patio cover offered some shade. Everything about the place was generic and so very different than their mountain home. But it was okay. The real estate agent, Nanci Booker, was a little put off when Edison didn't especially want a room-to-room tour. But her mood brightened quickly when instead, he wanted to get some paperwork going, make a down payment. He and Marcy had discussed it already, as they huddled in a corner of the kitchen, away from Nanci, as she was prepping the other rooms for her tour, the freshly painted cabinets still smelling of acrylic paint. Marcy knew there was no point in arguing with Edison about it, or to insist on looking at other homes.

With surprising speed, not wanting her impulsive clients to have a change of heart, Nanci was able to get all the paperwork filled out, and the Nabors' were ready to pay asking price. The agent was not accustomed to such speed, and a total lack of negotiation, but she knew not to be too curious or inquisitive, to cause any delays, and create hesitation from the buyer. She got their signatures on the last page, and asked Edison how he would like to pay the down?

"I'll write a check, tomorrow".

"That'll be fine Mr. Nabors, but did you mean a personal check?"

"Yes, that was the idea. I'll just get one of those temp ones til my printed ones come in. Don't worry, I'm good for it".

"Well, I am quite sure you are, but if you don't mind, would it be too much trouble for you to go to your institution and get a cashier's check?"

"Well, no, I suppose not. Do you know of a good local bank I could go to? I need to open an account".

Nanci, thought a moment and said, "Yes, there's the Johnson Bank, that has two branches in town, and one in Phoenix, if that would be adequate for your needs?"

"The Johnson Bank? It's a good one?"

"Yes, they deal with a lot of the small businesses here in town".

"Great, that'll do just fine".

"Oh, good, so you folks from far away?"

"No, not too far. We're from, from Arcata".

"Arcata?"

"Yes, that's up the coast, in California, and we always wanted to live in the desert, get away from all that rain and cloudy damp weather, you know?"

"Oh, why certainly. Arcata. I'm not familiar with it".

"That's okay. No need to be. Too many damn hippies moving in anyway. Probably a bunch of fucking commies".

That last comment took Nanci by surprise, not to mention Marcy, which was the intent. Edison figured if he said something blunt and raw, maybe with a taste of radical politics mixed in, it would shut Nanci up, make her stop asking questions. It worked.

Edison had almost said Oregon, or Washington, wanting to place themselves from even further away, but then realized the California plates on the Caprice would be a giveaway. Marcy stood nearby, mute as a rock, but studying this new and strange creature inhabiting Edison's skin.

Nanci stood a moment, holding the paperwork in her hand, and could not help herself. She had woven into all her sales pitches the history of the area, as a way to romance the prospective client, but this client, had leapt over most of her material, and almost reflexively, she had to share.

She said, "They were established, the Johnson Bank, in the early nineteen-hundreds, around 1910, I think. Johnson was a cattle baron, needed to invent a place to stick all his money. Quite a character from what I have read. Was gunned down by some Mexican ranchers after they thought he had cheated them. Right here, about a mile away. On old Alameda

Street, next to City Hall. In 1932, I think? There's the Presidio, the museum of art, lots to see, I mean, if you like history?"

"Yeah, always been a fan", said Edison.

"Oh yeah? Well, there's lots here. I'm third generation Tucson. There's a lot of colorful history to this town, you know, the Spanish and Mexicans, the land grants, the native Indians, the old west, all that kinda stuff. Really interesting".

Edison had let her ramble, because he needed time to figure out a plan. He had to transfer his bag of cash from his car to the bank, in broad daylight, without Marcy knowing anything about it. It had to be done later that day or first thing in the morning, so he could create a down payment check for their new house.

As if a spontaneous thought, "Hey Marce, I have an idea. I have to go to the bank, the Johnson one I guess, to open up the account and do all that money transfer stuff, which'll take some time, and be pretty boring for you - maybe you could go with Nanci and take a look at the Presidio, and other places?"

Nanci, caught off guard by the idea, realized that in order to seal the deal, she had better do all she could to facilitate it. The deal was not a deal until the money came across the table.

"Sure thing, that sounds fun, haven't been there for a while", said Nanci.

Marcy, shrugged her shoulders, "Yes, that would be nice, I mean, I don't want to take you away from your work".

"No problem at all, Mrs. Nabors".

"Marcy".

"Okay, good, Marcy".

Edison's diversion worked almost too smoothly for belief, but it would give him the window he needed. There would be many other hoops to jump through, such as making up a credible story as to how he came by so much cash, but he was confident he could snow almost anyone.

With no time to lose, Nanci took Marcy, and off they went to the old part of town, for the history tour. Meanwhile, Edison made his way to the Johnson Bank with his two duffle bags. He figured, why not? He had spent enough time in the Navy and at the JPL campus to know, that if he walked into the place with authority, nobody was going to question him, or doubt his word. It had to do with body language and the look in the eye. Edison used to be a more imposing figure when he was younger, but now at first glance, he'd be considered old or perhaps even "elderly", but that could work to his advantage. He indeed was an older guy, seventy years old, but people rarely give older folks a hard time, especially if they are dressed nicely, and white.

He went directly to a young woman behind a desk at the bank, figuring she must have some rank, some authority, put his bag down on the chair while still standing, and said, "I'd like to make a deposit".

The woman, Alice Broomfield, a youngish and reasonably handsome woman, appearing to be of Native Indian descent, looked up, somewhat startled, and said, "Why, of course, I can assist you with that".

What ensued was a gently couched, and long, Q and A, as to Edison's personal history, plans, intentions, why he chose Johnson's, about his new home, his wife, kids, all of which were answered in the most positive but vague terms by Edison. Part of it, was out of old-fashioned cordiality on the part of Broomfield, but the other part was a matter of getting a feel for the customer, what their future financial plans and needs might be, how long they planned on staying in town, and where all that cash had come from. Edison knew to be soft spoken, direct, and keep constant, but not overly constant, eye contact, and to not fidget with his hands or feet, as much as he wanted to. Everything went off like a breeze, and forty minutes later, his cash and checks were counted out in front of him, and gladly deposited.

The single biggest fabrication on his part had been as to why he had such a large amount of money? This had been the largest single deposit in Broomfield's memory. When Alice had begun zeroing in on that particular aspect, Edison was ready, and began a long rambling story, as if talking to himself, the kind an old man might tell, who's beginning to lose his wits. Alice sat, not wanting to interrupt the old man, to offend him in some way, to make him get up and leave with his money, so she sat and listened, hoping that there was a point to his story, and more importantly, an ending.

He had done a quick study of Tucson. He knew to make mention of Tucson's colorful past, with distracting tidbits of history, sure to derail Alice's line of questioning. He talked with familiarity about the first Paleo-Indians of the region, some 12,000 years ago, about the Hohokam Indians and their irrigation canals, about the Jesuit missionary Eusebio Kino, who established a mission upstream from present-day Tucson, about the town's capture during the Mexican-American War by Phillip St. George Cooke, with his Mormon Battalion, establishing a road to California, used later by many of the settlers headed to the California Gold Rush. It had a long history of stagecoach holdups, and was the place where Wyatt Earp's brother, Morgan, was fatally shot. Wyatt, an assistant U.S. Marshal to his other brother, Virgil, rode to Tucson and found the cowboys responsible, and gunned down most of them. Later, Virgil was tracked down and shot and beaten by the survivors of Wyatt's attack. Edison could have gone on for an hour, until finally, Alice had to politely detour him back to the paperwork.

As a throwaway line, Edison had muttered something in the middle of his soliloquy, about inheriting the money from an eccentric uncle in New York. That vital bit of information was heard by Alice, but before she could do a follow-up question, he was already two sentences into discussing the iconic saguaro cacti seen throughout the region.

It all timed out well, for Edison had only had to wait about thirty minutes in the parking lot with Rusty, for Nanci to show up with Marcy. Apparently, they had had a delightful time, with Marcy picking up some turquoise jewelry, and a Navajo-style purse. While in the safe air-conditioned confines of the bank, Nanci accepted the cashier's check, signed over the final paperwork, now headed to the sellers, for their signature, and the deal was all but done. All Edison and Marcy had to do was wait for the short escrow, which Edison had insisted upon, and they could move out of the Holiday Inn to their new home.

At times, Edison's thoughts would drift over to Forest Falls, wondering how things back there, were? It had only been a couple of days, but even so, perhaps by now, the pastor and others, had figured out the cause of their cash shortage. He was very curious about that, but knew he could not attempt any contact, but had to lay low. His beard was just beginning to take shape, having been spared a razor for almost a week. He would need to give it another month for it to really look like something, and be an effective disguise.

There was an outdoor mall nearby, and they paid a visit so Edison could get some new clothes, outside of his comfort zone. His attire had always been quite conservative, but as part of his disguise, he wanted something much louder, something he would have never chosen to wear. He picked up some jeans, probably the first he had owned since before the Navy, and four loudly patterned Aztec-style shirts. All this, as Marcy stood by, amused by this sudden shift in taste. He also picked up a bone-white felt Stetson "Range" cowboy hat. He could have easily picked one cheaper, but he said to Marcy, "it speaks to me". He refrained from cowboy boots however, but did give it a lot of consideration, before deciding against. After this uncharacteristic shopping spree, they headed to the optometrist down the block so he could get a pair of eyeglasses. Mary was not the only one to question this, but also the optometrist who said that he had only the slightest correction necessary, but Edison insisted, ordering two horn rims in tortoise-shell, that were practically clear glass. They went back to the hotel to drop off the purchases, and then across the street to the Denny's for an early supper. Rusty, all the while, was their constant companion, and being such an affable and pleasant-looking dog, was welcomed everywhere.

During all of this activity, Edison had not spoken a word to Marcy as to the over-arching reason they were there, that is to say, the part of the reason they were there that he could tell her. He was very conflicted, and worried constantly about his deceit. Mary knew he had a calling, but what about the money he had acquired for years? Would she understand any of that? At what point would he be directed to end the charade, and reveal to her, why it was he came to so much money. As far as she knew, his so-called nest egg from his JPL years was the only money he had deposited, and that they were now living on. She hadn't a clue that this amount had been dwarfed by his impounded sum, now resting comfortably in the Johnson Bank along with the nest egg, that he had pulled out of their joint account the same day he had wiped his secret account clean. He would next need to make arrangements, discreetly through a third party, for the sale of their home in the mountains. He had heard tell of a new technique, called a "pocket listing", in which the home is put up for sale, without fanfare, not even a real estate sign, out front.

Edison had felt re-directed all of this time, as if he had been silently urged from Above to concentrate on more terrestrial matters for the time being, all concerning their new town, house, attire, and banking, and allow the celestial to take a pause. And now, he sensed, it was time to begin the next phase of his journey, his purpose, which included, but was not limited to, eluding the authorities that were sure to come.

As he put his head on the Holiday Inn pillow each night, he fought away his anxiety about being apprehended in a raid, with the door being battered open, police surrounding their bed, guns drawn, flashlight beams blinding them, ordering them to stand, turn, and be handcuffed, with Marcy at first screaming in complete horror and then crying, watching her husband being escorted out of the room, and both of them deposited into separate police cars so they couldn't compare stories and alibis. He would go over this possible scenario, many times, imagining every detail.

Sometimes these thoughts kept him awake for an hour or more, and occasionally forced him out of bed and down the hallway to the vending machine, so a bag of Fritos or a sleeve or Oreos could calm his jangled nerves. He would stand in the hallway, all alone in his tee shirt and pajama bottoms, leaning on the vending machine, looking down at the geometric design on the indoor-outdoor carpeting, and try to tune in to his Great Director.

Lately, his antennae had seemed to work well, receiving a word of confidence and support, but only at times, and at most other times, he would not pick up a signal at all, leaving him to feel abandoned. Edison knew that he was mortal, certainly not a god, or even an overly special person in most ways, and that he was humble before God, awaiting further instructions. He knew he had been chosen, and was doing his level best to fulfill his directives, but his mind ached with anxiety, and a sense of being lost. He knew that he was not in charge of the operation, and that sometimes his weaker Human self would be caught short, and he'd have to wait, and it was his cross to bear, so to speak. He counseled himself that he should expect to become impatient or anxious, like he was now, standing in the hallway, munching nervously on Corn Nuts, and that it all had to be okay, this feeling of being stranded and without purpose. He coached himself on this numerous times, reminding himself that his primary purpose was not to evade the police, for he would be given instructions on how to do that, or make a new home, or to even comfort his wife, but to forge ahead on his pathway, wherever it might lead him. The anxiety he felt, was all part of the plan, he told himself, all designed to prompt him forward so he could navigate the next bend in the pathway.

The next day, while at the Chevron station filling up the Caprice, he turned to Marcy, who was sitting in the front passenger seat, with the visor down, looking in the mirror, adjusting her lipstick, and said, "You know, hon, maybe we need to get a different car, something a little less spendy with the gas, something more modest…"

She looked up at him, wondering why he was saying this. "Really? It seems fine and it is so roomy. You're sure about this?"

"Well, no, not sure exactly, I was just thinking that, is all".

Edison had rehearsed his "Andy Taylor" to perfection, seeming as spontaneous and natural as possible, not even disclosing a hint of his pre-meditated intention to ditch the wagon. She seemed disappointed with this new idea, but as always, was not there to impede her brilliant and mysterious husband, but to support his ambitions. Had she been able to peek inside his head, to hear his thoughts, she would've been horrified by his impudence, to think he was somehow, in some way, in direct communication with God himself, and taking direct instructions for every aspect of their life. It would have made her seriously doubt her husband's grip on reality, on his very sanity.

But of course, none of that crossed her mind, for she was utterly clueless about his inner life. Some of this was due to how clever Edison had become with deceit, but much was her own doing. She automatically acquiesced to his plans, and some of this was due to her everlasting optimism and sweetness. It would be nearly impossible to find a person of better or more uplifting attitude or demeanor. She forever forgave, at every turn. She knew that people, all people, were imperfect in any number of ways, and she prayed daily for forgiveness for her own shortcomings and her lack of understanding or cooperation, even though she was one of the most understanding and cooperative people you could ever meet.

To say that Edison took advantage of this quality of hers, would be an enormous understatement. Had he become cynical? Conniving? Dishonest? Immoral? Reprehensible? Well, yes, of course, but the means to his end, were forgiven, in his mind. He was able to rationalize his every dishonest step, for these "steps" were not truly his, but were simply the reaction to what he was being told to do. He was a device by which others would ultimately benefit.

As they walked together in the lot of Carmichael's Chevrolet Dealership, with the newly washed Caprice parked over on the side, Edison and Marcy scanned the lineup of "gently used" cars on display.

There were over three dozen, in various sizes, styles, colors and prices. The Caprice had been driven many miles, kept in good shape, but had depreciated considerably due to the high mileage. Edison didn't care if the place stabbed him on the trade-in price, and did not reveal his family's history in the car business. With a gentle firmness, Edison steered Marcy toward the kind of car he thought they should have, and once Marcy had chosen their new car, Edison did not negotiate a price, but simply informed the salesman as to what the car was actually worth, at retail. Edison was resolute and did not surrender a dime. He had come up with a fair and reasonable price in his head, and knew it to be so. It took the salesman, and his manager, about two hours, and with great reluctance, to reach the same conclusion. After the required and seemingly endless paperwork, they drove off the lot in their three-year-old, low mileage Chevy Cruze sedan, in enamel white. Edison had at first been leaning toward getting another Impala, in metallic burgundy, for that was what Marcy had dearly wanted, but realized it was a bit too flashy for discretion, and coaxed Marcy away from that choice and toward the Cruze as the more practical choice. He appealed to her thrifty side, for if he had he said to Marcy, "The Cruze will allow us to evade the police more effectively", it might not have gone over so well.

The same cigar box that he had used to purchase the Caprice, he used again, to pay the difference on the Cruze.

"You think it's safe to have all that cash on you like that, Edison?" said Marcy, as they drove back to the hotel.

"Yeah, I think so".

"Oh, okay…I was just thinking, it's a lot of cash…".

"It's okay".

"…Sometimes I worry, Edison…"

"Yes, I know, but you really don't have to, we have a purpose, a trajectory".

"But Edison, you know, you're what they'd call an older gentleman now, maybe all these changes aren't healthy for you, for us…?"

"Don't think I haven't given that a lot of thought Marce, but I have a calling, I have to keep moving forward…Do you like the car?"

"Yeah, sure, it's fine, it's a lot smaller but it makes sense, it's more practical I guess".

"That's what I thought".

"Well, yes, I know that's what you thought, that's why we got it".

"Are you mad about it?"

"No, no, it's fine, but sometimes I get the feeling you aren't telling me everything".

"What?"

"It's just a feeling, but sometimes I'm not sure...".

"Marce, I wouldn't ever deceive you".

CHAPTER 6

The escrow closed and they moved in. Marcy found some good deals at the local thrift stores for furniture and accessories, while Edison sought out a small work space, apart from the house, where he could begin creating his *Palm* newspaper. The months ticked away.

Although Marcy had inquired numerous times in different ways with Edison, as to how much money they had on hand, and from that, could design a house budget, Edison was always vague and elusive. She made the assumption that they had little to spare, which is why she had found deals at the Salvation Army and Goodwill, instead of exploring JC Penney or Sears.

Edison could be gone for hours, absorbed in setting up his small rented workspace in the rear of a barbershop. It had been a storage room with one window and a rear door, but had been largely ignored for years. The barber, Les Samuelson, had put a small ad in the paper, advertising it for storage. Edison showed up, offered to pay a bit more than the asking price, so he could use it as his workspace. Edison didn't volunteer what work it was he was doing, and Les, assessing the appearance of the old man with a loud shirt and a beard, didn't see it as any kind of a threat to his business. Before long, Les and Edison became friendly, with a key to the place handed over, so Edison could come and go as he pleased.

Edison set up a desk with his typewriter inside the small space, and began pounding out his message. He hadn't entirely formulated a plan as to how his first publication would be distributed, but like most of his plans, he knew that it wasn't up to him, and he would receive instructions as he needed them, not before.

Edison and Marcy slowly established themselves in the community, but only skin deep. They never discussed their lives much, or divulged their opinions. They laid low. They joined a church, and attended on a regular basis, and beyond that, they kept to themselves. After much resistance, Edison tolerated Marcy joining a church Yoga group. Their life was a boring routine, each week being the same as the previous one. They had lots of time to reminisce about happier days, more active times. They were both getting older, of course, but both were in unusually good health.

They rarely spoke to the boys, and they came to visit even more rarely. Marcy blamed Edison for this. The boys didn't like being judged for their lack of fervid religious belief, and Edison resented them for not being so. He felt he had failed in the worst way possible. He was still an agent for God, and would receive directives once in a great while, but the constant daily messaging had ended abruptly, once they had settled into their new home.

What few friends Edison had, had either passed away or he had lost touch with. Quentin was an exception to that. He visited a couple of times, enjoying the expanse of the desert, and the beauty of the nearby Saguaro National Park. But Quentin was still a young man with lots on his mind, and the friendship with the old man was fading, which was understandable. Edison had known to keep the subject of God out of the conversation, sensing that to do so, would only speed Quentin's exit from his life. But there was more to it than that. Edison had not ventured to the marina in many years, using his old age as an excuse, but in truth was disgusted by Quentin's Godless lifestyle. Supporting the continuation of the friendship had become an act, defying gravity, and both men were weary of it.

The only other person in Edison's life that seemed to have ever liked him at all, was Tony, his nephew. Tony was decades from being a kid, and now in his late forties, a software designer, and living in Palo Alto. They were all but estranged now.

The last time they had seen one another had been many years before, when Rachel had come up with him to visit Forest Falls in the snow. Quentin had greeted them stiffly, only agreeing to their visit due to his sister's insistence that they do so, for it had been so very long.

At one point during the visit, Edison had invited Tony, then in his early twenties, to go on a little hike with him. Tony was glad for the invitation to be alone with his uncle, someone he had long admired and looked up to. Although they had rarely seen one another, Tony felt a strong bond. It wasn't quite that way with Edison.

Tony tried to fire up a conversation about the "limitless universe" that his uncle had always spoken to him about. He enjoyed hearing about other dimensions and portals, about time travel and the "illusion of the world we know". But Edison didn't seem very interested in talking about any of that.

They reached the half way point on the hike, which was a rock formation up the hill about a mile, with a nice view of the community below. They looked at the creek, and the snow pack on either side of it, the frosted pine trees with icicles melting on their limbs, and the nature walk turned into something else. Edison began to ask him questions, not subtle ones.

"So Tony, you ever think about Jesus?"

"Uh, well, no, not really. What do you mean?"

"I mean, do you realize that he is the most important person in your life?"

"No, I don't. I mean *haven't*, haven't thought of him that way".

"Why do you think that is?"

"I dunno. Maybe I just know about him, but I haven't really thought about it much...".

"Uh huh. Maybe you should Tony. The devil is who keeps you from thinking about him. It's important you get to know Jesus. He's all that really matters, everything else is just a pile of crap".

This kind of talk puzzled and frightened Tony into silence, for the remainder of the hike, and when they got back to the house, he was all too glad to accept a mug of hot chocolate from Marcy, and distance himself from Edison. His uncle had turned into someone scary, and didn't seem to care for him at all. He wanted to go home.

This incident serves as a good example of how Edison treated many people. By the time he had decided to flee Forest Falls that morning, long ago, he had already burnt most of his bridges in the mountain community, and most avoided him when they saw him coming. Even his friendship with Michael had waned, and the people in the church office barely glanced up when he came in, as if he was another piece of furniture. His decision to leave was based on other concerns, obviously, and even if he had been beloved by most up on the mountain, all it would have done is make the departure painful.

The years had passed, and their life in Tucson had become a low budget routine. The anticipated visit by the police never took place. The realization that he had stolen money from the church was probably by then a firm conclusion, and perhaps there had been an attempt to track him down, but he had left no trace. Every item that could have possibly tipped the authorities off, he had removed from their mountain house. The real estate brochures and maps, had been the only real indicators, and they had all been taken away and stuffed into his bag.

The police had tracked Billy down shortly after the realization, living with his older brother in Redlands, but he didn't have a clue as to where they had gone, just "Someplace else, I don't know where, they wouldn't tell me", he had stated when interviewed. The other kids were even more clueless when interviewed. The parents had simply vanished. When they had driven down the mountain to the 7-Eleven, and dropped Billy off, he didn't "know if they had headed east or west after that".

The fruit doesn't fall too far. All the kids, of course, had known where their parents were, and like any tight knit crime family, they weren't about to roll over and help the police out. The kids were not implicated in the theft, so the police had no leverage, no threats they were able to make. The kids knew that their dad had his reasons, and they stood behind him. It didn't mean they agreed with his extreme views, the ones they knew of, but none of that mattered. The fact their dad had apparently committed a crime, came as a certain surprise to all of them, but they all knew that their dad was highly principled, and if he had stolen money, it was for a good reason.

Once in a while, when they would visit, they would take circuitous routes to Tucson, ever wary of the possibility of being tailed. What they hadn't realized is that the search for the "church thief" had all but been called off. The FBI and Riverside County Police had newer and bigger crimes to pursue. That didn't mean it was filed away entirely, just put on a high shelf, collecting dust.

Rachel, older than Edison by four years, had passed away quietly the year before, with her son and some other family members in attendance. It was met by Edison, with a stiff sense of destiny. Edison had, years before, cut his ties with everyone who did not see Jesus the way he saw Jesus. This had included Rachel. His disappearance into the desert of Arizona only served as a function of this, for he had no desire or need to continue any relationships. He was judgmental, and resolute. The irony of this is tremendous, considering who he thought he was representing, considering the footsteps he thought he was walking in, but Edison didn't see it as irony, but as simply the truth, the only truth.

He knew that anyone not in line with his thinking, the true thinking, was doomed. He didn't necessarily believe in a fiery hell, but knew the next life would be extremely unpleasant for those who had not given themselves fully to the truth. Maybe they would be returned to re-experience life on Earth, be placed in some hell hole of a location? He saw it as his mission, his purpose, to communicate the truth, using whatever skills he had. His knowledge served as a dividing line, between those who knew the truth and accepted it into their hearts, and those who denied it, or even doubted. His clear position made him popular with some at their church, but it put him into a state of resignation, and at times, even sadness, knowing that many in his orbit would succumb to the devil, no matter how hard he tried to show them the truth.

This code of conduct spread across all his relationships, oozed over all boundaries of what was considered normal social norms. He offended many, but could not care about that. He knew that all of the social norms, all the "good manners", were constructed by people, for the purpose of avoiding the truth, and it was the work of the devil. He wanted no part in deceit, or the denial of the actual truth, and if it meant severing ties with loved ones, dear friends, old chums, so be it.

And then, the messages from God started rolling in again. God was pleased with him apparently, for having fired up *The Palm* again, and wanted him to get serious, and get the word out.

The message being imparted from his *Palm*, was predictable. It centered around original sin, the separation of Man from God, and Man's need to seek redemption. It was the central theme of most evangelical messages, and Edison did not see himself as breaking new ground with new information. He wasn't trying to stand out in the crowd, or be noticed. He had a job to do, that was it. He began walking his pamphlet around, randomly choosing neighborhoods that he thought could use a good dose of God. Sometimes it would be low-income neighborhoods with worn down older homes, and other times, affluent ones with large and impressive looking homes. It didn't matter which he chose, for the acceptance or denial of Christ, came in all styles and colors.

There was always the needed element of urgency in his wording. The Earth, he would state, would be coming to a catastrophic and sudden end, and it was vital that any who wished to be on the last train out of town, better get their tickets now. This is not a sarcastic interpretation from the author, but in fact, Edison's very words: "I am warning all who read this, that our mortal existence is threatened, and will be obliterated at any moment, and if we wish to travel to paradise, we must first board the heavenly train with our tickets in hand, tickets that we must purchase by paying with our total surrender, and to leave our Human selves, and walk into the light of the Creator".

Some readers thought that Edison might be a little demented, but for those who had met him in their doorways, they wrote it off as the scared words of an old man. They did not take offense, therefore, that he would tell them to "flee their careless security" and to "abandon their vain Earthly possessions and corrupt beliefs".

When Edison had finished his fifth newspaper, he felt better about it. It was twice as thick and packed a punch. He felt that the first ones had been too small, and overly vague, not direct enough. He didn't like the references he had made about trains, thought it corny, and had wanted to come up with something that would really grab people. He decided on a thunderbolt, instead of the train. People would need to jump on the thunderbolt, he would write, in order to ascend to the next Heavenly life. He wasn't fooling around, for he had an important and urgent message, and the image of a thunderbolt better expressed the power, and danger, of God.

He would drive around in the car, select a neighborhood, and walk a block up, and a block down, distributing his *Palm Newsletter No. 5* to mailboxes, front porches, and the occasional person caught at home, as he had done before with his first four publications, and up in Forest Falls. He would then drive a couple of more blocks, and repeat. He reasoned that if he was directed to do otherwise, he would, and until such time, he would do what he had always done.

The days were exhausting for Edison, not being the young man he once was, and would return home tired, legs weary, his shirt soaked in sweat. Marcy would always admonish him, but he was insistent. He had never had a weight problem, but now, his physical health was in question, and his body had become smaller, weaker, and his large framed build was becoming overly thin. He ate, but only as a necessary function to ingest protein, and other nutrients, never for pleasure.

T he years had passed, and Edison was beginning to look at the undeniable age of eighty. He could hardly believe it. But he kept doing his deliveries.

It was only after he had been discovered collapsed on a hot sidewalk, with copies of his 54th issue spread all around him, likely thrown into the air when he had lost consciousness and collapsed. The paramedics arrived, he was rushed to urgent care, and was diagnosed with severe dehydration. It was no wonder. The air temp that day had been 104 in the shade.

While he rehabilitated at home, for even he had to recognize the limits of his body and age, he reasoned that this too was a directive for him to stop walking the newsletter around, and to chart a different course. But that was only part of it.

Once he felt up to it, he resumed his *Palm* deliveries, but at a much more moderate pace. That's when he began to notice a plain tan sedan tracking him. In the following days, he would notice it again. Sometimes the sedan was white, and other times, black. Sometimes, when he had gone into the bank for a small cash withdrawal, he would spot a man in a suit over in the corner, ostensibly filling out a deposit slip, but taking glances at Edison, one time too many. Edison's disguise was in full bloom, with a well grown-in white beard, eyeglasses, that by now he actually did need to wear, a Panama hat replacing the Stetson, and his trademark loud shirt, but by now, he had switched from the Aztec theme, to Aloha. He would climb into the Cruze, and spend a lot of time looking into the rear-view mirror, and would think he had spotted a car following him. He'd stop at a corner, and look around, his head on a swivel. He would do diversionary moves, taking various different routes to home, but again, was never positively sure anyone was tailing him. Sometimes, he became so confused, so upset, trying to shake off the tail, that he would become panicked, and get lost in the labyrinth of streets in their enormous 1960's tract development. But he knew something was up, he just knew it.

On one afternoon, Edison returned home, certain that he had been followed, but had managed to elude the plain-looking silver sedan. Marcy was in the kitchen, putting some cut flowers in a vase, when Edison said what he said, as he sat in the recliner in the living room. When he said it, she dropped the vase on the floor, and somehow, it did not shatter, but bounced, spilling water and the flowers, but the vase remained intact.

He had said, "Marcy, we're moving".

He had not gotten around to painting the white front door a dark blue as Marcy had wanted. Had not installed window boxes for flowers, had not replaced the bright white gravel in the front yard with something more appealing, had not painted the living room a soft pastel green as Marcy had asked, had not purchased an artificial Christmas Tree as requested, and had not re-painted the kitchen cabinets. It had been a long list, and admittedly, he had not devoted much time to it, for he had had another calling of a higher order. But now, his calling was to flee his home, once again. There was still a substantial amount of money in his account, enough to last them for at least two decades more, but of course, at their age, he knew that would not be necessary. He had already drawn up a will, giving the money to all his children. His estranged children. The children that he had not seen in years, due to his intransigent position on the God Thing. As a man, a mortal, it hurt him every day to not have his children in his life, and Marcy had become hollowed out, with no children in her life. But Edison knew that his purpose on Earth, at this time, in this form, was not to cave to the baser instincts, but to answer his calling, which required sacrifice.

It was this pivotal issue, that had divided and conquered their family unit, years ago. Things had never been the same between Edison and Marcy. She wanted little to do with him around the house for years, and much less of him anywhere in the vicinity of their bedroom. In fact, for the past few years, he had been exiled into his own bedroom. He rationalized that this was not all that uncommon with older folks, that sometimes they need their space, their privacy, and that sleeping behaviors by some, can be annoying to others. But it still broke his heart. He knew that he had pushed Marcy away in the name of his path, but one that he was required to take.

All those years had passed, and the fuel he had developed, had been reformulated a number of times, improved, and was carrying gigantic missiles aloft, allowing the exploration of the heavens. It would make it possible to land on Mars in the next few years, to explore into ever deeper regions beyond the solar system. They'd never try for Venus. What was the point? It was a molten globe, with immense surface pressure. It could crumple a car like it was an aluminum can. But Mars? That was the one.

They were designing the Europa Clipper module for the astronauts. He liked that name. It would be built at JPL, in their clean room. Outside, there were a million micro-particles floating in a single cubic foot. In the clean room, there were only 10,000. Once built, they'd ship it to Florida, to the Kennedy Space Center, for cleaning, and inspection. They'd have to launch it when Earth and Mars were the closest together. That happened every twenty-six months. And then it would take six months to travel there. The astronauts would live there for another twenty-six months, until they could launch and travel back to Earth. Thirty-eight months in total. They'd need lots of "space food", but wouldn't need water. They had recently confirmed that there was water on Mars.

Lots of it, under massive ice sheets. Drinkable clean water. It was obvious to everyone now, even the most skeptical, that Mars had water on it for millions of years. There were ocean beds, rivers and deltas, and lakes. *What was it like there, back then,* Edison would think? Had there been life? There must have been. Maybe it had been teaming with life, like on Earth? Maybe, when the Earth was incredibly hot, and molten, Mars had the temperate surface, suitable for life? Maybe then, is where life had been in the solar system? Maybe, as the Sun cooled ever so slightly, the Earth had cooled enough for life, and Mars had gone cold, barren, lifeless? When the space shuttle program was shut down in 2010, it had killed the spirit of NASA, and had affected the American national identity. Edison knew that the Mars missions would restore that identity, especially once they landed astronauts on it. He had read that NASA was planning on 2030 as being that year. Maybe that was possible, he didn't know for certain, but was reasonably sure he'd be gone by then, to his "reward". But he kept reading articles on the topic, every chance he got. For instance, he read that MIT was experimenting with an oxygen-maker, for Mars. It was still in the early stages, but was looking quite hopeful. They called it the Mars Oxygen In-Situ Resource Utilization Experiment, or "Moxie" of short. Edison preferred Moxie.

The quest had not come cheaply however. Most notably, the crews of the two shuttles, the Columbia on reentry, and the Challenger at launch, were horrific tragedies, and Edison would say a daily prayer for their souls, and thank them. He was almost as devout about space exploration as he was for Jesus, but he never dared actually think that.

But when he thought about exploring Mars, he felt a deep pride, and was glad the space programs had at last turned to his fuel for their exploration, having shunned it in decades past. The other missiles, the terrible deadly ones, ready for launch in their silos, were still in existence and perhaps one day, they would usher in the cataclysm he predicted in his newsletter? *Wouldn't that be the supreme irony,* he would think to himself. That he, the skinny kid from Brooklyn, would turn out to be the facilitator of the doom he predicted. It was too much for coincidence he reasoned, and it was, quite obviously, all part of the ultimate Plan.

God had other people he utilized, thought Edison. Some were complete unknowns, like himself, and others had been immortalized by their brilliance, their vision and accomplishments. For Edison, his favorite had always been Copernicus. A highly intelligent man of God, a mathematician and doctor, a Catholic Canon, denounced by Protestants for his findings, but a gifted man, born in what is now Poland, who had, just before his death, published his "Revolutions of the Celestial Sphere" in 1543, establishing a new model for the solar system, placing the Sun in the center, not the Earth. It changed everything. It thrilled Edison to think about this man, so enlightened, so open to God's directives.

Edison had always held strong beliefs about other unseen worlds, worlds that could involve other dimensions of existence, perhaps even time travel, but he had kept those beliefs under wraps at JPL, and at the churches he attended, for it conflicted terribly with his avid knowledge about Jesus and the correct path. *It is one thing to have a belief,* he would tell himself, *but quite another to have actual knowledge.* If there were other dimensions, other planes of existence, if it were possible to seemingly travel backwards or forwards in what people called "time", then all of it was of God's creation, and it was God's intention for Humans to discover it, when they were ready. And what of other-worldly beings? Of alien spacecrafts? At this point, there was no denying their existence, so these beings, wherever they were from, from whatever place or time they had ventured from, they too were all part of God's plan. And what of the other Earth-based religions, that did not include Jesus? The answer was easy. Jesus was everywhere, at all times, and was infused in all Human thought and belief. If a particular culture did not consciously think of Jesus, but of another, that was okay, for behind it all, was Jesus, but simply in another form. To Edison, it was as if Jesus had written a Universal Directory of Life, and had published it in the 7,151 recognized languages on Earth. Regardless of the language, the directory was the same.

Edison had thought this out quite thoroughly, and was confident of his convictions, for he knew it was all part of The Plan, which he was honored, humbly honored, to be a small part of. If it were simply about him, he would have thrown in the towel years ago, would have probably not created his impound account, wouldn't have gone on with his *Palm*, and a lot of things would have been different.

He felt the anguish of a man who had forsaken many relationships and experiences, all because he had believed in a higher calling for his short and relatively unimportant life. He was not regretful, for it couldn't be about regret. He had had a mission, a purpose, just like when he was a Lieutenant on the Iowa, just like at JPL. But this calling was much higher, and required him to subordinate everything else. But he was still Human, and had Human feelings, those he could not avoid.

Once Marcy had made it abundantly clear that she had no interest in moving again, and that in her opinion, she was far too old for such things, and for that matter, so was he, Edison came to realize that he would need to leave by himself, leave his wife, his new home, and listen for direction, as to where his path would take him next. He knew, that wherever that was, it was because people needed to hear from him, needed to hear his knowledge, and from that, be saved. The idea of leaving his wife was so grim and horrible, creating such a dark hole inside of him, he could barely bring himself to think about it. He knew, he simply had to do it, and not look back.

He went to the Johnson Bank, withdrew a large amount of cash, leaving some for his wife, enough for her to get along with, for a long time. The Forest Falls home had sold years ago, and the money had been wired to his Tucson account. The agent in Redlands, Jimmy Vane, he had sworn to secrecy.

What Edison didn't know, is that when two FBI agents had walked into Jimmy's small real estate office, retracing steps their predecessors had taken, trying to solve the rather ancient case, he had just about fainted, instantly forgetting about any long-ago promise he had made with Edison as to secrecy, and told them every detail he could think of. They thanked him for his cooperation. Their boss back at the FBI's Palm Springs field office wanted to impress his superiors, by closing the books on a few cases that had grown cold. He figured, that if he could get his agents to double-back, and solve a few, then he would look like some kind of investigative genius, and be able to escape the dreary confines of that office, and get promoted to a much more prestigious office, perhaps in L.A. County.

Edison returned home from the bank, mechanically, emotionally shut down, said a few words to Marcy, kissed her on the forehead, let her know that there was plenty of cash at the bank, and she would be okay. She was taken completely by surprise, but then again, her Edison had been a very mysterious and immutable person for years, so the fact he was telling her that he had to leave, that he had to continue his mission for God, did not shake her to the core. Normally, a person in her position would have been devastated, would have fallen to their knees, would have wept, but not Marcy. She had been resigned to this new Edison, carved from stone, for a long time.

What he hadn't mentioned is that the actual reason he was departing, and so abruptly, wasn't due to yet another message from Up High, but because it was obvious that the authorities had figured out his whereabouts, and his crime of embezzlement, which sounded better than saying "thievery" or "robbery".

He left the house with the casualness of someone leaving to go the grocery to pick up milk and eggs. He closed the front door behind him, walked to their car, dropped in his suitcase, and carry-on backpack, stuffed to the gills with hundred-dollar bills strapped with their mustard-yellow bands. He also had a small plastic case. Each bundle had $10,000, and he had many dozens.

He drove to the self-parking lot at the airport, all the while being on the lookout for a tail, none of which he had noticed. It had struck him odd that the Feds, assuming that was who was following him, had let him have lots of leash, and had not swept down in some dramatic fashion, as in his nightmares, and hauled him off to the hoosegow. *Why would that be?* He thought to himself as he walked across the lot to the terminal to catch his flight. He had arranged for a neighbor to take Marcy to the airport the next day, so she could retrieve their car. He had left the keys on top of the left rear tire.

He walked into the terminal of the Tucson International Airport, and scanned the departure sign, looking for his flight number. It was Flight 2015, departing in one hour, bound nonstop to Denver. From there, he had booked a flight to Miami, and from there, to Panama City. From there, he had booked a cruise on Royal Caribbean that would take him down the length of South America, around Cape Horn, to Buenos Aires. An odd circuitous route. He was so excited at the prospect of such a wonderful trip, it made him feel very unsettled and nervous with anticipation. If only he was really going on it. He had purchased all of the tickets at Allan's Travel Shop in Tucson, and had enjoyed talking to Allan about all the places he had been, before opening up his shop. The two FBI agents had also enjoyed talking to Allan.

In addition to Edison's suitcase, which he checked at the front desk, he also had his backpack carry-on, and a smaller, plastic case. It contained his unloaded .38 pistol. It was a Pelican case, the type that professional photographers use to safely house their camera equipment. They come in bright yellow, orange, and white, as a rule. Edison's was yellow. He had packed it properly, according to all the TSA requirements, and had chosen an airline that did not have even more restrictive rules, should he be apprehended. Edison brought the gun with him because he didn't want Marcy to come upon it one day, by accident, or have a AAA roadside tow truck driver discover it in the trunk, or worse yet, if she had been pulled over, and the police for some reason, had decided to inspect the contents of the car. He could have simply hidden it in their garage, or thrown it out, but both of those options had seemed, at the time, to be bad options, and he had decided to bring it with him. It wasn't something he had invested much thought in, for his head was swimming with far weightier matters, involving God, destiny, his messaging, his escape, and leaving the love of his life behind.

Ordinarily, a man traveling with a hand gun, and a bag packed with cash, would raise red flags, had anyone inspected the contents of his bags, but Edison was looking old, was certainly no longer an imposing figure, seemed a little frail, and did not present himself as someone hiding a secret, or trying overly hard to be pleasant, talkative, and nonchalant. He didn't come across as nervous, because he wasn't. He had the demeanor of someone who does this every week, routinely.

Edison made his way into the men's room in the front section of the terminal, placed his small plastic case in a stall, and left. He went to the checkpoint, and while the TSA agent was surprised to see the bundles of cash, and conferred with his partner, they let him pass. Again, nothing about the old man seemed suspicious or something to be concerned about. Edison had perfected acting befuddled and harmless.

Once past the checkpoint, and inside the terminal, Edison walked to the men's restroom, which was accessed by one of two entrances, one in the front, where most people entered and exited, and another down a short hallway, that some people used, but not many. Mostly employees from the kitchen used that one, since it was just a few short steps further down that hallway to the main kitchen, where many of the hot dishes for the various food vendors were prepared. It didn't matter if it was a Mexican dish, or Thai, or Chinese, or a hamburger, most of the food was prepared by the same cooks in the same kitchen. All the dishes had an odd bland similarity to them, due to the same mild spices being used on all the food, regardless.

Edison walked in the usual, and most-used entrance, availed himself to the urinal not because he had to, but as a ruse, to see who came in after him. There was a large man, dressed in a casual short sleeve button-up shirt with colorful images of tropical drinks on it, appearing to have just arrived from someplace very sunny, judging by his burnt forehead and cheeks. Another man entered, looking somewhat bewildered, and after a moment's indecision, chose a urinal. Was he from some other country, that did not have similar public restrooms? He was dressed in a standard dark suit and tie. He could've passed for an agent, but didn't seem to fit that role, he was too convincingly nervous. What Edison didn't know is that he had just been fired from his law firm, and was headed back home to Pennsylvania, to be with his brother, and felt lost and alone. He would've been the perfect vulnerable target for Edison's knowledge, if Edison hadn't been on a rather tight schedule.

Edison pretended to finish up, went to the sink with his backpack, rinsed his hands, being sure to look to his left and right, carefully and discreetly. He dried off his hands, looked in the mirror at himself, and behind him, and all seemed quiet and in order. He exited by way of the side door, that lead to the small hallway, hung a left and zipped into the kitchen. He did so with authority, as if he belonged there. Hardly anyone gave him even a glance, and he moved with sure footedness, not too fast, not too slow. It was as if he had done this before, and as a fact, he had, about a week earlier, when rehearsing these very steps. He crossed to the opposite door, about thirty feet away, went through that into a hallway, which took him past various behind-the-scenes offices, all with their doors closed. At the end of this long drab hallway was an exit door to the outside, that took him to the far end of the terminal, across a small parking area for employees, across a parkway, and into the front of the terminal again. He made his way to the restroom where he had stashed his small plastic case, went to the stall, relieved that no one had detected it in the seven minutes and thirty-two seconds he had been gone, grabbed it, and walked down the length of the terminal to a side door, and exited. He made his way across the employee parking lot, hugging the walls of the building, not wanting to stand out, and made his way to the bus terminal. All of this had the timing of a secret agent movie. It had taken him a week to figure out the exact choreography, and took full advantage of the Tucson airport, not being an overly busy facility, nor very sophisticated. It was surprising how easy they had made it for him.

He reached into his inside coat pocket and pulled out his Greyhound bus ticket, handed the attendant his plastic case, but kept the backpack with him, took the three metal steps up into the bus, found a roomy seat about half-way back on the right, sat down, and looked out the window, just to be positive he had given the slip to any agents that might be, and that likely were, on his tail, but walking in circles someplace near the gate to his outward bound flight to Denver. As for his suitcase, presently being loaded onto flight 2015? No worries. He would resupply himself in clothes the first moment he had a chance to do a little shopping. Time was on his side.

The bus departed four minutes later, was only about a third full, but no doubt would begin to fill up once they hit their next main stop in Las Cruces, New Mexico. This would be followed by El Paso, Midland, Abilene, Dallas, where he would change buses, and then onto Shreveport, Jackson, Tuscaloosa, Birmingham, Atlanta, Augusta, and at long last, Savannah. He had contemplated going from Atlanta up to New York, and then working his way back down to Savannah, but it would have added another three days to the trip, and at four days, this trip was plenty long enough already. He had thought of this, as an extra added measure of security, and that by taking an unanticipated turn toward the northeast, would shake off any remaining tail, but he figured he had already done a pretty good job of it, and if he hadn't, then a leg up to New York wouldn't have helped any. He was fatalistic about his route, seeing as how, it was not his invention in the first place, but had been told what to do, where to go, and when.

A wide slice of America had sat next to him, as people had gotten off at their stops and others had boarded. They engaged him in conversations, folksy anecdotes, awful jokes, confessions about their true politics, or proudly showing him wallet-photos of grandchildren, or a pie that had won them first place at the fair, a new puppy, a waterfall on their last vacation, or their restored 50's pickup truck. Naturally, people were curious about the elderly man seated next to them, and had questions to ask. Edison would tell them how he was going back to Orlando to visit his grandchildren, and that he had been an art professor at the Lichter School of Graphic Design, which sometimes he'd call Lowenstein, or Lightner, or Luckinbill, as the mood struck him, for it didn't really matter, since it was all fiction, just words to pass the time. The school was located just outside of Detroit, he would tell them, or in Victoria, British Columbia, or in Bismarck, North Dakota, and was very exclusive, and not many had even heard of it. And he was correct in that, for no one had.

The bus pulled into Savannah at three in the morning, and the weary passengers slowly disembarked, waiting for their bags to emerge from the underside storage compartments, and be on their drowsy ways. Not Edison however. He was energized, having a sense of accomplishment at having come all this way without a hitch. His only regret, but he knew it to be a vain and immodest regret, was that he had not been able to impart his special knowledge to a single person. And in many cases, it would have been so very timely and helpful to them. There had been people with broken hearts and compromised internal organs, with guilty consciences and bucket lists not fulfilled. But he knew he was not being asked to take this journey for that reason, else he'd be asked to get on another bus and head the other way, going back and forth, crisscrossing the country on buses, saving lives. That was not his path.

He took a taxi to the Planters Inn on Abercorn Street, a lovely place, embodying the charm of old Savannah. Part of him wished he could call this his final destination, as the hotel and the city seemed so very welcoming, and ripe with potential fellow Earthly constituents. The Planters Inn had seen better days, there was little doubt in that, but his stay was to be for what was left of this day, plus one night, and then he'd be on his way the next morning. The building itself had no Civil War history or participation, as it wasn't built until 1913. Edison had chosen this hotel, one of dozens available, because it had been originally called the John Wesley Hotel, after the 18th Century evangelist.

He checked in at the front desk, hauled his backpack and case up the creaky staircase to room 212, sank into bed fully clothed, and slept until noon. A light lunch followed, with a walk around the block to take in the local sights. On his walk, digesting his French Onion soup and sourdough bread, he thought about Marcy, what she might be doing right about now, and if she was heartbroken or depressed. He felt terrible about all of this, and had certainly not intended for things to turn out this way. He knew, that at any moment, and definitely within a few short months or years, they would both be called to Heaven, and meet again, and then she would understand what all the subterfuge and sacrifice had been about. He passed by a local clothing store, and walked in. About half an hour later, he emerged with a smart-looking duffle bag packed with essentials.

After a light supper, he laid on his bed, gave a glance to his gun case, and opened up his backpack and examined his bundles of hundred-dollar bills. He counted them again, and pulled one out of a bundle, a fresh one, for the housekeeper. He figured she deserved a break. He placed it on the side table under a water glass. He opened the gun case and stared at the gun. He closed the case, unzipped a side pocket on his backpack and pulled out a small box of .38 caliber bullets. He considered loading the gun, but thought the better of it. He closed the case, put the bullets back. He put his head down on the fluffy pillow, stared out the window, listening to some young people walk by on the sidewalk below. They were laughing about something. He drifted off to sleep, woke up early, just after dawn, took a shower in the tiny stall with miserably low water pressure, got dressed, and made his way downstairs. Virtually everyone he had passed since arriving, the people in the lobby of the hotel, the people in the cafe where he had his soup, on the street when he took his walk, and the salesman in the clothing shop, had been younger than him, and everyone had been pleasant, given him a friendly nod, or gotten out of his way, as if he was special. He didn't think of himself as special, just old.

He took a taxi from the Inn to the Savannah Hilton Head Airport, checked his small gun case, took his backpack, his duffle, flashed his coach seat ticket, and walked down the corridor to the plane, found his seat, and settled in for the flight. It first took him to Miami, as the one stop, and then continued on to Lindbergh Bay, where the Cyril King Airport was located on St. Thomas, in the Virgin Islands, and from there, he took a taxi to the other end of the island, to Red Hook, and took a ferry to Road Town, Tortola, in the British Virgin Islands.

It had been an exhausting trek for the old man, and he looked it, by the time he stepped off onto the pier and took in the view of the old town. He had gotten through his labyrinth without a problem, excepting some British customs agents at the dock back at Road Town. They were accustomed to large sums of cash passing under their noses, sometimes drugs, and on occasion, weapons.

Edison was prepared for the unexpected, however. Once he was in the line, the first thing they did is flip open his passport, and compare the photo of Dr. Peter Mockingbird to the man standing before them, and then proceeded to inspect his duffle, full of boxers, socks, a pair of slacks, two nondescript short-sleeve shirts, and then turned their attention to his backpack, stuffed with bundles of cash, and finally, the gun case. They took note that the gun was unloaded and that the only bullets belonging to it, were in the small zippered pouch on his backpack. Staring at the old man, you could almost see the gears in their heads spinning, and then locking up, over-heating, trying to figure out where the missing clue was. But, as odd as this new arrival was, everything seemed above board, but then again, maybe not? As the agent, that appeared to be the senior in charge, considered pulling Dr. Mockingbird aside for questioning, he noticed that the old man had carelessly dropped one of the bundles of hundreds on the floor, under the table, right at the agent's feet, by accident of course. The agent made the snap decision that things might go more smoothly if he let the old doctor pass, and then discover the bundle, but too late, as the doctor would have already walked away, and had gotten lost in the crowd.

There was the Island Bank and Trust, which was his first stop, and after paying them a visit, with his backpack much lighter, and his small gun case in hand, and the duffled slung over his shoulder, he made his leisurely way up Waterfront Drive to the roundabout, and then by way of some walkways, to Pickenin Road, past the Royal Virgin Island Police Department, taking in the wonderful trade winds, carrying the scents of flowers and salt air, the puffy white clouds drifting against the bright blue sky, and glancing at the people. Of course, lots of tourists were roaming about, looking over-dressed. There were taco stands and chicken stands, poor old drunks sitting against walls at the ends of alleyways, in stark contrast to the expensive rental cars zipping by, full of expectant American or South American tourists, their children in the back seat, looking eagerly out their windows at the marina, and hills decorated with brightly painted houses.

This was not the kind of place that Edison would have thought up as a destination for himself, but he had had lots of help and direction from Upstairs. His idea of someplace where he could hide, while saving lives, would have been more obvious, such as Denver, or Minneapolis.

He made his way to Horse Path Road, where his rental was. It was a four-plex, converted years ago from a once-elegant single residence. It was painted a cheery Kelly green with turquoise trim, which ordinarily would have stood out, but to the right was an orange unit with white trim, and to the right, a cobalt blue unit with yellow trim.

His unit, a moderately priced one bedroom, was on the ground floor, thankfully, and inside it was somewhat antiseptic, with a hodge-podge variety of essential furniture pieces, but clean, that he had arranged for on a long-term basis. It had a view facing out, toward the marina and the ocean beyond. He could make out Peter Island and Norman Island. It was indeed a wondrous place, a paradise. He got down on his knees and thanked God for delivering him to this destination. He could have been sent to a much worse location, where no doubt, people needed saving, *such as Haiti or Sudan,* he thought.

He had booked it surreptitiously, like all of his bus tickets, airfare, and ferry tickets. The only thing he had booked transparently through Allan, back in Tucson, was his flight to Miami. He had confirmed his theory, that paying by cash, and paying a little extra, had the amazing effect on people, such as Allan, that were booking you on transportation. They suffered temporary amnesia, and furthermore, did not require credentials, credit card numbers, or identification. For an additional fee, they gladly chaperoned the creation of a passport by an anonymous third party, with the correct photo, but a new and creative name and birthdate. They were spontaneously motivated, after the completion of making the itinerary, to destroy all evidence of the transactions. How far that amnesia would go, he wasn't sure, and how deep it would go, if that person were put under the scrutiny of questioning authorities, he wasn't sure, but like with everything else, he had an imperative, a path, all supplied to him. His role was that of the simple and humble valet. He splashed some water on his face, and headed down the road to the local neighborhood market.

After returning with his backpack full of basic foods, he began to settle in. He put his mustard and mayonnaise in the fridge, put the loaf of white bread on the counter, put away the iceberg lettuce and small jar of pickles, and the pack of sliced turkey. There was a six-pack of 7-Up, a small carton of orange juice, and a bottle of vodka to add to the fridge as well. He realized that he thought of himself as a much younger man, capable of such exertion, but this errand had forced him to a chair, with a generous pour of vodka and a dash of juice.

He sat, looking out at the distant islands, the sailboats cruising in the bay, and did an inventory of his situation. He looked down at his left palm, freshly scraped, and then at his left pants leg, at the knee, ripped open, with a scrape on his knee, and bleeding slightly, and only then, he began to tremble, with tears forming, and he remembered, what had just happened.

There had been one hiccup, in his otherwise smooth transition to his new home on the island. A large hiccup. Apparently, he had caught the attention of a man, a drunken and desperate man, his mind addled by the drink, his reasoning foggy with the booze, and hunger, who had elected to follow Edison, all the way from the bank, up the circuitous route to the four-plex. Edison had noticed the man right off the bat, as soon as exiting the bank, but at the time did not give him special attention, for he was one of about a dozen people that could have fit that description, some of them sitting, leaning on a wall in the shade, and others walking, meandering. On occasion, Edison would find an excuse to look back, and sure enough, there was that same guy, a few hundred feet back, who happened to be walking the same route as he. It was when Edison had decided to pop down to the small market, that the man had made an unfortunate decision.

There was a cluster of bushes, about five feet tall, next to Edison's door, which offered some privacy to the entrance, but also it turned out, offered a good hiding place for someone to leap out from. But Edison, his antennae turned on, had decided to unpack his gun, load it carefully with six bullets, and conceal it under his windbreaker, draped over his arm. He thought himself overly cautious, paranoid even, but the same directives that had delivered him to this spot, were talking to him then, and he followed the instructions.

About two steps out of the door, the man lunged at Edison from the bushes, smothering him with his body, knocking Edison down onto the concrete walkway. Edison broke the fall with his left knee, and by reaching out with his left hand, which is where he came up with the scrapes. The man, struggling to wrest the backpack away from Edison, still containing a single bundle of hundreds, did not notice Edison's right hand, holding the .38, as it turned toward his belly. Edison's right hand got tangled up in the man's belt, which was not a belt at all, but some hemp rope, and as the man struggled to wrench the bag away from Edison, and with his gun hand caught up in the rope, inadvertently, he pulled the trigger. The sound of the gun firing was muffled by the man's body, who received the single bullet point blank, the barrel of the gun pressed into him, and he writhed in excruciating pain, rolling away from Edison into the bushes, holding his stomach, and in remarkably fast time, became still and limp. The report of the gun had sounded not so much like a gun firing, but more like the sound of a heavy wood crate dropping from the tailgate of a pickup, a fairly loud sharp "thud" of a sound. The man's belly had served as a muffling pillow, and hadn't alarmed a soul. Edison, sweat pouring from his face, out of breath, and terrified, got to his feet, stared at the now quite obviously dead stranger, and looked around for witnesses to the fight, or people made curious from the sound. But there was no one. No one came. All was quiet. All he could hear was the hustle bustle of the town below, with the traffic, boat horns, and some sea gulls.

Fortunately, below this cluster of bushes, was a fairly steep downslope leading to a larger cluster of bushes and tall grass. Impulsively, Edison walked over to the man, now splayed out on his back, and shoved him with his foot, once, and then once more, until the man rolled very cooperatively down the slope and into the tall grass and bushes. He was gone. Obviously, at some point, someone would discover the wretch, but it would be nearly a hundred feet away from Edison's front door, closer to other front doors than his. It was then that he proceeded to the market, picked up his orange juice, bread, turkey slices, lettuce, condiments and vodka.

It wasn't until he was sitting in the arm chair, examining his scraped palm, looking at his torn pants, that he had begun to tremble. He interpreted this sudden act of violence as necessary. This man, no doubt an agent of the devil, had been dispatched to interrupt his plan, The Plan. And he was sure the desperate man would find his niche in the afterlife. It was not for Edison to worry about him, or to bother with him, but to remain rational and calm.

In order to do this with some sense of rationality, he had to recognize that his mission had forced him to objectify everything in his life. He had already done so, incrementally over the years, with his kids, his rocketeering work, his time at the Forest Roots church complex, and of course, with his ability to appropriate a large sum of money from the church. The action he took, not with the violent mugger, but with his wife, essentially abandoning his wife, could fill him with self-doubt and recrimination at times, and yes, not to mention, dispatching a man to the afterlife, had also caused him to sense a crack in his resolve. It was a small crack, nothing to get too alarmed about, quite yet, but he didn't like what he saw through that crack. He saw an old man who had deluded himself into believing he had some kind of special receiver inside of him, that could hear God's transmissions.

He had convinced himself that his every action was being created and supervised by his Lord's invisible hands. He had been able to plaster over his horrible guilt about being a common thief, and now, about being someone who was capable of leaving his wife, all by herself, and now, ending a mortal's life.

He had cinched down on their married life so severely in the last number of years, he felt a shame beginning to wash over him. He thought about all the restrictions he had placed on their lives, from the gigantic decisions, such as leaving their lovely mountain home for the drab confines of an old tract house in Tucson, and about his decision to steal large sums of money from a church that claimed to believe in what he did, more or less. All of these decisions he had made, perhaps hundreds of them, trickled down to the insignificant. He had insisted that they buy powdered milk, for example, to save money. One thing Marcy loved was her glass of milk at night time, and she had had a hard time, with the awful tasting powder mixed with water, but she went along with it, like with all things. When he had afforded himself some spare time, apart from his job at the church consulting, and his embezzlement trips, he had managed to accomplish one large chore at the house, but only the one.

When they had arrived at the place, it had a dirt back yard, with the concrete slab for a table and BBQ. He decided to brick-in the entire dirt area, which measured about twenty feet deep from the backside of the house to the fence, and about fifty feet wide, from the concrete slab on the right, to the fence on the left. It was a thousand square feet. The orange-vested guy at Home Depot had calculated that he'd need over 6,600 standard-sized red clay bricks to do the job, factoring in the mortar between them. Edison didn't like the imprecision of that, and wanted to lay down a bed of sand, and then place the bricks side by side, tightly, with no mortar or sand between them. This required an additional 732 bricks to be delivered on top of the 6,600.

Edison had opened up the side gate to the yard, and had them set down the two pallets of bricks as close as they could get to the back yard. He then, two bricks at a time, began to lay them down, after his laborer had smoothed out the delivered sand over all the dirt. It took Edison over two months to achieve his goal, and once done, he stood proudly, looking over his precisely laid bricks, flat as a pool table.

He didn't have anyone to show it off to right away, and when one of his kids had managed to drop in, he would march them out there and let them take in the majesty of his precise accomplishment, to which they paid many compliments, wondering to themselves, why he hadn't used any mortar? Then, he showed it to their agent, Nanci, who had come by for a visit, holding a tray of home-made cookies. Nanci seemed a genuine person, happy that they had moved to Tucson, happy that they had found a nice home to call theirs, happy that she had gotten a nice commission with the minimum of effort, and was all too aware that word of mouth was king in her business, so a neighborly offering of cookies seemed the appropriate thing to do. She was careful to not make even a casual mention of hippies.

She stood with Edison, at the glass slider patio door, admiring his brick work, and quite impressed with his decision. She too thought it odd that there was no mortar or sand between them, but she didn't know a whole lot about such things, just knew what she liked and didn't like, and she liked his work. Marcy had poured a glass of milk for Nanci, to go along with the chocolate chip cookies, and Nanci had a sip, surprised at the watery bland taste, but didn't indicate that to her clients. She was a polite person, aiming to please at every opportunity.

Beyond that, the brick yard didn't see a lot of action. They had had one BBQ, which they had invited Nanci to, and ate grilled chicken with green beans and rice at the weathered wood picnic table that came with the place. Edison spoke of how much he was beginning to love the dry desert air, and how they ought to go visit the nearby Saguaro Preserve, maybe take some photos of the elegant large cactuses. Marcy was agreeable to this, and Nanci was flattered that they had thought to include her. They began to plan a picnic lunch for the occasion.

Edison could remember Nanci pulling a note pad from her purse and beginning to write down the things they'd need for the picnic. Some imported water. Napkins. Some bread and cold cuts. Brown mustard. And just about then, he came out of his daydream…and was still seated in the arm chair, in his brightly painted rental unit, drained the last of his drink, watched the clouds painted with the colors of the sunset. He looked at the backside of his weathered hand, with veins pronounced, his old age spots from all the ultraviolet radiation he had received, like anyone who is outdoors for any length of time, over the years. His fingers looked frail, his wrist thin, and he wondered how much longer he could carry on this mission for God, and wondered how much longer he could justify objectifying everything and everyone in his life? It concerned him that he was doing any "wondering" at all, since up until now, his pathway for God had seemed sure and straight. Well, not straight perhaps, but planned out and determined, however serpentine God's path for him had been. He thought about the dead guy in the bushes. Did he ever have a wife? Any kids? How long had he been on the island? Was he well known? Was he liked? He was a thief, a mugger, he knew that much. Had he rolled other visitors as well? Had he spent any time in jail? Was he known to the police to be dangerous? Edison stopped thinking about the man. He didn't want to know any of those answers. He wanted to forget all about him, as if he had never seen him.

He got up from the chair, with some effort, and bargained with himself for a second drink, but declined. He didn't want to get plastered on his first day in his new home, and wanted to be bright and fresh the next morning. He had a job to do, that's why he was sent here, and although it seemed like paradise, especially if you cast your eye away from the drunks in the shadows, away from all the repressed and abused, and away from the man he killed. That was obviously why he had been sent here. Not to kill someone, but to help. These people needed an opportunity to raise up their heads, to see into the future, and realize they could hope for a better life, especially the one waiting for them should they take the call. He could think of one of them that had decided on a different course, had hidden in the bushes, and he had been met by Michael, the Archangel, bless his eternal soul. Edison thought more about the man in the bushes, even though he didn't want to. He remembered what a pastor had told him, a long time ago, when he had gone to a small church with his mom, out in the country someplace. The pastor, seeing that the young Nabors boy was upset with the sermon, that had centered around death and Heaven, crouched down to the boy Edison, and said, in a warm and soothing voice, "Just remember Edison, nobody passes alone, there's always somebody there to greet them, to show them the way".

E dison sensed, that doing what he had done before, printing out a pamphlet, might not be the most effective way to reach his audience. Something simpler, easier to access, less wordy, might be the better choice. He was on an island, and like most islands anywhere, it was totally dependent on incoming sources, that supplied the island with whatever it needed, from gasoline, to furniture, to his vodka. But if he kept *The Palm* simple, he might not need anything from the outside world, might not have to be dependent on the next container from a ship. Maybe, if he kept it small and simple, he could do it all himself, right here?

The next day, he got a taxi to take him to the Mr. Nice Guy Variety Store in town. Edison found what he needed. After a few minutes, he exited with a box full of large index cards, a variety of pens and narrow-tip markers, and some Ziplock baggies. It was the perfect angle. If he had gone to the effort to produce a professional-looking pamphlet, with all the time and fuss it would have required, having it typed up and printed off-island, being shipped to him, hopefully without mistakes, it might come across as too professional, too slick, too suspect. He had all the time in the world, figuratively speaking, and could hand-print his messages, his knowledge, on the cards, one by one, and then hand them out individually. The baggies would protect his cards from the frequent flurries of rain that would pass over the island, and the entire presentation would come across as non-threatening and homey. It was not *The Palm* of old, but this would contain the same message, but more simply, more directly. The medium indeed was the message. Without the correct medium, the message would never be read or heard.

Certainly, underneath his message, it was anything but homey, and was essentially an ultimatum, but he had to grab their attention, trigger their fear, and then their trust. He knew that his physical appearance was non-threatening, and he didn't mind adding a little limp or a bent back to the act, to evoke some sympathy.

He knew that people in a hurry, whether visitors or residents, and preoccupied, are not predisposed to listen to a sales pitch, even one about eternal Heavenly life, but they will give an old man a moment of their time, almost without fail. All he had to do was say a sentence or two, hand them a card during that, and he'd be in, the package would be delivered. That's all he needed, that's all he was there for. To plant the seeds. As with car sales, the Supreme Manager, would be the closer.

Edison didn't want to stall the debut of his cards, but labored over the name. He felt he had to give them a name, as he had with his newsletter. But what name? He knew if he entitled on the top, with a colored Sharpie, something such as "Word of God", or something equally humorless or somber, he'd likely get people waving the card away and moving on. The appearance of a 4x6 index card, with colorful writing on it, and perhaps some crudely drawn palm trees, would not be off-putting, in fact, the receiver might be charmed by it, especially when handed to them by a sweet old man, was his thinking. He could ruin the entire effect if it was headlined with some kind of overly serious title. After a vodka with a dash of orange juice, over the rocks, he gave up trying to invent a name, and simply decided to write, "The Best Message You'll Ever Get" on the top line. He would use various colors, not black, and do his very best job of printing. Upper and lower case, to make it look less imposing.

Following this, he would print a passage from the Good Book, avoiding sentences that foretold of apocalypse or damnation. He was by DNA, a salesman, he couldn't help it, and wanted to "sell" his idea to the people on the island that occupied the lowest rung on the ladder, he had come to decide. Was this penance for his dead mugger? Perhaps it was. The cards were not all the same, but he usually wrote one of these three passages, to launch the campaign, all about faith and hope:

Joshua 1:9 "Have I not commanded you? Be strong and courageous. Do not be frightened, and do not be dismayed, for the Lord your God is with you wherever you go".

John 16:33 "I have said these things to you, that in me you may have peace. In the world you will have tribulation. But take heart; I have overcome the world".

Timothy 4:10 "For to this end we toll and strive, because we have our hope set on the living God, who is the Savior of all people, especially of those who believe".

Edison felt that these three nailed it pretty well, and he would begin his walkabouts once he had finished a short stack of them and zipped them up in baggies. There were a multitude of passages he could pick from, enough for a fresh batch of three on a weekly basis for a year or two. He wasn't looking that far ahead, but wanted to get on the street and give it a try.

The taxi took him down to the center of town, near the roundabout, and he began trolling for the forgotten and unwanted. They weren't too hard to find. They were up shaded streets, in public park areas up against a tree, or huddled in a makeshift tent near a wall. The Chamber of Commerce got help from the police to keep these unfortunates away from the tourist's eyes as much as possible, but they could only do so much. In many instances, a poor unwashed soul was a distant relative of the cop assigned the duty to sweep them away, so unless a crime had been committed, such as an attempted mugging, the sweeping was gentle and not on any kind of regular basis. The police wanted to demonstrate they were addressing the problem, and the local politicians wanted to be plausible in expressing their frustration at the unsolvable problem it presented to the Chamber, retailers, travel agencies, cruise lines and car rental outfits. No one expected anyone to solve the problem, or help these unfortunates in any lasting and significant way. No one was trying to kid anyone that they had an actual solution, or really gave a damn.

Edison wanted to be systematic in his distribution, and not repeat his steps if at all possible. The roundabout seemed the best starting point, and sure enough, there were three lost souls leaning up against the back of the gas station, and four more hanging out in front of Bobby's Marketplace. Edison handed them the cards, all neatly zipped into a baggie, and spoke to them very briefly, not wanting to over-sell. He figured his presence, and what the cards said on them, was more than adequate, to get the job of seed-planting accomplished.

"Here you go brother", or "Have some hope friend", or "You're not lost", were typical phrases he'd use while handing a scruffy looking islander the card. Sometimes, the taker would be so glassy-eyed from drink or hunger, they'd just gaze at the out-of-focus card, while others would read it, and glance up at Edison, gratefully. It warmed Edison's heart, to know that he was reaching some people, and informing their souls of a better life coming.

He did not limit his hand-outs strictly to the lowly and desperate, but once in a while, to a well-dressed tourist. They'd always take the card, for he was a sweet and gentle looking elderly man, and once in a while they'd take a look at what it said, but more often than not, be distracted in conversation with their spouse or kids about where to have lunch, or if the tee shirt they bought for uncle Bill was large enough, or promising the kids they'd take them to the beach tomorrow. Edison knew it was his job to distribute these cards, but also knew he was allowed discernment. He far more related to the lowly than the lofty, and with the lofty in particular, it amused him that none of those people would have ever imagined that the old sweet man who had just handed them a hand-wrought card with a message about Jesus, was the same person who helped to make traveling to distant planets possible. Edison enjoyed the anonymity of this, and was thankful that he had been sent to this distant outpost. He felt purposeful here, much more than when he had distributed in Forest Falls or Tucson. He was needed here.

CHAPTER 7

U prooted from her home in the mountains, estranged from her children, deposited into an arid desert city with no friends and no sense of culture she could relate to, and abandoned by her husband, who she had been unfailingly loyal to, was not the future that Marcy had envisioned for herself. It was so horribly unfair. The only upside was when she made her first trip to the bank, out of curiosity.

Edison had been gone for over two months, and not a word from him. None of her checks had bounced, but Edison hadn't told her how much money was in the account. The money from the mountain house sale had no doubt been deposited long ago, and Edison had taken some, so she was curious, as to how much was in there. Who wouldn't be? Edison had requested that the bank not send any notices or statement to them by mail.

On the drive over to Johnson Bank, she was running through her inventory of options. Should the balance be getting perilously low, and she was required to make a decision, such as selling the new house, she wanted to know about it. Edison had quit-claimed the whole place over to her, signed off on the car, and the bank account, so she was unencumbered in terms of the paperwork, or of any bills beyond basic utilities, which were modest. This gave her some solace. When she had arrived at the bank, gone in, and quietly asked the teller to tell her the balance on the account, the teller wrote it down on a slip of paper, and slid it toward Marcy.

Marcy, not wanting to see impending financial doom, hesitated a moment, but then looked at the paper. She was hoping to see a five-digit number, not a four digit, and was hoping it was fairly high, which would buy her some time. Over $70,000 would be, of course, wonderful and fantastic. But she was being realistic, and hoped that the sum was at least $30,000. That would give her some breathing room. Her needs were modest and she knew how to scrimp. But she needed a little time, some wiggle room, should she need to off-load her desert house and find an economical apartment, for example. Would she stay in Tucson or go back up to the mountain, to Forest Falls, maybe rent a room from an old friend or church member? That sounded appealing.

When she looked at the slip of paper, her eyes involuntarily blinked, for surely, her vision was off. There were not four digits, or five, but six (not including the pennies). $332,328. She tilted on her heels, her head feeling light, but grasped the counter edge and steadied herself. How could this be? She knew that Edison had squirreled away a lot of money, about $50,000 during his JPL days. She knew that the net profit of the Forest Falls house would be about $150,000, but knew also that Edison had taken a sizable chunk from this before he left, or assumed he had. How was this even possible?

Yes, abandoned, left alone to fend for herself, her children far and away, but now, with a large sum of money that she had no explanation for. Had Edison been making far more money at JPL all those years without telling her? Had he invested wisely and made a large profit? Had he bought some commercial real estate, that paid a lease? She walked out of the bank in a daze, got in her car, and drove toward the grocery for some eggs and marmalade. She kept going over and over the amount in the account, trying to figure out how there could be so much there. She came up short on answers, other than remembering that Edison had had that part time consulting job at the church, which paid a stipend. He was being grossly underpaid, she had known that much, for it had included sharing his strong organizational skills, his bookkeeping abilities, his weekly drives for bank deposits, and she knew the church to be quite thrifty when it came to paying their employees. She got out of the car, walked a few steps toward the grocery store entrance, and then stopped in her tracks.

"Bank deposits? Oh, my Lord, bank deposits!", said Marcy out loud to herself, with a gasp. *Was it possible? Was it possible that somehow, in some way, Edison has helped himself to some of the church's money? No, no, that is impossible, unthinkable. But did he?* If he had, and she was sure he hadn't, but if he had, it would have been an unspeakable sin. He may as well have denounced Jesus, shaved his head, and become a Buddhist, or fornicated with dozens of under-aged children, some of them boys. He'd have to be deranged to have taken money. She didn't want to use the word "stolen". She knew that his zealotry was unwaveringly strong on the subject of Jesus, but this? Was it possible? No. No, it wasn't, and the sooner she stopped thinking such horrible sinful thoughts, the better. The moment she got home, she told herself, she would kneel down and pray for forgiveness for having such thoughts, obviously supplied to her by the devil himself, for he was so skillful at introducing doubt into a person already unsettled, as was she.

She aborted her grocery trip and headed home, wanting to get to the praying as soon as possible. But something was different, as she pulled into the parking area in front of the detached garage. There were two men standing at her doorstep, as if having just rung the bell. They turned to see her pull in, having heard her car, and stood, stiffly, observing her. They wore dark suits, sunglasses, and seemed to be in a bad mood, judging by their unwelcoming stances. This helped to bring Marcy's thinking into focus about the church, and about all those deposits over the years.

She got out of her car nervously, and stood at the open car door, giving them a steady look. Nothing about this could be good, she thought to herself. Nothing.

There were some introductions by the two men, who turned out to be very polite and soft spoken. They displayed their FBI badges to her, and she invited them inside for some ice tea, and to get out of the hot sun.

Once inside, she invited them to sit down in the living room, which they did, and she went to the kitchen to pull the pitcher of iced tea from the fridge, and brought it with two glasses, to the coffee table in front of where they sat on the davenport. There was a time when Rusty would have barked at the two men, and he could be quite intimidating when he felt like it, but Rusty was gone. It was just her alone now. She didn't want any tea, or to consume anything, as she was on the edge of being ill, and didn't want to projectile vomit all over the nicely dressed men. They politely declined the offer of iced tea, following protocol.

She sat, her hands clasped, her feet nervously wiggling, in a wingback chair, as the two agents informed her that they wanted to know the whereabouts of her husband, who had apparently made off with a sizable sum of money from the Forest Roots Church and Retreat. They were testing her. She knew that much.

Maybe if they said something, she'd have a reaction, a twitch, look away, and then they'd know she knew something. She knew to offer no reactions, no facial expression beyond blank, like a mannequin. She felt caught in the cross hairs. How could Edison have done this? How could it be true? Why would he leave her in this horribly precarious position, and quite possibly, a criminal one, should they suspect her of collusion with her felonious husband?

They asked questions, a lot of them, and she answered them truthfully, although not fully. Her loyalty was, in this order, to the Lord, to her husband, to her children, to her country as both an aspirational concept and as a reality, and somewhere much further down on her list, to these two agents and the FBI. She looked down at her hands, also dotted with age spots, and thought that any time now, perhaps in a moment or two, she would meet her maker, and that all of this would become vapor, frivolous unimportant vapor. She knew that while her husband could be rightly described as a religious fanatic, he was nevertheless her husband, under the watchful eyes of God himself, and to him and to Him, she had allegiance. She knew that money, like everything material, was a fleeting thing, and in the grand scheme of things, was unimportant, and she refused to befriend the two frustrated agents. They knew that she was withholding, and they were obliged to advise her of the legal dangers to that. "Accessory after the fact" is how they described it. "Accomplice" was another word advanced. They were saying utterly horrible things to her, in kind and calm voices. They were good at this, she thought.

From what they could discern, Marcy Nabors, a kindly and sweet elderly woman, was as much a victim to her husband's criminality, as was the church. They didn't detect any markers that would make them suspect otherwise, although they were not infallible, and cautioned her to "not do anything extreme".

"Extreme?" said Marcy.

"Yes, such as decide to take a trip out of town, or withdraw a large sum of money from an account. You do have an account, right? Any of those actions might make you look suspicious..."

"I can barely rub two nickels together. Do you have any proof of what you have told me today?"

"Proof? No, no absolute proof, but once we fit all the pieces together, we will have. Let's just say that your husband is a person of interest. There is a high probability that your husband has pilfered a very large sum of money from the church's bank deposits, for years, incrementally, and we would sure like to talk to him about it…are you sure you don't know of his whereabouts?"

"No, I don't. He didn't tell me. He just left one day, told me there would be sufficient money for me in the account, you know, to live on, just a few thousand dollars, that's it, and then he kissed me on the forehead, and left".

"We've checked all the account holders on all the major brand banks in Tucson. You don't have an account in any of them. Do you have money in a smaller institution, such as a credit union?"

"Screw off".

The agents gave Marcy a long stare. One of them spoke up, "So, does he know anyone in Miami?"

"Miami? No, I don't believe so. Why do you ask that?"

"How about Panama? Does Buenos Aires ring a bell? Know anybody down there, in those places?"

"Why, goodness no".

"Just wondering. Turns out, he didn't use any of those tickets, you know, to throw us off maybe, but we thought it interesting that he chose those places, so maybe he went there, but just by another means".

"I have no idea what you are talking about".

Almost completely believing her, and having arrived at a dead end, the other agent said, with just a trace of sarcasm, "Yeah, I didn't think you would".

Currently, the United States has about 250,000 unsolved murder cases on file. Some are "open" and some are "cold". That's just the single murders, either premeditated or spontaneous. There are other major crimes involving organized crime, racketeering, serial killers, thefts of highly valuable art, remarkable jewelry, rare automobiles, gold coins, archeological treasures, and even cash. When these are totaled out, it involves vastly more than 250,000 unsolved. The FBI and the Department of Justice have not released those numbers, but it probably sits at about one million. And in this ocean of crime, sits Edison Nabors, comfortably situated in his arm chair, looking at the Caribbean sunset, sipping on his vodka and orange juice, and contemplating how many lives he may have saved today, and how many more he might tomorrow, and conversely, how many more, if any, he'll have to kill?

At that same time, back in Tucson, after the two agents had left, Marcy had to have a large glass of cold water, and then sat down. She got up, went to the bathroom, and downed two aspirins. She went back to the living room, was too agitated to sit, and instead, pulled aside the curtain and looked out the window to the yard, decorated with small pieces of colored gravel, one or two larger rocks, and a cactus. She squinted against the sunlight's reflection against the concrete sidewalk, the hot asphalt street, and the sidewalk on the other side. No one was walking around, as it was just too damn hot. Further down the street was a car, parked. Two people were seated in it. Were they the two agents, or different agents, or just people sitting in their car? She began to cry quietly, the tears slowly coming from her eyes, and then erupting. Her right hand searched for the small gold cross that hung around her neck, given to her by her mother. She clasped it. She had to sit down, and breathe, and breathe again. She returned to the bathroom and placed a wet cold wash cloth on her forehead, on her face, on the back of her neck. Out loud, she screamed, "Ed, what the fuck!?"

Three thousand miles away, Edison's body complained without stop. His joints ached, his knees would freeze up, his neck hurt, his eyes would go in and out of focus, and on occasion, he felt heart palpitations. He was getting to be pretty old, even he had to admit that. He had learned quite a bit while on this planet, had made some friends along the way, had contributed to Man's quest to the stars, had inadvertently contributed to Mankind's possible demise, had had a wonderful and loving wife, three kids that wanted nothing to do with him, but they were probably good kids, who might accomplish something of importance one day, and perhaps, think back about their dad kindly?

He saw his life as a metaphor of the shuttle program which had been cancelled in 2010. There had been too many accidents, and it had become an unacceptably high risk, for a decreasing return. Years before, in 2003, the Columbia tragedy had occurred. NASA had fallen into complacency, and had figured that a mere "foam strike" couldn't bring down a shuttle, couldn't damage the reinforced carbon-carbon shell. Their real failure had been their inability to admit failure, after the disintegration of the shuttle. Was that an apt description of Edison now? Not that he had necessarily failed, but that he could not admit it? Was that the larger sin? Failing, or not admitting failure?

He had handed out thousands of newsletters, and now, hundreds of his index cards. He knew that he had affected some people, had changed their lives and destinies forever. He had pulled them from the fire, so to speak. But what had he really accomplished? He thought, *am I merely a pawn, a small piece of a much larger machine, that is highly expendable?* He remembered the poisoning of the American women, during World War Two, who worked in a watch factory, who had blithely painted military clock hands and numbers with paint that glowed. It glowed because it was radium, and every time they wet the end of the paint brush with their tongues, every time they painted themselves for fun with the paint, on their noses and foreheads, on their fingers and cheeks, and turned off the lights so they could laugh at one another, they didn't realize they were killing themselves. No one had told them. Was it known, that radium was radioactive, that it could kill them? One has to believe the answer is "yes". *Is this me,* Edison thought.

He viewed everything in his life, all the things he had learned, as nascent, as if those things were just now springing into life, into his consciousness. Maybe it was the heavy pour of Vodka, or maybe he was onto something, and had pulled away a curtain, now able to see beyond into another world of some kind? This kind of thinking had always been the pebble in his shoe. The thing that nagged at him, teased him.

Perhaps, he thought, he had at last come upon his own personal "termination shock". Out in space, just as near space becomes deep space, right at that demarcation line, when a satellite, such as the Voyager, is hurtling away from Earth at 32,000 mph, the solar wind has virtually stopped, slowed to only about 60 mph, almost dead still, and it is there, by definition, that the influence of the Sun is left behind, and where deep space begins. That's what the term meant. That's how it was now, for him. The influence of his former life no longer had a grip on him. He was traveling outward bound, and was in God's hands.

He knew how to sail a boat thanks to Quentin, how to organize ledgers thanks to Marcy, how to lay down thousands of bricks in a precise manner, knew how to make a bed, wash dishes properly, make an omelet, BBQ chicken, and felt he knew about people, what made them tick, what motivated them, what their weaknesses were, and their strengths. His list was impressively long, and he reviewed it, while watching the sun settle into the Caribbean Sea.

There was one thing however, he did not know. And that was at what point Allan, his travel agent in Tucson, would snap and crumble into a thousand little pieces. The FBI was good at scaring the bejeezus out of someone, and good at applying steady pressure like a bench vice, onto someone such as Allan. Edison had never committed a crime of any size at all as an adult. Not once. The most dishonest thing he had done as a child, was in fourth grade. The teacher wanted to know who stole her liverwurst sandwich. It had been his best pal, Tommy. He told the teacher he didn't know who had taken it, and then added, "Who'd want to eat that nasty old thing anyway?" This earned him some time in detention after school, but he didn't rat out Tommy. And, oh yes, stealing he Snickers bar. The most dishonest thing he did as an adult was to get away without paying a parking meter, and cheating the municipality out of an hour's parking fee, from time to time. That was about it. To say he was a bland and rather uninteresting person, would not be unfair, or inaccurate. He had no sense of adventure. No desire or ability to risk anything, take a chance, put himself out there, in harm's way. So, when he was presented with a bundle of fresh hundred-dollar bills, $10,000 worth, and offered it again and again, his for the taking, he felt he had earned it. He felt he had karmic credit, had some kind of refund coming, for all his many years of adherence to society's rules, for conforming, and for tolerating society's dismissive attitude about God. He was going to tip the scale back in favor of the Almighty.

The FBI agents had a different perspective on the subject, and put a lot of pressure on Allan, the independent non-franchised Arizona travel agent, trying to eke out a living. The prospect of going to prison for a minimum of eight years for aiding and abetting a major criminal, was coming into ever sharper focus for him. They didn't want to hurt him, they said.

They didn't want to ruin his life, or destroy his business, or his personal reputation, they said. They would keep this information that he was about to divulge to them, a secret, just between the two agents and him, nobody else had to know.

"So, Allan, where did Mr. Nabors book his travel to?"

Allan looked up from his desk, his face blanched, having already unsuccessfully told them "Miami, a flight to Miami, and then Panama, and then a cruise". They knew better, and they were becoming impatient with the lie. They began to raise their voices, one of them pounded Allan's desk with a fist. The other them kicked his metal waste paper basket across the room. They began to raise their voices. They were playing bad cop, bad cop. They began to describe how wonderful it was to live in a prison and make new friends. What it would be like the first time he was raped. And the fourth time. And the fiftieth time. Maybe at some point, "you'll like it?", they said. A lot of what they said was cliche' crap, straight out of a formulaic movie script, but that didn't mean it didn't scare Allan significantly, or that it wasn't essentially the truth.

Allan buckled, and the vibration that sent out, could be felt all the way over to Tortola, delivering a "mind quake" to Edison, who bolted up out of bed at three in the morning, sweating, suddenly afraid that his cover had been blown.

He prayed that God would allow him to continue the good work, spreading the Good News. He prayed that his wife would be okay, and that his kids would be okay, and that he wouldn't be apprehended. He assured himself that it was just a bad dream, and that God had supplied him with just a dash of paranoia, so he could continue the good work, straight as an arrow.

The knock on the door came just hours later, at about seven in the morning. Too early and too rudely. Edison crawled out of bed in his boxers and a "Tortola" souvenir tee shirt, and went to the door, peeking through the peephole. He could see two uniformed constables in a distorted wide angle, and they were not smiling. One was tall, the other short.

He opened the door, and the taller one said, "Are you Edison Nabors, from the United States?" This was spoken with an English accent, but with just a hint a Creole accent, mixed in.

"Yes, that's me." The dream from hours earlier, had formed into a foreboding, a heavy and dark feeling over his head. He looked up, to see if he could see it. He looked back down, and stared wide-eyed at the two constables. "Why do you ask?"

"We have reason to believe that you are wanted back in the United States for felony charges, Mr. Nabors".

"Reason to believe?"

"Yes. We were notified two days ago".

"Two days?"

"Yes. Paperwork, all the paperwork, takes time".

It almost sounded as if they were apologizing to him, for having taken this long to come to his door, and presumably, arrest him.

"We're very sorry about this Mr. Nabors, but we regret to inform you that we must detain you at our station house until further directives arrive".

"Detain? You mean, like arrest?"

"Well, yes, that would be another word for it, but we're very sorry about this, this isn't our idea, this is just our job, you understand, right? We've observed you handing out your cards for the last few weeks, and it's obvious you are trying to be of help, and we appreciate that, but we have to carry out our orders, you understand that, right?"

At last, the shorter one spoke up. He had a flat, American-sounding accent. "That's right Mr. Nabors, we feel bad about this, didn't want to come here, we even got into an argument with our sergeant, but you know how it is, we have to do our job…"

An apologetic arrest was not what he had been expecting, should his identity and whereabouts be discovered. *Allan, it had to have been Allan* he thought to himself. Edison invited the two contrite officers in, offered to make them some hot tea, which they declined, and he asked if he could go change into some street clothes. They stood in the entryway, and waited.

Once he was out of earshot, they began to bicker about the ethics of carrying out this arrest. The tall one stated that Edison was too "damn old" be to arrested and detained in the station house, and the other one said the whole matter "was immoral, and at worst, he should simply be put under house arrest in his condo, adding that "this extradition process could take weeks, it's ridiculous".

"Well, perhaps to you it is ridiculous, but this is what we do Arnold, this is what we are paid for".

"Then I guess we're a pretty sorry lot".

"And what does that mean?"

"It means that while real crime is going on all around us, we are told we have to arrest an old man, and stick him in a cell for God knows how long, it disgusts me".

"Well, I have an idea, why don't you just disgust yourself right off this island, and quit?"

"Why should I quit?"

"You don't seem to like it much".

"I like it fine".

"Then do your job damnit, you think I like this?"

"Can't say as I'm sure about that".

"Oh, really now? You think I enjoy this kind of a thing?"

"It's just a pile of money Carl, just a big damn pile of money, it's not like he hurt someone".

"He stole the fucking money Arnold".

"Yeah? And? A bunch of fucking money, from a fat cow church someplace in California".

"Stealing is stealing Arnold, simple as that".

"Oh, why thank you for the nursery school lesson, Carl".

Understandably, these two decent fellows were not keen on arresting the old man, but in the end, knew it had to be. The process was overly complex, in that they had to take Edison down to the main island headquarters station, near the marina, and book him. Then, they had to transport him to the "Royal" police station, just about a block from the rental unit, to formalize his arrest. Since Road Town was the capitol of the British Virgin Islands, and because Edison would need to be transported out of country, they would need to contact the United States consulate, the closest one being in the American Virgin Islands, on St. Thomas. No doubt this would become politicized, the moment certain special interest groups heard of it, and would make an already bureaucratic process even more sluggish. There would be commentary of every stripe on social media, a podcast or two no doubt, and maybe a "special investigative unit" would be dispatched from a major network, to interview the police and the suspect? In the end, Edison would no doubt be returned to the States, and put under American custody, awaiting his arraignment.

This was the first time either of the constables had made such an arrest. Their days were usually filled with responding to reports of petty theft on tourists, vandalized rental cars, unwanted drunks sitting too close to the entrance of a store, fights that would on occasion break out between some of the town's drunk and downtrodden, and issuing parking tickets on a frequent basis, to entitled visitors. But hauling away a frail old man, was unseemly to the both of them. For Edison, it was the first time he had stolen a golf cart.

While the two constables had been squabbling about the ethics of arresting Edison, Edison had no such internal argument when it came to slithering out the bedroom window and purloining his neighbor's cart. He sped down the road, and headed to the marina. He had his carry-on backpack, containing a small vinyl pouch of what was left of his bundle of hundreds, the balance was in the bank, and his small duffle bag with some clothes, and a book he had been reading, *The Second Mountain* about a man who had found Jesus. And the gun.

Edison, the precise and careful person that he was, had always kept a ferry schedule in his pocket, so he knew the comings and goings of his only escape route, should it ever be necessary. He had almost made it to the ferry landing, when he realized, he was leaving behind a fortune in the bank, and turned the cart around and made for the bank. Maybe this move would get him caught, but without the money, what good was escaping going to do?

During this, the two constables had begun to get curious, as to exactly how long it should take the old frail man to change clothes, and after politely calling out for him, and then knocking on the bedroom door, then delicately entering, then knocking on the bathroom door, which was locked, they came to realize that the old man had given them the slip. They looked at one another in astonishment, realizing this could mark the end of their not so illustrious careers on the island. Carl bounded out the back door, went around the pathway to the street, looking everywhere, and Arnold bounded out the front door, heading around the pathway, with both nearly colliding into one another as they met. They ran to their Ford Escape patrol car, not appreciating the irony.

Arnold and Carl got on the radio, called in their "escaped felon" report to the station house, and sped down the road, keeping a wary eye out for the devious old man. They decided that they would not share with their sergeant, the tiff they had with one another in the entryway as the old man had been making his escape, but would perhaps modify their account somewhat, condensing the timeline, to their favor. It was possible that their sergeant would take a dim view of the actual facts surrounding his escape, they had reasoned, correctly.

Edison had taken the suggestion of the teller, and her manager, and had a counter check drafted, rather than carrying out a large bag of cash. He walked out of the Republic Bank just as the patrol car had sped by. Arnold and Carl didn't spot him, because as timing would have it, the "Chicken Shack" blocked their view.

Edison double-checked the departure time of the next ferry, and he had, unfortunately, just barely missed the ferry, and there was a leisurely forty-five minutes to wait for the next one. As he carefully walked toward the dock, he realized that forty-five minutes would be more than enough time for the police department to get organized, to place constables at the ferry, and no doubt, patrol the streets. He was not nearly as frail as they believed him to be, but nevertheless, he was in his nineties, and not the fastest walker around.

He would dart into stores if he saw a patrol car coming, or turn his back and bend down as if to tie a shoe, or pet a little dog.

It was becoming glaringly obvious that attempting commercial public transport off the island was foolish. Had he been able to go directly to the pier, he could've hopped on the ferry, without his fortune, but probably have been apprehended at the next stop, Coral Bay on Saint John Island.

He had stashed the golf cart in a small alley between "Candy World" and "Rick's Sportswear", and did an about-face, heading back to the golf cart. About seven minutes later, he was behind the wheel again, headed along Blackburn Highway, to the airport. His cart had to hug the shoulder, as it could only do a top speed of about twenty. At times it was perilous, almost being blown off the road and down a steep embankment twice, once by a bus and another time by a large SUV piloted by a distracted tourist. No doubt, the police had thought of this escape route as well, and had people posted at the terminal, at each gate perhaps.

It occurred to Edison that the hunt for him seemed less earnest than it could have been. He should've been easily spotted and apprehended by now, but judging by the less than enthusiastic duo who had come to arrest him, perhaps this sentiment was something that the entire department shared? Maybe their hearts simply weren't into it, pursuing him the same way a "real criminal" on the run would be pursued? He wasn't sure about that, but the results were clear, for not a single patrol car did he come upon on, during the twenty-two-minute drive, to the airport.

Being a popular tourist destination, there were many dozens of private airplanes parked in the southwest section of the Terrence Lettsome airport, with its own entrance and hangers. The terminal and commercial jets were a quarter mile away, accessed by Beef Island Road. He turned left onto the driveway leading to the private hangers, calmly got out of his cart, and walked to the first hanger.

There were some mechanics working on a Cessna Citation private jet on the far side of the hanger, and in the middle of the cavernous space, were some couches and a coffee table. Seated there, were two casually dressed American-looking men, middle-aged, drinking some Scotch. There were a couple of additional Cessna's, and one Phenom. All were private jets, and worth many millions each.

Edison had considered a couple of tall tales as he drove the highway to the airport, each one evocative and full of sympathy for a misunderstood old man, trying to evade the unethical police. None of them rang true, so he kept finessing them, molding them into something more plausible, more endearing, worthy of sympathy and help.

As he approached the two men, he decided on a different approach. He walked straight up to them, opened up his pack, pulled out a bundle of hundreds, and slapped it down on the coffee table.

"I need to get out of here, now".

Both men, looked up at him wide-eyed, and then glanced down at the bundle.

"What's that mister?"

"I need transport out of here, to anywhere I can get, but I need it now, no questions".

The two guys glanced at one another, trying to suppress smiles, and looked back at Edison.

The older of the two, Jimmy, took a while to form his sentence, and finally said, "My home base is Miami Exec airport, outside of Miami - that sound good to you?"

Edison nodded.

Jimmy gave a glance to his friend, sitting across from him on the other couch, then looked back to Edison. "So, what's your story? Why you duckin' out of here? The police hot on your tail, or maybe you got a real pissed off girlfriend?"

Why do people always have to make cracks about girlfriends and sex to old men, he thought to himself.

Edison thought, okay, he's maybe willing to do this for him, for a price, but he's also a smart ass. Poking fun at him wasn't appreciated. That stupid joke wouldn't work nearly as well if Edison were forty. "No, no, no girlfriend, friend, I just have to protect myself from unfair and unwarranted invasions of my privacy and business".

Jimmy surveyed him a little more carefully now, taking note of his somewhat elevated, educated, way of speaking. After another few moments that felt like an hour to Edison, Jimmy looked up and said, "Okay, you're on".

Edison could exhale. "Great, thank you".

Jimmy, picking up the bundle, said, "No, thank you partner", and then, as a tag said, "And we don't ask questions, and you don't ask questions, right?"

"Right".

"Okay then, no time like the present" said Jimmy, rising from the couch. He looked at his friend, "Okay Bill, looks like we got ourselves a job".

Edison knew, just as a general fact, that running illicit drugs, arms, and people, to and from the Caribbean islands and the mainland, usually Florida, was a commonplace thing. Just about as common as having a poker game at home for money, or making a friendly bet on the golf course, both illegal in some states. These two characters, both looking very "American", plump, and sporting plaid, short-sleeve shirts, jeans, and cowboy boots, could easily be guys who are in the practice of making some side money. The fact that Edison, appearing to be much more frail than he actually was, and in need of a haircut, and a beard trim, helped with his plea. The $10,000 bundle also helped. The flight would take nearly three hours.

The two men escorted Edison to their Cessna twin-engine jet, white with blue stripes, and helped him up the fold-down stairs, and settled him into a large comfortable seat. The bundle of hundreds had been taken by Jimmy and stuffed into his jeans pocket. The two men made their way into the cockpit, and the hanger attendant pulled up in his small tractor, hitched up the plane, and gently pulled her out of the hanger into the bright sun. Edison, buckled in, looked out the window and saw the abandoned golf cart, that he should have stashed someplace out of sight, not in plain view as it was. Too late to do anything about that now.

Jimmy, serving as the pilot, radioed the airport tower for takeoff clearance, and got the go-ahead. Bill was busy double-checking the instruments. They didn't seem in a hurry and had the measured efficiency of pilots being careful and thorough. The airport was very quiet at the time, with no commercial jets arriving or departing. For Edison, this escape had seemed too easy, without the customary showing of papers to authorities, or what he assumed would be customary. Was it really this easy to simply leave a foreign country, even if it was British, and just fly away, without being identified, cleared, checked and approved? Apparently so. About four minutes later, Edison was pressed back in his seat with the swift ascent, and off they went. It was just the three of them, no other passengers. After a few minutes, they leveled off, and Edison quietly made his way back to the restroom. Once inside, he pulled some scissors, and his razor from his bag, and went to work. About twenty minutes later, he emerged from the bathroom, with much shorter hair and no beard. He felt lighter and younger. Looked younger too.

Bill craned his neck and looked back into the cabin at Edison. "Well, well, well. A whole new man. Don't even recognize you". It wasn't said sarcastically, but as a compliment. Edison beamed. "I'm not quite finished, but do you guys have anything to drink?"

With a chuckle, Bill got out of his co-pilot's seat and came back, opened a cabinet, and asked, "What'll be your pleasure?"

"Well, how about a Scotch, neat?"

"I think we can handle that". Bill poured Edison a double, and asked, "So, this the first time on a private jet?"

"Yes, first time. I like it".

Bill gave him a smile, and returned to the cockpit. Edison took a large swig, polishing off the Scotch, and returned to the bathroom. Once inside, he pulled out from his "escape kit", some men's hair dye. It was the type for taking out the grey, and would last maybe a month or six weeks. That's all he needed. If he had gone to solid jet black, it would look fake and maybe draw attention, but his face still looked roundish and younger than his years, so a salt and pepper appearance might look very convincing. After a few minutes, he again emerged from the bathroom, sat down in his chair, and looked out the window at the clouds and deep blue sea.

They landed smoothly at the Miami Executive Airport, which was surrounded on three sides by retirement developments: "Country Walk", "Three Lakes" and "The Hammocks". On the fourth side, to the west, was open farmland. Once the Cessna had rolled to a stop, Bill came back to the cabin, went to the small closet and pulled out a blue pair of overalls. "Here, put these on".

"What?"

"Put 'em on. We're going to position the plane so the door faces away from the tower and administration building, and you're gonna step out, and do a three-sixty around the plane, like you're a maintenance guy, you know?"

"Oh, got it. I like it".

"Good, I'm glad to hear it. And take this hat too", handing him a dark blue ball cap with an embroidered "MEA" patch.

As instructed, Edison walked down the stairs, and did a circle around the plane, as if checking the fuselage, landing gear, engines, tail, and so forth. After a few moments, he was followed down the stairs by the two. Jimmy approached him with a clipboard and said, "Here, pretend you're checking things off, and then hand it back to me". Edison did just that, handing the clipboard back at which time Jimmy said, "Okay, say goodbye to us, wish us 'happy trails', turn around with the clipboard and walk through that gate, over there, behind you. No! Don't look over there, just go ahead and do it like you've been doing it for years. Once through the gate, you'll see a utility shed. Go inside, slip out of the overalls and cap, hang 'em on the hook, and walk out. Okay, give a little wave. Bye bye".

Obviously, Jimmy and Bill were not new to this. God knows who else they had transported. Certainly, graded on a curve, Edison thought he'd have to be near the bottom of the rung, in terms of what crimes the others had committed, or why they were eluding the authorities.

As Edison walked away from the two men, now both engaged in conversation and walking toward the parking lot, he realized that he had been led to these two men, that it was no accident, or simply coincidence. It was complete bold daring that had made him march up to them, and plop down the bundle of hundreds. He must've known inside, that these were the men. He had been directed by God's invisible hands, yet again.

He said a short prayer of thanks after hanging the overalls on the hook, before stepping out into the sunshine. There wasn't a soul in sight, and he walked down a pathway and around a building, to the front entrance area, where he could get some public transport.

It had been about four hours since he had first arrived at the airport back in Tortola, and had approached Jimmy and Bill. He wondered, how much progress the police there had made? It didn't seem that any eyes were on him now, so it appeared he had given them the slip. They had underestimated the frail old man.

What he didn't know is that the police department on Tortola had been thrown into pandemonium over his escape, and when a report was filed about a stolen golf cart, little attention was paid to it, in the chaos, with no connection made to the old man. No one had known of his bank account, or the withdrawal, so it hadn't occurred to anyone to inquire. And then, in the middle of this, came a report from a resident on Horse Path Road, who had come upon a dead body in the tall grass while searching for their stray miniature Poodle. All forces were pulled off the "old man" search and were dispatched to the site of the dead man, blocking the street on both sides, rolling out the rarely-used yellow police tape.

Only after the body had been retrieved and driven away, did the sergeant call for a resumption of the "old man" search, but after two hours, he called it off, and reported back to the American Consulate, that "the suspect had cleverly eluded them, but was likely still on the island and they would continue their search in the morning".

Because of that wildly incorrect statement, the FBI stateside had no inkling that Edison had stepped foot back in the States. To be thorough however, they started the long process, going through the usual channels, to investigate departures from the airport and ferry terminal. It would take hours. Nothing turned up. During this activity, Jimmy and Bill took their wives out for a steak and lobster dinner at the Capital Grille.

What now? That was the big question rolling around in Edison's head. His mission to spread the word, to impart his divine knowledge on the unwitting and/or downtrodden, had been a success by any measure. He had certainly fulfilled his assignment, but he was now left to the wind. Ordinarily, he had the luxury of time to ponder such questions, but at the moment, he didn't have time to waste, and had to hurry to his next destination.

When a Prius taxi pulled up, he waved it down, got in, and instructed the driver to take him to Tucson. The driver turned, incredulous, and the obvious back and forth conversation fired up, with Edison declining the taxi driver's advice to rent a car (for which a credit card, and presentation of an I.D. would be required, which would have tentacles leading back to the FBI) so no, Edison insisted, and helped to convince the cabby using another bundle. His driver slowly reached for the cash, examined it, had an amazed look on his face, then smiled, and said, "Okay my friend, buckle yourself in".

Edison's crime had not been all that remarkable or large, for there were many open cases far more egregious than his, involving much larger sums, and in many cases, physical violence, injury and even murder, and that is to say, premeditated murder, not accidental spontaneous self-defense from a homeless island predator, murder.

So, looking at the big picture, Edison's felony theft and embezzlement charge, attached to a conspiracy to commit theft and embezzlement, coupled with forgery and interstate travel with stolen goods, known as case No. CA889344-11, from Redlands, California, was now being digested into the data base at the FBI. The FBI has 22 categories of crimes, each with sub-categories. They are classified by the type of incident, whether it was a single isolated incident or tied with other incidents perpetrated by the same individual (or individuals). As luck would have it (or was it another example of Intervention?) the FBI was in the throes of overhauling their entire computer system, which is called a NIBRS (National Incident-Based Reporting System). It is intended to be a byproduct of local, state, federal and tribal automated reporting systems containing all data collected, listing each of the 22 types of offenses, and broken down into 46 specific crimes, that they call Group A offenses. Thus far, the attempt to update and streamline the system was only 13% accomplished due to myriad complications between different jurisdictions and software glitches. It might take the FBI years to untangle the mess.

Given all that, with the key person of interest in case No. CA8893411-11 being an elderly man, a former rocket scientist, and a former WW2 veteran Naval officer, who served on the iconic USS Iowa, who had stolen money, and not committed a crime of violence, there was not a lot of motivation to track him down and bring him to justice. It seemed politically incorrect to do so. It seemed a waste of law enforcement resources. The dirty little secret, held close by certain law enforcement department heads, was that they were cheering for him.

The only thing that made the case stand out at all, was the suspect himself, not so much the alleged crimes. He was far from being the usual type of person who engaged in this type of behavior. Usually, there would be a rap sheet on this type of individual, showing a history of crimes, perhaps some prison time, and almost without exception, a horrible and deprived childhood. Sometimes there would be a mob or "family" connection. Since Edison's profile was light years from the norm, it since it was a paradox, it stood out, earning more attention than it ordinarily would have.

Also, there was the simple matter of pride. The FBI, as a culture, and down to the man (or woman), had their image to consider. The notion, that an elderly amateur crook could so successfully elude them, smacked them in the face. They weren't going to make a spectacle of it when they apprehended them, and weren't going to let TV cameras or iPhones anywhere near them when they cuffed him, for it would make for some very bad public relations. They were going to get their man, they had collectively decided, or at the very least, give every outward appearance that they were determined to get their man.

Edison and his cabby made good time, and stayed in reasonably nice motels along the way. Edison would usually keep to himself, and let the cabby dine alone and retreat to his own room, all paid for, incrementally, by Edison. He had faith that the guy wouldn't decide to knock him out, and steal all of his money. He had faith that he had been led to this one person in particular, and that he was graced.

During the four-day journey westward, there was little in the way of unexpected delays or unpleasant surprises. They ate together at diners for lunch, ate separately, their breakfasts and dinners, near their motel. They didn't stop to look at any roadside attractions, even though Edison was sorely tempted to do so when they came upon a facsimile of the marble Edicule. It was something Edison dearly wanted to see. The taxi slowed to a stop as they looked at the exhibit from afar, through the windows of the car.

Edison leaned over the front seat of the cab and explained to Berezat, his driver, Zat for short, "…The inside of the real Edicule is where Jesus was laid to rest, atop a slab of flat rock. It's now in old Jerusalem".

Zat was not well versed in Christian objects or history, being a devout Hindu from Pakistan (which is why he and his family had to flee).

"It's a space", explained Edison, "like an altar, usually set between two walls or columns made of marble, or in this case, stone, with a cross piece over, like a beam, called an entablature, and the Edicule is set inside, like an altar. Behind the real Edicule, are remnants of the stone walls that made up the man-made cave, into which he was placed, it was about six feet high". Zat looked at Edison, soaking up the information. It was the first time a customer had ever said more than three words to him.

Edison continued, "Six feet seems low, but back then, the average person was only about five foot six, so it made sense. Theologians are pretty sure Jesus was about that height as well"

Zat nodded, having not expected this to be an educational or theological road trip. An extended one at that.

The facsimile claimed to be an exact replica. Edison didn't know this to be true, for a fact, and could only go by photos he had seen, and the billboard that proclaimed, "See Where Jesus Was Laid to Rest Before the Resurrection - Turn Right in 500 Feet - An Exact Replica! Souvenirs! Free Lemonade". They had had some advance warning that the display was coming up, as there had been the large billboard plus 18 small "Burma-Shave" type signs put up, about three hundred feet apart. "Here-is-our-rule-come-see-the-Edicule-where-Jesus-was-laid-to-rest-it-is-the-best".

Zat had wanted to pull into the lot, for "just five minutes", but Edison knew that to stop there, in the middle of this lonely stretch of Oklahoma highway, was not the wisest thing to do. Stopping somewhere, even somewhere as tantalizing as this replica, would only invite well-meaning curiosity and conversation from other travelers, which could then easily lead to those people being interviewed by the FBI. Edison was not about to underestimate their ability to track him down. Also, the Prius was an eye-catcher, done up with loud green and yellow stripes, and with "Miami-Dade Taxi Co." plastered all over it. To his regret, he knew it best to keep moving, and draw as little attention to themselves as possible. As he looked out the back window of the cab, he promised himself he'd come back there one day.

It was this caution that prompted Edison to always have Zat pull around to the back of their motel, and why he never sat with him for meals at their motel location. The lunch stops were risky enough, and if asked, while they sat in a booth or at the counter, Edison had rehearsed Zat to say that he was Edison's son, his adopted son, taking his dear old frail dad to Disneyland, a lifetime dream. This always got "ooohs" and "aaahs", with the story serving as a complete distraction from other more salient details, such as the plate number on the cab, or why they were in a Florida cab in the first place? This pair of travelers were not the typical, and Edison was always concerned that their unusual pairing would be the hook, be the detail that people would remember, that would cause them to be apprehended. At one point, Edison had nearly asked Zat to pull into a bus station, so he could go the rest of the way on his own, and not draw any more attention to himself, paired as he was with the middle-aged Hindu Pakistani. Something told him to not make that move, but from there on, he insisted they never sit together while having lunch, and not even go into the mini-mart at the gas station together.

Zat was an agreeable sort of person, and pleasant to talk to. He related much family history to Edison on the trip, regaling him in stories about home life in Multan, in the Punjab district of Pakistan. He told of his wife and children, and how many goats he once had. He mentioned the horrible dust storms that would come through and destroy his yard, and make life miserable for days at a time. He carefully avoided the unpleasant, political topics, such as why they had to leave their homeland. He would say vague things like, "We wanted to be in a safer place". Life had taught Zat to keep his cards close, and to back out of a tight spot, slowly and smiling. His home city, one of the most ancient in Asia, and conquered throughout history by a variety of other countries or roving armies, from the Greeks, to White Huns, to sects of Hindus, and finally, as part of the Islamic conquest. The British had their hand in as well, but in 1947, they backed out and Pakistan had won its independence. Most of the Hindus fled to India, with a small number of Hindus and Christians remaining there to this day. But the more strident Islamists took a dim view of those religions, and Zat realized, they needed to take an exit. Edison was humbled, and couldn't help but to compare this to his life as a kid growing up in Brooklyn and Manhattan. Zat explained that now, his family lived with him in a modest one-bedroom apartment in the Bronx. Edison was tempted to share his history, but knew he had better keep his lips zipped.

From this, Zat segued to his religious beliefs, in response to Edison's tutorial on the Edicule. While Edison politely listened, he first realized, that he was *listening*, and politely. For the first time he could recall, he listened to alternative thinking and spiritual belief, with this man detailing for him the high points of his faith. He sat in the backseat, and not once, did he interrupt or try to steer the talk to Jesus. Zat must have spent nearly half an hour going through the various "isms" of Hinduism, each one a denomination, so to speak. Some espoused the absence of a belief in God, or gods. That was Nontheism. Others, in degrees and types, espoused a belief in a higher power or intelligence, such as Henotheism, that worshipped a single supreme god, but that did not deny the existence of other deities. Edison's head began to swim after Zat had gotten through explaining Polytheism, having not yet delved into Panentheism, Pantheism, Pandeism, Monism, Agnosticism, Atheism, not to mention the four major Hindu traditions of, Vaishnavism, Shaivism, Shaktism and Smartism.

Once through listening to this exhaustive list, Edison began to think, perhaps this man, and his rather thorough and dizzying knowledge of his faith, and all of its disparate sub-categories, was yet another example of the Supreme Being having a hand in this? Could it be, that Edison's absolute and harshly judgmental self was melting away. and in its place, a kinder, and more tolerant Edison was emerging? Could it be that The One, the King of Kings, was demonstrating that indeed, faith and Heaven had many rooms? A certain time ago, and it hadn't been all that long, Edison would've considered even *thinking* such a thing, as blasphemous. But not now. It was turning into a strange new world for him, and he leaned back in the seat, and let those thoughts seep in.

As they neared the Arizona border, having just passed through Lordsburg, New Mexico, Edison began to get white knuckles. His head started pounding, his heart rate shot up, and his knees shook uncontrollably. All of this was unknown to Zat, who drove straight ahead, with his AirPods tuned to some Elvis Costello. Edison thought, *should I go straight home, or should I hide out, in case the place is being watched? What if Marcy has moved away? What if she passed? I would know if she passed, I would've been signaled, I know it.*

Edison clenched his eyes shut, seeking a transmission from above, but received nothing. He looked out the window, worried that he had lost contact. But, just as quickly, he realized that the reason he had cooked up this entire idea, had taken a cab across the country, was not his idea. He had been directed to do this, and if it was meant for him to go directly home, then that's what he would do. No more worry, no more indecision. He closed his eyes, and tried to relax, doing deep breathing. Before long, he had drifted off to sleep, and was only stirred from his dream when Zat's door slammed shut. They were at a gas station, and it was time to fill up. Even a Prius needed gas once in a while, and this was their fourth stop since leaving Miami. The day was late, and there were some high storm clouds. He didn't know exactly where they were, but it couldn't be far from Tucson, maybe only a few more miles? He looked out the window and saw "Green Valley Mini Mart" on the glass door of the service station. Green Valley was a short distance from Tucson, so it would only be another few short minutes until they pulled up in front of his house.

Zat exited the mini mart, holding a can of Rockstar, pulled the gas nozzle from the Prius and hung it back on the pump, climbed into the cab, turned to Edison and said, 'Hey, Ed, you want something from in there? You were asleep, didn't want to bother you".

"No, no, I'm fine, thanks".

"We're almost there, I'll need the address?"

Edison told him the street and number, not wanting anything on paper for future inspection. Zat put it in his GPS, and pulled out of the station.

Only eleven minutes later, they were in front of Edison's house. Or rather, Marcy's house. Dusk was coming on quickly. Edison peered out the window at the place. He got out, and asked Zat to hang around for a minute, and that he'd be right back. He walked up to the door timidly, not knowing what to say to Marcy, or what he should say, having been away for so long, for having left so abruptly. His heart raced at the prospect of seeing her again, and tears welled up in his eyes. He knocked on the door. The porch light was flicked on and the door opened, revealing a large Hispanic woman, or perhaps of Native heritage, he couldn't be too sure, what with the light in his face.

"Yes?" said the woman.

Haltingly, Edison said, "Is Marcy home? Is she here?"

"Who?"

Edison was completely deflated, and didn't need to ask another question. He turned and started back toward the cab.

The woman thought a moment, then said, "You mean the lady who owned this place?"

He stopped and turned, hopeful. "Yes, her, yes".

"Who you?"

"An old friend". The lady assessed him for a long moment, as if she could see into his very self.

"Oh man, yes, she go back, I think".

"Go back?"

Yeah, go back, up to the mountains I think".

"Thank you, thank you, you're so kind". Edison turned and started to make his way back to the cab. He glanced up and saw, parked on the street, about two-hundred feet away, a four-door sedan, the shape of which was an older Ford or Mercury, the kind the police and FBI drive around in, in order to be invisible. He wasn't sure of the make, and it was either silver or white, he couldn't tell in this light. He stood, frozen, scared witless. There was no movement coming from the car. He couldn't tell if someone was behind the wheel or not, or if there was also a passenger. It was too dark, and his old eyes weren't helping much either. He ambled quickly to the Prius, told Zat that they had someplace else to go, and jumped into the back seat. "Go, go, let's get outta here".

"Okay Ed, don't want to be rude or nothing, but you know, the pay was to get you here, to your place in Tucson, so…"

"Yeah, yeah, I know - more pay, don't you worry about it - just go, now, please!"

The Prius sped off, and the plain wrap car remained still.

After Edison and his cabby had turned the corner, Debbie Gaston, age 19, bounded out of her house and went to her car, a retired undercover car from the Tucson Police Department, bought at auction by her dad. They didn't have a whole lot of money, and her dad figured a good solid war horse of a car is just what his daughter needed, to be safe around town.

By then, the Prius was blocks away, carrying a puzzled cabby and a panicked old man. Edison kept looking through the back window, and as they turned onto a boulevard full of traffic, his heart calmed down. He wiped sweat from his brow, but knew that they were onto him.

But that was okay, it had to be okay. He was an old man, a very old man, and he had done his work, done his assignments, spread his knowledge, served his time, and now it was time to go see his wife, his beautiful, lovely, kind, generous, loyal, and adoring wife. He knew he had taken advantage of her goodness, and felt terribly guilty about it all. He also knew that he had followed the directions given to him, had reacted to the people and places put in front of him, and felt fulfilled by it. He had answered his calling. And now, it was time to complete the circle, to seek out his wife.

Apparently, she had gone back to Forest Falls. But where, exactly? Was she living in the church's compound somewhere? They had apartments there, but usually they would be rented out for their seminars. Perhaps she found a small rental house, or a room in a friend's house? The direct approach would be the only way to handle it, to just go and ask at the cafe, as to her whereabouts. It wouldn't take long for word to spread, for the church to hear of his return, and for the police to be summoned. But if he moved swiftly enough, he would get to see Marcy before being hauled away. That's all that really mattered anymore.

About every five minutes he'd glance through the rear window to check for that sedan following them, or any other type of suspicious vehicle. Had he been closer to the sedan, back near his former house, he would have realized it was pretty worn looking, had a cracked windshield, had regular plates, not government, no radio antenna, and if he had stepped even closer, he would have seen Debbie Gaston's Letterman jacket, given to her by Troy, her high school boyfriend who had joined the Coast Guard, and left just three weeks ago. The night before he was to report to duty, there had been a dinner at Luigi's Ristorante, Green Valley's finest Italian-American restaurant, followed by a visit to Yogurtland, so she could have her favorite flavor, Caramel Macchiato, large cup. Afterwards they said a tearful goodbye in the backseat of her oxidized silver 2001 Mercury Marquis, ending with some very intense humping, which resulted in Troy's left foot slamming against the windshield and cracking it, but they had hardly lost a beat. You couldn't have asked for anything more romantic. The point is, Edison, had he dared to look more closely at the sedan, could have saved himself a tremendous amount of anxiety.

Edison dozed off in the back seat, as darkness descended, and Zat forged ahead to the final destination.

As they entered Redlands proper, it was nearly midnight. Edison stirred, and asked Zat to find the Comfort Suites, a 2-star rated hotel, that served a hot breakfast. There was no point in arriving in Forest Falls in the dead of the night. They parked the cab discreetly, and walked around to the front entrance, slapped the bell, got two rooms with cash, and bunked down for the night. Edison woke up early, went down to the breakfast, gobbled down scrambled eggs, a bagel, and some black coffee. Went upstairs to roust Zat, who was still dead asleep. Zat came down a few minutes later, looking rumpled, had some breakfast and they headed out. It was 9:00. On the way to Mill Creek Road, Edison had him pull into the Bank of America lot. Edison got out, asked the cabby to hang loose, and went into the bank. He went to the first available window, pulled the counter check out of his pocket, signed the back of it in front of the teller, and slid it in front of him. "Nate. Would you please deposit this check into the Forest Roots main account for me?"

Nate, a well-seasoned teller, on the cusp of being promoted to assistant loan manager, glanced down at the counter check, and that's when his eyes bugged out of his head. He had never seen a check with so many numbers. He took a quick look at the old man standing before him, and then said, "Sure thing, Mister...Mister..."

"Nabors. Edison Nabors".

"Sure thing. Give me just a sec." Nate walked with the check over to his manager, Lydia Margolis, and showed her the check, she almost choked on her Danish, gave a glance to the old man at the window, stood up, and walked back to the window with Nate. "Hello, Mr. Nabors, hello. Nate tells me you'd like to deposit this check, in the Forest Roots main account, is that right?"

"Yes, Nate got it right, and now, I've got to go. I endorsed it on the back, you can check it, it's good." Edison turned and walked briskly to the front door and exited. Zat was waiting for him with the engine running. Edison got into the front passenger seat, and they took off. This entire transaction took less than four minutes, and for Edison, it was far too long. At one time, with the former staff, he had been well-known at this branch, but by now, surely, the word would have been spread about the wanted criminal, Edison Nabors. He had not recognized even one of the tellers. Had never laid eyes on Lydia, the chief teller, and had kept his head down, hat on, in case there was someone at a desk who might recognize him, and call the cops. Perhaps the salt and pepper dyed hair had helped?

He had caught them off-guard, which was the idea. After he left, they would talk amongst themselves and it would take them all of five minutes to realize who he was, and of course following that, calls were made to the church, and to the police. The police showed up twenty minutes later, and began asking everyone for details, of which there were few. No one had seen how Edison had left the property, whether on foot, or by vehicle. No one had immediately recognized him, or his name. The only thing that stuck in their mind was the enormous counter check, which after a phone call to Tortola, was confirmed to be good as gold.

Edison and Zat made their way up the mountain, with Edison giving furtive glances behind them, checking for flashing lights. There were none. He looked at his carry-on pack, nearly depleted of his cash bundles save two, and then he looked at the road ahead, looked down in the wash, remembering Frank Hollis and how he had pulled his car out of the mud years ago, which had led to sailing, meeting his son, and more sailing. Those were good days. This took him back to JPL and the camaraderie he had enjoyed here, and the pure adrenalin rush he would get with some new accomplishment, he and his team had created. His daydreaming came to an end, as they entered the community, and before long, they were coming up to the Mexican cafe on their right. He asked Zat to pull into a parking slot and wait for him. He got out, walked up the cement stairs to the cafe, and entered. It was 10:28am.

At first, no one gave him a glance, and then the daughter of the owners, and the principal waitress, Maria, noticed him. She dropped a tray heaped with huevos rancheros, and a side of chilaquiles, to punctuate the moment. The plates hit the floor with a loud explosion of shattering porcelain, and pieces of egg, refried beans, and salsa, flying everywhere. The cafe was somewhat crowded, being late-morning, past the busier breakfast time, but there were still about fifteen patrons present, and all conversation stopped. Everyone first looked at Maria, who stood frozen, and then to who she was looking at, who also stood frozen.

There was a moment of complete and stunned silence in the room as everyone was taking in the scene. Then, erupting out of his chair, was Leo, a middle-aged, and large Hispanic man, who knew who Edison was. He should know, for he was the most popular handyman on the hill, having done myriad jobs for Edison over the years, plus for virtually everyone else.

"Nabors! You stinking son of a bitch, what the hell are you doing here? Tienes un puto nervio, viniendo aqui, donde has estado todo este tiempo, hijo de puta?"

"Hey, hey, you don't understand, nobody does, I'm just here to see Marcy, then I'll leave, really, can somebody tell me where she is?"

Within seconds, most everyone in the room had stood up and charged Edison, all of them red-faced, lips curled, teeth bared. Edison thought they looked like a bunch of chimps. The small room had exploded with cursing and threats, all of them hateful, over what he had done to the church, and how he had left Marcy in the desert.

"No, no, you don't understand" pleaded Edison. "I didn't leave her in the desert, she had a house, a nice house, and lots of money".

People reached into their pockets, reaching for their cells, wanting to be the first to call the police…

As Edison stumbled backwards, shocked at the enormous hateful reaction to his appearance, one woman shoved a slip of paper into his hand, with a wink.

A thought entered his mind, for just an instant, perhaps a continuation of his daydreaming of a few minutes before. *How funny and ironic life can be.* Here he was, the focus of a mob scene in the small cafe, that couldn't be more than six-hundred square feet in size, and there he was, someone who could hear God, who had knowledge, who had done the right thing, the moral thing, except for murdering the transient, and stealing the church's money, yet someone who was special, most special, and had been able to harness an exotic mix of chemicals into a powerful sludge, capable of sending equipment, robots and people to distant planets, out into the limitless and boundless sky. And it all boiled down to this showdown in the cafe, as if he was in the old West, being challenged to a gunfight.

He clenched his fist around the scrap of paper, turned, and flew out the door, down the steps, to the awaiting cab, which had been idling in suspense. They sped up the street. Zat was getting pretty good at this.

He looked to his left and saw his old house, now re-painted a depressing dark grey, with a black Suburban parked in the drive. He looked down at the scrap of paper, and on it was, "47 Marcy Road". He blinked, checking his eyesight. Yes, there was a Marcy Road in town, and was his Marcy living there now?

He told Zat to hang a right in three streets, as he prepared to see his wife for the first time, in what seemed ages. He flipped the visor down to give himself a quick look, slicking his unkempt hair down with a wet palm.

He had given back practically all that had been left of his impound money for God, not seeing a purpose for it any longer, and wanting to do the right thing. When convicted, they might go easier on him, but that was not the main motivation. He was so old now, getting to be pretty worn out, a lighter sentence would not make much of a difference. He just wanted to square things, if he could.

They passed Wood Road, and then, around a blind curve, appeared a State Ranger pickup, parked sideways, blocking the road, lights flashing, and the Ranger standing in front of the truck, holding a shotgun. Zat slammed the brakes on, and the Prius fish-tailed into a dirt berm on the side of the road, with a hard jolt. The Ranger advanced on the car, ordered both men to get out. Zat, rattled, stumbled out. Edison, desperate to see his Marcy, only two blocks and a few steps away from him, rolled out of the passenger side, stood up, and began pleading with the Ranger. As he was talking, he was also walking up the side of the street, toward Marcy Road, and the Ranger kept telling him to 'halt', but Edison kept walking, and the Ranger started to walk briskly to Edison, to intercept him.

Then, as if a rock had been thrown at his chest, Edison crumpled in pain, clutching this left side, groaning, falling to the ground, and passed out. The Ranger called for an ambulance. By then, people had come out of their houses, had run up the street to see the commotion, and some of the more outraged patrons of the cafe, had gotten into their cars to follow the Prius. Four Redlands Police cruisers showed up, their tires screeching to a stop, cops jumping out, breaking up the crowd, telling people to disperse. The County fire engine had just come back from Redlands on a grocery errand, and right behind it, the paramedics arrived. The crowd did not disperse, but only backed up a few feet, their eyes riveted to the scene, watching Edison being placed on a gurney, being slid into the back of the ambulance, cops trying some crowd control but it was futile, and the light bars flashing their colors on the nearby houses and trees. The cabby was handcuffed and placed in the rear seat of a cruiser and taken away. A tow truck showed up to move the Prius to the impound yard. The ambulance did a five-point turn, burping the siren a few times, lights flashing, and sped down the road to Redlands. No one knew if Edison was dead or alive. The police cruisers departed, one by one, with some officers staying back, collecting statements. After about an hour, everything had turned back to normal, with the most activity being a squirrel, perched on a rock, watching a plumber drive up the road.

If you were standing there, at the scene of the incident, while it had been going on, and had walked a little further up the street, you'd have come to Coffey Road, and then to Marcy Road. It was about a thousand feet from where the Prius was, tops. It's where Edison had wanted to go. And then, if you'd have turned to the right, and travelled another two-hundred-feet or so, to 47 Marcy Road, which was on the left, you'd have seen Marcy at her small kitchen sink, in her small remodeled cabin that she was renting, at a very reasonable price, from a church member. You would have seen her drying a dish, and placing it back in the wall cabinet, but then being distracted, and looking out the window at her hummingbird feeder, and straining to hear, thinking, *what is all the noise? Sounds like lots of commotion…*

CHAPTER 8

Time had slowed down for Edison. He spent most of his days outside, weather permitting, tending to the vegetable garden, that measured thirty feet deep by thirty-seven feet across. He would sometimes calculate how many bricks it would take to fill that space, without mortar. With mortar, he knew the calculation. It was 7,650 bricks. But without mortar, he could only guesstimate. He figured it would be another 900, or close to it.

But it was not going to be a brick yard, but remain a garden, that had dry un-nourished soil, was acidic, some sections hard as cement, with very limited irrigation. In spite of that, he was doing well with the beefsteak tomatoes and yellow squash. He would wear a wide brim straw hat, since there was no shade and the sun could beat down very hard. He'd carry a bucket of water out from the shower, to hand water his plants when it was especially hot, and when the garden hose had especially low pressure. It always had low pressure, but sometimes, was worse than other times. It was intermittent. He had asked if a plumber could come out, look into it. His guess was that the water lines were old, probably made of galvanized pipe, and over the decades had become clogged, like an artery, reducing the pressure down to a trickle. He was told, "No". He was especially happy with his artichokes, but in order to feed the entire prison population, he would've had to give over most of the garden area, to just that one crop, for one artichoke to each inmate. So, the harvest was limited to the staff at Dublin State, and select inmates.

Months before, he had had his arraignment and trial in the Redlands Superior Court, and was sentenced to three years in a federal prison, but due to the numerous extenuating circumstances of his situation, he was given the opportunity for parole in two years. His defense attorney cited his very advanced age, his having returned a large portion of the stolen funds, his state of health following his extreme anxiety attack (which had mimicked a heart attack), and the purpose behind his theft of funds (to serve God).

All of these line items had fallen upon the sympathetic ears of Judge Cornwall Stevens, just months before. He was elated to have Edison's case in his courtroom, because, for the nearly retired veteran judge, the last several years had been a constant parade of repeat offense drug dealers, wife beaters, flashers, stalkers, small time con men, burglars, and perhaps most horribly, a crime ring involving grossly mistreated pit bulls, trained to attack. The sight of the old man, looking puzzled, with a kind grin on his face, puzzled the judge at first, wondering how it was such a kindly-looking man could have ended up before him that day? No mention had been made of the dead mugger back in Tortola. Edison had reasoned, correctly so, that to bring that topic up to his attorney would have only started a chain reaction, complicating matters considerably.

It didn't take the D.A.'s office long to lay out all of Edison's crimes, framing them as if he were San Bernardino

County's version of John Gotti. Edison had employed Rule 23 in the Federal Rules of Criminal Procedure, and waived his right to a jury trial. He knew he had committed a crime, and pled "no contest" on the advice of his court-appointed practitioner, and felt that the motive for it, would exonerate him.

During the trial, the prosecutors had over-played their hand, and the judge realized, that while Edison had indeed committed a serious crime, many dozens of times over, with the intention to keep the funds, and then elude the authorities, he would need to receive a sentence. The judge knew that some of the money had been returned, which helped, and could be defined as restitution in advance, but it didn't make the crime disappear. Edison had been correct in his belief that the judge would be responsive to why Edison had done, what he had done.

The FBI had given the case over to the D.A.'s office, not thinking it worthy of their most needed attention, knowing it would also draw much negative press. The FBI was in a public relations repair mode and did not want to be seen as unfairly punishing an old man who had only wanted to serve God, not buy a yacht, a penthouse, or have a young girlfriend.

Judge Stevens heard both sides presented, with testimony given by a parade of various individuals, such as Marcy, Pastor Ragnoli, Edison's cabby, Zat, (who was also brought up on charges), the managers of both Redlands' banks, an assortment of tellers, motel managers strung out along the length of the #10 interstate transcontinental highway, also known as, moving from west to east, the Rosa Parks Freeway, Blue Star Memorial Highway, Sonny Bono Memorial Freeway, Pearl Harbor Memorial Freeway, Maricopa Freeway, Papago Freeway, Pima Freeway, Katy Freeway, East Freeway, Atchafalaya Swamp Freeway, and the Pontchartrain Expressway. Due to various complaints filed by Native Americans, the California designation of the Christopher Columbus Intercontinental Highway had been removed by 2022. Edison's attorney had gone down this list, entering the information into the court records, in order to make a point. By the time he had reached the end of his list, he had forgotten what the point of it was, and sat down, with an apologetic nod to the judge.

Under cross examination, everyone who testified said the most wonderful things about Edison. They talked of his generosity, his kindness, his amazing mind and inventions, his time on the Iowa, his devout Christian belief, and how helpful he was to everyone. As much as the prosecutors wanted to paint him as someone evil, with a devious criminal mind, they simply didn't have enough on him. At one point, Pastor Ragnoli apologized to Edison. It seemed, that in spite of Edison's thievery and deceit, in spite of his fire and brimstone beliefs, and in spite of his often cold and clinical demeanor, everyone loved him. Everyone called him a rocket scientist. The Assistant District Attorney, frustrated by the near-adulation he was receiving from the witnesses, asked the judge to ban the term and not allow its use. Judge Stevens replied, "All right, would you prefer they call him a war hero?" That was the end of that. The key defense witness was none other than Michael Fontaine, who gave a full throated and kind description of Edison. It was so sincere and moving, that Edison could not help but cry.

The strangest testimony came from Braxton Bernhard, the owner and operator of the Pecos Motel and Lounge, located about forty-one miles west of Pecos, in Scroggins Draw, which is where the motel is actually located, giving no end to confusion by users of Travel Advisor and other booking sites. Braxton gave a colorful account of seeing the Prius pull up and park behind his motel, and watching the two occupants through his kitchen window, as they snuck around to the front motel office door. He stated that he had greeted them in his usual friendly way, and played dumb.

"Howdy neighbors".

"What?" said Edison, startled to hear his name.

"Howdy. You come from far?"

"No, well, yes, I guess I meant to say".

"Oh, okay, that's fine by me. It all is. Got a car?"

"Yes, yes, we do" with Edison giving a nudge to Zat, to remain silent.

"Oh, all right then..." with Braxton pretending to peer out the door to spot their car parked in front. And then with a laugh, "you guys musta walked here".

Edison with a fake nervous laugh, "No, no, we just parked out back, weren't sure where the office was...".

"Well, okay then, got you handled - one room or two?"

The testimony rambled on like this for another twenty minutes, detailing what the two travelers were wearing, their grooming, their shoes, the sound of their voices, how they had seemed nervous, but also very tired, and how Edison had paid in cash with a fresh hundred-dollar bill, and all of this, nearly putting the judge to sleep. What the prosecution wanted to demonstrate, was Edison's willful intent to conceal his whereabouts.

At the end of Braxton's testimony, the judge wryly stated, "Yes, yes, good, thank you Mister Bernhard", and then to the prosecutor, "I'm sure we are all aware of Mister Nabors' intent to conceal himself, and the vehicle, which was obvious three minutes into the testimony. Can we attempt to be more concise with the next witness?"

The case droned on for another three days, further condemning Edison to his un-admitted guilt from the one side, and displaying his Godly intent from the other. His attorney emphasized Edison's wartime service aboard the Iowa, and made him out to be a rockstar in the field of space exploration. While there was much hyperbole thrown around, the judge recognized that Edison had been "somebody", had served his nation loyally, and deserved leniency, especially in view of his motives for stealing the large sum of money. The prosecution pushed back hard on this sentiment, which only further cemented the judge's sympathies. He handed Edison a three-year sentence with an opportunity for parole in two.

He was incarcerated at the Federal Correctional Institution in Dublin, California.

Dublin was nestled between the Bay Area and Livermore, in a rural farm setting. The facility itself was considered to be one of many "white collar crime" prisons, and low security, what some refer to as "resort prisons". If this place were a resort, it would go out of business inside of a weekend. As compared to maximum security prisons, it was much nicer, but it was still a prison, where the inmates, in this case about six-hundred and sixty of them, were told what to wear, when to shower, when to sleep, wake, eat, what to eat, when they could go outside, when they could watch TV, or engage in some type of low impact exercise such as handball, tennis or jogging. Most of the equipment was worn to tatters, with the tennis rackets missing their webbing, the rubber handballs replaced with old tennis balls, and the workout room shut down due to all the treadmills being non-operative, and the "weights" consisting mostly of old-fashioned leather wrapped "medicine balls" from the Jack LaLanne era. There was a community room, which featured orange-colored leatherette cushioned chairs and couches, a TV mounted on the wall with very limited channel selection, a coffee table and a coffeemaker in the corner, and Styrofoam cups. There was a view through the barred window to the tennis courts. The best news was that it was not prone to violence, and all of the inmates were there for non-violent crimes, often having to do with drug dealing, car theft rings, racketeering, and in two cases, arms dealing. Those two were white guys, gun dealers doing bad things, and brothers, and wealthy, politically very well-connected, but thrown under the bus by their connections, like sacrificial goats. They had sold and transferred military arms, such as assault helicopter parts or missiles, from one country to another, often times, countries considered to be enemies of the U.S. And they had moved and laundered the resulting cash, all at the behest of their connections in high places.

The majority consisted of Blacks and Hispanics, and one Italian immigrant.

Edison was fortunate, for most of his fellow inmates took an immediate liking to him, partly due to his advanced age, but also because he was far from the run of the mill criminal. Most of his new friends had nicknames. There was Rocco, Toneeze, Big, Shooter, The Man, Donkey, Juice, Strawberry Jam, Tex, Catfish and Preacher. Edison was anointed with a nickname after he was in for about a week: Snake.

The two arms dealers, tried to immediately glom onto Edison, thinking him "one of them", and sitting next to him in the cafeteria, but Edison made it clear he wasn't, by saying to them over the lunch table one afternoon, "He also will drink the wine of God's wrath, poured full strength into the cup of his anger, and he will be tormented with fire and sulfur in the presence of the holy angels and in the presence of the Lamb (Revelation 19:20)". The brothers looked at Edison blank faced, speechless. But this had not adequately dissuaded them. The next day, they intercepted Edison while he was sitting in the community room, reading a dog-eared paperback of "Al Capone, the Myth and the Man". They sat down across from him, teasing him about his "God talk". Edison stopped and looked at them, with the deadliest stare he could make, saying "And if your eye causes you to sin, tear it out. It is better for you to enter the kingdom of God with one eye than with two eyes to be thrown into hell (Mark 9:47)".

Edison had embraced the brimstone approach decades ago, alienating most everyone around him, but of late, in the last few years, he had adopted a much kinder approach, but that didn't mean he hadn't memorized certain grim passages.

The two dealers backed off after that, thinking him a "crazy old fool" which suited Edison just fine. In his life, he had managed to unwittingly export death, or potential death, with his chemical formulations, with an eye toward space travel, so the last thing he wanted to do is be around people who did their deadly work with foresight and intention, for profit. As for his paperback, he put it down after two chapters, thinking, *this guy doesn't know how to write.*

Prison staff recognized Edison's unusually high level of education, and ability to organize, which led to some minor assignments in the room they euphemistically called the "library", for a week. This is where Edison had pulled his Capone book from a shelf, not spotting anything more interesting. Most of the books were paperback, and usually not well known, and often about crime or criminals, fiction or non-fiction. After this, they had him in the kitchen reorganizing the assembly line of dirty plates and cookware. This assignment lasted a week, and finally, he was assigned to the "garden area", and asked to remedy the sad-looking patch of dry dirt.

It was there that Edison found solace, could have long conversations with God, while nurturing some life in the form of vegetables. His new friends thought it not coincidental that he had befriended a gopher snake in the garden.

Marcy would come and visit, about once a month. Edison didn't want her to come even that often, it being a long trip and to a husband that had, in the end, not served her well. It was true, that she had been left a substantial amount of money that she had cleverly hidden with the help of their kids, soon after he had left, and was never detected by the authorities. Financially, she was set, but he felt a tremendous weight of guilt, for emotionally, she was far from "set". He would often pray at night, not for forgiveness, for he knew there was none, not yet, while still inhabiting his tired old body on this tired old planet, but for understanding. And for knowledge. He was always so big on the knowledge thing, and now, he was confused, left in the dark, forsaken it seemed to him, on his gloomier nights.

The kids would visit from time to time, and it was always stiff and forced, but he did get to meet his two grandchildren from his daughter, the sons having never had any kids, and both divorced.

Edison loved his family, but had to admit having failed them, having been a lousy father, and a weak example of what a father should be. But he knew that he had been put on the planet for other things, and he wasn't bitter about that in the least, and knew that the path he had been on, had led him to this place, this moment, and he accepted it. The fact he no longer could hear the Heavenly transmissions, bothered him, he had to admit, but it was all part of the plan, he knew it, and had to accept it.

She had laid out her best dress, something she hadn't worn in more years than she could remember. She stepped into it, glad that her slender body still fit into it comfortably. She stepped to the mirror and swiped her palm across the front of it, to straighten out a wrinkle. "This'll need some ironing" she said to herself. She liked how she looked in the cobalt blue dress, accented with faint white crosshatched lines, and large white buttons. The last time she had put it on, her hair had been not nearly as greyed out, but it still worked. It was important she look her finest, as she had made an appointment with Edison's attorney, and had to make her best impression.

She drove in the Cruze, from her mountain cabin down into Redlands, parking on the street, and entering the old five-story brick building where the attorney had an office on the third floor. She entered his outer office, was greeted by an empty desk, as years ago, the attorney had dispensed with having a secretary.

The attorney, a one Mr. William Gaines, not to be confused with the White, and bearded, former publisher of MAD Magazine, was a fifty-something Black man of above average height and weight, and had been effective in dampening down the sentence that had been handed out by the judge. Through a steady quiet voice, and humility, he was successful in painting an empathetic picture of the religious fanatic old man embezzler. He thought that he had done a pretty good job, allowing Edison to receive a relatively light sentence, all things considered. This is why her visit puzzled him. What did she want?

Marcy wanted more than a "relatively light sentence". She wanted Gaines to approach Judge Stevens, and submit to him a plea for "special circumstances". She had been reading up. She expressed to attorney Gaines her unwavering belief that if the judge were to consider what an exemplary inmate Edison had been for the last year and two months, and took into consideration the improvements he had made to the facility in terms of operation and appearance, that it was likely the judge would reduce his sentence. Attorney Gaines didn't see it that way, and did a considerable amount of polite pushback, but Marcy was resolute, and insisted. He succumbed to her will, and promised to make an appointment with Judge Stevens, to discuss the matter, "But don't be holding out any hope. Besides which, he's eligible for parole in about ten months, and he's got a pretty good shot at getting it". This last comment, was greeted by a steely glare.

After hearing Gaines out, the judge said, "Yes, yes, I see your point counselor, and I was not aware of Edison's contributions to Dublin, nor was I aware of his overall behavior there...I will look into it". Judge Stevens was not about to move an inch without first speaking to the warden at Dublin. It seemed that everything Gaines had told him, that had been told to him by Marcy, held true. The judge determined that his sentence would be reduced, effective immediately, to one year and a day. Edison had already served one year and sixty-seven days.

Marcy was elated, and Edison was shocked. It took about two weeks of paperwork to process his release, but at last, on a sunny but cold day in March, Edison walked out of the facility and climbed into the Cruze, with Marcy at the wheel, beaming. They went to a celebratory lunch at IHop, ordered Edison a stack of buttermilk pancakes with bacon, while Marcy confined herself to a grapefruit with black coffee. They stayed in a motel in Livermore that night, took the #5 interstate south, and stayed in a motel another night, this time in Buttonwillow. They had lots of time to catch up, as they drove along, or stopped for some lunch or dinner. They talked about the kids, the grandchildren, and Rusty, how he had passed away quietly about two years ago, about her friends on the mountain. What was noteworthy, perhaps ground-shaking, was that every time Edison brought up any subject pertaining to "plans", of what they should do next, or what he felt about his life's mission, his "path", Marcy would shoot him down. "Ed, I'm not going to listen to a word of this, I mean it, not a word".

"Ed?"

"Yes, Edison, you've forbade me from calling you that for decades, and to be honest about it, I don't like that, and I'm going to call you Ed if I want to, and I damn well want to".

Edison stared at her blank faced, and said not a word.

He hadn't been around her for quite a few years and it took some getting used to, and he was beginning to feel claustrophobic, being so close to his wife for the last two and a half days. It wasn't a bad thing, to the most part, but suddenly, it was too much all at once.

Also, she seemed to have changed. He realized, that he had foisted so much "change" onto her, it wasn't surprising that she would have adapted, been forced to change in order to survive. Anytime he began to think about this, the crushing weight of guilt descended upon him. He knew that his choices had been made in response to communicating with God, but he also knew that he was simply a man, who had Earthly obligations he had not met. The time in their two motel rooms was spent playing cards, watching old movies, and cuddling.

They arrived at 47 Marcy Road late in the afternoon, tired from their journey. They walked together up the steps to the small porch and then inside. Edison was expecting a homey and cozy little place, with simple furniture and a fireplace. Instead, he was greeted by a dozen cardboard boxes full of belongings and clothes, all the surfaces stripped bare, the cabinets empty, and sheets placed over the furniture.

"What is going on Marcy?"

"Ed, we're moving, tomorrow".

"What?"

"I have it all arranged. Tommy down the street helped me get everything packed really well, and our things will be shipped to us. He'll take everything down to FedEx Freight tomorrow."

"What are you talking about?"

"I'm talking about us leaving here"

"Why?"

"Why? You're asking why? For starters, everybody up here hates you, okay maybe not everybody, I think you might still have one or two friends, but that's about it".

"Hate me?"

"Yes Ed, hate. And besides which, we need a change in scenery, we need a new life".

"Where did all this thinking come from, why do you want to do this?"

She leveled a deadly stare at him. "Ed, you stole money from the church, you lied to me about that for years. You moved me from my lovely home up in the mountains, I cry every time I drive by the place, and moved me to the desert in a run-down little tract house surrounded by sand and cactus, and then, you left me, dropped me like an old rag to fend for myself, and yes, you left me some money, I'm not forgetting that, and I sold that awful house, but you left me Ed, you *left* me. And then, after you were caught, not two blocks from here, I was interrogated by the police and by the FBI. The *FBI* Ed."

"Marce, I am so sorry about all of this, about..."

"Shut up Ed, just shut up".

"What?!"

"You heard me. We're doing this plan, Ed, we're doing this plan".

"What plan?"

"I'm in charge now, Ed. I'm going to call the shots from here on out. You want to discuss it with your God, go ahead, but I'm in charge".

Edison had to steady himself, and he sat down on a kitchen chair.

"You want some water, Ed?"

"Yeah, yeah, that would be good, some water..."

What could he do now? He had nowhere to go. All the money he had had in his carry-on, had been seized. He had a $200 debit card in his pocket, the "gate money", supplied to him by the State when he left Dublin, but that was it. No car, no house, no bank account. Nothing. He had his clothes, that he was wearing, and a pair of jeans and a tee shirt in his bag. And one pair of shoes, the sneakers he was wearing. He was ninety-four years old. He did have his health however. He had had a complete physical while in Dublin, and he had checked out fine, more than fine. He could walk out right now, he thought, and go where exactly? If he walked down to the Mexican cafe', if his last visit there was any indication, and if Marcy was even half-right, he'd probably get attacked. It seemed that Marcy had a plan in place, and she had all the purse strings. She had whatever was left of the money he had left for her, unless it too had been seized, and the money from selling the Tucson house, if that money hadn't been seized, but it sounded like nothing had been seized, so that meant that she had a lot of money. And had the title to the Cruze.

He realized, that he had better capitulate to his wife's demands, and maybe that wasn't such a bad thing? He had done his tour of duty for God, he had enlightened many people, probably saved a few souls along the way, no question about it. Even with the murder factored in, it had been a net gain of several saved souls. That's why he did it, that's why he had been directed to do it. And he loved his Marcy, loved her through and through, even this new version of her. He was still struggling with being called "Ed" though.

M arcy met Tommy at the Redlands Airport and handed him the keys to the Cruze, for all the help he had given her over the months. He needed a reliable car for going to and from Redlands University. It took nearly eighteen hours for the old couple to arrive at their new home.

First, they boarded a small prop jet that took them to Phoenix, and after a three hour wait, boarded a jet to Miami, with a stop in Atlanta. From Miami, they made it to Saint Thomas in the Virgin Islands, and then from Red Hook, took a ferry to Cruz Bay on Saint John.

As part of his early release deal, Edison could not leave the country, and his passport had been revoked. Marcy had gone to the Arrowhead Credit Union in Redlands the day before, and cleaned out her account. She held back a little cash but had most of it broken down into large counter checks.

There had been a fog of chaos that existed between the police and FBI, the British police on Tortola, the church and the banks, with no one agency or person in charge of the investigation, and Marcy had taken full advantage of that. The unusual and long-running crime perpetrated by her husband, the most unlikely of suspects, helped her in a similar fashion, to conceal the funds.

For years, Edison's outward appearance and demeanor threw suspicion off of him, and likewise, that same outward impression aided her. Her bewilderment was genuine at the time of the discovery of the crime, and she had been a quick study in how to react, how to conceal.

Upon arriving at Saint John, they took a taxi along North Shore Road a few miles, past Honeymoon Beach and the revered Caneel Bay Resort, to a gentle beach with a row of four small cottages, all but one set back from the shore about two hundred feet.

This location was not chosen haphazardly. There were many remote locations to choose from in the fifty states, and territories. Hawaii was too crowded for them, she reasoned, Guam too distant-feeling and foreign. Regions in Alaska too cold. Other areas also too cold or barren, or too hot, or too populated. And even the smallest and most isolated towns in the lower 48, were too easily subject to intrusion from reporters, and authorities wanting to do a follow-up, pursue a lead, or a tip. Saint John provided a U.S. based home, that was quite remote, isolated, and provided the beauty and healing of nature, they both adored and needed. There were no airports on the island, and no accommodations for cruise ships. Laurence Rockefeller had purchased the island long ago, and donated the vast majority of it to the U.S. government, as a natural preserve.

They were both becoming quite old, virtual relics, and as far as she knew, even though they both felt well, they had only days to live, maybe only a year or two at best, so why waste them on anywhere second-best? They had earned some privacy, and some of God's beauty, she reckoned.

Also, whether he knew it or not, she knew that Edison had a book in him, and that to the best of his ability, he could write it. When she would visit him in prison, he would say to her that he felt too depressed to start such a task, and had he served his full term, and finished it in prison, he couldn't have sold it, there were laws about that. But she had always encouraged the idea, and now, the story could be told, and within a few months she figured, "The Rocketeer for God" would find a publisher. She had thought up the name, and insisted that he use it. "Don't you worry about the title or finding a publisher, just leave all that to me. You just concern yourself with writing it, I'll do the rest" was what she had told him. He began writing on the second day they were there.

Their cottage was located in the pocket of Hawksnest Bay, and rarely visited by tourists, who usually stay in Cruz Bay, the main town, or go directly to a resort, or visit the world-famous Trunk Bay, and snorkel or scuba around the small island just off shore, along what's called "the underwater trail".

People that were full-time residents were quite friendly to the old couple. No drive into town could exclude passing peacocks, chickens and donkeys, that roam freely. Most of the original inhabitants of the island were descendants of slaves, that the Danish had kidnapped from Africa, to work the sugarcane and cotton plantations. But now, it was made up of mostly the extremely or moderately affluent, usually White but not always, who fancied a home on the stunningly beautiful island, or people in the service industry, supporting the handful of restaurants and shops.

As for the part-time residents, there are many, and their homes are often rented out on a weekly basis to the scores of tourists, coming mostly from the U.S. Saint Thomas is far more developed, and attracts a substantially larger number of visitors, who like having a wide array of places to choose from for dining out, St. Thomas having about four times as many restaurants as St. John. The shopping opportunities are equally imbalanced, with people arriving to St. Thomas on enormous cruise ships almost daily, in the high season, and being catered to. As a result, the personality of St. John is much quieter and humbler, and Marcy knew that it would fit Edison's needs quite well.

She had not included Edison in any of her planning, quite intentionally, for she was fed up. She had supported him through all his years at JPL, with him working tirelessly, often into the night, not being there as much as he should have been for the kids, and suffering along with him during his years of discouragement. She had supported him when he decided to leave the mountain and devote himself to God, spreading the Good News, and put up only the meekest of protests when he decided to uproot them and stick them in the Arizona desert.

Many people in this kind of a situation, would have left years ago, but not Marcy. She was as loyal a person as they come. She had stuck by her husband even during the most confusing and frightening of times. She had almost grown used to being followed by the FBI, to and from the grocery market and other errands. It was only after Edison had been apprehended and sentenced, that the heat on her had subsided, allowing her more mobility, with the undercover agents, in their ridiculously obvious cars, or dressed as residents, no longer hovering around.

Almost instinctively, she knew to transfer all the money he had left to her, to the credit union. That same instinct directed her to do likewise when she sold the house. She had chosen the smallest and least-known credit union in Tucson, correctly figuring that they would be about the last place any of the authorities would look for hidden funds, for she knew that the FBI wanted to back out of the case, and pursue more important criminals, and the D.A.s office was not keen on nailing an old man for skimming funds from a wealthy church, that made money hand over fist, enjoying a non-tax status with the government. She did all her banking in-person, never online, and waited to visit the credit union only after the smoke had cleared. Of these two nonagenarian criminals, it must be said, she was the cleverer one.

Due to the complete lack of enthusiasm the authorities had for this case, Edison had become nearly untouchable, not due to his cunning, his ability to confuse or evade, or his overall untapped talent at being a criminal, but simply because it made for bad politics to go after him. That didn't entirely stop the unruly legal mechanism of course, and had he not popped up in Forest Falls that day, and instead had laid low for a year or two, other more important cases would have risen to the top, and taken the attention of the authorities, glad at not having to deal with this ticklish case. Edison, lurching desperately toward Marcy that day, had forced their hand.

Macy understood all of this, even if Edison remained bewildered by his strange odyssey.

When they had arrived at Cruz Bay, word had just come that the U.S. had just landed a spacecraft on the Moon, on the south pole. The Odysseus (the brilliant and versatile hero from Homer's *Odyssey*) lunar lander had touched down, not manually piloted by the likes of Armstrong, but a highly sophisticated robot, that had been sent aloft from the Kennedy Space Center, a joint venture of NASA, SpaceX and Intuitive Machines. They use the company's Falcon family of rockets. It was the first time a U.S. spacecraft had landed on the Moon since 1972, over fifty years before.

China's Moon landing had been successful just weeks before, and although Boeing's "Starliner" capsule launch had been scrubbed twice before, the third attempt proved successful. It blasted into the Florida sky from the Cape Canaveral Air Force Station, using the launch system developed by SpaceX's competitor, the United Launch Alliance, also in partnership with NASA. It passed the most critical stress point for the vehicle at the two-minute mark, simply called "max two", bound for the International Space Station. It carried critical supplies for the astronauts housed there, including a replacement pump motor for the urine purification system. For the last number of weeks, the astronauts inside the Station resided with numerous secured bags of weightless urine.

All of this was in preparation for a manned Mars landing, which is not meant literally, for of the two astronauts in the Starliner, both Air Navy test pilots, one was a woman.

The heavy launch vehicle used, was the Saturn V, which they used as a replacement for the Atlas V. The first stage of the rocket carries over 203,000 gallons of a special kerosene mix fuel, along with 318,000 gallons of liquid oxygen that is needed for combustion. When liftoff occurs, the first stage's five F-1 rockets give out a deafening roar, and the ground trembles. It's no wonder, for it produces 7 ½ million pounds of thrust. Once the rocket, with the space capsule atop, reaches forty-two miles up, the engines shut down and explosive bolts fire, severing the first stage. It now travels at over 15,000 mph. Intricate math goes into calculating the power of thrust, the atmospheric conditions, the mass of the vehicle at launch in relation to gravity, and the reduction of mass as it pulls away from Earth. The first stage drops down and lands in the Atlantic, to be retrieved later by Navy ships. The second stage carries 260,000 gallons of liquid hydrogen fuel and 80,000 gallons of liquid oxygen. No solid fuel propellant in sight. It burns more fuel in one second, than Lindbergh used to cross the entire Atlantic. After a few seconds, the second stage's rockets are ignited, and a "skirt", acting as an air foil, is jettisoned. After nine minutes of flight, the second stage is discarded same as the first, and the third stage's rockets fire for another two minutes. By then, the spacecraft has attained Earth orbit, and the engines shut down. About two and a half hours later, once in optimal position, they are re-ignited so that the vehicle can head to the Station, and once it is securely in near-space, with Earth's gravity less powerful, the third stage is jettisoned. From there, the Starliner is guided to the Station using thrusters, until they dock.

This is the long way of saying, that the ultra-complex world of rocket technology had passed Edison by. This new generation of rockets, used exotic new mixtures of fuel, involving methane, kerosene, liquid oxygen, and liquid hydrogen, for more efficient and reliable fuel consumption, and with rocket thrusters designed for that specific type of fuel.

It wasn't that Edison's solid fuel was obsolete. Far from it, for it was still in use, or an improved version of it, with heavy-load rockets that would carry people back to the Moon, and to Mars. The Artemis (named after the Greek Goddess of the Moon) family of rockets would be used for that purpose, developed for NASA by SpaceX, it had been recently announced. It thrilled Edison to contemplate such a glorious and exciting thing. It would make for a good ending to his book.

And of course, his fuel, or a variation of it, was still used in most ICBM nuclear warhead missiles, and so popular, that China and Russia had copied it for theirs.

Not long after this, it would be announced that Russia had launched a "counterspace" satellite, likely armed, to shoot down other satellites. It had been launched from their "Cosmodrome" station in Kazakhstan, using their Soyuz-2 rocket booster. In particular, the Russian's had their wary eye on the "Keyhole" series of U.S. military satellites, referred to as "imaging assets". And all of this, against the backdrop of an ever-worsening climate change event taking place on Earth, with over a dozen successive months breaking heat records globally.

It seemed to Edison, that the relatively short existence of Humans on the planet was being threatened by the Humans themselves. They were highly capable and full of potential, but seemingly inclined, to destroy themselves, whether it be by a nuclear exchange, the collapse of modern civilization, or, by destroying the Earth's thin and protective membrane, with pollutants. Maybe all three? He would marvel at Man's unwillingness to protect their very own existence. He never thought of it as their inability.

The taxi slowed and turned into a dirt parking lot that faced the ocean. It was a gorgeous view, that looked out onto turquoise water, and white sand, framed with palm trees. The beach itself was not very broad, only about twenty feet before it came to the water, which was all that they needed. The bay quieted the swells and surf, so that by the time the waves came ashore, they were small and gentle. The breeze was always present, and the water warm, and inviting.

At his ripe old age, snorkeling was probably not on the menu, but certainly he could wade into the water, and dip his face down into it, with a mask, and see the occasional fish dart by. Most of the fish would be found further out, along the rock and coral outcroppings, but every once in a while, a Barred Hamlet could be seen (a member of the Sea Bass family, about four inches long, distinguished by brown bars of color on a background of white and yellow, with bright blue lines and spots on the head). They also happened to be hermaphrodites, using their reproductive organs interchangeably. On one occasion, Edison was startled by the sudden appearance of a huge black Ray, emerging from the dark water, and sailing just over the turtle grass. Speaking of which, he was thrilled that on occasion, if he stood very still in about four feet of water, a Sea Turtle would glide by. Thanks to Marcy, he had been delivered to paradise on Earth.

Edison became quite the expert at fish identification over the next number of months, slowly taking on a dark tan, and growing accustomed to bare feet, or sandals if necessary. He could also chart the constellations quite well, and would speak to Marcy dreamily about time, space, and other dimensions. He would also speak of God and Jesus, often, interlacing his adventurous path, his experiences, with quotations.

When thinking back about all of the types of people he had consorted with, or helped, many of them undesirables, or of questionable backgrounds or morals, he would think of a translated statement of Jesus, *"Those who are well have no need of a physician"*.

He would spend about three hours a day penning his book. He had never written an actual book, let alone, had ever expressed anything about himself, so at first, it was a very difficult undertaking. Marcy encouraged him, and told him she'd get an editor, and to not worry about poor grammar or typos, that he should simply "let it pour out". So, pour he did.

In the back of his mind, he knew that at some point, toward the end of the book, he would have to confront the horrible scene with the violent stranger, and the murder. At first, he thought he'd simply skip over it, but then, realized that if it were to be truthful, then he had to write about that, he had no choice. What were they going to do, arrest him? The book, after all, was not meant to be an expression of his ego, showing only his best traits and actions, but to serve God, with humility.

They shared their small cottage by the bay with other cottages, each one painted a different bright color. Theirs was bright lime green, while on the left was bright orange, and on the right, bright blue. Theirs had cost a small fortune, but Edison never inquired as to the details. They were all wood-framed, but improved with metal roofing and imitation wood siding. Inside, they were comfortable, with modern amenities, making life pleasant for the old couple. Their neighbors were younger, how could they not be?

One couple was part-time from Miami, and the other cottage occupied by a serious looking young man, who was a novelist. Edison would chat with him about writing, and come away with thoughts of "structure", "arcs", "plot development", "exposition" and about "avoiding redundancy", which he thought especially funny.

For Edison, life was all about redundancy. For him, it meant he was consistent, and had stayed the course. He considered his life to have been the most redundant thing imaginable. As for the novelist neighbor, they had looked him up, and he had written a few titles, fiction mysteries and sci-fi primarily, and had sold quite a few copies. Obviously, the money it took to buy his modest cottage came from other revenue streams, as he was far from a household name.

Edison would take walks along the gently curved shoreline, walking barefoot on the fine-grained sand, usually in the direction of the neighboring beach, Gibney Beach. Once in a while, he'd walk in the other direction, and get to the end, where it turned to steep rock terrain, and became inaccessible.

There was one lone cottage, a fourth one, down at that end of the beach. It was separated from the three, and obviously something built decades ago, that appeared abandoned. It sat very close to the water, much closer than building codes would allow currently. It was partially obscured by mature palms and broad leaf plants. There were empty openings, where there were once doors and windows, and it looked uncared for, and forgotten. Some vines had wound their way inside, and some broadleaf plants, tropical ones that

Edison had not learned the names of yet, had taken root inside, through the many cracks in the concrete floor.

When he was bold enough to walk up close to it, close enough to peer inside, he could see only some haphazardly placed tables, some folding chairs, and some long-handled tools for yard work. It certainly didn't appear to be a home, but more of a storage facility for the island's maintenance crew, he figured. The outside wasn't wood, but concrete, all concrete, like a bunker. Perhaps it was concrete troweled over cement blocks, was his guess? The roof seemed newer, but not by much. It was made of corrugated sheets of metal, rusted out most everywhere from what he could see. He was fascinated by the place, and wondered if it had ever been a home? If so, who had lived there? Why it was here? He wanted to know its history.

Marcy had not divulged how much money she had stashed away, and he only knew that she had made deposits in the two banks on the island. There was the First Bank of Puerto Rico, and Merchants Commercial Bank. She would visit those banks on occasion, but never went online. She didn't trust the browsers to keep her financial business secret, and was always fearful of someone deciding to re-open the case, to probe around for additional stolen funds. She, like Edison, had rationalized the thievery, and now, after so much suffering, time, and sacrifice, felt entitled to whatever amount remained as a result of his impounding. Looked at from her perspective, Edison had sacrificed mightily, but willingly, for his Lord, and had followed the path that had been laid out before him, without questioning.

As for Edison's viewpoint, he had wisely decided to recede back into the shadows, and ceased his proselytizing, and further, did not question her, or challenge her, regarding anything to do with money. But he noticed the details.

She would often behave in a very thrifty manner, choosing only the grocery items on sale, passing by her favorite regularly-priced brands if not on sale. She turned off lights, even though the cottage was so small, and couldn't possibly be using that much electricity. It would take her two days of raking, to clear a patch of sand in front of the cottage of fallen leaves from the Plumeria trees that inhabited the area. Edison, always curious, had looked up the tree on Marcy's laptop, and came to find that the tree was a member of a very large species, many of them highly toxic, if not deadly poisonous. Natives had used the sap from some varieties to poison the tips of arrows or spears. Others would become poisoned quite by accident, having touched their hands to their mouth after handling or pruning. As for the leaves that fell from the beautiful things, she could've hired someone to do it, but defended it by saying she needed the exercise. But that wasn't it, it was the money she was saving. There was a lone thrift store on the island, in Cruz Bay, that she would buy all her clothing, and his. She never shopped in a regular store, never paid regular retail.

Edison would often find himself sitting in a beach chair on the shore, under a swooping palm tree, in front of the concrete house. He felt a kinship to the old rundown place. Only once did he see a crew show up, driving an old rusty pickup, and grab a couple of hand tools and a wheelbarrow, that was it. He'd sit there, in front of it, have a legal pad in his lap, and a pocket-full of sharp pencils. He had managed to begin his "Rocketeer" book, and was now on chapter three. He had named each chapter, and called this one, "Pass the Ammunition, Praise the Lord". He wasn't entirely sure what it meant, but figured that "ammunition" could mean missiles.

Also, he wanted to devote a chapter to the moons of the solar system, simply entitled "Moons". There were so many of them, 293 according to NASA's last count. All of them were created about 4.5 billion years ago, along with all the planets, emerging from an enormous and violent cloud of gas and dust. *They deserve their own chapter*, he reasoned. NASA's Cassini orbiter taught scientists much, on its twenty-year mission through the solar system, discovering for instance, that Titan, Saturn's largest moon, is the only moon discovered thus far, with its own atmosphere. It has abundant amounts of nitrogen and methane, and gigantic wind storms comparable to those on Earth and Mars. There are moons with underground oceans, and perhaps made of clean drinkable water, such as with our own Moon? Moons with raging volcanoes, others made of rock, others of ice, some with enormous sand dunes, and some shooting plumes from hydrothermal vents, made of hydrogen, carbon, nitrogen and oxygen, the "Big Four" ingredients of life. Some simply spew water vapor, sometimes one-hundred miles out into space. For Edison, the moons were nearly as fascinating as the planets they orbited.

He'd write some more, and when tired of that, he'd read an article about the latest development over at JPL or with NASA, or take a nap, or choose to have a short walk up or down the beach, maybe take a dip into the water to freshen up, and start the cycle all over again. Marcy was not nearly as fond of lounging around, and always busied herself with chores. She'd bring Edison his lunch, usually a sandwich of some sort, with a few cut wedges of mango or pineapple, saying, "Here you go Ed, lunch time", turn around, and head back to the lime green cottage.

The former owner of the lonely concrete cottage had, years ago, willingly and joyfully escaped to the solitude that this island, and this beach, had offered. His life on the mainland had turned into a nightmare. He had created a monster. He had been given much help and encouragement to do so, by way of his considerable ego, his hubris, and for that, he was not ashamed or regretful, not at first. He was born in 1903 and had grown up in an age of amazing new inventions and technological advancements. As an adult, he had been supplied with misconceptions about the ultimate purpose of his work. He had been deceived about how his work would be used, and not told of the plans to exploit it, to expand it. All this while having his ego bolstered with endless praise, for his genius, and invention. But it seemed he had turned a blind eye, that he had wanted to be deceived. He wanted to go forward with his invention, for at the time, he believed in his work, believed in its righteousness, only later denouncing it. And the denouncing of it had caused him and his family tremendous grief, recriminations, and banishment from places that formerly greeted him with open arms. There had been panic and desperation in the air during this, and it made people in the military, act out of a tremendous sense of urgency, some would say panic. He understood that, he knew of the urgency, and forgave them their trespasses in his later years, but could not forgive himself. And then, after all of this, with his invention, and its future versions having been put into full use, he had to escape, and fled to this beautiful place with his wife, his children, for peace and tranquility. It seemed to make sense.

And then he became bolder, not as quiet as before. He befriended the locals, and so very out of keeping with his former personality, hosted parties for the wealthy and poor, for the Whites and the Blacks, hiring the local Mariachi band to play, and he danced, they all danced, became drunk with the booze and happiness, and they were boisterous, and later, the party having faded out, he'd walk to the shore and point out the constellations to his remaining guests. Was he over-compensating for creating the monster, for his carelessness, his willing blindness? Perhaps, but he didn't see it that way, not entirely, although it was true to a large extent, for he couldn't escape his deathly sense of guilt, could not erase what he had done, and now his creation was completely unleashed, and threatened all of mankind. His hair had turned prematurely white when he was in his late fifties, and when he had been older, thinning and gone. He had become an old man, a very old man. Would someone else have come along and invented what he had invented? Yes, very likely, yes. In fact, others were close on his tail back then, other countries, only months away from developing a monster of equal horror. But that wasn't the point. He had been that someone.

He had built their family cottage near the water, listened to the surf, hung out hammocks, and took long walks along the shore, and years later, Edison would walk those same steps, sit at that same beach, and stare at the old concrete house, wondering why it attracted him so? The original owner died of throat cancer, having overdone his Chesterfields. He had only been sixty-two at the time. Thirty-two years younger than the old man who stood at his house, staring into the square spaces that used to be windows, wondering of its history. The man had been a very complex person, of high intelligence and curiosity, and had followed Hinduism at arm's length, learned how to read Sanskrit, quoting later from Hindu scripture, "Now I become Death, the destroyer of worlds". The locals had named the beach after the man, a beach name that Edison was completely unaware of. He would have known the man's name, a little too well. Marcy had known the name. In fact, that's why she had chosen this particular beach, this particular cottage, for them to live out the rest of their lives. She thought it appropriate that Edison, her dear sweet Ed, should be here, next to the old abandoned cottage, on Oppenheimer Beach.

Edison never did know about the name, partly because he rarely came into contact with anyone who might know the name. Their two neighbors knew it incorrectly, as Gibney Beach or Hawksnest Beach. They didn't know the local name either. The other names seemed logical to Edison, since the bay was called Hawksnest. Why think otherwise?

On one particular afternoon, Edison died there on that beach, and it had been a quiet passing, with his legal pad splayed out on his chest, a half-empty can of soda fallen from his hand, the surf gently lapping up against his ankles, and drifting under the beach chair. It had all been so quiet. Marcy had come upon him, a plate in hand, delivering his lunch. She knew, from twenty feet away, that he had gone away, leaving his old tired body behind. She bent her head down, and said a prayer for her troubled and determined Ed.

The previous owner hadn't had it so lucky. He had been rushed to New York, poked and probed, operated on, given chemotherapy and ironically, radiation treatment. He did however, manage to pass quietly at his primary home. His wife, Kitty, spread his ashes in the bay that Edison now had a commanding view of. Marcy chose that option as well, and remained living there in their little cottage until the remarkable age of 102, in terrific health, before drifting off early one morning, just before dawn.

In that time there alone, she had managed to keep her mind sharp by memorizing all of Shakespeare's sonnets, which on occasion, she would recite to her entranced neighbors.

She would at times, look up at the stars, so very pronounced and dramatic in the Caribbean sky, and think about her Ed. Other times, usually in the early morning, she'd walk down the steps of their cottage, and find herself by the water. She'd look up at the sky and know that he had been right about the Lord, and that he had heard his transmissions, and had followed the path that had been laid out before him. But she wondered, had he also been right about time and space, about other dimensions? He must have been, for those messages, that knowledge, was all part of the larger package that had been delivered to him, were they not? Was it all part of God's plan? Could he, somehow, see her now?

The End

The author wishes to thank his dear longtime friend

Rev. Patrick Vance

for his invaluable help with breathing life
into this story

About the Author

photo by Kristen Pietro

Brian has lived in Malibu for the last many decades, has come from a long line of artists, has done a fair amount of acting, along with some writing and directing, owned and operated a locally iconic general store, is married, has three kids, all grown, has had many wonderful dogs, and has fallen in love all over again with writing. This is his fourth novel, with a few more to go.

Made in the USA
Las Vegas, NV
11 June 2024

90971416R00223